Hester Thomas worked as a journalist, copywriter and trained people in business writing skills. She now works on her own creative projects and with 26 Characters, a group of writers who share a love of words.

The Rollercoaster Year

Hester Thomas

First published in Great Britain in 2021 by Cloche Editions

Copyright text © Hester Thomas

Hester Thomas asserts the moral right to be identified as the author of this work in accordance with the Copyright, Designs and Patents Act 1988

This is a work of fiction, although its form is that of an autobiographical diary. Any resemblance to persons living or dead is coincidental.

Grateful acknowledgement is made to Penguin Random House LLC (US) for permission to reprint an extract from Elizabeth Berg's short story 'What Stays' from her book of short stories *Ordinary Lives*; and to Danny Penman co-author with Mark Williams for permission to reproduce extracts from their book *Mindfulness: A practical guide to finding peace in a frantic world*.

A catalogue record for this book is available from the British Library

ISBN 978-1-5272-7168-5

All rights reserved. No part of this publication may be reproduced, stored in a retrieval system, or transmitted, in any form or by any means, electronic, mechanical, photocopying, recording or otherwise, without the prior permission of the publisher.

This book is sold subject to the condition that it shall not, by way of trade or otherwise, be lent, re-sold, hired out or otherwise circulated without the publisher's prior consent in any form of binding or cover other than that in which it is published and without a similar condition including this condition being imposed on the subsequent purchaser.

Typeset in Garamond, printed and bound
in Great Britain by KMS Litho Ltd.
The paper is Arena Ivory Bulk from Fedrigoni, Italy.

To Buffy and Julius
with love

The Rollercoaster Year

January

Tuesday 1st January
This was what it was like at the end. Breathless. My heart was out of kilter, missing a beat, then making up for it by crashing down extra hard with the next. All provoked by a mixture of pure excitement topped with a small dose of anxiety that I was trying hard to ignore. Because if this was the end, then it was also the beginning. And that was the amazing part.

Of course, George hadn't a clue. He was fast asleep beside me, lying on his back, a regular clicking sound rising from his mouth as the breath caught in his throat.

It was the usual New Year's Eve in the Baxter household, celebrated in bed, asleep. Well, some of us. I was wide awake, energised about the year to come.

As midnight struck, I slipped out of bed and snuck between the curtains and window to watch the night sky alight with fireworks shooting and screaming their way above south London. They woke George who, unaware of where I was, trundled round the bed on his way to the loo. As he came back, I decided to go too and stepped out from behind the curtains.

'Happy New Year!' I said cheerily.

He stopped, momentarily. 'What the hell! I thought you were in bed. I could have had a heart attack!' Then he continued his night-time shuffle, climbed back under the duvet and was asleep, instantly.

I was about to open the bathroom door when I realised Tillie was inside. I leaned hopefully against the radiator in the hallway, but it was cold.

'Happy New Year!' I greeted her as she came out.

'Humpf,' she replied, sleepwalking her way back to her

bedroom.

Only Lucas snoozed on unaffected by the fireworks, the significance of the hour or his bladder.

*

The brilliantly sunny day matched my mood perfectly. We donned our coats and walked over the common to the park with its fine views of London. Even Tillie came. At eighteen, she's wary of being seen too often with us ageing and *so* uncool parents.

The air was crystal clear and every building stood out: the Shard, the Gherkin, St Paul's, the Walkie-Talkie, the Cheesegrater, and the skyscrapers in Docklands. On the far horizon lay the gentle slopes of Hampstead Heath.

The good weather had lured everyone out.

Tillie called, 'Hey,' to a teenage girl who resembled a sumo wrestler.

'Who's that?' I asked.

'Emma.'

'Emma who?'

'Emma from Lucas's old school.'

'*Emma?*' I asked in amazement.

'Yes!'

Lucas left at the end of year 2 when Emma was small and fairy-like, with a fine bone structure. I could not match that child to her hefty, fifteen-year-old self. I was about to turn round and stare, my mouth dropping open but Tillie, who knows all my foibles, hissed in my ear, 'Don't you dare.'

*

I'm committing my New Year resolutions to paper, this being a thrilling year of liberation as I embark on a year off. The first ever in my entire life. Which means no more work. No clients. No demands. No long hours. No stress. Just freedom.

So here they are:
1. I will end a lifetime's bad habit of agreeing to every piece of freelance graphic design work I'm offered. *(I did love this job, but it's lost its gloss. And I'm tired of being stretched in too many different directions – job, children, George, home – and stressed by it all too.)*
2. Instead I will do something wonderful, new, unexpected and stimulating. *(But what??!!!)*
3. ~~Lose five kilos in weight.~~ *(Well, that's a start.)*
3. Embark on The Body Beautiful Project and lose weight. *(Anything would be good.)*
4. Take more exercise to support the third resolution.
5. Write this diary to chart the progress of my year. *(And oh, what might it hold?!)*

That's enough. If I manage one of those resolutions, it'll be a minor miracle.

Wednesday 2nd January
George was up at the crack of dawn, back to work at his law firm. I lay in bed brooding on his profession: a lawyer specialising in money-laundering. I picture his colleagues, all those men and women in smart pin-stripe suits, taking off their jackets and rolling up fine cotton sleeves of dazzling white shirts in order to plunge their arms into vast communal sinks of dirty bank notes. A good wash and rinse followed by drying on wooden racks hoisted ceiling-high. Then a quick iron to remove the wrinkles before sorting them into size and type. Their return to the Bank of England sees the financial world transformed into a cleaner place.

The truth is more mundane. George handles concepts, not money. He peers over the edge of the current legal framework to see what changes may be in the offing, not just in the UK but worldwide. Then he lobbies for what his firm would like to either change or stay the same.

That's my crude version. It's far more technical and complicated. Occasionally he attempts to tell me exactly what's involved, but by the time he's explained which White Paper he's working on – the section, subsection, point and paragraph – my eyes have glazed over.

*

Although I wouldn't normally be back at work yet, I would be checking my emails and texts for messages from keen clients. I didn't do either of those things because I've slowly dropped them. I didn't tell anyone I was taking a year off *(oh, it does sound good)* – in case. *(In case what? In case I bottled out? In case it turns out I need my clients?)* I said I would be busy for a few months and thus unavailable. They all presumed I meant busy with work for another client, and I didn't disabuse them.

Anyway, there was no one to spoil a leisurely day in which Tillie and I went to central London and mooched round the sales. In Paperchase, we scoured the shelves for discounted greetings cards.

'I've found just the thing for Great Aunt Vi,' said Tillie triumphantly, handing me a cellophane-wrapped confection. The front cover announced, 'Happy Birthday you barmy old woman.'

'Spot on!' We both laughed.

But as I'd already sent her something, we left it behind.

*

After dinner, when Tillie and Lucas had gone upstairs, I told George about the card and Tillie's idea of sending it to Great Aunt Vi. She's the kind of person who others politely refer to as 'interesting' or 'a character'. George, who has witnessed my decades-long, turbulent relationship with her, is more forthright, 'Her default mode is nasty.' But he smiled at Tillie's suggestion nevertheless.

'I wonder who you *could* buy it for?' I pondered, trying to imagine what sort of relationship was sufficiently robust to withstand that kind of humour.

George thought for a moment and then, without changing the contemplative expression on his face said, 'I suppose someone could buy it for his wife.'

Thursday 3rd January
As Tillie was out with her friends, I decided to give Lucas a treat.

'Let's have lunch at Pizza Express on the high street.' It's his favourite restaurant.

The place was heaving with adults, young children – and us. A little girl, about eighteen months old, was sitting in a high-chair at the next table. She tried to chew on the children's menu and then, when it was taken away, lowered her head until it was level with the table and gnawed that instead.

Lucas ordered the biggest pizza I have ever seen. With The Body Beautiful Project in mind, I chose a healthy salad. Lucas followed up his main course with a return to starters: dough balls and garlic butter. The waitresses never fail to be amazed at his method of ordering. It has the logic of a fifteen-year-old.

It was lovely to spend some time with him, knowing that all I had to do was concentrate on him and me. There was nothing and no one yattering away at the back of my mind: *you should be getting on with such-and-such a project* or *so-and-so will be expecting an update*. It was just me, Lucas, the food, and a little girl who'd discovered a taste for wood.

Friday 4th January
Great Aunt Vi's birthday. I phoned but didn't say anything about my year off. *(I don't want her thinking I'll be visiting more.)* At 94, she's as sharp as a knife, as bright as a button and, today, was on her best behaviour. I'd sent her an extravagant bouquet of flowers and she was pleased.

I've thought a lot about why I love her when she can, at the flick of an invisible switch, become extremely unpleasant. I've concluded it's because she's my only surviving elderly relative – the very much younger sister of my paternal grandmother. She's also the one person who has known me from my earliest years and who knew my parents too. The familial ties run deep.

Today she was mellow with fond memories, talking about her early years as a lowly civil servant in her home town of Leicester. It was an era in which few roles were open to women. She never married but carved out a career and rose to giddy heights. Well, giddy for Leicester.

Her holidays often included a brief stop at our house in Yorkshire, passing through on some jaunt to an ancient monument: Fountains Abbey, Lindisfarne, Hadrian's Wall. She'd park her red Mini, rattle the letterbox on our front door and swan in for afternoon tea. She would then cast a critical eye over my mother, my father and me while wolfing down an inordinate number of scones for someone so breathtakingly slim – even for those days. We always had the impression she found us wanting, though what we were wanting in was never specified or apparent to us. And then she'd waltz back out to her car, never giving us another glance. We were a pit stop: the pit more important than the people.

Despite our failings, she kept in touch – always prompt with birthday and Christmas cards including accompanying treats for me – money, mostly.

Today's conversation was pleasant. But as I put the phone down, I thought how she is like the little girl with the curl in the middle of her forehead: when she is good, she is very good, and when she is bad, she is an absolute horror.

Saturday 5th January

Family birthdays come thick and fast between November and January, with George's – his 57th – the last in the run.

He sat in bed, running his hand over his chin to test for stubble as we plied him with gifts. Well, 'ply' isn't the correct verb. George is a man who owns little and wants less. Hence his presents were few. Tillie gave him a bumper bag of M&Ms. Lucas had chosen several packets of flower seeds, there was a cheque from his mum, Edith, and I gave him a book.

I also baked a chocolate birthday cake *(relaxed and without any pressure on my time)* which we ate with the birthday tea.

'This is scrumptiously delicious,' he said, helping himself to a third slice. He managed four in total. I had a miserly one. *(Oh, sorrow.)* George is now lying in a corner, groaning. He says they're happy groans.

Sunday 6th January

We took down the Christmas decorations, the cards, the various table and mantelpiece centrepieces including the three wise men and the robin beside its nest. We removed the wreath from the front door which, each year, becomes thinner as the postie pushes its branches through the letterbox along with the post. And then we took all the tinsel and baubles from the tree.

Christmas is a strange time which I'm never equal to but always running after. I've just about caught up with the season – done the shopping, wrapped the presents, put up the decorations, prepared the food – when suddenly, it's all over and everything is to be put away again. And I want to say, 'Stop! I've only just got here. Let me sit down and savour the moment.' But it's already gone.

Monday 7th January

A very late Christmas card arrived from David, an old friend of my parents who has outlived them and most of his peers. He enclosed a Round Robin letter detailing his extraordinarily busy life in retirement. He's an active member of his local church, where he's on various committees and he's joined the Rotary

Club, where he attends every meeting and goes on all outings. Beyond that he looks after himself: shops, cooks, washes, irons, cleans the house and tidies the garden.

I showed the letter to George when he got home at eight thirty after a day slaving away on money-laundering law. He was a third of the way through when he said, 'For God's sake, why can't he just sit and relax?'

At the end, he slapped the letter down on the table. 'When I'm retired, my first Round Robin letter will contain just one triumphant sentence: "Did fuck all this year."'

Tuesday 8th January
Both children are back at their respective schools. As this would normally be the signal for me to start earning a living, I marked my new role as a woman of leisure by going out.

Frankie and I headed up to London for a guided tour of English Heritage's Apsley House on Hyde Park Corner, the home of Arthur Wellesley, the first Duke of Wellington.

To come clean on my sparse knowledge and greater ignorance: I knew about Wellington, Waterloo and Napoleon. But I had no idea that Wellington was regarded as such an important figure in the late eighteenth and early nineteenth centuries, that he was involved in the Peninsular Wars *(what Peninsular Wars?)* or that he became Prime Minister. Later, when I said all of this to George, thinking he'd be similarly ignorant, he shook his head and asked how come I'd missed this huge chunk of history? Then I felt doubly dim though cheered up a little when I remembered that Frankie had been as uninformed as me.

After the tour, Frankie and I walked to the Royal Academy and, as we tucked into sandwiches, I told her my breaking news. She was astonished *(she knows what a slave I've been to my job)* but very pleased for me.

'You'll become a lady who not only lunches but has coffee and afternoon tea too. And sometimes all of those in a single day,' she mused.

'With a bit of luck.'

'I'm quite envious, but in a nice kind of way. What will you do instead – after you've had the coffee, lunch and tea?'

'I'm not exactly sure. It took all my energy and resolve to give up the day job. But I'm working on what comes next,' I lied. *(What am I going to do???!!! It's taken so many months to steel myself and down tools that I haven't thought about what wonderful thing to do next – or to tell anyone else about taking a year off. Isn't it enough for the moment to be not doing what I used to do? Aren't I allowed an interlude?)*

We moved on to gossip: the hopelessness of husbands, the vagaries of our respective children – Archie and Seb in Frankie's case – her work and Christmas. Then we went home because those same children were due back from school and, despite the fact that they're all near-enough grown-ups, we still like to be there to greet them.

Wednesday 9th January

Having dropped Lucas at school, I headed home, went to my office and checked the emails.

The Victoria & Albert Museum had sent one about an art history course on the Late Medieval and Early Renaissance era. It's a period about which I know little, though I'm a keen follower of art and culture. I sat back in my chair, contemplating the screen. From the deep distant past of my childhood, a series of memories bubbled to the surface.

My parents enjoyed paintings. An occasional treat was to order a catalogue from Sotheby's in London. We'd leaf our way through it, swap opinions on our favourite paintings and how much we'd bid if money was no object. Our preferred era was early twentieth-century British paintings from the Bloomsbury Group, Brangwyn and the Nicholsons – Winifred and Ben – through to Ravilious and Nash.

Then, in my mind's eye, I saw a woman lying on a velvet chaise-longue, scrutinising a Sotheby's catalogue and deciding which of the works she'd place bids on. The woman was me: the grown-up I'd imagined I'd become as a child – and, until that moment, quite forgotten.

(Is this what taking a year off does? Allows the mind's gatekeeper to let through memories which can now be considered?)

And had that been my ambition? It hadn't worked out. But I have always loved art and wanted to know more. Why shouldn't I take up at almost the same place where that child left off? Why shouldn't I learn more about art history?

I checked my diary. Yes, I could attend once a week for all of the spring term. Then, fearing lassitude *(which can leave me dithering for days)* I signed up. That's it! I'm already on my way to fulfilling one of my New Year resolutions: do something wonderful, new, unexpected and stimulating!

Thursday 10th January

I'm reading *Mindfulness* by Mark Williams and Danny Penman which offers meditations and practices to 'find peace in a frantic world'. *(I need this after years of stressful work.)*

Today, I tried the first of two mindful eating exercises. It involved – believe it or not – the hard task of consuming a whole bar of chocolate! *(Well, maybe not the whole bar, but it was impossible to stop once I'd started.)*

The idea is to live in the moment, rather than do things on automatic pilot and therefore fail to experience them fully – or even at all. The exercise involved spending ten minutes unwrapping a bar of chocolate and then eating it. It had to be done very slowly in order to savour everything: the weight of the chocolate, the feel of the packaging, the sound of paper crackling as the wrapper was removed and the rich scent of the chocolate as the foil was peeled back.

I put a small piece of chocolate carefully in my mouth and

let it melt slowly on my tongue, rather than bolt it down as per usual. Though this was a brand of chocolate that I eat regularly, the taste was different – bitter and harsh. I tried another tiny piece. And then another. They were all equally unpleasant.

Finally, just to see whether the taste changed if I ate it at my normal rate, I chomped and swallowed the last piece in two seconds flat. It tasted fine.

Oh, what horrible conclusion can this lead to? Do I like most foods because I don't take any notice of their tastes? And if I do take notice, will I discover that I don't like them at all? Is mindfulness going to lead me to a life of miserable revelations where the only conclusion is to decide not to be mindful?

Friday 11th January
Frankie phoned. I told her about the V&A course and then honed in on the mindful chocolate-eating exercise. She thought I was having her on. She'd just come back from a health assessment at the doctor's where she'd been told to lose weight. I thought *she* was having me on. Frankie is as thin as a slim-line bar of Weight Watchers' chocolate. If she's considered fat, the rest of us might as well slit our throats right now.

Apparently her Body Mass Index is fine, but her waist measurement is more than the 34.6 inches which medics take as the indicator for being at risk of Type 2 diabetes.

In view of The Body Beautiful Project, and since I had struggled to get into my skirt this morning, Frankie's words struck a chord. *(And oh, how awful would it be to find out, just as I'm savouring freedom, that I'm a diabetic and about to die?)*

I went in search of a tape measure and was about to stretch it around my waist when I stopped. What is the point of discovering I am too large? I know that already. And, anyway, I've set my sights on losing weight and exercising more. *(The mantra of every woman in the western world.)* Isn't that enough? What else can I do? I rolled up the tape and put it away.

Saturday 12th January
Spent the day cleaning the house from top to bottom. *(Does this count as exercise? I definitely sweated.)* I've agreed to take on this mammoth task now that Dora's retired. It'll reduce our household costs in the face of my lack of income. I miss her already. After 17 years, working first as a mother's help and later as a cleaner, she'd become part of the family.

Sunday 13th January
Have caught The Lurgy. My tonsils are enormous. One has a white puss-filled spot on it and hurts viciously. I also have a hideously sore throat, though this is somewhat compensated by a husky voice which makes me sound like a different person: sexy and irresistible. Until you look at me.

I woke up feeling sorry for myself. *(I haven't taken a year off just to be ill.)* George was eating breakfast feeling even sorrier for *himself* having listened to me battling for breath all night and thus disturbing his sleep. He sat hunched over the table. A black cloud hovered over his head, threatening to drift my way.

I do understand how miserable it is to feel tired. *(After all, that's how I'm feeling too.)* Compassion, though, is something that eludes George.

He said, in a chilly tone, 'I suggest you take it easy today. Stay warm and drink lots.'

Good idea. But he wasn't forthcoming about who was going to run the house in my absence. So, while he did some gardening, I changed our bed, put several loads of washing on and hung it on the indoor racks, then cleaned the bathroom.

I shall sleep in the spare room tonight and, if I die, I hope he'll be stricken with guilt and remorse, and never get over it. *(Fat chance.)*

Monday 14th January
I didn't sleep in the spare room. I decided that if I got to bed first, that meant I had made my choice of where to spend the night and it was then up to George to make his decision. He climbed in next to me.

Tillie, who floated through to return the hairdryer to our room, remarked lightly, 'Why are you sleeping together after this morning's run-in? It'll be World War Three tomorrow. And you'll only have yourselves to blame. 'Night.'

I dosed myself with Paracetamol and slept well. Consequently, George slept well too. So, no war today.

*

Strange things are happening to my voice. If I try to speak at my usual level, hardly anything comes out. If I don't try and instead let my voice go where it wants, I have a very low and decent pitch. Is this my normal timbre? Perhaps I'm turning into a man. *(Please God, no. Not on my year off.)*

Frankie phoned and we had a curious conversation.

'What are you doing home?' she demanded.

I paused, wondering for a moment why I *was* at home. But I couldn't come up with a decent answer.

'Why shouldn't I be?' I replied hoarsely.

'Why aren't you at school?'

I paused again. Was there some appointment I'd completely forgotten about at one of the children's schools?

'I don't know. Should I be?'

Silence.

'Frankie, it's me – Jill. I've got a really bad cold.'

'Oh God,' she replied, shocked. 'I thought you were Lucas. Shall we start again?'

We discussed this season's ballets at the Royal Opera House, decided which we'd see and what our maximum price was for a ticket. Then Frankie booked everything and I put money into her account. All done and dusted.

Tuesday 15th January

The Lurgy was still doing battle but, as this was the first day of my Late Medieval and Early Renaissance course at the V&A, I wasn't going to miss it. I packed my bag with hankies, mints and a notebook, picked a favourite fountain pen and headed off.

I was met by the course director, a friendly woman about my age who congratulated me on my choice and handed me the reading list. *(She's hopeful.)*

The three lectures, with lunch after the first two, were on medieval furniture, tapestries and jewellery. I've never taken to tapestries but now that my attention was being directed to how they were made, what they showed, how and where they were hung, and what happened to some of them after they fell out of fashion, I was captivated.

The fourteenth-century Apocalypse Tapestry, which belonged to Louis I, Duke of Anjou, was eventually used to insulate orange trees against the chill of long, northern French winters.

I could just imagine an eighteenth-century Yorkshire head gardener and his apprentice eyeing citrus trees for the first time.

Head gardener: Them new-fangled trees, in t'orangery, wot Spanish Ambassador give t'gov'nor, won't mek it through t'winter.

Apprentice: Nay.

Head gardener: Wot thems needs is sommat to coddle 'em.

Apprentice: Ay.

Head gardener: Any ideas?

The apprentice thinks and a light goes on: T'under scullery maid says there's a knackered auld tapestry in't one of t'attics.

The head gardener turns to give him a keen look: Oh ay?

Apprentice: Reet big it is. Med of wool. If we wrapped that round trees, it'd keep 'em warm.

Head gardener: By 'eck lad, that's a reet good idea. They'll be snug as bug in't proverbial rug.

By the end of the afternoon, I felt both enlightened and much better.

Wednesday 16th January
My voice is almost back to normal, though a little huskiness still remains. I quite like it. It may be the only sexy bit of me and God knows, it too will go soon enough.

Thursday 17th January
In case any ignoramus *(me before I started out on this year off)* thinks that the life of a woman of leisure is just that, here is a typical day:

06.45	Get up. Take pile of white washing down to kitchen. Make breakfast. Call George and children down to eat. Empty dehumidifier.
07.15	Load dishwasher, load washing machine, put both on. Get dressed, put on make-up to look human.
07.45	Drive Lucas to school. Drive back via Morrisons. Do midweek top-up shop.
08.55	Get home. Put shopping away. Empty washing machine. Hang washing on indoor drying racks because it's raining. Collect two more loads from upstairs. Put next load on.
09.20	Clean teeth for second time and drive to dentists.
09.45	See new dentist. Very young, very gentle and very complimentary about my teeth-cleaning standards and state of teeth and gums. He can't find anything wrong. Like him instantly.
10.25	Drive home. Take out next load of washing and hang on racks. Put final load in. Make coffee and take to office.
10.45	Answer emails, deal with snail-mail and pay bills.
12.30	Take out third load of washing and hang on racks. Make sandwiches for lunch. Eat. Make breadcrumbs from leftover crusts and put in freezer. Wash up. Clean sink.
13.55	Clean fridge. Discover alien-like blue food. Put on

	Marigolds and throw in bin.
14.45	Write shopping list. Trawl through cupboards to check what's in short supply. Choose recipes to cook. Add ingredients to list.
15.00	Put shopping list on Ocado.
15.25	Empty airing cupboard. Redistribute clothes, towels and bed linen to appropriate wardrobes, drawers and cupboards.
15.40	Select bed linen and make up spare bed – in case.
16.00	Children arrive home. Have a drink with them. Try not to eat too many biscuits.
16.20	Play piano – which I should do more often. *(Why? What does it matter?)*
17.20	Make dinner: chicken casserole with potatoes and green beans, followed by apple crumble and custard. Wash up cooking utensils while food cooks. Lay table.
18.20	Call children for dinner. Put George's in oven. Chat about day, putting into practise how-to-have-happy-children-and-a-secure-home school of psychology.
19.00	Dinner finished. Children go to do homework. Play game of Patience while listening to The Archers.
19.20	Still no George. Sort out clothes washed this morning. Start ironing.
19.45	George home. Wash up while he eats so we have some time together and, simultaneously, I complete another task.
20.15	Finish ironing. Put it in airing cupboard.
20.35	Check emails and send replies. Close computer.
21.05	Sit in bedroom and flick through Evening Standard. Attempt sudoku.
21.40	George getting jittery as 22.00 approaches – official Baxter-residence moment for lights-out. *(It gives George almost nine hours of sleep before the onslaught of the next day.)* Loathe being chivvied, so dawdle in bathroom,

anointing The Body Beautiful with various creams. Kiss children goodnight, lingering for last hugs. Head for bed.

Jeez, I'm lost without Dora. It was because she did so much that I had the hours I needed to earn a living. But – horrible thought – where am I going to find the time to do lots of wonderful things in my year off if I have to work this hard?

Friday 18th January
Back to normal. No Lurgy, sore throat, sore ears, tickly throat, cough or sexy voice. Bliss. Ordinariness is much overlooked.

*

Great Aunt Vi phoned. I knew exactly which version I was getting when she started in her chair-of-the-important-meeting voice.

'I've written my will and you're the sole executor,' she announced, dispensing with any preliminaries such as 'hello' or 'how are you?'

I was taken aback. One: I'd prefer to be asked, so that I could say no. Two: I was struck by a ghastly vision of her house filled to the brim with seventy-odd years of knick-knacks and clutter. And three: even worse, a nightmare vision of me having to clear it out.

'I thought of making George the executor but decided against him, blood being thicker than water. He can, at least, use his legal background to assist you.'

'Yes, his knowledge of money-laundering will be very helpful,' I offered, starting to recover.

'Don't be facetious. It doesn't suit you. I've also made you the sole beneficiary.'

Instantly, my heart lifted. Great Aunt Vi would never be forthcoming about something inherently private. She was fibbing. And if she was fibbing about that, there was a good chance she was fibbing about me being the executor. She's great at saying one thing and meaning the opposite. I bet she's left her estate to the RSPCA or The Salvation Army. As she loathes animals and can't stand Christianity, they're both likely recipients. Still, it was best to take her at face value.

'That's extremely generous of you,' I said politely.

'You're setting your sights rather high, aren't you?' she cut in sharply. 'Doubtless you imagine I'm living in a valuable house and sitting on a pile of money, both of which will make you rich.'

(Actually, Great Aunt Vi, I'm not. But don't let me put you off.)

'Will you send me a copy of the will?'

Silence. And in that silence, a tidal wave of contempt rolled towards me. It's interesting how much Great Aunt Vi can convey in no words at all.

'Certainly not.'

'Where will I find it then?'

Silence again. I could hear her disgust at what she regarded as not so much a practical question, but my money-grabbing ambitions.

'At my solicitor's.'

I could have left it at that, but there must be dozens of firms of solicitors in Leicester and how would I know which to go to, presuming that there was any veracity in this call of hers?

'And who would that be?'

More silence. If she could have spat at me down the phone she would. Then she gave the name, but said it at such speed, I didn't pick it up. I was thinking: four words – third word is 'and'.

'Can you repeat that?'

'Oh, for goodness sake,' she said and slammed her phone down.

Great.

Saturday 19th January
A paradox of family life is that despite living together, there are periods when we hardly see one another. We meet for meals, but the rest of the time we do our own things. Homework for the children on weekday evenings, while on Saturday, George works in the home office before doing some gardening, Tillie stacks shelves at Morrisons and Lucas is off with his best friend Max. Sunday tends to be more homework for the kids, George catching up with paperwork and me reclining on a lounger. *(I made that last bit up. Bleating on about housework, making meals, washing up, putting the washing on and ironing is irksome.)* So, it's a pleasant experience for me to spend some time with one or other of the children or, on even rarer occasions, George.

Today, Lucas asked me to buy new clothes with him. We headed to Oxford Street and cruised H&M, Gap and Next. It's the first time he's purchased men's clothing, as opposed to older children's. Once decked out with new jeans and two warm sweat-shirts, he needed sustenance.

Caffè Nero provided coffee and hot chocolate, along with a fattening Danish bun. *(Lucas only. I'm on my no sugar, low-fat diet.)* After three hours together, we came home.

What a lovely boy he is. Mind you, he's as daft as they come – larking about on the train insisting I play Rock, Paper, Scissors. After a while, I tried snipping his coat with my finger-shaped scissors.

'What are you doing?' he asked in mock alarm.

'I'm scissoring you.'

'That's not how you play the game.'

'It's how I play it.'

'Gerroff.'

But he laughed all the same.

To my amazement, he rested his head on my shoulder and, when I rested my head on his, he let me keep it there. Just for a few moments. Pure treasure.

Sunday 20th January

Snow. And not just a sprinkling, but hours and hours of fat flakes falling throughout the day. The world is white, clean and surprisingly quiet.

Late this evening, with the snow deeper and the hush more pronounced, I couldn't bear to stay inside. The new me who doesn't have to work tomorrow morning was free to break old boundaries.

'Let's go for a walk and take the sledge,' I suggested.

'Can we?' asked Lucas, knowing that bedtime was nigh.

And Tillie, for all her eighteen years, jumped up and down on the spot with excitement.

The familiar world was transformed: the trees etched in white, their branches weighted with the fall. Snow creaked under our feet. The side streets were pristine. This could have been London in any age: the 1980s or the 1960s. If you ignored the parked cars – easy to do when most of them were blanketed by snow – it could have been the 1890s.

We chose the street with the longest hill. The place was deserted: no passers-by and no traffic. Just us.

George has definitely missed his calling: he should have been a bobsleigh runner. He pushed Lucas and Tillie at great speed until the sledge went so fast he couldn't keep up and, while they disappeared south, he rolled into the snow.

Tillie turned into a child again. She was free and happy, laughing like she used to do. *(What is it about adulthood that makes her more withdrawn and sombre? Why and when do we forget about playfulness and delight?)*

I listened to myself laughing as I watched our antics and I knew, even as it was happening, that this evening was special beyond words. Just as the whole day has been beautiful beyond the capturing of its image by a camera.

Monday 21st January
Despite the snow, Lucas's school, which is set on the semi-rural fringes of London, was open. He was profoundly depressed. I left him to catch the bus as I won't drive on snowy roads. We knew Tillie's would open as it's in the heart of the City with multiple public transport connections.

Tuesday 22nd January
The snow has gone. Just like that. What was white yesterday is now wet pavement drying quickly in today's sunshine.

But this was my V&A day, and off I went. I'm particular about how I dress. I choose the kind of smart clothes that I think a serious student of my age should wear: a tailored shirt and jacket over an A-line skirt, plus my favourite – albeit old – boots whose heels go clip-clip as I walk up the street. I even sound smart. I walk through the V&A with my papers and pens in my best hobo handbag and I imagine I look the part: a professional art history student. *(Can you be professional and a student?)* I'm the star of my own fantasy.

We learned about European Gothic architecture and, in particular, Milan Cathedral. Its construction involved the kind of unhappy relationship between client and consultancy which governs many major projects today. The Committee of Patrons, managing the build, went through numerous architects until they found one who would build them what they wanted: an outstandingly tall spire. Prior to that they were told that it was too high for the building to support, out of proportion, wouldn't look right and might well fall over. Eventually they got what they wanted, it does look good and, so far, it hasn't fallen down.

Wednesday 23rd January
Sue, a fellow long-suffering great niece, phoned. There's a decent number of us cousins – though I only keep up with Sue.

I'm very fond of her. She's a big, cuddly, character – one of those motherly women who should have had six children, two dogs, a hamster and a hard-working husband, all of whom she would have loved with blind devotion. But life didn't work out that way. Still, she's got the next best thing. She's in seventh heaven working as a teaching assistant in a primary school. Whether she's helping the little ones read or cleaning cut knees while wiping away tears, she is what every child needs: a solid, capable person who cares.

'I thought you'd like to know that Great Aunt Vi called last night,' she said.

'Ah.'

'That's a very diplomatic "Ah". It tells me you probably know what I'm going to say next.'

'Well, I might do. But just in case I don't, do go on.'

'She was in one of her taking-no-hostages moods and I was informed that not only had she written her will but that I'm the sole executor and the sole beneficiary.'

A huge weight lifted from my shoulders.

'Of course it's all a load of baloney,' she continued blithely. 'There's a possible chance I may be the executor but there's no way she'll be leaving me her estate. The last thing Great Aunt Vi would do is be frank about such personal matters.'

I smiled, recalling my identical thoughts on the subject.

'God knows what she's really up to,' said Sue. 'The point is, she's up to something.'

'I had a similar call last Friday and was told *I* was the sole executor and beneficiary though clearly, if I ever was, I didn't last long.'

'I suspected as much.'

'I did ask for a copy of the will, in my capacity as executor.'

'That was brave. I'm surprised you're still alive. What happened?'

'A tsunami of contempt rolled down the line.'

'Brilliantly put, darling. But did she agree?'

'No. Though she did give me the name of the solicitors.'
'And what is it?'
'Something, something and something. She said the name ridiculously quickly and I didn't catch what it was.'
'The "and" will prove very helpful.'

We both started laughing and once we started we couldn't stop. Girlish giggles combined with anxiety: the fear of being Great Aunt Vi's victims.

'Can you imagine being the executor and having to clear out her house?' I said when I could catch my breath.

'The same hideous thought had occurred to me.'

'Oh, the horror of going through all the clutter and junk.'

'Quite,' said Sue. 'But the real question is: what *is* she up to?'

I thought about that for a moment.

'Maybe nothing. Maybe she's really trying to wind up her affairs and is just looking to find a suitable relative to sort it out. At least I'm off the hook. And I'm pretty sure you will be soon, if not already.'

'I hope so. Keep praying.'

The thing with Great Aunt Vi is that we are so used to her Machiavellian ways that we always look for ulterior motives. But she can be straightforward too. Do I believe that's the case here? No. Definitely not.

Thursday 24th January

I'm not making much progress with *Mindfulness* and its associated meditations. It's hard to find time for the latter. But I'm not feeling as stressed as I was a month ago. Maybe it *has* helped.

Friday 25th January

George was cross when I was still in the bath after the curfew hour. He stepped into the bathroom to chastise me for my tardiness.

'I don't believe it!' he remarked tartly.

I turned round to find him stark naked. I wasn't sure I believed it either.

'Is this what you do to avoid coming to bed?'

I was blowing bubbles through the circle formed by the forefinger and thumb of each hand. I didn't reply as I was in the process of producing the most amazing bubble. It grew until it reached the bath taps and then burst.

'Did you see the size of that? Brilliant, wasn't it!'

'Do you do this every night?' he asked, in a world-weary kind of way.

'Only when I have a bar of Chanel No. 5 soap. You gave it to me for Christmas. It's the best soap in the world for blowing bubbles.'

'And how long do you spend doing this?'

Another vocation that George has missed is that of prosecuting barrister, though clearly he'd have to throw on some clothes.

'I only do two bubbles a night: one for each hand. Sorry darling, but I have to get on with the other one before all the soap runs down my arm.'

He shook his head and left me to it.

A few minutes later, I bounced into bed and he almost bounced out.

'Oh for God's sake,' he grumbled, settling himself back down again.

And I had the audacity to laugh.

Saturday 26th January
How can four people produce such copious quantities of washing? Nine loads. Nine loads of bloody washing.

Sunday 27th January
Another glorious day. Not.

We were all at sixes and sevens. Tillie and Lucas spent hours sniping at one another like an old, embittered, married couple. *(Not, I hope, like George and me, even on our worst day.)* George was miserable because he hadn't slept well. And I was grumpy because they were all out of sorts. And that's all I'm going to say.

Monday 28th January
I did the next eating mindfully exercise – necessary after yesterday. It involved a sultana. The idea was to quietly contemplate a sultana before eating it.

A sultana is not a beautiful fruit. In fact, if I'd never seen one before I'm not sure I'd want to eat it. I thought how trusting children are when we introduce new foods to them. *(Or not, in the case of my two who have never let a sultana, a raisin or any other dry and wrinkly fruit pass their lips.)*

What was astounding was the smell. It was sweet, rich and enticing. I wondered why no one had made a perfume from it. Eau de sultana. Women could dab it behind their ears and men would swoon at the scent. *(Well, not George, who is far too practical for such things.)*

And then the taste when I bit into it: sweet, rich and enticing. Just like the scent, but yet so different from it too – much stronger and fuller. My whole mouth was bursting with it.

So, this is *being* – not doing. Being alive to *what* I'm doing and the wonders of my small world. If I pay attention to it, I will see it as not at all ordinary, bland and unexciting but filled with extraordinary, rich experiences beyond anything I could imagine. This is part of putting my life on a fresh path, being aware of the new world that's literally at my finger-tips. Right here. Now. *(Amazing.)*

Tuesday 29th January
On the Tube to the V&A, I sat and took out my book. As I did so I noticed, in the seat opposite, a young man – perhaps in his late twenties or early thirties – and his slightly older male

companion. The young man was thin and pale, his eyes red raw. His head was shaved and, as he moved it, I saw a perfectly straight line running from the top centre down the back of his scalp. It was neatly stitched, though small amounts of blood had escaped and clotted into a narrow ridge of scabs. Taped around the base of his skull, running from ear to ear, were fine white gauze bandages. Beneath them were more dressings, rising like low white hillocks, semi-transparent and hinting at an intricate network of more scalpel-cuts and stitches crusted with more blood. The two men shared a few words as if nothing was awry.

The shaved man clutched a new plastic carrier bag from the Co-op on his lap while the companion held two enormous roll-bags. *(Full of more bandages?)*

I tried not to stare and read my book instead. No one else in the carriage noticed the bandaged man. *(How could they let him out of the hospital? Or was he returning? What was the 'back-story' as they say in The Guardian?)*

The two men got out at Sloane Square, still chatting, as if this was just any old day.

The course was interesting, but not as interesting as the man.

Wednesday 30th January

A day at home catching up with paperwork: bills, diary, household budgets, emails, letters and phone calls. Late afternoon, Sue rang.

'I'm off the hook,' she sang happily. 'According to Robert, Great Aunt Vi has done the decent thing and decided *he* will make a finer executor and sole beneficiary than me. He rang to tell me the good news last night.'

Robert is yet another of us cousins.

'Congratulations. You must be celebrating your freedom.'

'You bet. I'm clutching a full wine glass as we speak.'

'And how did Robert greet his appointment?'

'Rather flattered, actually. But that's men for you.'

'Is he not even a tiny bit worried about clearing her house and managing her effects?'

'God, no. That's housework, darling, and he's never done any. He'll regard that part of the contract as Elizabeth's.'

His wife.

'Not that it'll last,' she continued. 'You and I do, at least, know what Great Aunt Vi is up to. It's her new game: Upset the Great Nieces and Great Nephews. I expect that at this very moment she is flicking through her contacts book in search of the next victim who will find that they – temporarily – have received the poisoned chalice. Anyway, the main thing is that you and I have nothing to worry about.'

We rang off and I wondered, for a few minutes, where this would all end. Then gave up and went to make a pot of tea instead.

Thursday 31st January
I met Fay, as arranged, at the British Museum. It's some time since we worked together as designers for Ellis Hatcher: she as an employee, me as a freelancer – but we remain firm friends.

We bought coffee in the Great Court and settled down for a chat, talking about old times, past projects, the battles lost or won. It used to be fun working on corporate magazines before the Internet became the ubiquitous medium for almost all communications. With its arrival, much of the old creativity was displaced by prescriptive, limiting software.

It was good to remember this because I'm still recovering from years of finding the freelance, Internet-dominated design life less and less enjoyable.

Only George, Frankie and the children know that I've quit for this year. I decided to tell Fay, though I heard myself adding, 'Of course, I could still change my mind.'

Fay congratulated me on my decision. But I felt awkward, worried that she'd return to her office, tear my contact details out of the digital equivalent of a Rolodex and throw them in the bin. I said as much.

'Don't be daft. We'll always be friends.'

And she hugged me there and then.

I nearly burst into tears. I hadn't realised that stopping work would make me vulnerable.

It's curious how the job I loved gradually turned into the job I loathed. Before the children were born, it provided a decent income and, once they were here, the flexibility to work part-time.

But its appeal was wearing thin even when Lucas arrived. By then I'd spent almost twenty years doing the same thing year in, year out.

I carried on but my heart started sinking. I'd hear myself saying cheerily to a client who was talking about new work, 'That sounds interesting,' when inside I was thinking, 'Ohhh nnnnnnno.'

I know I'm lucky. I couldn't stop without George and his income. But also, I couldn't have gone on.

*

A highlight of the day – beyond that of seeing Fay – was the scene outside the British Museum as we left. The rain had just stopped and the sun was out. It transformed the forecourt's wet pavements into a vast silver mirror in which was reflected a watery image of the Museum's classically-columned entrance. As we walked closer to it, the image retreated, though it was still there. Entrancing.

February

Friday 1st February
I had every intention of addressing The Body Beautiful Project today but couldn't because – and this shows just what kind of a callous person I am – Lucas has caught The Lurgy. Instead of thinking 'poor boy' I thought 'damn'.

I reported Lucas's absence to his school and then attempted a change of attitude. While Lucas watched David Attenborough's latest series on iPlayer, I plied him with warm drinks, baked his favourite Betty Crocker chocolate cake and thought about what I love about not working.

The really big thing is: NO STRESS. It's an enormous relief not to have to worry about:

- racing back from the school run to start work
- spending too long hanging the washing out when I should be working on a client's account with a same-day deadline in sight
- disciplining myself to work one hour on fee-based work, then taking a break of fifteen minutes to go to the loo and, afterwards, manage some of the admin that goes with being a working woman, mother, wife and complete manager of a family and its finances – then carrying on throughout the day in the same vein
- popping downstairs to see the children when they've come home from school and hoping they won't tell me too much about their day or see the anxiety in my face because I really do need to get back to the office to do more work
- how much work I can get done and still leave myself enough time to make the evening meal
- chasing up invoices from rogue clients who, more likely than

not, are using the money they should be paying me to fund their business
- how I'm going to get enough work next month to keep the wolf from the door.

Horrible. I was stretched too far, too thinly and in too many conflicting directions with too few rewards: financial, emotional or psychological. And even if there had been wonderful rewards *(which there weren't)*, I'm not sure anything was worth feeling as over-worked and stressed as I did.

Saturday 2nd February
Lucas is still unwell, but as his throat is less painful he can talk more easily. *(The house is an eerie place when he's silent.)*

He spent much of the day on the PlayStation, in games with school friends. They take sides in hideously violent battles, shooting one another with large weapons, blood splattering the television's screen – albeit from the inside.

I loathe these war games. I worry about the harm they may do and whether his sweet nature will be irrevocably damaged. It's a constant battle, ironically, *(George and me versus Lucas)* to limit his time on the PlayStation. We feel we're always on the losing side. *(Though Lucas probably feels the same.)* Does anyone win in a war?

Sunday 3rd February
Although Lucas was still coughing, he said he felt more like his old self. I reminded him, now that he's improving, that his school shoes need cleaning and his school blazer is still lying on the hall floor where he dropped it on Thursday evening. I gave him half an hour in which to sort these two things out. Without a strict time limit, nothing gets done.

Tillie went to work stacking shelves at Morrisons, then spent the rest of the day on homework.

And I was bored. Bored of the washing, the housework, the ironing, the emptying of the airing cupboard, the washing up, the putting away, the laying of tables, the writing of shopping lists, the cooking of food and all other matters related to the smooth running of the household.

I know I agreed to do the housework when Dora retired, but I hadn't realised that combining what I used to do on a day-to-day basis with what she did three days a week would be as time consuming as it is – *and* do nothing for my ego.

Monday 4th February
Took Lucas to school, then drove to the sports centre to advance The Body Beautiful Project. I signed up for Total Workout and, a tad nervous, joined a class of athletic looking people with the kinds of bodies I'd swap mine for. We stepped up and down on plastic platforms *(easier said than done after the twentieth step)*, bent, stretched, waved our arms and legs, and ran around throwing and catching a netball which looked normal but was weighed down with a lead lining.

I was fine after they took me off the life-support machine, though my legs were still shaking. I was hallucinating about a large latte and Danish pastry but resisted and stuck to boring water from a boring fountain.

Tuesday 5th February
A bizarre thing happened on the way to the V&A. I stepped onto the Tube, sat down and discovered I was opposite the same young man and his slightly older companion who I'd seen a week ago. This was weird: you never see the same random people twice in London.

I rationalised it by telling myself we were all clearly on regular trips at regular times and that the coincidence was that I'd happened to step into the same carriage as them – albeit in a different part of the train from last Tuesday.

The young man didn't look as ill as he had. His scalp wounds were healing, the stitches had been taken out and there was no blood or scabs. He was still bandaged in semi-transparent gauze, but it all looked far less scary.

As before, the shaved man clutched a new plastic carrier bag from the Co-op on his lap while his companion held two enormous roll-bags.

They were both dressed casually in jeans, sweatshirts and sneakers. They passed the occasional comment and I had a sense of two good friends, as opposed to a gay couple.

I don't think they realised they'd seen me before. Certainly there was no sign of recognition. But then I didn't give any sign of recognising them either. Just like last week, I tried to read my book while surreptitiously watching them until they exited at Sloane Square.

*

There was a table at the back of the V&A lecture theatre at which a woman, a little older than me, was sitting. I went up and asked if the seat next to her was free.

We started chatting and carried on between each lecture as well as through lunch. She's a retired GP, is passionately interested in art history, has two grown-up daughters – one an artist, the other an academic – and is married to Victor, an accountant, who is still working. Oh, and her name is Annabel.

The lectures on illuminated manuscripts were excellent, particularly one about the Limbourg Brothers' Très Riches Heures created in about 1412. But it was Annabel who enriched my day – and those strange men who unsettled it.

Wednesday 6th February

I can't stop thinking about the two men on the Tube, particularly the one with the damaged head. If he was my son I'd make him a hearty, nutritious meal. And I'd buy a large flask and fill it with hot chocolate, knowing the milk would do him good.

This is ridiculous. If he's capable of taking the Tube, he's capable of looking after himself. Anyway, he's got his friend. And he's probably got a mother as well, while I've got my own children to take care of. What's getting into me?

Thursday 7th February
Frankie and I went to see the Royal Ballet perform *Onegin*. Or One Gin, as George calls it. She didn't mention her weight or diabetic waistline. Her bugbears at the moment are a leaking loo, a burglar alarm system that goes off for no reason in the middle of the night and a husband who enjoys cooking but hates washing up. *(She thinks she's got problems – at least hers cooks.)*

Onegin, the man, wasn't an ambassador for the opposite sex, being cold, manipulative and, ultimately, murderous. However, the dancing was sublime. Tears ran down my cheeks in the final act as Onegin and Tatiana expressed their intense love for one another. Even Frankie, who rarely shows her emotions, preferring a more laconic style, said she was moved.

Friday 8th February
I'm losing my voice. Not because of a nasty germ but through lack of use. With no one to talk to between eight-thirty and four, it's drying up. The kids come home, I croak, 'Hello'. And they laugh! It takes a good few sentences for my voice to warm up until I speak normally.

I never had this problem when Dora was here because we chatted over lunch, coffee and tea breaks. I miss our discussions. I miss the fun we had. Being alone can be lonely. It's easy to lose your focus. Not to mention it's frightening to find I'm turning into a frog.

Saturday 9th February
Lucas slept until midday. When the phone rang, he leapt out of bed guessing, rightly, it would be Max arranging to come round.

I might employ Max to phone every school morning as it looks like he has the knack of separating Lucas from his sheets. None of us do. You take your life in your hands when you wake him. Step close and he'll take a swipe at you.

George spent most of the day in the office – home, not City – catching up on emails and work matters. And I went from reading The Times, to putting the washing on, making lunch, reading some more, playing the piano, cleaning the bathroom, reading some more, eating dinner *(a hot meal made by George – yes!!!)* and then going to bed. Oddly satisfying.

Sunday 10th February
An outing for George and me to the National Gallery! We hardly ever go out as his job is too demanding. He arrives home late most evenings and, after a meal, goes up to the office to work at least another hour. He also works around four hours on each of Saturday and Sunday. In total, he does about seventy hours each week. Consequently, going out is a treat.

We wandered round the Impressionist rooms, these being our favourites. The works of Degas, Renoir, Manet, Monet, Morisot and Pissarro are so familiar to us, it's like returning to see old friends. In fact, going out with George was a reminder that he's a good friend, too.

'Can't you work less?' I asked him, tucking my arm companionably into his on the way home. 'Can't you give me and the children a little more of your time?'

He sighed. And I saw how he's torn between two enormous demands: work and home.

'We've been through this before,' he said, turning to me with a sympathetic smile. 'I go in early to speak with my Far Eastern colleagues before they go home, and I stay late to talk with my US colleagues who've recently arrived at work. In between those I catch up with everything that's happened in the UK and Europe, and attend a ridiculous number of back-to-back meetings. I come home to have dinner with you and take a break before sorting through emails ready for the next day. I'm doing my best.'

I grimaced.

'And we've got half term off together from next weekend,' he reminded me.

True, but I wasn't consoled. George remains intransigent. He sees no room for lee-way. And perhaps there is none. As I didn't want to turn an enjoyable time with him into a battle ground, I didn't pursue the subject. Nevertheless, the score was: work: 1, home: 0.

Monday 11th February
I was tired out by ten this morning – possibly caused by the continuous housework. My thoughts flew to Dora. I do wish she was still with us. Not just because she worked hard but because she was one of life's good, strong anchors. I realise now how much, in my mother's absence, she mothered me as well as the children. That did it: I was overcome by loss and started crying.

Great Aunt Vi must have a direct line to my emotional barometer because, just as I was mopping myself up, she rang.

She was in her sergeant-on-parade mode: barked instructions, responses needed instantaneously and no questions asked.

'Jill!'

She said it in such a commanding voice, I actually stood to attention.

'Yes.'

'I need a decision.'

'Excellent. I can do it. How are you, by the way?'

'Never been better. Now listen. I'm having a clear-out. Is there anything you'd like from this cesspit of excess that I call my home?'

'That's a bit harsh.'

'Possibly. But I have far too much of everything and need

to down-size.'

'Are you planning to move?' I asked startled. She's lived in her house since before I was born. In my mind, the two are inextricably linked.

'I'm planning to die,' she said slowly and venomously. 'At 94, it's what you do. Now, is there anything you'd like before I put it all in a box and send it to Oxfam? I need a decision.'

I racked my brains, mentally racing through her home from room to room, trying to recall what was in each. Was there any item I coveted? Simultaneously I considered the accumulation of excess here. More stuff would be excessively excessive.

I was also aware that this could be one of Great Aunt Vi's traps. She has firm beliefs about want. Basically, you must never want anything. And if you do, then you must never be given whatever it is as punishment for wanting it in the first place. So, if I said I wanted something *(even though she had asked)* there was a good chance I'd never receive it.

Oh, what the hell. I decided to give a straight answer to an apparently straight question.

'Well, you do have a very nice set of bone-handled fish knives and forks.'

'You're not having those,' she retorted testily. 'I'm keeping them for myself.'

(Hah! I knew it!)

'And you have an attractive dark-coloured glass vase. The one on the right-hand side of the mantelpiece in your back bedroom.'

'I'm keeping that too.'

This was pointless and dispiriting. I felt even more tired. Apart from which, I didn't want or need anything.

'How about a dinner service?' she prompted.

My mind started racing around our house. George and I each had a flat before we met. In combining the contents of our respective households we ended up with a lot of duplicates, including dinner services, together with his best service. We still have those. Since then I've bought a large quantity of Denby for our daily use and, a while ago, when I was going through a white phase, I purchased an additional set of plain porcelain.

'I'm embarrassed to admit this, but I have five dinner services and use just one of them.'

'Well you've got to have something,' she replied irritated.

'Why don't you just find a tiny memento? A jigsaw that we used to do together when I was a child. A button from your tin of buttons – if you still have that. Or an old coin we used to play Shove Ha-penny with. That way it'll remind me of holidays at your house *and* be a lovely keepsake.'

'Hopeless,' she snapped. 'You're unutterably hopeless.'

(Well, so much for love and sentimentality.)

'Has George ever told you how *useless* you can be at times?' she asked with venom.

(Tired or not, I wasn't taking this.)

'No. Actually, never.' I took my metaphorical sword out of its metaphorical scabbard. 'By the way, who did you settle on as your executor and sole beneficiary in the end?'

'It's not you. *And* it's none of your business,' she said tartly.

The phone went down.

Tuesday 12th February

My V&A day. I walked, deliberately, to the far right-hand side of the platform in order to step on the Tube at the opposite end to where I normally join it. Blow me, but there were those two men again. I sat opposite them, drawn irresistibly. I had a horrible sense of being stalked, except that it seemed to be me stalking them. How was I managing that? What strange force was at work?

I didn't even bother with my book. I just stared, openly. Curiously, they didn't seem to notice me, but then they were chatting away to one another. The young man looked much better this week. There were no bandages on his head and his wounds were healing nicely into trim scars.

He still clutched a new plastic carrier bag from the Co-op on his lap and his friend still held two enormous roll-bags. And then they got out at Sloane Square. What is going on?

*

We had three lectures on the development of oil painting in northern Europe but my mind was on other matters: those two blokes and pancakes, it being Shrove Tuesday. I hurried home and made enough to feed a small army. We ate them in no-seconds flat, as hungry soldiers do.

Wednesday 13th February
I've banned Lucas from his PlayStation for two days and I've reduced his play time to one hour a day after that. This is because he verbalised a horrible thought about Tillie. I think it's related to all the brutal games he plays. Either that or he's a psychopath.

Talking of disturbing thoughts, the penny finally dropped with a resounding clang. On Monday, Great Aunt Vi said she was clearing her house in preparation for dying. And I didn't make any comment, ameliorating or otherwise. Is she ill? Should I be worried?

Thursday 14th February
Valentine's Day. George and I never used to bother with sentimental tripe, but age has withered our disdain. Now we offer each other a votive card and then ignore the rest of the commercial rubbish that goes with the day.

*

I tried another class at the gym, having found Total Workout totally knackering. I went for yoga on the basis that much of it is done either sitting or lying down. I mean, what can be hard about that?

Well, I don't want to sound like a complete wimp but

sitting down with your legs straight out in front and your back ramrod straight is agonisingly difficult when you've spent decades sitting round-shouldered, hunched over a computer.

There are people in that class who can do things with their bodies that shouldn't be possible. And, worse still, they make them look easy. I was trying hard not to cry out in pain when we went into 'swan' position. Everyone else looked graceful and serene. I was inelegant and felt like a wounded duck.

It was far worse than Total Workout.

But who cares because here's the good news! I weighed myself afterwards and – yippee – I've lost a kilo! My mood switched instantly from downcast to elated! I'm on my way to a beautiful me.

Friday 15th February
Sue phoned just as I was in the middle of drinking a late afternoon mug of tea and writing the shopping list.

'I've had Great Aunt Vi on the blower asking me what I'd like out of her self-styled flea market of a home.'

'I've had that call too,' I replied.

'She rather put me on the spot. Told me I had to decide there and then. Did you make any requests?'

'I did, though I found the idea of asking rather off-putting, knowing her contempt for people who want anything.'

'Quite. Rather hard to know whether you'll be hanged for asking or hanged for not asking.'

'I plumped for her fish knives and forks, which she promptly told me she was keeping. And then I suggested the glass vase, the one on the right-hand side of the mantelpiece in her back bedroom.'

She paused and thought for a moment. 'No. Can't say that comes to mind.'

'It doesn't matter because she's keeping that too.'

'Ah, just as we thought: you must never get what you ask

for. Even if you've been asked to ask.'

'Exactly. And, frankly, I don't *need* anything. It's not as if I've missed out. In the end, I suggested she send me a small memento from when I stayed with her as a child to remind me of those times. Did you ask for anything?'

'Yes, I did – in a not dissimilar fashion to you. I've always been partial to her set of Dickens. They're the green, hard-back version she keeps in the glass-fronted bookcase in the sitting room. There's nothing special about them beyond the fact that I used to read them on wet days when I stayed with her as a child. I'd pull out a book, sit behind the settee with my back against the wall and read. It's where my love of Dickens stemmed from.'

'That's a nice idea.'

'But she said she'd already got rid of them.'

'They'll be in her local Oxfam. That's where she said she was sending everything.'

'Did she? I might give them a call and see if they've still got them.'

'She told me she was having a clear-out in preparation for dying. It took me two days to realise what she'd said and then wonder if I should have shown sympathy for the dying bit.'

'Oh, when she brought that up I told her she was good for another few years yet,' replied Sue dismissively.

'Do you think she is?' I asked. The idea of her lasting many more years was … well, lowering. I realised that in some dark corner of my brain I'd counted on her dying, sooner rather than later.

'Who knows? But she's as fit as a fiddle. There's no reason why she shouldn't celebrate her centenary. Anyway, is your family alright?'

And we moved on to other matters.

*

Lucas has not yet gone back to the PlayStation even though he's now allowed on it. I asked him why and he shrugged his

shoulders. Then I asked him how it felt not playing on it.
'Dunno.'
'Well, does it feel different from those days when you *do* play on it?'
'Not really.'
'Have you missed it?'
Another shrug of the shoulders.
'Have your friends asked why you haven't been on?'
'No.'
He's not quite monosyllabic, but it's a close-run thing.

Saturday 16th February
Half term. Tillie stacked shelves at Morrisons this morning then came home, picked up the bag she'd packed last night and headed off to Bristol Uni. She's staying with Carina, who she met at playgroup when they were both three years old.

They're going clubbing tonight – the first time for Tillie. I must have given her the 'keep-your-hand-over-your-drink-all-the-time' lecture at least six times in the last two days.

Lucas had Max round for half the day, playing on the trampoline then kicking a football about.

I've managed a few mindfulness meditations – twice yesterday and once today. The idea is to do the first meditation practice two times each day for a week. Then, the following week, you move on to the next meditation until, eight weeks later, you've completed the series. *(Then you have a complete nervous breakdown. Just kidding.)*

The thing is, I don't feel stressed any more. Do I still need to do the mindfulness exercises? Or is it because of them?

Sunday 17th February
Lucas was in a foul mood – exceedingly cross and exceedingly unpleasant – and I've no idea why. It was exceedingly trying. There are times when it's hard not to be worn down by the

mean minutiae of family life.

George refused to react and was resolutely positive – and kind – in the face of Lucas's grimness.

*

Tillie texted.

Clubbing fine & fun. Pub tour of Bristol today. Clifton suspension bridge to city docks. Not sure plan for tomorrow. xxx

Is this how it will be when she leaves home for university later in the year? Clubs and pubs plus abbreviated sentences sent digitally?

Monday 18th February
I half expected George to return to work given how horrid Lucas was yesterday. *(I would have.)* But George is made of sterner stuff.

It was a beautiful day, though bitterly cold with a hard ground frost. As George fancied a walk in the countryside, we made a picnic and then he drove the three of us to Chartwell – Winston Churchill's home. We walked from there to Emmetts Garden, about two and a half miles away, where we chose a table and bench in the sun and ate our lunch.

Lucas is now refusing to speak to me or George, replying only with a nod or shake of his head. We're not taking any notice in the hope that he'll tire before we do – and revert to normal.

It's such a shame. He usually loves it when Tillie goes away and there's just him and us. He also loves spending time with George. And now he's spoiling it.

*

No text from Tillie. It's not the same without her – a light goes out. *(Well, it does for me.)* I shall be heartbroken when she leaves for university.

Tuesday 19th February

There was no sight of the young man with his mending head and his slightly older companion on the Tube. It was one of the open trains, and I walked its length to check. If they were on it, I was going to ask them what was going on. Though, on reflection, they could have asked that of me – and perhaps with more reason. But they weren't and my heart sank. *(Why? What do I care?)*

*

I had to queue to get into the V&A because of the half-term crowds – mostly mums and offspring, with the latter becoming increasingly silly and the former fractious at the silliness. Just in front of me was a mum with two boys aged about six or seven years. They were larking about, pulling faces at one another, talking in gibberish and finding themselves very amusing. Beyond them a baby, about ten months old, sat bolt upright in a pram, eyes like saucers, watching them.

'Stop it before one of you gets hurt,' the boys' mum snapped.

As if on cue, the taller boy tripped and bumped his head against a pillar. He ran to her and buried his head in her stomach. She rubbed it vigorously. He pulled away and, with his face contorted in pain, yelled, 'You're doing that too hard. It's making it worse.'

The baby was still watching, its eyes now almost out on stalks. At least one person was learning a lot.

*

The three lectures were exceptionally good, but the fact remains that I'm not keen on too much religious art. The multiple saints are beyond me.

As a lapsed Catholic, Annabel has a much better grasp of who's who and what they did. At lunchtime she tried to explain, but the hard drive of my brain was full and what she said slipped off the edge.

Back at South Ken station, the mums, dads, grandparents

and children were wending their weary way home, back-packs empty of food, buggies laden down with souvenirs. There was a low-level scent, brown and warm, of full nappies.

Wednesday 20th February
Tillie arrived home this evening. She'd had a wonderful time in Bristol: clubbing, sightseeing, eating, shopping, not getting enough sleep and generally having a good introduction to student life. And oh, so happy. *(I am oh, so happy too.)*

Thursday 21st February
Spent the morning catching up on paperwork, while Tillie and Lucas spent it catching up on homework. Briefly, George and I went down the garden to look at the plants. They were hunkering down. It's too cold to do anything other than try to survive. The odd flurry of snow drifted out of a grey sky.

*

Lucas is starting to act normally towards George and me. Such a relief.

Friday 22nd February
It started snowing this morning, slowly and lazily. At first, I thought it was blossom drifting past the bedroom window – even though it was the wrong season. Then more white things appeared. Some danced leisurely in circles as if they couldn't be bothered to make it to the ground. Others spun upwards and disappeared beyond the window frame. It wasn't so much snowing as messing around. And it didn't settle.

Saturday 23rd February
Tillie went to work at Morrisons, Lucas went to Max's, and George and I went back to bed. Only rarely do we have the opportunity to make love in a house devoid of anyone but ourselves. It's liberating to know no one will burst into the room

with a query about homework or a sudden need for the hairdryer.

There's nothing George likes more than making love. I can see from the expression on his face that he's transported to some other sphere. My mind, on the other hand, remains on the domestic. I've always found it to be a short distance between sex and the shopping list, though I have learned over the years not to ask if George has finished the Shreddies, whether he needs more razors or if he'd prefer Italian to French salami. Nevertheless, these and other questions hover.

But it was nice to be naughty!

Sunday 24th February
Still snowing, still not settling and still bitingly cold. Tillie's bedside alarm clock incorporates a thermometer, which indicates it's 15.7 degrees Celsius in her bedroom. The rest of the house will be about the same. That's when the central heating is off. It's on for two and a half hours in the morning and six hours from the late afternoon. We don't usually put it on for longer as both George and I are from the north of England, where frugality and suffering are integral to everyday life.

Monday 25th February
Tillie went back to school, but Lucas had an extra day off. While he made the most of his lie-in, I went to a Pilates class. I was still deluding myself that anything which involved sitting or lying down was going to be easy. After half an hour, I rolled up my mat and walked out. Every head turned.

Pilates is similar to yoga, only worse. Much worse. I mean, how can you brace your stomach muscles and still breathe? They're mutually exclusive actions.

I grabbed a coffee and Danish pastry, then drove home. Miserable, frustrated and angry. Why can't I do any of this?

*

I tried to tempt Lucas out to see a film but he decided to stay at home and do his schoolwork. *(Honestly, he said that!)* He then proceeded to play on his PlayStation. I told him to do his work. He stomped into our bedroom, threw himself on the bed, face down, moaning and groaning. He eventually dragged himself to the office and, shortly after, announced he had learned all the required French. And then he decided he was hungry, even though he'd only had breakfast an hour earlier. It's a hard life being a teenage boy.

Talking of which, and according to George in whom Lucas confided, Lucas was turfed out of Max's house after lunch on Saturday because Max was taking a girl to see a film! Max with a girl! A girl with Max! Unbelievable!

When you've seen a boy grow from a toddler to this curious in-between stage that Lucas and Max are currently at, it's impossible to believe that they could be attracted by or attractive to anyone. That sounds harsh, but these are children in adults' clothes. They're hovering on the edge of childhood wondering whether or not now is the time to leave it behind and, mostly, deciding it's not. They mess around like nine-year-olds, have a puerile sense of humour and next to no social skills. They're lovely boys, but they're as mad as March hares.

Tuesday 26th February

I know this is ridiculous, but I was still hoping to spot the young man and his mending head, along with his slightly older companion, on the way to the V&A. Yet again, I walked from one end of the train to the other in search of my man. *('My man'?? What am I talking about?! This is lunacy.)* He wasn't there. Sadly. I wanted to ask, 'What happened? Can I help?' Too late.

*

We learned about medieval guilds, art markets, Erasmus and his colloquies. *(I'm not exactly sure what they are but didn't like to say in case everyone else knew, and they thought I was an idiot.)*

*

On the crowded Tube home, a young woman bumped into me and apologised.

'Too tired,' she said wearily. 'It's been a long day.'

'A bad one?' I asked.

'Don't even go there. How about you? What's your day been like?'

I explained about the V&A course and how much I was enjoying it.

'I've just started something which is a change for me,' she said. 'And it's great.'

But she didn't say what it was.

The Tube slowed down as it approached the next station. She put out her left hand towards me. I wasn't sure what she was doing.

'Shake pinkies,' she prompted, and moved her hand closer. She'd curled her little finger into the shape of a hook. I curled the little finger of my right hand round hers and we shook little fingers. She had long, pink, perfectly painted nails. I wondered whether this was how people do things now. I lead such a sheltered life that subtle changes in etiquette pass me by.

The train stopped. She picked up her bag and left, waving.

At dinner *(George was working late, again)* I asked Tillie if shaking little fingers with your friends was something girls did at her school. She looked at me as if I had taken leave of my senses, then burst out laughing. Lucas joined in, and then I did too because I could see it was funny.

When we'd calmed down, Tillie said, 'No. That's really weird. Anyway, why do you want to know?'

I explained about the young woman on the Tube.

'You *talked* to a stranger?' asked Lucas.

'Yes.'

'And then you *touched* them?' he pursued.

'Yes.'

'I don't believe this. You go out and you do *all* the things you tell us never to do. I suppose if she'd asked you if you wanted a little blue packet of something you would have said yes.'

'Possibly.'

From the look on his face I realised he might not understand I was joking. I added, 'No. Probably not.'

And then, worrying that this might not be strong enough or set a good enough example, I continued more soberly, 'No, definitely not. I'd definitely *not* do that.'

I sounded like someone who had no morals and, having just discovered that, decided she needed to find some quickly.

He shook his head, disgusted.

'I suppose it was innocent,' said Tillie.

But her voice was full of doubt.

Wednesday 27th February

I looked up 'colloquy' in the dictionary. It means conversation or discussion. In a religious context, it refers to a meeting to settle differences of doctrine or dogma. No one uses it now or, if they do, they're not in my small orbit.

If I said to the children, 'I'm going for a colloquy,' they'd think I was off to the loo for a major session.

And then – unbelievably, just as I was writing this down in my diary – George butted in.

'It would be C, O, L – that is, a word with only one L – if it was to do with the bowel or colon,' he said, emphasising the last word.

I turned round to find him resting his hands on the back of my chair and reading my diary over my shoulder.

'Do you mind? This is my personal, private, most intimate diary. It's meant for my eyes only,' I said, outraged. I covered the pages with my hands to stop him reading any more. 'I could have been writing about one of the six lovers who entertain me while you're out messing with laundered money.'

'Just to correct you once more, I actually mess with *the law* on laundered money rather than have anything to do with the money itself.'

'But what of the six lovers? If you'd read about them, just think how you'd feel!'

He was silent for a moment as he drew himself up to his full height.

'On reflection, I'd say good luck to them.'

And he walked out of the room.

(Really!)

Thursday 28th February
Phoned Frankie to see if she'd like to meet up for coffee. She sounded terrible, her voice gruff and flat.

'What on earth's the matter?' I asked, concerned.

'I had that norovirus thing last week as well as a fever and it beat the shit out of me. Worse still, Sam and I had to cancel a surprise trip to Paris for the boys.'

'Oh, Frankie, what bad timing.'

'Yeah. But I'm getting better.'

'I was calling to see if you'd like to meet for coffee, but perhaps that's not a good idea.'

'Not this week. Or next. I'm still spending half the day in bed.'

'Did Sam and the boys make a fuss of you?'

'Sam went to work once he knew Paris was off, and the boys managed to bring me the odd glass of water. But that was only when I called out repeatedly for help. To be honest, it was bleak.'

'Frankie, that's awful!'

'I've been planning revenge. It's the only thing that's kept me going between the bouts of vomiting, fierce chills and sweat pouring off me. I'm waiting for one of them to get sick. Really sick, so that they're glued to their beds. Then I'm going to discover I must watch all the films in The Bourne Trilogy without a break. After that, I'll have to check my social media, answer my emails and texts, see how I look in the mirror, make myself a meal, play a quick game on the PlayStation, which turns into a long game because I've met up with all my friends online and then, finally, I'll remember that it's twelve hours since I last looked in on the ill person. Then I'll promptly forget.'

'Sounds like you've worked it out.'

'Of course, I'll never manage it,' she said wearily.

I'd never heard Frankie sound as despondent. I changed the subject.

'We're meeting in early March for another ballet, aren't we?'

'Yes. I'll be OK for that. On the positive side, I've vomited my way to a smaller waistline. I needn't have any diabetic worries.'

'Well, that's something.'

'Yup.'

She sighed and we rang off.

*

Talking of weight loss, I ran upstairs to the bathroom, stripped off and stood on the scales. Another kilo gone! Oh, happy day! I'm in control of my life, eating less fat and sugar, exercising *(just)*, losing weight, studying at the V&A and not working! All my resolutions and everything I ever wanted for this year!

(Everything, that is, except for the never-ending, sodding housework. And what can I do about that that doesn't involve the expenditure of money?)

March

Friday 1st March
Dora came for lunch. We haven't seen one another since she retired at Christmas. I love Dora – though I could never say that to her. I can't imagine which of us would be more embarrassed. But the fact is, she has been one of the best people in my life ever since her very first day with us. Tillie was three weeks old and crying inconsolably. Dora picked her up, held her firmly, rocked her and within five minutes she was asleep.

Dora looked after Tillie and then Lucas while I worked upstairs in the office. She was a gem. The eldest of ten children and the mother of four boys, she knew exactly how to play with a toddler, care for a sick child or entertain a group of children. She was happy to adapt, too. As the children grew up and needed her less, and just as George and I were wondering how we could keep her employed, our cleaner left and Dora took on that role instead.

She was my right hand. If the dishwasher needed emptying, she'd empty it. If there was a pile of ironing, she'd work her way through it. If the airing cupboard was full, she'd remove everything and put it in the correct wardrobe or drawer.

Beyond all that, she was strong, wise, kind and loyal. Of all the people she cared for, it was me who benefited most. When she left, we were all sad – but no one was sadder than me.

Knowing how much she likes food, I'd prepared home-made cannelloni and a side salad, followed by good old Yorkshire parkin and fruit.

After we'd eaten, and with a cup of tea held between her hands, she confided, 'I just didn't know what to do with myself after I left here. I became a complete fidget. I couldn't settle to anything. It just didn't feel right being stuck at home.'

'It's not the same without you,' I said.

'I have to say, though,' she continued, looking round the room, 'you're managing to keep the place nice and clean.'

'Thank you.'

'Anyway, I'm fine now. I'm spending time with the grandchildren and that's lovely.'

We're in the process of developing a new relationship, the old one of employer and employee having ended. We agreed to meet next month. When she left I watched her walk down the drive – a small, solid, good woman.

Saturday 2nd March

Naively, I believe that weekends are for relaxing. But I'd like someone to run a time-and-motion study on me to determine exactly how many hours I spend on housework. Whatever it is, it's too many.

Take the washing. *(And I wish someone would take the washing.)* I've done nine loads this weekend. I estimate each load takes fifty minutes of my time. That includes:

- sorting the washing into different piles (whites, colours, woollens)
- taking it to the kitchen and putting it in the machine
- taking it out and hanging it either on the line down the garden or on the indoor racks
- taking it off the lines/racks and sorting it into ironing and non-ironing piles
- doing the ironing
- putting everything in the airing cupboard
- removing it and sorting it into piles according to whose clothes they are
- redistributing them to the appropriate bedrooms plus, in Lucas's and my own case, putting everything away in

cupboards and drawers.

Those nine loads take 450 minutes, which is the equivalent of seven and a half hours. Each week. And that's just the washing, never mind everything else.

If I ever inherit a shed-load of money *(pigs might fly)*, I am moving into a suite in Claridge's, where my every need will be catered for by lovely people. I will never touch a washing machine again in my entire life. And I will not miss it.

Sunday 3rd March
Miserable, being burdened by all the stuff that needs to be done to keep the house and us going. George was miserable too because his relaxation time involved reading just fourteen pages of a novel. It doesn't help that he's a workaholic trapped in a hamster-wheel world of workaholics.

Monday 4th March
A trial lesson of Zumba. What can I say? It's a completely bonkers kind of group dancing. Plus, I really am the most uncoordinated person in the world. I have not two but three left feet, one of which I was constantly tripping over. I did manage to last the full fifty minutes but by the end I was just jumping around waving my arms and legs like a mad woman. Like all the mad women in the lesson.

I'll stick to Total Workout. At least I can catch the ball.

*

I'd intended to clean the ground floor windows but didn't have the energy. Oh, but surely there's more to a year off than this? I know it's partly my own fault. I was so engrossed in making the decision to stop work that I didn't focus on what I was going to do instead. Taking on Dora's role in an attempt to reduce our household costs seemed eminently reasonable. But, on my worst days, I think all I've done is switch one unhappy *paid* job for another unhappy, *unpaid* job. Shit.

Tuesday 5th March

Well, at least the V&A day gets me out of the house and away from its associated work. Plus, I feel special. I'm an academic: serious, knowledgeable and with an enquiring mind.

I don't know why I'm continuing with this fantasy *(other than it's fun)* because no one else among the elderly student body appears to have delusions about themselves. But I do have a sense of being a different version of myself *(not a graphic designer, not a mum, not a wife and definitely not a cleaner)*. I'm born-again. I could be anyone to any of these people.

Today's lectures were about sculpture. I now appreciate the extraordinary skill that goes into the casting of bronze – a process so lengthy, awkward and difficult to achieve that one wonders first, how anyone invented it and, second, why anyone continued with it.

Wednesday 6th March

Finally finished cleaning the wretched windows. They gleam. Well, they would if there was any sunshine.

*

Tonight, Lucas announced that we must all stay out of his bedroom as he was expecting a call and would be taking it in private. He was talking to Emma – the girl we passed on our walk on New Year's Day – for an hour. According to Tillie, they've been messaging one another on various social networking sites.

Briefly, *(because even if it's fascinating, I do know it's rude to listen)* I stood outside his door to hear what he was saying.

'No, I don't have any gossip from my school day. We don't have gossip at my school.'

I smiled because he and his friends *do* gossip but it's usually brief, and then they move on to other things. That's boys for you. Girls are a completely different matter. They chew over who said what to whom, what the motives were and what the implications may be.

'No, we don't do that either. After lunch, we go to the playing fields and kick a football about. Or have a fight. It depends on the weather and what mood we're in.'

Pause.

'No, a play fight. We're not nasty. It's just fun. Though Gozo did break his arm last year. But that was a mistake. He fell badly. Stupid, really.'

I was impressed he could hold a conversation for that long. He's never talked to any of us for an hour.

Thursday 7th March
Every year, Tillie's school has a day dedicated to preparing the year 11 girls for work. In the morning they learn how to write a CV and covering letter to accompany an application for a fictitious job. Various parents, representing different professions, write the job specifications and then do mock interviews with the students who have applied. I go along in my guise as graphic designer looking for a junior.

This afternoon, I read five job application letters and CVs, then interviewed the girls before selecting one for the 'role'.

All my candidates had excellent GCSE art portfolios, though there was an inevitable similarity through studying the same course with the same teacher. I could detect her preferred style and how she was building their skills.

In the interviews, two of the students were diffident, though one warmed up as we progressed. Another was confident, witty and opinionated. The fourth girl had a most beautiful nature, and the fifth was the one I chose.

Not only was she good at art, but she was superb with ideas. I'd taken along three teen magazines and asked the students to describe what they saw. This open question left some of them reeling, while others plunged in with a host of interesting comments about the format, the fonts, the ratio of photographs to words, the number and frequency of ads and so on. My chosen candidate gave a soliloquy making insightful comments while brimming with enthusiasm.

I'm deeply impressed by how smart and confident these girls are. If they're strikingly good at fifteen or sixteen, what will they be like at twenty-one when they hit the job market with even more skills and greater maturity?

I love meeting them. Yes, I have two young people in my life, and I do see their friends. But I spend too much time either on my own or with other adults. It's a breath of fresh air to meet a different age group whose ideas are expressed with a sparkle that's missing from my peers.

Sadly, though, this is my last year doing the interviews. When Tillie leaves school, they will look for another parent. I have reached my sell-by date.

Friday 8th March
Frankie phoned late afternoon. She's ill with a heavy cold she picked up just as she was getting over the norovirus and can't come to this evening's ballet at the Royal Opera House. I called George to see if he'd like to join me, but he's not a ballet fan. The kids aren't either. I called numerous friends, but no one was free at such short notice.

Consequently, I went alone and, though I'd taken a book to keep myself occupied before the ballet started, I listened to the elderly couple sitting to my right. Their interest in one another's activities revealed them to be old friends, so familiar with each other that they anticipated what each was about to say and then interrupted. Sentences were truncated, vital nouns were missing and the subject of the conversation never expressed fully.

Him: You were going to tell me about your visit to the —
Her: Ah, yes. I'd gone about the —
Him: Yes, you gave me the details last time.

Her: And they said it was working marvellously. They've asked other people to use this new —

Him: Is that the thing that pulses?

Her: Yes. Rather strange at first but then you get used to it. I'm wearing it now.

It's hard to stare at someone sideways, but I did my best. I could only see her in profile, but I scanned her from the top of her white-haired head to the tips of her black court shoes. Nothing was pulsating.

When she left for the bar in the interval, I followed. She was tiny and wearing particularly thick black stockings over slightly swollen legs. *(Was she wearing pulsating stockings? Are there such things?)*

*

The ballets – *Apollo*, *24 Preludes* and *Aeternum* – were extraordinary. The dancers combined athleticism with strength, poise and beauty.

Afterwards, in Covent Garden's piazza, a man in a duffle coat had set up his evening's spot and, accompanying himself on his guitar, was singing Carole King's *You've Got a Friend* in a deep, rich and melodious voice.

Saturday 9th March

Tillie's school's Easter Fair – the main annual fundraising activity – is held in the primary school. The children and I have always gone, but this year they baulked.

The gym was heaving with parents and offspring. A bevy of under-sevens was racing around excitedly clutching newly-won Easter eggs. Elderly couples were clustered round stalls selling old novels. Young mums, with babies strapped to their fronts, were sifting through boxes of children's books. Dads were serving coffee. Other mums were at a variety of stalls selling raffle tickets, running the bottle tombola, managing the second-hand uniform stall or sliding mouth-watering cakes into cellophane bags – just as I had done years ago.

Suddenly, and horribly, I had an out-of-body experience where I saw the happy throng and then myself, totally alone. There wasn't a single person I knew and, without an accompanying child, I was completely out of place.

Though I'd been there less than three minutes, I turned tail. Just as I did, I passed the entrance to Tillie's first classroom. When it was home time, the children used to rush to the door. They were small and even standing on tiptoes, their noses just about reached the base of the window half-way up the door. They'd peer out, eagerly looking for whoever had come to collect them that day.

I walked past all the other classes in which Tillie had studied, then past the cloakrooms and the tiny toilets, past the colourful artworks that lined the walls, past the stairs and landing, past reception and out of the school.

Tears pricked my eyes because it's over: all the loveliness of the children being little with everything to look forward to in, literally, small, incremental steps. The next step is large. Too large. Tillie will go to university. I know it's wonderful and exciting for her. But it's without me. And I'm grief-stricken.

Sunday 10th March
I asked George whether he shared my feelings about Tillie leaving home.

'What do you mean?'

'Well, I've given the children my all over the last eighteen years. Yes, I've had my job but the mainstay of my life has been them: their care, their health, their happiness and my love for them. And with Tillie leaving – well, I know it will be amazing for her – but it's an awful loss for me.'

He reflected for a few moments on what I'd said and then gently shook his head.

'No, I don't feel that at all. I'm looking forward to having you back.'

I was surprised. I thought he'd be sad too. As for 'having me back' well, I didn't know I'd been away. Though I should have. He's definitely been a poor second to the children.

Life for George and me has been very different since they were born. I've spent far more time with them than he has, not least of all because my work was based at home.

Plus, there were times when George saw very little of any of us. For several years, he commuted between his firm's offices in London and Frankfurt. His absence made me even closer to the children and even more grateful for Dora's help.

George's role has been to provide the main income for us all, and I'm eternally grateful for that. *(We'd be in the poor house if we'd been relying on mine.)* But in doing so, he missed out on too much. Not cuddling the children every night. Not reading them night-time stories. Not seeing Lucas trip in the fifty metres race on sports day, pick himself up and limp, with great dignity, to the finish line, blood dripping from a cut knee, tears running down his face. Not seeing Tillie as one of so many angels in the primary school's nativity play that a fight broke out and several angels fell off the stage.

I have lived for the children. They have been my life.

*

My devotion hasn't necessarily been reciprocated. Today was Mother's Day. Tillie remembered and gave me a lovely bunch of carnations. Lucas forgot and then said the carnations were from him too. Tillie was sufficiently gracious not to contradict him, but Lucas was mortified and wouldn't look me in the eye.

Monday 11th March

Went to Total Workout and have signed up for two classes a week. Some of the women recognised me and came over to chat. I felt welcomed, part of the crowd.

*

The postman delivered a parcel wrapped in brown paper, addressed to me in Great Aunt Vi's unmistakeable and old-fashioned looping handwriting.

I sat on the stairs and, under the wrapping, discovered a shoe box. The paper, pasted on the narrow end, showed that it had once housed a magnificent pair of size six, black patent stiletto shoes from, I'd guess, the 1950s. I've only ever known Great Aunt Vi to wear brogues. The idea of her tottering around in elegant footwear hinted at a person beyond my ken.

Resting on top of the box was a folded sheet of blue Basildon Bond paper on which she had written a brief note: 'Thought you might like these keepsakes.'

Removing the lid, I discovered, in date order, dozens of letters, birthday cards, Christmas cards, get-well cards and holiday postcards. She had kept everything I had ever sent – from my very first 'thank you' to the birthday card I posted in January.

I read through them all and was unravelled by being presented with my childhood self. I'd written the earliest letter when I was just five years old. A shakily penned 'Thank you' wobbled its way across a thin sheet of pastel-coloured sugar paper. My mother had written the rest around it.

'Jill wants to "Thank you" for the money you sent her at Christmas.'

It was a shock to see my mother's hand and style. She'd signed off with a small illustration of snowdrops. This was typical of her: a modest but pretty and seasonal end to a letter. It was from her that I inherited my graphic design skills.

I'd written a note to acknowledge every gift including 'spending money' for our annual family holiday. There were postcards from Bridlington, Scarborough, Whitby and Filey.

Dear Great Aunt Vi,
Thank you for the £2 postal order. I am spending the money on donkey rides. My favourite donkey is Willow. She has long

eyelashes, blue ribbons on her reins and is always pleased to see me. I hope you are keeping well.
Love, Jill xxx
P.S. I can afford two rides a day for six days.

The images on the postcards were a history of their own. The oldest, from the late 1960s, were in black and white and made the resorts look as attractive as funeral parlours. By the 1970s, colour photography was all the rage but the photographers had forgotten to include holidaymakers in their images. Beautiful flower gardens were caught with not one person admiring the blooms. Scarborough's famous beaches were captured before the first tourists had started their breakfasts. Whitby's small, picturesque harbour showed a number of boats from modest trawlers to tiny yachts, but not even the ghost of a sailor strolling any of the decks.

In addition, there were letters thanking Great Aunt Vi for having me to stay. God knows, she should have sent me the odd thank you for putting up with her. Doubtless she did her best, but she was a confirmed spinster: happiest with her own company and soon irritated by a child's constant presence. Her temper flared and I was regularly roasted.

The years rolled over and on. We were still corresponding when I was at college – the cost of a phone call being beyond my meagre student finances.

Dear Great Aunt Vi,
Many thanks for the £5 you sent. Riches! I went out straight away and bought myself a beautiful, purple, wide-brimmed hat. I look great! I'll try to remember and wear it next time I see you, then you can enjoy it too.
I'm working hell for leather on my latest assignment – a double-page spread for a leisure magazine about Paris as a tourist destination.
There's a group of us going to a disco tonight. Tomorrow, if it's

sunny, we're having a picnic.
I hope you are keeping well.
Love, Jill

I was deeply touched that Great Aunt Vi, that gorgon of rudeness and *(let's not beat about the bush here)* intermittent cruelty, had a heart soft enough to keep everything carefully all these years. It revealed a side I'd always hoped was there but had never discovered previously.

Tuesday 12th March

I bumped into Annabel on my way to the V&A. We were both dressed in multiple layers of clothing for it was a bitterly cold day.

Fortunately, the lecture room was warm and we enjoyed a series of talks on Brunelleschi and other early Renaissance architects. Afterwards, I went on an associated gallery talk about Donatello given by the same young man who, last week, gave a lecture on Donatello's sculptures. Then he wore a smart dark grey suit, a white shirt, and a red patterned tie. He carried a leather briefcase and exuded the air of an elegant professional.

Today he looked as if he'd stepped straight off an old dinghy. He sported worn-out, blue sailing shoes, baggy grey trousers and a tatty, loose-fitting orange polo neck jumper plus scruffy orange sailing jacket. His papers sagged within a tired plastic bag. But he had the most enormous grin and such wit, warmth and knowledge that nothing else mattered.

If I'm brutally honest, my own clothes aren't much to write home about either. I ran my work wardrobe down to almost nothing last year. I own about three smart things and they're all beginning to look jaded.

Only two more weeks left of the term. What shall I do?

Wednesday 13th March
I phoned Great Aunt Vi to thank her for the keepsakes.

'They brought back some lovely memories,' I said. 'I was surprised at how many cards I recognised.'

'I read through every one before I returned them to you,' she responded. She sounded to be in a good mood. 'They reminded me of wonderful times too.'

'And did you really wear the stiletto shoes illustrated on the box?'

She was surprised.

'Why, yes I did! I was quite a goer in my hey-day, though by the time you were born I was forty and, in those days, that was ancient spinster territory. But I've always loved beautiful shoes. I may not wear them now, but I can still admire them.'

I was about to launch into an extended conversation covering various trivia when she interrupted.

'Sorry, dear heart, but I must go; I have more clearing out to do.'

(Dear heart?!! She's never called me that before. She's hardly ever tender, never mind down-right loving. Was something up?)

'Great Aunt Vi, before you go, are you OK? I mean, are you unwell or anything?'

'Never felt better. Absolutely tickety-boo.'

And off she went.

No plans for dying this month, then.

Thursday 14th March
My life is being taken over by all things to do with the venerable aunt. Shortly after school kicking out time and, just as I'd nipped down to the kitchen to make a mug of tea, the landline phone rang.

'It wasn't Oxfam.'

I sighed. Sue, like Great Aunt Vi, launches straight into a conversation without any preliminaries and, worse than Great

Aunt Vi, doesn't give any clue to what she's talking about.

'What wasn't Oxfam?'

'You said it was Oxfam. Remember? When we were talking about Great Aunt Vi last time? About a month ago? *You* said that *she* said she was taking her unwanted household goods to Oxfam.'

'Yes,' I replied, the penny dropping. 'That's right.'

'Well, you were wrong.'

'I was only telling you what I'd been told,' I said, a tad defensively.

'Oh, I know that,' she responded breezily. 'But have you any idea how many Oxfams there are in Leicester?'

She didn't wait for a reply.

'Three. I found them all via Google Maps, called each up in turn and explained my story – great niece of great aunt clearing out house, and had they by any chance received a complete set of green, hard-backed novels by Dickens?'

'And had they?'

'No.'

'And there I was about to be impressed by your sleuthing abilities.'

'Ah, yes. Well, it doesn't end there because by then I'd got the bit between my teeth. I thought about it for a day or two, and then I called them all back to double-check – in case the old horror had donated them in the meantime. Which she hadn't. Plus, none of them recognised my description of her. Then it occurred to me that it was probably a ruse – her telling you it was Oxfam. I mean, how many times has what she said turned out to be true?'

'Not many.'

'Quite. I asked them what other charity shops there were in Leicester and then I called each of them in turn.'

'You're keen.'

'I don't like to be beaten.'

'And how many other charity shops are there?'

'Too many. Believe me, like every other town in this beleaguered country, Leicester's shopping streets are thirty per cent regular retailers, thirty per cent empty and the rest charity shops.'

'Blimey, Sue. I know being single makes you carefree, but don't you have better things to do?'

'Of course I have! But I was hooked! The more shops that didn't have Great Aunt Vi's junk, the more determined I became to find the one that did. As I had to be getting closer, it seemed madness to stop. Anyway. Back to the story. Many calls later, I finally tracked down the charity to which she's been going. She's brought in such quantities of stuff, that they treat her like an old friend.'

'And which one is it?'

'Leicester Loves Llamas in Lebanon. Otherwise known locally as The Five Ls.'

I was busy counting on the fingers of the none phone-holding hand.

'There's only four Ls.'

'Pedant. There's two in llama and they count them both. It's a small charity and it has just one shop nationwide.'

'I didn't know there were llamas in Lebanon.'

'Well, there weren't originally. But what I don't know now about those llamas isn't worth knowing. I've become great pals with the people who run this little charity. Well, are you sitting comfortably and then I'll begin?'

'Hang on,' I said. 'Let me grab my mug of tea.'

I went back to the kitchen, picked up my mug, dragged a chair with the other hand and settled in for the long haul.

'OK. I'm here.'

'Suffice to say, llamas are *not* an indigenous species of that country. But back in the late 1960s some rich Lebanese man – whose name I can't recall and even if I did I couldn't pronounce it and how racist is that – decided to set up a zoo on the outskirts of Beirut. He imported ten llamas. From Peru. All well and good.

'Fast forward to 1975: the good burghers of Leicester were in the process of twinning their city with Beirut. But then all hell broke loose with the civil war which ultimately put paid to the zoo's survival. The animals were either sent to other zoos, put down or in the llamas' case, let loose to fend for themselves in the Lebanese mountain range.'

'I'm beginning to feel this is turning into both a history and a geography lesson.'

'Just hang on in. So, the war raged and Lebanon descended into chaos. But up in the mountains the llamas were doing well, breeding and becoming a small herd. Finally, a ceasefire was agreed in 1989. Back in Leicester, a woman who'd been on the town-twinning committee in 1975 heard the story about the zoo and the llamas and, don't ask me why, but she decided to go and see them. The herd was now rather large and, with refugees returning and farmers resuming the tilling of the soil or whatever it is that farmers do in Lebanon, there was competition for the land. She came back to Leicester, set up a charity to buy some land for them – llamas not farmers – organised the rounding up of as many llamas as the locals could capture and she now pays the said locals to care for them. If you live in Leicester, you can even volunteer as a helper and head out to sunny Lebanon. Apparently, it's very popular with gap year students. The charity shop provides the ongoing funds.'

'You're not making this up are you? If you are, it's a hell of a good story and you should definitely give up the day job and start writing novels.'

'Hand on heart, it's all true. But the point is that they had Great Aunt Vi's set of Dickens. And now they're sending them to me. I couldn't be more chuffed.'

'That's amazing. Well done, Sue.'

'I did ask them if they'd seen a sort of dark-coloured glass vase.'

My heart rose. Perhaps I too could benefit from Sue's detective work.

'And had they?' I asked hopefully.

'No.'

(Oh, for goodness sakes.)

'Well, I'm glad you're getting the set of Dickens.'

'Me too. Financially, they're worthless but they mean a lot to me emotionally.'

I told her about the shoe box, the letters and postcards. She was as surprised as I had been by the aged A's show of sentimentality, but agreed it was touching.

Unlikely as it seems, both of us will have got what we wanted: things that mattered.

Friday 15th March
Total Workout again and, as before, I was made welcome by a group of women. This is the best part, this sense of belonging after years of working on my own. I'm still struggling with the exercise, still massively hungry afterwards and still resisting the sugary snacks.

*

Have encouraged Lucas to go on a one-week university taster course during the summer holiday. I want him to think about potential subjects that he could eventually study, as well as a career he might pursue. I don't think it's dawned on him yet that in just a few years he'll be fending for himself. He's looked at a few educational websites but nothing's caught his fancy.

There are more pressing matters in his life. Tonight he showered, sprayed on quantities of deodorant, put on his best jeans, tee-shirt and sweater, then headed off to the cinema to meet Emma. He has sworn us all to secrecy about his friendship with her. We are not to tell anyone, anywhere, ever. Not friends, not family, not a soul on earth. Cross our hearts and hope to die.

Saturday 16th March
Highlight of the day *(and this is not sarcasm)*: George and I walked to the high street where I took a pair of boots to the menders. We then called in at our favourite café, Flavours. In total, we spent a whole hour together. It's times like these – simple times – when I realise just what a nice person George is and how fond I am of him.

*

Lucas refused to talk about last night's adventure to the cinema with Emma. He wouldn't even tell us about the film. I'm hoping he did see it.

Sunday 17th March
Made love tonight. Making love is the only reason *(in George's eyes)* for breaking the 10pm curfew. Over the years, we've discovered that Sunday evening is the one time in the week when both of us find it hard to sleep: we each lie worrying about the coming week's work. In the make-good-use-of-every-waking-minute world in which George and I live, we've decided that making love is a good way of using that time. *(Ye gods, and how romantic is that?)* Plus, with all those lovely endorphins swimming around afterwards, we fall swiftly into sweet sleep.

Monday 18th March
Tonight, Emma phoned Lucas and I answered the phone. She sounded very young and very sweet. Lucas came running into the room, grabbed the phone from me, made shooing motions with his hands and then they talked for an hour. Again.

At bedtime, he referred to her as his 'girlfriend'. Up until now she's been described as 'a girl who's my friend'.

'Have you kissed her?' Tillie asked bluntly.

Lucas pulled a face and made a disgusting noise.

'You have to kiss her if she's your girlfriend.'

'No, he doesn't,' I said, interrupting.

'Yes, he does.'

He thought about that for a moment. 'I don't think I do.'

She raised her eyebrows at him and gave him a withering look.

'You do what you want,' I said to him, supporting his apparent chastity.

'Don't worry, Mum. I will.'

I wasn't sure whether to be encouraged. Or not.

Tuesday 19th March
In the lift at the V&A, I was joined by two employees. One was telling the other that they'd decided it was too wet to hold today's falconry display in The John Madejski Garden and that instead they were going to have it in a gallery. I was about to butt in and ask which gallery as I'd like to watch it, when the pair of them reached their floor and stepped out.

It reminded me of a birthday party that Tillie went to when she was nine. The parents had invited an entertainer: the keeper of a hand-holding zoo of animals. These included a snake, a lizard, a chinchilla – which had beautiful padded furry feet and which we all wanted to take home with us – and a little white owl. The owl flew round their small sitting room and pooed.

I did wonder what the curators of silverware, statuary, paintings and tapestries would say when they discovered the falcons had behaved similarly.

*

Annabel and I joined a group of four other women on the course for a picnic lunch in the lecture room. *(As with Total Workout, I'm now part of another friendly group.)* They're all retired except for Lillian, who works as a part-time psychiatrist. They've had high-flying careers: Audrey as headmistress of a large comprehensive school, Rachel as a company secretary of an international blue-chip organisation and Mabel as a senior social worker. You'd never know any of this from just looking at them. There's not one inflated ego. *(Oh and how easy is it to underestimate women?)*

A week left and then my time is up. Shall I sign up for the summer term?

Wednesday 20th March
Snow. Large swathes of the country are covered and transport is severely disrupted. George's mum, Edith, is due to travel from Manchester at the weekend to stay with us and then go to a Women's Institute meeting on Monday. I'm wondering if she'll make it.

Thursday 21st March
The first day of spring and the snow has frozen.

Friday 22nd March
Edith phoned to say she's not coming: she saw the snow and her courage failed. She's transferred her ticket to tomorrow, hoping for better weather.

*

Tonight, Lucas went to Pizza Express with Emma. I wanted to follow him in order to peer from the dark exterior *(in which I'd be hidden)* into the bright, revealing lights of the restaurant to get a better look at the pair of them. They must make an odd couple: long, lanky Lucas and Emma, the sumo wrestler. Suffice to say, I didn't stalk them. I'm better behaved than that. *(But I wish I wasn't.)*

Saturday 23rd March
It's still snowing but in a giving-up-the-ghost kind of way. George collected Edith from Euston while I prepared lunch.

Afterwards, she asked, 'Where's your ironing?'

Despite us urging her to relax, she was having none of it. She ironed and chatted for a good ninety minutes, then decided a pot of tea was called for.

Tillie produced a skirt which needed altering: waist nipped in, hem raised. Edith, who is a dab hand with a needle and thread *(unlike you-know-who)* sorted it out in no time at all.

Then, before it became dark, she went down the garden to watch Lucas on his trampoline. She came back singing his praises.

'He's grand, isn't he?'

'He certainly is,' I replied, while George raised his eyebrows in a way that could have meant anything.

'Gran had a go too,' said Lucas.

'You didn't,' I responded, aghast.

'I did,' she confirmed, smiling.

I thought they were kidding but Lucas had filmed her on his phone. Sure enough, there she was bouncing gently up and down.

'Go on, Gran! Jump higher!' urged Lucas in the background.

'I'm going high already!'

'Bounce harder and you'll go even higher.'

She did, and she did.

'Hell's teeth,' she said, promptly sitting down.

'Are you all right, Gran?'

'I think so,' she said, clambering back up. 'But that's me done for today.'

Lucas stopped the film.

'Well, Edith. You did better than me,' I told her.

'I can see it could do wonders for your pelvic floor,' she commented, 'given enough time and presuming it hadn't fallen out already.'

Sunday 24th March

We had lunch at Marco's on the high street. Edith said it was the kind of family meal she'd always hoped we'd have one day. That is, everyone found something they liked on the menu, the conversation involved us all, people said what they thought, were listened to with interest – and we were all happy.

We've had plenty of other meals out but, almost invariably, the children have been far too picky about the food, or someone's been out of sorts and battling with whatever mood was dominating their day. Today, though, humours were set fair, social graces worked and Edith saw her family in their best light.

Monday 25th March
Unusually, Edith was nervous about her journey to the Women's Institute meeting in central London. Which station did she need to go to? And then which Tube line? Where did she need to get out? Then how did she get from there to the meeting? These are things that could concern anyone who is unfamiliar with London, but Edith knows the city from years of visiting us and they've never bothered her before.

We went over it several times, but she remained worried.

'I tell you what, Edith. I'll take you,' I said.

'Oh no, you couldn't possibly.'

'Of course I can.'

'No, love. I know you have lots planned for the day and you don't want your mother-in-law spoiling it for you. I'll be right as rain. Now, just tell me one more time and then I'll be off.'

I was unsettled by this new Edith, lacking in her usual confidence. I realised that behind the robust Lancashire woman is a shadow of another person, unsure about herself and her abilities. *(Probably a Yorkshire woman.)*

She made it back in time for tea, relieved that she'd survived.

Tuesday 26th March
As I was due at the V&A, I couldn't take Edith to Euston. Fortunately, today she was confident about her ability to negotiate the journey and, this evening, sent an email saying how friendly everyone was on our local bus.

I didn't like to tell her that sometimes they're too friendly and end up stabbing one another. We came home one evening to discover a police team scouring our front garden and those of our neighbours, searching for a knife. A young boy had been murdered as he stepped off the bus.

*

It was the last day of term and we learned about Renaissance drawings, including those of Leonardo da Vinci. I love these practice pictures of his: disjointed legs, headless bodies or heads and no bodies, hands held in various poses and details captured in just a few lines.

I've signed up for next term's course. It's not just the course that I like but the people I meet on it, and even on my way to and from it. I like who I am at the V&A, the sense of purpose that I have, the self-esteem that comes with being part of a group of successful and dynamic people. I feel like someone who matters.

Wednesday 27th March
I've stuck to my goal of doing Total Workout twice a week. The agony's decreasing but the body looks much the same. I hopped on the scales and – oh misery – I've put on a kilo! How can that be when I'm exercising, resisting sugary snacks and eating almost no fat???

George, who's a human encyclopaedia *(irritating at times, but useful at others),* explained that my body is burning up fat and converting it to muscle, which weighs more! How cruel and counter-intuitive is that?!

Thursday 28th March
The last day of term and Lucas came home on a high. The front door burst open and he yelled in his best Jamaican accent, 'Bladderins, I is home, man.'

He threw his school bag and games kit on the floor, took

one look at me and pretended I was firing a gun at him. He let his body judder and then fall to the ground, a few more spasms passing through him until he lay dead.

I pushed my foot gently against his side.

'Aghhhhh! And now she's kicking him.' Football commentator voice. 'And he's fighting back, though he's down.'

He writhed on the floor some more.

'No! He's mortally wounded and now he's …'

Dead. Again. I waited a moment or two, then he got up as if everything was normal.

'Hash-tag me YOLO swag, mum-pants.' His own voice.

'Do you fancy a hot chocolate?'

'Tanktastic. Need a poo first though.'

And he raced upstairs.

A normal day in paradise.

Good Friday 29th March

What's special about Good Friday when you're stuck at home?

I've done nothing but washing this week. It breeds in the washing basket. Certainly the socks are up to no good: there's more of them each week.

I started on jobs that Dora did at this time of year: polished the brass on the front door which refused to shine, polished the brass on the fender in the front room which begrudgingly shone a little, and cleaned some of the kitchen cupboards. I am worn down by the housework.

Of course, I'm not just a cleaner. Here – in no particular order – are some of my other roles:

- Cook
- Taxi driver
- Party planner
- Buyer (of everything from loo rolls to holidays to cars)
- Travel agent

- Counsellor
- Financial manager
- Nurse
- Homework helper
- Cheer leader
- Project manager of all repair and building works
- Car maintenance manager
- … and general good egg/dogsbody.

I've been juggling this lot for years and am a dab hand. *(Though it was the juggling combined with working as a graphic designer that was truly stressful.)* If I did this job professionally, I'd be paid a fortune. But I don't and I'm not. And I've come to realise, in this my year off, that what's unpaid is unappreciated. Money counts for everything. It confers status and worth.

The question is: how do I regain appreciation, status and worth without going back to the old job?

Saturday 30th March
Sue phoned, mid-afternoon, in great excitement. The staff at The Five Ls had just called her to say that among Great Aunt Vi's latest donations is a small, coloured vase.

'It's about eight inches tall and made of glass,' she said, breathless with her news. 'And it's dark blue-stroke-black and has goldy-green lines running down and around it as if lava's flowed over it in a random kind of way. This is the one you wanted, isn't it?'

'Yes! That's it! And it's a perfect description. Amazing!' My spirits lifted.

'Well, the darling aunt brought it in a few days ago, but they've only just got round to emptying this particular box. And there it was. It's £3.99 plus post and packaging, if you'd like it. What shall I tell them?'

Suddenly and unexpectedly, I felt diffident. Yes, I had

wanted the vase but when Great Aunt Vi said she was keeping it I'd accepted that – even if I'd been irritated with her game-playing. The fact that it could now be mine, and behind her back, didn't seem right. If Great Aunt Vi wanted The Five Ls to have it, well, so be it. Apart from which I didn't *need* a vase and, goodness knows, George wouldn't approve of another frivolous acquisition. Plus, there was the issue of getting it here. How likely was a glass vase to arrive, via the post, in one piece?

'Oh, Sue. I'm grateful for you asking The Five Ls but I'm going to leave it with them.'

'I thought you wanted it!'

'I thought I did too. But I wanted it to come from Great Aunt Vi. And now that she's decided The Five Ls should have it, well, maybe they should keep it.'

'But they still have to sell it to someone. Why not you?'

'I'm thinking George won't be thrilled and, most of all, that it's quite likely to be broken in the post.'

'Certainly, the latter's a consideration. George isn't.'

I laughed.

'Why don't *you* buy it?' I suggested.

'I can just about remember the vase from The Five Ls description and, if it's as I recall, then I've never been able to stand it. A horrid, ugly thing.'

'Beauty lies in the eye of the beholder,' I reminded her, somewhat sententiously.

'Quite. Oh, what a shame. And there I was thinking that we'd both come away with something from Great Aunt Vi, despite her trying to keep our mitts off her precious junk.'

Part of me felt sad and torn. I *had* quite wanted the vase, but then on the other hand – it was only a vase. Nothing special. Unlike the postcards and letters, which really did matter.

Easter Sunday 31st March
In true family tradition, George and I hid twelve small Cadbury's eggs round the house then, after breakfast, Tillie and Lucas went hunting for them, racing from room to room, each eager to find more than the other and both ridiculously excited. This was followed by a ritual opening of boxes from Edith and Great Aunt Vi, each containing large eggs for the children – all well-wrapped and none broken. *(Perhaps the vase would have made it intact after all.)*

*

The clocks went forward to British summer time, but the weather forgot to keep up. It was another bitingly cold day and, yet again, it snowed. In a bitter poetic moment, I wondered if the weather was a metaphor for my mood. For a millisecond, I was satisfied by this thought, then told myself to stop being a prat.

April

Easter Monday 1st April
By chance, I noticed the date on my computer. George was working on his laptop, next to me.

I turned to him and said, 'You've got a black mark running all the way down your left cheek.'

He ran a finger down his face as if trying to locate it.

'Here?' he asked.

'April Fool!' I sang.

'Very funny,' he replied, unamused.

I was on tenterhooks waiting for the children to wake up so I could trick them too, but they slept in until after midday.

*

Tillie, Lucas and I were in the office this afternoon when we heard a persistent meowing. Lucas went to the window and announced that a brown cat with white paws was sitting on our front doorstep.

He adores cats, unlike the rest of us. He rushed outside where the cat wound itself round his legs, meowing, and then purring as he made a fuss of it.

When he came in, it remained meowing outside. Lucas meowed back at it through the closed door. George, coming in from the back garden, asked in an exasperated voice, 'Lucas! Why are you meowing at the front door?'

'Dad, there's a cat out there. It could be a stray. Oh Dad, say we can have it.'

'No.'

'It's lovely and furry and is just the kind of cat I've always wanted. Oh, Dad, it's incredibly cute.'

'It's probably one of the many that poo in our garden. It's

not coming in.'

George walked away while Lucas and the cat continued calling to one another.

Tuesday 2nd April
No sign of the cat though Lucas walked down the front garden making 'come hither kitty' noises.

Meanwhile, I have turned into the last person on earth my children wish to be with. Actually, that's not true of Tillie. She doesn't mind being with me, but she's got her social life sorted out and puts her friends first. As for Lucas, I'm definitely uncool.

It took a few years before I realised that school holidays were precious. I stopped working in them and, instead, devoted my time to the children. I'd take them on day trips to English Heritage and National Trust properties. Or we'd go for a walk in the park, swing on the swings, have a picnic, feed the ducks, go to the cinema and generally have a fine time.

Now I'm the only one interested in going out. Even if I hit on an idea that appeals to Lucas – for instance, taking the Emirates Air Line across the Thames – I find he likes the thought, but not the proposed company. I'm a dud.

To say I'm feeling low would be the understatement of the century. Since I stopped work my ego has steadily shrunk to almost nothing. It wasn't as if I had the most ego-inflating job, but it did give me a sense of purpose and self-worth.

And now, what am I doing? OK, I'm fulfilling my New Year resolutions but, in retrospect, they don't seem very ambitious. An *adventure* would be nice but how, and when, and with whom?

*

The only good thing to report is that Lucas is spending at least an hour every day on the phone with Emma and hence less time on the PlayStation.

Wednesday 3rd April

I'm miserable. Let's face it: first, I'm no longer the focal point of my kids' lives and second, this year isn't the thrill-a-minute I thought it would be.

I took my misery out on the freezer and was in the middle of chipping away the accumulated frost *(a peculiarly satisfying job akin to picking scabs)* when the phone rang. It was Dora.

'You'd laugh if you could see me,' I told her, thinking I could do with a laugh myself.

'What are you up to?'

'I'm defrosting the freezer.'

'I hope you've got plenty of towels on the floor to mop up the water as the ice melts. It goes pretty quickly at the end.'

'I'm discovering that.'

We arranged for her to come round for lunch next Wednesday. I felt better already.

Thursday 4th April

Lucas spent the day with his friend Arak. As part of The Body Beautiful Project, I went for a swim then took Tillie to Flavours for a light lunch and to give her a break from the hours of revision she's doing for A-levels.

As we walked to the high street, she announced that Amy's family has invited her to join them on holiday in Derbyshire at the end of the summer. She's said she'll go.

I was miffed that she hadn't asked George and me first. Then I realised that the reason she'd left it several days to say anything was because she knew she should have done just that. I was going to tick her off, but she is eighteen and able to make up her own mind. And then again, she's also in loco parentis. Should I tell her off or be pleased? I plumped for pleased, it being the most positive, least acrimonious reaction.

Then I thought: that's one more week when I won't see her before she leaves for university. I was like a child holding a bright balloon that suddenly burst.

Tillie chattered on about how her summer was filling up nicely with various trips and how Adele – another school friend, who is now at Nottingham University – and she are thinking about a few days away in the summer too. In addition, she reminded me that she and Kaya are going to the Gentlemen of the Road festival in Lewes.

I had a light-bulb moment: I should go with the flow. I suggested I book a short trip abroad for the two of us once her A-levels finish and while Lucas is still at school.

'We could go to Rome, or Amsterdam, or Berlin,' I suggested, suddenly excited.

She considered these for a moment, screwing up her mouth and biting her right cheek.

'Nah. I don't think so. Sorry, Mum.'

My excitement evaporated as quickly as it had arisen. Tillie's busy creating her future, unlike muggins. I'm being left behind. Literally.

Friday 5th April
A catch-up day on letters, emails, paying bills, doing the washing and making meals.

The phone rang at four o'clock, just as I'd made myself a drink.

'A week's a long time in antiques.'

'Is it really? Hello, Sue, and how are you?'

'Amazed, bemused, excited, elated, startled and breathless. I have got to tell you the most earth-shattering, extraordinary and gob-smackingly ridiculous thing you have ever heard in your entire life.'

'You're pregnant.'

'Oh, stop it. You know damn well I'm a virgin and intend to stay that way forevermore. No, this is far more interesting than my non-existent sex life. Seriously. I want you to sit down.'

I plonked myself on the floor, back against the wall.

'Go on,' I said wearily, wondering what preposterous thing I was about to hear.

'It's to do with You Know Who.'

I actually felt exhausted, just at the thought.

'I could have called you earlier this week, but the plot has changed almost by the hour and now I have the full story along with the conclusion.'

'Are you going to tell me or not?'

'Of course I am. Stop being ratty! Well, are you sitting comfortably?'

'Yeeeeesssss.'

'Then I'll begin.'

She took a deep breath and I had a vision of what she must be like with her class of little children when it's story time.

'You know the glass vase that Great Aunt Vi took into The Five Ls and which you decided you didn't want after all?'

'Yes.'

'Well, on Tuesday, one of the volunteers – a retired nurse – thought it looked unusual. Not your regular tat, to put it bluntly. So, she took it down the road to a local antique dealer who gave it the once-over, peered briefly at the base and offered her a tenner.

'Apparently, she would have taken the cash but for two things. She'd seen his pulse in his neck and noticed that, as he looked at the vase, it suddenly went much faster. Also, when he handed the vase back to her, he'd left sweaty finger-marks on it. She concluded that he was excited about it.'

I couldn't help it: I started laughing.

'This is like something out of Miss Marple,' I said when I got my breath back. 'Perhaps you and the nurse could team up and open a detective agency.'

'Sneer not, oh ye of little faith. Are you listening, you little horror?'

'Yeeeeesssss.'

'Then I'll resume. The retired-nurse-cum-volunteer said she'd think about it. She took it back to The Five Ls put it on their shelf of odd items in the back room and stuck a 'Do Not Sell' note on it.

'Now, as it happens, Bonhams, the auctioneers, were visiting Leicester this week, offering valuations. Using her initiative, the retired nurse took the vase to them. The valuer took out her little spy glass thingy and scrutinised its base. Then she said, exactly like they do on Antiques Roadshow, "This is a Lava glass vase, made in about 1918, and the marks on the base tell me that it's from Tiffany Studios. If you were to sell this at auction, I'd put an estimate on it of between £30,000 to £40,000."'

'WHAT?' I shouted. 'That little vase is worth a fortune? BLOODY HELL.'

'Quite,' said Sue, satisfied. 'Amazing, isn't it? And that wily antique dealer had offered a measly and immoral £10. The first thing the shop did was to phone the Aged Aunt, tell her the story and offer to return the vase.'

'That was decent of them.' *(My mind was racing. Perhaps she was, at this very moment, sealing it in bubble-wrap to post to me. This was possible on the basis that her sense of humour was sufficiently warped to enjoy the idea that she was sending me a ridiculously valuable item which I'd think was a bit of pretty but valueless junk. But she doesn't know that I do know! Hah! I'll sell that darned vase and take the money. Oh, riches! But the alternative was a possibility too. And it was likely to be back on her mantelpiece. I made a mental note to snaffle it the moment she popped her clogs.)*

'But the Aged Aunt was having nothing of it. Said she'd given it to them and that they should sell it, via Bonhams, to the highest bidder, and enjoy the proceeds.'

'WHAT?!' *(Christ! Thwarted! No Tiffany vase for me then. Neither now nor ever.)* 'Well, I suppose it's generous of her,' I added, feeling distinctly ungenerous myself.

'Potty more like, if you'll excuse the almost-pun.'

'Had she known it was Tiffany when she gave it to them?' I was trying to hide my irritation: it's not every day I discover a valuable item could have been mine for a song.

'Apparently not. She'd picked it up in a village hall bring-and-buy sale back in the 1950s.' She added, almost bitterly, 'And to think you could have had it for £3.99.'

'Plus post and packaging.' I reminded her through gritted teeth.

'Oh, do stop being fatuous,' she snapped.

'You could have had it too,' I retaliated, crossly.

'But I don't like it!'

'Anyway, even if one of us had bought it, we'd still be none the wiser that it was Tiffany. It would have mouldered on a shelf and then either been accidentally broken or eventually sent to one of *our* local charity shops.'

'Why didn't you spot that it was something special?' she asked me, angrily. 'You're the designer. You've got a good eye. Surely, you must have realised?'

'Sue, I'm a *graphic* designer. I am not a specialist in early twentieth-century glassware.'

'Oh, well. There's no point either of us getting upset,' she replied, trying to control her annoyance. 'As you say, how were we to know?'

We both paused, each sighing deeply while watching several ghostly stacks of rich, red, crisp and new £50 notes float past our respective eyes.

'Hell's teeth. What happens next?' I asked, trying to regain my composure.

'It'll sell at Bonhams. Apparently, The Five Ls has never had such a 'find' before. It's quite something.'

I shook my head at what could have been and tried to salvage something positive.

'It's brilliant that Great Aunt Vi's Machiavellian ways will finally serve someone well. By the way, am I right in thinking that *she* doesn't know that *we* know about the Tiffany vase?'

'No. She has no idea about my relationship with The Five Ls. She'd shoot me if she did: she'd think I was spying.'

We put our respective phones down. I looked at the brown powdery dregs of coffee lying at the bottom of my mug. I moved them in a slow, small circle so they ran round the perimeter. Could I ever have guessed it was a Tiffany vase? If there's one thing the V&A course has taught me it's to always look at the base of objects and scrutinise the maker's mark. But I never had the chance to do that with the vase. And, even if I had, I probably wouldn't have bothered, simply presuming it was yet another of Great Aunt Vi's old cheap and cheerful possessions.

I sighed deeply, crossly, sadly. And put the mug in the sink.

*

After dinner, when I was on my own with George, I told him about Sue's call. There is nothing related to Great Aunt Vi that can surprise him. I asked him if he wished I'd bought the vase while it was at £3.99.

'Not particularly. In all likelihood, you'd have thought it was nice and I would've been annoyed about the pointlessness of having yet another piece of clutter. And then we'd probably have had a row.'

But, as he concluded, 'It's a funny old world, isn't it?'

Saturday 6th April

The sun is shining and the temperature has risen above three degrees Celsius! I spent much of the day cleaning and catching up with the washing while trying *(unsuccessfully)* not to think about that damn Tiffany vase. George did some gardening and came in at coffee time to tell me that the cat had been sitting on the front doorstep meowing, and that he hadn't shooed it away. Which is nothing short of a miracle.

*

Tillie went with friends to Camden Market in search of a vintage ball gown for the school's Leavers' Ball in June. She came back with a wonderful 1950s black dress with a cinched-in waist and a full, long skirt. It fits her like a dream.

Sunday 7th April
Another beautiful day. I made coffee mid-morning while George put the garden chairs in the corner against the brick wall. With the sun directed straight at us, it was positively warm.

It's not often we sit down and relax. The experience was extraordinarily pleasant and made us wonder why we don't do it more often. Which made us realise that most of the time we're haring around the house keeping it clean or managing running repairs while our delightful offspring contribute next to nothing.

And that sparked my brilliant idea.

'Let's share the dusting and hoovering. If we all set about it once a week, we could have it done in no time. Two people could dust and two people could hoover.'

George didn't look convinced.

'Tillie and Lucas need to learn these life skills,' I added to bolster my argument. 'And why should you and I flog ourselves to death while they swan around?'

The flaw in my argument – which I didn't express – was that I was proposing something which would help me but would require more of George's time.

'OK,' he said, a little cautiously. 'We'll give it a go. We certainly need to get the pair of them off their backsides.'

'Oh, thank you, George,' I said, wrapping my arms around him and kissing him on his cheek.

*

And that's what we did this afternoon. Tillie and Lucas were not pleased but they did do as we asked. The four of us set about the house at four o'clock and, fifty minutes later, we'd dusted and hoovered it from basement to attic. I was utterly thrilled *(even if the three of them were tired and depressed)*. That's one hundred and fifty minutes of work that I don't need to do. Each week and every week!

Monday 8th April
Lucas has found a summer course he likes. It's a week of criminology at the University of Birmingham. I don't know why he's chosen criminology. He never watches any crime-related programmes on television. Still, better a criminologist than a criminal. I signed him up.

Tuesday 9th April
Tillie and I spent the morning applying to Student Finance for the tuition fee and maintenance loan she needs for university. Given the interest rate which kicks in the moment she borrows her first penny, the debt on her fees alone will have increased by over £3,000 when she graduates in three years' time, taking the total to well over £30,000. And then there's the maintenance loan on top.

She's relaxed about the idea of this colossal debt. It's large enough to be meaningless. And the years in which she will repay it lie in the far distance, beyond her imagination. Plus, all her friends are in the same situation.

'It's life,' she said blithely, 'and it's not worth worrying about.'

(But that Tiffany vase swam into my view and I thought how useful £30,000 would be and how £40,000 would be even better. I must get a grip on myself. It is not mine. It never will be. Greed and bitterness are not attractive attributes.)

Wednesday 10th April
Dora arrived at midday. She hasn't seen the children since

December and was amazed to find that Lucas is now taller than Tillie.

We ate fishcakes with peas and broccoli, followed by Eve's pudding and cream. When the children excused themselves, Dora and I got stuck into a catch-up of news and views: who's ill in her family, the government, buses, woks versus pans, marmalade and the weather.

She looked well and is enjoying caring for her grandchildren. She's a natural with all children, knowing how to manage them regardless of age, background or mood.

I suddenly realised how well she'd managed not just Tillie and Lucas, but me too. I was enormously grateful. It's curious how much I'm learning after the event.

Thursday 11th April
Emma hasn't called Lucas for days. I asked him if she was away.

'I don't want to talk about it,' he said, shaking his head and putting his fingers in his ears. 'La, la, la, la, la. And I don't want you asking me anything either.'

'I won't. Promise.'

I went to Tillie instead.

'What's happened?'

But she's too loyal to betray any of her brother's confidences, though she offered some wisdom from the lofty height of an eighteen-year-old.

'At fifteen they're too young to be going out together. As soon as you say you're girlfriend and boyfriend, it kills it.'

I wondered if she was speaking from experience. Sometimes I feel like I'm living with strangers.

Friday 12th April
Out of the blue, I had a call from a housing charity in Ludgate Hill asking if I could do a small amount of work. They'd got my name from someone who knew someone who knew me –

the usual networking route. They need help with the design of emails to corporate supporters. They sent me samples which were dull, complicated, cluttered and difficult to understand. Would I help?

As my heart stayed in place, rather than falling to my boots, I said I would. We've arranged a meeting for next Wednesday.

I put the phone down and felt pleased because someone wants me and self-satisfied because I am, after all, an expert in my field. *(Shocked too at how quickly my ego re-inflated. But oh, how good it felt!)*

Saturday 13th April
The four of us went to the Saatchi Gallery, which I thought was home to Charles Saatchi's collections of paintings.

Wrong. The main gallery was dedicated to a newly opened exhibition, *Now You See It, Now You Don't* made up of contemporary works by the photographic artist Iggie Aitchison. None of us had ever come across him, and we were unsure whether or not to see what he had to offer.

Tillie and I went to talk to the women at the information desk, who persuaded us it was worth viewing. We had just turned away to walk back to George and Lucas when I became aware that they were whispering to one another in an urgent, excited kind of way. For a horrible moment I thought my skirt was tucked in my pants. I ran my hands over my bottom: everything was in place. But the women were definitely watching me and there was a look of amusement on their faces too.

Although we weren't thrilled about seeing an unknown artist's recent work, it turned out to be not that bad. He's a still *and* occasional moving image photographer who concentrates much of his practice in London. The photographs featured people from around the city caught in everyday activities, but he had the wit to catch them off-guard. Consequently, they weren't posing but simply doing whatever it was, unselfconsciously.

Which is my way of trying to explain what came next in the form of a colour film seen on a large television. It showed people sitting on a series of Tube trains, face-on to the camera, completely unaware that they were being captured.

Most were on their mobiles, though some were eating, some were sleeping and some were talking to the person next to them. A few were reading, and one woman started off reading but then kept raising her eyes almost looking at the camera. You could tell she was fascinated by it or something nearby. She'd go back to her book and then, surreptitiously, take another look.

The reel went on showing other people, almost none of whom had any interest in the camera. Eventually it came back to this woman who had less and less time for her book and more and more time for staring almost at the camera and the thing to the right of it. You could see from the rigid muscles in her face that she was riveted. Whatever she was looking at had her in its grip.

Then there were images of more people and finally, the woman turned up again. This time she didn't even take the book out of her bag. Her eyes were out on stops. She couldn't believe what she was seeing.

And who was that woman? And what was she looking at?

It was me. And I was looking at the man with the bandaged head, otherwise known as Iggie Aitchison.

Lucas was first to the TV. He came back to find me and pulled my sleeve.

'Mum, there's this woman on that telly over there who looks just like you.'

I went over. And there I was. My heart almost stopped.

Tillie joined us. She leant forward to scrutinise the screen.

'It *is* you,' she confirmed. 'OMG.'

George ambled over.

We all watched in silence and then started laughing: I

looked ridiculously funny.

'Oh Mum, that's just like you! You're always watching people and hoping no one notices,' Lucas said.

'And finally you've been caught,' remarked Tillie. 'Serves you right!'

'Well,' said George, 'there's no doubt that your curiosity has been well and truly captured in full Technicolor.'

He wiped his eyes with his handkerchief.

'But what were you looking at?' Tillie asked.

Despite laughing, I was in a state of semi-shock. I gave a garbled explanation about the man with the bandaged head and how I'd seen him every week for three weeks sitting opposite me on the Tube to the V&A. The information panel, next to the television, showed his photograph as he had looked the first time I saw him, and it filled in all the information I'd not had previously.

Apparently Iggie Aitchison had undergone major surgery – a craniotomy to remove a benign brain tumour. He decided to make an artwork of people's reactions to him as he travelled on the Tube from his home to the hospital for weekly follow-up appointments and back again. He'd hidden a camera in a Co-op shopping bag he'd held on his lap, the eye of the lens poking through the first 'o'.

(Well, I'd certainly missed that.)

Two more images showed how he'd looked each week, and what I was staring at.

'I think you're the only person who noticed there was anything strange about him,' George noted. 'Well, you've certainly got your fifteen minutes of fame – to quote Andy Warhol.'

With that, Tillie and Lucas looked at one another horrified.

'Do you think *Mum* could be famous? Like famous in London?' asked Lucas, appalled.

'Or the world?' Tillie looked aghast. 'What if she puts it on Instagram? Or tweets about it?'

'I hardly use social media,' I reminded them.

'Anyway, what's wrong with your mother being famous?' asked George. 'A good woman like your mother. You should be proud.'

They were silent. Frozen: the horror of a famous mother too much for them.

'Oh, come on,' I said, smiling. 'No one's going to notice beyond us.'

Their shoulders sank back into place.

I walked out of the gallery, while they stayed behind.

'Is it really you?' asked one of the young women behind the information desk.

'Yes.'

'Would you like to leave your name and mobile number? Iggie's keen to meet the people he filmed or photographed.'

I thought for a moment. I was flattered, but I was flustered too. It's not every day you find yourself inadvertently featuring in a major London gallery. It was sufficient to take that in without having to contemplate anything beyond it. Also, I'd worked with enough people in the media to realise that Iggie could use the news of my identity as a great story to publicise his exhibition. I had a vision of my staring face splattered over the arts page of the Evening Standard.

'You give me Iggie's contact details and I'll think about it,' I said.

They're in my handbag. George knows, but Tillie and Lucas don't.

Sunday 14th April
I've had far too many thoughts and emotions flying through my head because of yesterday. It was bizarre to find myself part of an exhibition, and I was rattled, too. Iggie had nailed an aspect of me: the watcher who's not very good at hiding what she's doing. But should he even have been filming me and all those other

people? Is it exploitation? Should I be outraged and defend my right to travel privately on public transport? Or is that the point? That there's no such thing as privacy in public these days?

I googled him and found his website. Although he's only thirty years old, he's already a successful commercial *and* contemporary art photographer. He's from Grimsby, he studied social anthropology at the University of Essex and became hooked on photojournalism and portraiture while working on the student magazine. After that he went to Goldsmiths, studied photography and, since then, has had commissions from The Sunday Times, The Guardian Weekend Magazine and FT Magazine, photographing everyone from celebrities and business people through to ordinary folk who make it into the news.

Away from the commercial world he's interested in issues of identity – marrying his study of social anthropology with that of contemporary concerns. His preference is for colour images: direct, crisp, underplayed and often poignant. The foray into moving colour film is a relatively new one and, as his website claims, is the highlight of his latest show at the Saatchi Gallery.

Quite some guy. But a craniotomy can't be nice. You wouldn't choose to have someone rootling round in your brain even if they were putting you to rights. Still, he'd turned a bad situation to his advantage in making an artwork of the aftermath.

As to whether I'll contact him, I'm considering it. But I am flattered to be part of the highlight of his show. *(Even if I do look ridiculous. And how pathetic is that?)*

*

Sunday afternoon family house cleaning. We did it in just 45 minutes this week.

Monday 15th April
Summer term – the last for Tillie and actually only half a term, then she's on study leave. My heart lurched. Lucas was nervous about going back, as he always is after a break.

I was wondering what job to start on first, then decided on a delaying tactic. I phoned Great Aunt Vi. No answer. Damn. I headed off to clean the bathroom. While there I stripped off and weighed myself. Down half a kilo. Yes!

*

Lucas came home far happier than he left. School was fine, friends were great and the homework was rubbish. In short, everything was normal.

Tuesday 16th April
I called Great Aunt Vi first thing, but still no answer. I tried at lunchtime too. No reply. I was starting to feel alarmed. What if she'd fallen over and broken a hip? What if she was lying on a floor, cold, conscious but unable to reach a phone? I decided to call one more time, at the end of the afternoon, before going into full-scale panic.

Bingo! She was in.

'I've phoned you four times over the last two days,' I told her, somewhat reproachfully.

'I was in the garage,' she replied equably, 'and couldn't hear.'

'What? *All* the time?'

'Almost. I'm clearing it out.'

'Oh, I see. Part of the greater clear-out.'

'Yes. I started off with one view in mind, which was to tackle the worst of the house. But I've moved on to something rather larger now – clearing out *all* the excess, everywhere.'

'How's it going?'

'Slowly. I don't know why I have collected five lawnmowers, only one of which works. Or three freezers, none of which has worked for many a long year. I've commandeered the council's Larger Household Items Disposal Department and, currently, they're arriving on an almost daily basis to take away all these extraneous items.'

'They're probably museum pieces.'

'I don't care what they are,' she said tetchily. 'I don't want them anymore. They can sell them on eBay for all I care. Just take them away from me.'

I wondered if that was how she'd viewed the Tiffany vase: getting rid of it being more important than its value or presence in her house. I sensed an edge of fatigue and despair as well.

'Would you like me to help?' I asked gently. 'I promise to only do as I'm told and not interfere.'

'A kind offer but no, I'd prefer to do this on my own. It's rather a private affair, clearing out one's life.'

'Well, don't go tiring yourself. There's always tomorrow and after that there's the next day.'

'Good advice for a young slip of a thing but for an old codger like me, you can't count on your tomorrows. I'm pretty much near the end of them.'

I had an unwelcome thought and decided it was best to voice it. 'Are you ill?'

'I'm perfectly fine, but that's not the point.'

She was irritable now.

'At ninety-four I *must* be nearing the end. That's not an illogical or profound thought. It's simply stating a fact. Anyway, returning to the main subject of my clearing out, I have just sent you a present.'

'Oh! Wow! Thank you.' *(For a millisecond I hoped it might be the Tiffany vase, but then remembered: it's at The Five Ls.)*

Still, I'm a sucker for presents. Not so much a restrained adult as an eager child. I don't need much *(though a Tiffany vase would be nice)*. A bar of chocolate, a small bunch of flowers or a paperback would suffice.

'You'll like it, I'm pretty sure. But I won't say more as I don't want to spoil the fun. Let me know when it arrives. Love to the family.'

Well, that's something to look forward to. I shall listen out for the soft thud of a small package hitting the doormat!

Wednesday 17th April
I rummaged in the darkest recesses of my wardrobe to find a smart outfit that hinted at the professional, creative working woman that I am. Then I remembered that outfit has been reassigned to my V&A day. So, feeling more V&A academic than graphic designer, I went to the housing charity in Ludgate Hill.

There I met a very nice communications manager called Lulu. We talked about the issues and I suggested, among other things, that they should make far better use of the attractive corporate logo, which appears as a very small, easy-to-overlook emblem in almost all their materials. Lulu listened, then made her own intelligent and sensitive suggestions too.

At home, I rattled out a new design for the standard 'corporate supporter' email. Bigger logo, larger heading, colour photograph from their library, clear hierarchy of information, simple use of three colours, lots of white space and an easy-to-read typeface for the words. Then I sent it to Lulu saying it would act as a template.

It felt good to be an all-knowing designer again, able to make a difference. I felt special, needed and valued, even if it was just for a few hours and very little pay.

*

Nothing arrived in the post. No large envelope, padded packet or small box. Just the usual bills and junk mail.

Thursday 18th April
Back to normal. *(Actually subnormal. Can a life this un-thrilling be anywhere near the average?)*

I did two days of housework, catching up on what I missed yesterday which probably only I will notice.

Still nothing from the postman.

Friday 19th April
In order to improve my fitness, I walked to the gym and was half-way there when a familiar-looking cat ran towards me. I made a brief fuss of it and then walked on, fearing I'd be late for the class. I wasn't, but I did feel half-dead with the total workout I'd done getting to Total Workout.

By the time the class ended, I was completely knackered. I staggered downstairs to the coffee shop where I consumed a large cappuccino and a chunky bar of chocolate – both at a disgusting speed. Then I raced home, fuelled by a zillion calories.

*

The postman came and went. Four letters but not even the tiniest, weeniest present. What's it doing? Walking from Leicester to London?

Saturday 20th April
Two emails re the Saatchi exhibition:

Jill, is that really you featuring in Iggie Aitchison's film at the Saatchi Gallery?
Love, Scruffins xxx
P.S. Found your email via your website. How's your love life???!!

Spotted you! You should win an Oscar for that staring – whoops, typo – starring performance.
Craig

Bloody hell. Scruffins is an old boyfriend. I mean *really* old. *(How could I ever have gone out with someone called Scruffins?)* Craig's a copywriter from one of many agencies I've worked with over the millennia.

I replied to both – curtly and discouragingly to Scruffins. I don't want that dead relationship rising out of its grave.

I was perturbed to discover that not only do people I know

go to the Saatchi Gallery but that they're recognising me too.

*

Still nothing from Great Aunt Vi. I felt like going out and wringing the postman's neck, though I realise it's the wrong neck.

Sunday 21st April
Another email.

Hello, media star! Did you audition for the role or is that boggle-eyed look natural?
(Only joking!) It was great to see you and such a surprise too. How's the family?
Amelie xxx

Shit. At this rate, everyone in my extended social circle is going to see that film and have a good laugh. At my expense.

*

Group house cleaning. I spent the full forty-five minutes hoovering and pondering on my emerging fame/infamy.

Monday 22nd April
As usual, Tillie and George were out of the house first. Lucas and I were about to leave for school when the light pouring into the house suddenly turned to gloom. I looked out of the sitting room window to see if a storm was on its way, but the sky was bright blue. What was blocking the sun's rays from entering the house was a huge Pickfords removal lorry, which was being reversed slowly up the drive.

Instantly I was furious that they'd come to the wrong house, worried that they'd hit a wall and anxious that they'd leave in order for Lucas and I to get in the car and go to school – which we needed to do straight away.

When I opened the front door, the vehicle had come to a

stop. I raced to the driver's door which loomed about six feet above me. The window slid down smoothly and a jovial face peered out.

'You've got the wrong house,' I said angrily.

His head went back into the cab as he consulted his papers and then it popped back out.

'Says 'ere 364 Blueberry Avenue. That's you, innit?'

'Yes,' I replied, perplexed. 'But we're not moving. We're not even for sale. There's been a mistake.'

He looked at his papers again.

'Mrs Jill Baxter?'

'Yes, that's me.'

For a moment I thought, perhaps I'm going mad and I've forgotten that we *have* sold the house and we *are* moving. But I stuck by my guns.

'I'm *not* moving.' An alarming idea struck me. 'And no one's moving in with us.'

He opened the door and jumped to the ground. On the other side of the lorry I could hear his mate clambering out too.

'No mistake, love. We're at the right address. And don't worry, we're not 'ere to move you out or anyone in. We're 'ere to give you summat.'

Oh God. My heart was leaping around in my chest. Lucas was beside me.

'What's going on? You didn't tell *me* we were moving,' he said crossly.

'We're not.'

'I hope you weren't going to do it while I was at school, because that's really sneaky and I'd be completely peed off. *And* it's child abuse to keep your only son in the dark.'

'Of course I'm not. It's not the kind of thing I'd do. And anyway, the house isn't for sale, it's not been sold and *we are not moving*.' I was talking through gritted teeth.

The Pickfords driver and his mate ignored the pair of us and opened the vast rear doors of the lorry. One of them pressed a button and a ramp descended.

I moved to peer up the ramp. Lucas followed. The lorry was full of furnishings swathed in thick grey blankets and tied to the lorry's sides with broad belts. There were a lot of tea chests.

'Now there's nuffink to worry about, Mrs Baxter,' said the driver. 'It's just a part load.'

'A part load of what?'

'A part load of what's in 'ere.'

My heart was now sinking.

'Three tea chests. That's all,' he called as, carefully, he braced his legs and back, picked up one of them and walked down the ramp. 'Where'd you like it?'

'In the hall.'

Lucas held the front door open while the driver and his mate carried the three tea chests inside.

'Exciting, isn't it?' said Lucas, smiling and happy now that he knew his home was safe. 'A bit like Christmas, but on a larger scale and without the tree.'

The driver came forward with papers for me to sign while his mate pressed a button to retract the ramp.

'Just put your mark 'ere to show what you've got and that it's safely ensconced in your 'ome,' he said.

My hand was shaking.

'But who is this from?' I asked.

He rifled through his papers. 'A Miss Violet 'Ar-Monds-Worth,' he said, careful to pronounce each syllable of her surname.

'I was expecting a small package in the post,' I said lamely.

'Oh no, dear. This is what she sent. I've got the rest for the others in 'ere.'

He patted the side of the lorry.

'What others? What else have you got?'

But he was climbing into the cab.

'Toodle-pip,' he called from the open window and gave a cheery wave.

The pantechnicon inched its way down the drive and, with a roar of acceleration and fumes, turned right into the traffic and was gone.

I went into the house.

'Shall I start unpacking?' asked Lucas eagerly, having already opened a crate and thrown the top layer of scrunched up newspaper on the hall floor.

'No. We're late enough as it is.'

I got him to school with thirty seconds to spare before the bell rang and detention slips were handed out.

Tuesday 23rd April
The rest of yesterday was spent dealing with Great Aunt Vi's gift. The crates contained the Wedgwood dinner service that she'd offered me back in February – and which I'd refused on the basis that I'd got more than enough sets of my own.

She'd sent a dinner *and* tea service as well as all the additional serving dishes. There were complete settings for twenty people to settle down to a banquet. *Twenty people.* Enough for a small hotel.

There were soup dishes, dinner plates, side plates, pudding bowls, cereal bowls, cheese plates, a cheese dish, teacups and saucers, coffee cups and saucers, milk jugs, cream jugs, sugar bowls, sauceboats, a gravy boat, several tea and coffee pots, three sets of salt and pepper pots, butter dishes, and various meat platters and tureens. I put everything out in the kitchen and, even though I'd stacked as much as I could, it covered every surface, including the floor.

The design is Westbury. It features a delicate floral motif in pale green and silver and probably dates back to the 1960s or early 1970s. I stood back and eyed it all. Part of me was pleased. It's attractive and I do have a penchant for elegant tableware.

But then there was the quantity. I have never entertained twenty people at any one time, and I'm not planning to start now. And where was I going to put it all? I don't have any spare cupboard space. What was George the Minimalist going to say? And to think I'd been worried about letting one small glass vase into the house.

I picked up the phone.

'Yes?' came a stentorian voice.

I moved the phone a couple of centimetres away from my head. The venerable aunt was in one of her worst don't-mess-with-me moods. I decided I'd go for an innocent, jolly, good manners and thank you approach.

'Great Aunt Vi! Hi! It's me!' I almost sang the words.

'Which me? The one I don't want to talk to?'

'It's Jill!'

Silence.

'Your great niece!'

Silence.

'Are you there?' I asked.

'It's not a séance: one knock for yes, two for no. What do you want?'

She was being her worst version: rude and abrupt.

'To thank you.'

Silence.

'For the generous gift of the Wedgwood service.'

No response.

'The one I said I didn't want,' I added, opting for a modicum of honesty.

'I thought you deserved it,' she said.

(Deserved it in what sense? Because I'm wonderful? Or because I'm such a loser?)

'Thanks.' *(I'm good at irony.)* 'I've just unpacked it all. Three cases. Rather a lot. Actually, *really* rather a lot. Far more than I knew you had.'

'You don't know everything, though you always think you do.'

I ignored this.

'Why did you have quite so much?'

'Once upon a time, I gave parties,' she replied tartly. 'Big parties with lots of people – colleagues from work, my friends and neighbours.'

(I noticed relatives weren't included in her list.)

'You haven't got it all. I kept four place settings for myself, for when I'm entertaining.'

(Crikey. I should look on the bright side: I could have been landed with more.)

'Twenty-four works very well,' she continued. 'Six sets of four, four sets of six, eight sets of three, twelve sets of two. It's a flexible number. Is there anything else you wanted to say?'

'No. I think that's it.' And then, in case I had missed anything I added, 'Just: thank you, thank you and thank you.'

'Idiot,' she said and put the phone down.

*

I was still wondering whether to be angry or amused when, bang on four o'clock, the phone rang.

'You'll never believe what she's done. She's gone far too far this time. I shall murder her in her sleep. Or maybe I won't even wait until nightfall.'

It was Sue.

'Has a Pickfords lorry just been to your place?' I enquired.

'Hideous. Absolutely hideous.'

I took that as a yes.

'She's given me that awful piano she's had since she was a child, even though I can't play the damn thing. It's old, dusty, dirty, knackered and I hate it. I've always hated it. She knows I've always hated it and now I've got it. And I don't want it.'

Sue was close to tears.

'That wicked old woman knows I live in a tiny flat and she

knows very well it's on the third floor, accessible only by stairs. There was no way those Pickfords men could carry it up. She's no right sending people things they can't take and don't want.'

'Where is it now?'

'In the communal hall, which will make me incredibly popular when the rest of the residents come home tonight,' she said bitterly. 'Oh, what am I going to do?'

'Are the guys still there? Because if so, you could send it back.'

'No, they're off to the next person.'

'Another cousin,' I said. 'I'm guessing the van is full of items each designated for a different relative.'

'You're joking.'

'No.'

'So, I take it they've been to you too? What charming memento did *you* get?'

'A Wedgwood dinner and tea service.'

'You lucky sod.'

'Not quite. She offered it to me back in February, but I turned it down. She's done the same to me as she's done to you: sent me something she knows I don't want.'

I explained about the quantity and how it was cluttering every surface in my kitchen. That cheered her up.

'Anyway, getting back to your question about what to do with the piano. I've got an idea.'

'What?'

'Give it to the school.'

'They've already got a decent piano in the hall,' she wailed.

'But they haven't got an indecent one for the playground, have they? If there's a sheltered area, it could go there. The children will be able to attack it with the kind of vigour that they'd never be allowed to do with the good piano in the hall. They'll love it.'

There was a pause while Sue thought.

'You're right. They will. *And* I know just where it'll fit.'

She started to sound brighter, but then was beset by another gloomy thought.

'But how will I get it from here to there?'

'Ask the parents for help. Someone will have a van.'

'You are a genius.'

'I try,' I said modestly, my halo threatening to sink over my face and lock itself round my throat.

*

We ate take-away pizzas for tea off vintage Wedgwood and supped Coca-Cola from matching teacups – while watching the television. George was gallant about the rest of the service cluttering the kitchen. That is, once I'd waved the smelling salts under his nose after he fainted.

Then we crammed everything back in the tea crates and put them in the garage, where all things go that have no home.

The only other thing to add is that cousin Robert received a Victorian triple door wardrobe which was too tall and too wide to go through the front door of his twenty-first century home. It is now being stored by Out of Sight, Out of Mind – a local company he found via the Internet and who turned up pronto to collect the said item.

God knows what the rest of the cousins received. I'd rather not.

Wednesday 24th April

Lulu, from the housing charity, called to say she liked my suggested design template, though she wanted a few tweaks made to it. She gave the go-ahead for me to create a series of templates for regular emails, news emails, press releases and membership renewals. It's a bigger job than originally envisaged with slightly more pay. Even better.

I settled down to work on what was a reasonably easy project. It made for a quiet, creative, productive and somewhat lucrative day.

Thursday 25th April
I emailed all the work to Lulu. She was pleased and accepted it without any further changes. Perfect. Then I tackled the very best part of any job: I typed up my invoice and sent it.

Friday 26th April
Three more emails about my appearance in Iggie Aitchison's exhibition.

> *You're 'looking good' Jill. Geddit?*
> *Sara*

> *Darling Pop-Eye, see you're turning into a media star. What next??!!!*
> *Robert xxx*

> *What big eyes you have, Granny! LOL!*
> *Little Red Riding Hood/aka your fave editor, Hank*

Granny? For God's sake, how insulting is that?! And what if my 'fave editor' or some other wit from my distant past, goes up to the information desk and tells them who the woman with eyes-out-on-stalks is in the film? I'll be well and truly 'outed'.

Saturday 27th April
Talked with George about my fame/infamy predicament and whether I should 'out' myself. He thinks it's something and nothing, and that I'm making a mountain out of a molehill.

Six more emails! Does everyone I know go to the Saatchi Gallery all the time? If so, why didn't they ever tell me?

Sunday 28th April
Ten emails. This is ridiculous. I'm spending half my day answering my in-box.

Monday 29th April
Fourteen emails! I've decided only to answer those from true friends. I've now heard every staring-eyes joke on the planet.

Tuesday 30th April
Summer term at the V&A and a blessed relief from unfunny emails. What a joy to be back learning, seeing works of art and chatting with friends – none of whom appears to have been anywhere near the Saatchi Gallery.

But how long before one of them does? And then what do I do? Or say?

May

Wednesday 1st May
A beautiful day: the sun was shining and the sky was wall-to-wall blue. I went for a walk and found the street where we'd sledged that snowy evening in the depths of winter.

The cherry trees were laden with a froth of pink and white blossoms. I stopped to look. Really look. Just as you should if you are living mindfully. And I saw the magnificence of this street, in this season, at this moment: the lavish blooms, their lovely colours and, in the distance, a lone tree, its boughs backlit and black, etched at its branch tips with that extraordinarily sharp, fresh green which is only seen for a very few days in spring as the first leaves emerge.

An elderly man, out for an amble, stopped to talk.

'I've never walked down these streets before,' he said in amazement, 'even though I've lived here for many years. Lovely, aren't they?'

We were both escaping winter's long cold grip and seeing that, at last, there was beauty. And joy too.

Thursday 2nd May
Three emails relating to my infamy. I ignored them.

Fay and I met for lunch at Wagamama near her design studio. She thought I'd hit a new low in doing email designs for a charity.

'If you're looking for work, I can find something for you that's far more challenging,' she said, as she slurped noodles from a dish the size of a washing up bowl.

'Thanks,' I said, tucking into a neat arrangement of chicken on a bed of rice. 'But much of the attraction of creating the templates was that it was easy, short and sweet. I wasn't going to have some client breathing down my neck for weeks on end and wreaking havoc with my layouts.'

'But it can't have paid much.'

'Hardly anything.'

'Well then.'

'Well then, what? I'm not looking for riches. I'm just doing someone a good turn and getting the equivalent of a tip as my reward. I'm happy with that.'

'Oh, Jill,' she concluded in a tone that implied there was no hope for me.

Oddly enough, I wasn't disheartened by her attitude. It made me realise that Fay has no idea of the gap that exists between those who want to work and those who don't. Once you've given up trying to earn a living or pursue a career, you're free to do what you want: glorious or otherwise.

As we were waiting for coffee to arrive, Fay said, 'I heard on the grapevine that you star in Iggie Aitchison's exhibition at the Saatchi Gallery.'

'Unintentionally. And I'm not exactly a star.'

'Iggie's very well regarded, you know. He's noteworthy among both commercial *and* art photographers. Not many people manage to straddle both of those worlds and with such success. You should be pleased to be associated with him. There's a lot of folk who'd give their eye teeth to be in your position.'

(Would they? Even if my role is minor and ridiculous?)

'Models and actresses queue up at his door,' she said, continuing her theme. 'But he's not interested. It's people like you who catch his eye.'

(In which case, we're well matched because the reason I stared as hard at him was because he'd caught mine. But she gave me pause for thought.)

Friday 3rd May

To break my usual routine, I went to Flavours for coffee, sharing the café with a dad and his pre-school daughter. I detected a man who spent little time with his child. He talked in a silly high-pitched voice that some people think is appropriate with children. At one point, his daughter told him that she was tired of his girlfriends. He looked like she'd socked him in the jaw.

Of course, it's easy to see the blatant faults in other people's parenting. I remain deaf, dumb and blind to nearly all of my own.

I did ask the children recently what they thought of me as a mum. They looked at one another in a sort of *shall we really tell her?* kind of way. Then Tillie said, 'You're OK.'

It wasn't a 'You're OK, you're fine, don't worry.' It was more a 'You're OK, but you'd be far better if ...'

All I ever wanted, when I embarked on parenthood, was to be good enough. It didn't take me long to realise that this was a standard way beyond my reach. Clearly my children think so too.

Saturday 4th May

Tillie came home upset and anxious last night. The year 10 GCSE art class is going to the Saatchi Gallery next Wednesday to see Iggie Aitchison's *Now You See It, Now You Don't.*

'Someone's bound to recognise you and, when they do, I'll be the laughing stock of the school. What am I going to do? Do you think I should leave now, move to another school and defer my A-levels for a year?'

She made me feel like a leper. And as for changing schools, well, it was melodramatic. I took a deep, calming breath.

'Why don't you tell the teacher that I appear in the film that goes with the exhibition and can she let the girls know in advance? That way, it won't come as a surprise to anyone. I'll be a five-second wonder. Believe me, you've nothing to worry about.'

She looked less concerned, but not exactly convinced.

'OK. But if it goes badly, this could end my wonderful time

at that school. And you'll be to blame.'
(As with everything.)

Sunday 5th May
Fifteen emails! What's everyone doing? Spending their holiday weekend at the Saatchi Gallery? I checked the website to see when the exhibition closes and it's not until the end of this month!!! I noticed that it's had rave reviews: rated five stars by all the major newspapers. A 'not to be missed exhibition' according to the Times' art critic.

That did it. I took the bull by the horns and sent an email to everyone I know telling them about my appearance in Iggie's exhibition. *(Everyone that is bar Great Aunt Vi who lives in a pre-digital world.)* Then I sent an email to Iggie asking him to contact me. I might as well take control of the situation rather than worry about where it will all end if I don't.

Bank Holiday Monday 6th May
Tillie revised all day for A-level exams, and Lucas did a much smaller amount in preparation for the two GCSEs – maths and RE – that he's sitting a year early. His first exam is this week.

He doesn't like to push himself too hard. In the weeks leading up to exams he's calm, disregarding any fears of George's or mine that he's not putting in enough work. But, at the last minute, he panics – viewing the volume of knowledge he's revised, through the other end of a telescope. What was large is suddenly reduced to almost nothing.

*

Frankie's invited George and me to her fiftieth birthday party on Sunday 16th June, at home. Frankie will be fifty?! That's too much. I think of her as young, energetic, vital. Now she's joining the rest of us on the slippery slope.

*

And, among the ridiculous number of 'I've-seen-you-at-the-Saatchi' emails, one from Iggie Aitchison. He's given me his number and can I call him?

Tuesday 7th May
On reflection, I may have started off defensively on my call to Iggie, telling him I didn't want to become the focus of any publicity surrounding his show. Now that I've written it down, it sounds embarrassingly self-centred, but it's how I felt and it's what I feared.

He was amazingly gentle, sweet, kind and reassuring. He hoped I hadn't minded him filming me as he had, and that he could always edit the film and remove the parts where I appear, but he'd prefer not to do that as it would change the balance of the overall film. *(It certainly would. The whole reason for showing me as the person who stares is that I act as a counterpoint to those who don't.)* Also, he said he was sorry if I was receiving too many emails from friends and acquaintances, but wasn't it wonderful that all these people were visiting the gallery and watching the film with such care that they actually recognised those in it? And, finally, he's having a party on the closing evening for everyone who's been identified either in the still or film images, as well as all those who have helped with the exhibition, and would I like to come and bring friends too?

As we were finishing the conversation I asked solicitously, 'Are you better now?'

'As good as.'

I was left with the impression of a quiet person with a beautiful soul, and I was completely won over. He's right: it *is* wonderful that many people I like and haven't heard from for ages have seen the show and are contacting me. My glass, that was half-empty, is suddenly half-full. Possibly more. Possibly overflowing.

*

Then I went to the V&A where three people asked if it was really me in the Saatchi Gallery show. To which I proudly answered, 'Yes'.

Wednesday 8th May
Tillie came home as high as a kite. The year 10 GCSE art class returned from the Saatchi Gallery declaring I am the coolest mum on the planet! Several of the girls mobbed Tillie in the corridor and said wasn't she lucky to have a mother who's a performance artist *(that's news to me, but, hey, I'll run with it)* and working with Iggie Aitchison, he being the coolest artist on the planet. And they want my autograph!

Tillie played it low-key but she was flattered by the attention and her link, via me, to Iggie Aitchison. The three of us are, right now, sharing a golden pedestal.

So, there you go. In five days I've gone from being a complete liability to a complete dream.

Thursday 9th May
I'm inundated by emails in response to mine about Iggie's exhibition. As well as being well and truly ribbed, I've also had all kinds of lovely, complimentary remarks. Even the redoubtable Sue thought it was an achievement. I'm walking two inches off the ground in a warm glow.

*

Lucas sat on the loo all evening with diarrhoea. His first GCSE exam – maths – is tomorrow.

'It'll be fine,' I said blithely, when clearly it's not if he's glued to the loo.

I'm telling myself it's worse for Frankie and her two boys. Archie's cramming for A-levels, while Seb is revising for his full set of GCSEs. Frankie's performing the motherly support act with food and drink at regular intervals, mopping sweaty brows, offering calm words of advice and generally tearing her hair out.

*

Tillie came home weighed down by eighteen A3 sketch books from the year 10 GCSE art students. I signed my name against the pages of illustrations they'd done while at Iggie's show: Jill Baxter, performance artist in Iggie Aitchison's *Now You See It, Now You Don't* at the Saatchi Gallery.

Talk about hamming it up. But Tillie was thrilled and, oddly enough, I am too.

Friday 10th May
I handed Lucas a packet of Imodium tablets – in case – and drove him to school. He took four calculators, five black pens and seven pencils to the exam on the basis that if one failed, he had back-up options. I didn't like to ask him what he'd do if his mind went blank, an alternative head not being available.

He came home in high spirits. There was just one question he couldn't answer and everyone else had struggled with it too. That was heartening. And the Imodium wasn't needed.

*

I'm attending Total Workout diligently. I'm part of a group of friends now. Sometimes I join them for a drink afterwards, but I only sip water and if I eat anything it's a banana from my bag. I'm turning into a food and exercise saint. *(Curiously, no one at the gym has mentioned my role in Iggie's show. Perhaps their interests don't extend to art.)*

Saturday 11th May
Still happy about yesterday's exam, Lucas tested George's mathematical abilities at breakfast with a sum worth an unusually high four points and which he'd found ridiculously easy. *(He didn't test me. The children know that, beyond the basics, I'm a mathematical basket-case.)*

'What was it?' asked George.

'It said: if there were 35,573 runners in last year's London

Marathon how many of them were likely to have been born on the 29th February?'

'That *is* easy,' agreed George. 'You divide the number of runners by the number of days in the year.'

'That's what I did,' said Lucas, satisfied.

'But it's a leap year,' I butted in. 'As it happens just once every four years, you need to divide by a different number.'

I was chuffed with myself for spotting something they hadn't.

'Ah, yes,' said George.

We all argued about what the division should be. George was adamant it was three hundred and sixty-five and a quarter, I wasn't sure, and Lucas looked despondent at losing four points that he thought he'd gained.

Sunday 12th May
Although Lucas was supposed to revise for his GCSE RE paper today, he spent most of the time playing on his phone.

'You're meant to be revising,' I said.

'Don't nag.'

'I wouldn't if you'd just get on with it.'

'I'd do it, if you didn't ask.'

Later, and still no sign of the RE textbook, he confided that he didn't think he'd done very well in the maths paper after all.

'Did you try your best?'

'Yes, I did.'

'That's all we ever ask of you, and what you get will be the very best mark for you.'

Those words were something one of my friends once said to me in relation to her children and their exams. When *she* said it, it sounded really good. But when *I* said it, it sounded flaky. And it didn't console him either.

This evening, Lucas was spouting questions and answers on RE topics, much to Tillie's amusement. She sat this exam two years ago, can still remember the answers and was quick to tell him whether or not he was correct. And he was – most of the time.

*

George complained about our lack of sex life. Now that I'm doing vast quantities of housework I'm physically tired and, most nights, hit the pillow and fall fast asleep. Recently, we've missed our minimal Sunday night slot. *(Is that a suitable noun?)* George's perfect world would be one in which we made love every day. We have tried this at different times in our lives and it worked a treat for conceiving the children. But other than then, for me it turns a special act into something so regular as to be functional. Still, we managed it tonight. *(Would it help if I thought of myself as a sex goddess, rather than a knackered woman?)*

Monday 13th May
Lucas went to school relaxed about the RE exam. He didn't even count how many black pens he'd got in his pencil case before he left home.

*

Late afternoon, I called Sue to see how she was getting on with Great Aunt Vi's piano.

'It's gone.'

'Where?'

'School. Like you suggested. The Head thought it was an excellent idea to have a piano in the playground. It's under cover near the bike sheds, protected from the weather.'

'And how did you get it there?'

'We put out a request to the parents in our weekly newsletter, and two Latvian dads turned up with a van.'

'Sounds good,' I said, pleased to know that my suggestion had worked.

'Oh, but there's more to it than that in terms of what

happened *before* it was taken away,' she continued. 'Far from being furious that an old upright piano was filling our communal hallway, my fellow residents were thrilled. It turned out that a couple of them – Lottie and Harry – were players. The ground floor flat owners suggested we had a soirée with the piano as the centrepiece.'

'Very *west* London, my dear,' I said, putting on a posh accent.

'Very. I'm surprised someone from *south* London would even know what a soirée is,' she retorted.

'That was going to be my next question.'

'The long and the short of it was,' she said, ignoring my comment, 'that we had the most wonderful evening where the ground floor flats were open to everyone. We all supplied our share of canapés and drinks, while the two pianists provided a musical miscellany followed by group singing.'

'Good Lord.'

'We were all pretty oiled by then. Consequently, it went off brilliantly.'

'Well, who could have foretold that yet another of Great Aunt Vi's seemingly malevolent acts could have turned out as fortuitously? You don't want part of a Wedgwood dinner service, by any chance?'

'Sorry. No can do. I'm sure the children will take it off your hands when they leave home.'

'They've already told me they can't stand it and will never use it.'

'Ah well. You'll have to find someone else who likes it instead.'

*

Lucas came home from school in a good mood. The RE exam was easy-peasy, he said. And beyond that, he refused to be drawn.

Tuesday 14th May
I do love the V&A. My heart lifts as I walk in. It's not just the

contents that are extraordinary, the building is too. It's such a privilege simply to saunter through the vast galleries and let my eye be drawn by the long vistas, never mind stop to enjoy any of the thousands of artefacts.

I love myself at the V&A too. I love sitting at the desk I share with Annabel. I love my notebook and my pencil case. I love my fountain pen and the pages upon pages of notes that I take. I love the fact that I'm diligent. I love my lunchtime chats with other women. I love the subject. And I absolutely love not being at home.

This afternoon's lecture on the Italian Renaissance painter Carpaccio was given by a young woman from the Courtauld Institute. She recounted how, when she was nine, she'd gone on holiday to Italy with her mother and seen Carpaccio's painting, *The Healing of a Possessed Man*. She'd fallen in love with it and begged her mother to buy her a book about it. The only book available was in Italian which, as her mother pointed out, neither of them could understand.

'But one day I'll learn,' said the little girl and, persuaded, her mother bought it.

Twenty-five years later, she's fluent in Italian and is a Carpaccio scholar. But how strange she should be drawn at a tender age to such a powerful image, one which would become central to her later life.

Wednesday 15th May

Tillie sat her A-level mechanics maths paper. She'd prepared long and hard for it, testing herself on multiple previous papers. I can honestly say she could not have revised more.

Soon after four o'clock, I heard her key in the front door lock and called down to ask her how it went.

'Fucking shit.'

This is not Tillie's normal language. I hurried downstairs.

'Really, Mum. It was awful. There was one question worth

fourteen marks, broken down into two sections of eight marks and six marks. You had to get the first section right to be able to answer the second. It was incredibly hard. At the end, they said "Pens down" but I took no notice as I was determined to finish the last question. I've never, ever taken up that much time answering the questions and not checking what I've done.'

I tried consoling her, saying that if she found it hard so would everyone else up and down the country, and that what was done was done. The usual clichéd guff.

I made her a cup of hot chocolate – the weather's cold – and squirted a whirl of cream on top. She dunked four Oreos in it and started to look less distraught.

Thank the Lord I only have to make the meals and drinks, and not revise or sit the exams. One turn on that educational merry-go-round was enough.

Thursday 16th May
I'm reading Elizabeth Berg's *Ordinary Life*, a series of short stories. In 'What Stays' an independent, easy-going mother in 1950s America is finding life increasingly difficult as she fails to meet the restrictive expectations of both her husband and the illiberal society of the time. He thinks she needs medical help and – surprise, surprise – it's not long before she's diagnosed as mentally ill.

Shortly before she ends up in a psychiatric unit, she says to her young daughter, 'You are children. And right now you are as smart as God. As you get older, something will try to take you from yourself. And you'll start stuffing your brain with numbers, with facts you'll need to memorize, and all of it will be something someone else has come up with. You will learn to ignore your own genius, let yourself wither on the vine out of deference to someone else's opinion. It's a damn shame.'

As well as being applicable to my children's lives today, it prompted me to recall paintings that Tillie did at nursery school. Three particular ones stick in my memory: the tornado from *The Wizard of Oz*, one of some friends, and a splatter painting. All of them were brilliant works of art. I didn't want her to learn any art beyond what she was doing because it would drill this innate, intuitive skill and beauty out of her.

I realised then that education's failing is what it takes away, before filling the gaps with conforming processes and inhibiting rules that only a few can manage well. When I look at some contemporary art, I see artists who have spent their lives trying to get back to where they started as children, seeking to find what they knew then and lost through education.

Friday 17th May
Even though the four of us now do the dusting and hoovering, I'm still left with cleaning the bathrooms and kitchen, the washing and ironing, the seasonal jobs and generally keeping the place smart. How can four people create such quantities of dust, hairs on the rugs and flecks on the carpets? It's turning me into a complete nag.

'Lucas, get your feet off the coffee table!'

'Oh, come on Mum. I'm relaxing. Why can't you just chill for once?'

'Because I'm the chief cleaner and you're making more work for me.'

Was I like this when Dora was here? No. Because it was her responsibility.

The only perfect house is one in which no one lives: pristine and flawless – like a room-set in a magazine. But then it's not a home, is it?

Saturday 18th May
Yet another nine loads of washing in one day.

Sunday 19th May

Cleaning is the only job that's not low status, but no status. I was working my way through the nine loads of ironing and ruminating miserably: people used to pay good money for my advice, and they listened to me. Now no one listens. No one pays for my labour. And, worst of all, I CHOSE THIS.

I turned the iron off, went into the kitchen and found a sheet of A4 paper along with some coloured pens. A few minutes, later I stuck my beautifully designed graphic instructions on how to use the washing machine on the wall above it.

At the end of lunch, I explained the new house rule: everyone is now responsible for washing their own clothes. I said I'd continue to do the bedding, towels and kitchen cloths, and for the time being, I'd do the ironing.

'Why should a man of my stature have to do the washing?' asked George.

I wasn't sure whether or not he was being ironic and, if he wasn't, whether I had the self-control to not hit him.

'Exactly!' I replied. 'You have hit the nail on the head! You perceive that you have status and I don't. That's why you don't do it and I do. But I am a woman of stature too. I'll do my washing and you can all do yours. It's called equality.'

Lucas looked appalled, while Tillie took it in her stride.

'It's no big deal,' she said waving her hand dismissively at George and Lucas.

I gave a quick demonstration of how the machine works and impressed upon them the importance of separating whites from colours.

*

When we were on our own, George asked, 'What happened to our agreement that you'd take on Dora's work now that she's retired and you've stopped earning?'

'I've decided I don't like it and am reviewing it. By taking on Dora's old role I've swapped one low-paid job for a no-paid one. Anyhow, it's not as if I'm handing over every task. I'll still be doing the bulk of the work. But I'm tired and fed up. Not that I want to go back to being a graphic designer either, but if I carry on like this I'll never have the time or energy to do anything wildly different in my year off.'

'And what *do* you want to do?'

'I don't know, George!' I answered crossly. 'But I do know I don't want to spend it cleaning and running round after everyone. I am *not* a skivvy.'

He didn't look happy. Lucas hadn't looked happy. I'm not that happy either. Only Tillie's reasonably happy and that's probably because she'll be leaving home soon and can't wait to get away from us all.

*

There is some good news. I weighed myself *(and I don't do it often because it can be horribly depressing)*. But today was good. I'm another half kilo down. Bliss!

Monday 20th May
After school, Lucas played on the trampoline then came into the office to do his homework. At quarter to six he gave a yelp and, having frantically searched his school bag, announced that he'd lost his pencil case containing his calculator, protractor, compass, numerous pencils and black pens. In short, everything he needs for tomorrow's second GCSE maths exam.

'Drive me to school,' he demanded.

'But it shuts at six.'

'I don't care. Take me.' He was panicking. 'I need my pencil case for the exam. Oh God. Where have I left it? I need to scour the school. Now.'

'It doesn't matter how fast I drive because by the time we get there school will be closed. Let's just take a moment to think.'

I thought while Lucas fretted.

'OK. This is what you'll do. First: call the school and ask if it's been found.'

He scrambled through the contact list on my mobile phone, his hands shaking. The receptionist answered and said, no, nothing had been handed in and there was no point coming to look. She was switching off the lights as she spoke, and the caretaker was locking up behind her.

'Second,' I said, 'is Plan B. Run up to Ryman's in the high street and buy everything you need.'

He held out his hand for funds.

'No, Lucas. You lost it, you buy it. I bought you a new set of everything for the exams. I'm not buying another.'

He groaned.

'As the shop closes at six, you'd better go now.'

A sweaty teenager returned within twenty minutes, Ryman's bag clutched in one hand.

'Cost me nearly fifteen quid,' he grumbled, tipping the bag's contents onto the table.

'If you find your pencil case tomorrow morning before the exam, then in the evening you can take this lot back to Ryman's and get a refund. But at least now you've got everything you need.'

I was trying to sound reasonable, not furious. Actually, I think Lucas was more furious with himself than I was. Which is hard to imagine as I was pretty much off the spectrum.

Tuesday 21st May
A chilly day at the V&A. As it's almost summer, they've turned off the heating. Too soon. I was one jumper short of being warm. Most people sat wearing their coats and complaining bitterly.

*

As soon as I was home, Lucas yelled to say that he'd found his pencil case before the exam, that the exam went OK and he'd already been back to Ryman's to return his purchases. All's well that ends well.

Wednesday 22nd May

I like Wednesdays. After the intense day of learning at the V&A, this is one in which I catch up with everything, uninterrupted. There's a pureness and clarity to it. Among other things, I invited Dora to lunch in a couple of weeks.

Despite – or perhaps because of – Sunday's meltdown, today I felt incredibly positive. I am taking control of my life and that in itself makes me happy. I have all I need: beautiful children, a good husband and a lovely house. We have our health. I want for nothing. *(Bit of a revelation, that. Of course, I could carp on about longing to be half a stone lighter. But I'm not going to be picky. Not today.)*

Thursday 23rd May

Tonight was Tillie's school's farewell party to year 13 pupils and their parents. I'd been looking forward to the party, planning to thank Tillie's teachers for all they've done for her but they were more interested in the girls than the parents. Also, I'm fragile on the subject of her leaving and wasn't sure I could say much to anyone without bursting into tears. I took the safe and cowardly route: I said nothing.

George and I talked with other parents whose daughters had joined the school in reception, when they were all just four years old. For us, it truly is the end of a fourteen-year era: of childhood and puberty; teachers and subjects loved and loathed; SATS, school entrance tests and public exams; school reports good and others best forgotten; concerts, plays, school trips near and far; friendships and falling outs; sex, drugs and rock 'n roll *(and that's just the parents);* the wonderful highs and, sometimes, the terrible lows. Finally, we've arrived at this evening where it all comes to an end, before our lovely girls take flight.

The headmistress gave a short practical speech followed by another from the head of sixth form who struggled to contain her tears. The girls themselves were upbeat. They're ready for the next step.

It's not the complete end of school but, to paraphrase Winston Churchill, it is the beginning of the end. The school is gently letting us all go – girls and parents alike. But go we will.

Friday 24th May
I lead an ordered life. Each day I make a long list of what I want to do, even though I rarely reach the final item – ambition being greater than time plus ability. Today I looked at the list and thought: *sod it*.

I skipped Total Workout and, instead, came home from the school run, made a jug of coffee and headed up to the bedroom to read *Sweet Tooth* by Ian McEwan. Two hours later, I made a second jug and added a plate of biscuits. *(Sod the careful eating.)*

It was Tillie's final school day and the start of Lucas's half term holiday. Tillie put on her glad rags and went off to a party. Lucas made a sandwich for himself and headed off to youth club. As George came home at a reasonable hour, the two of us ordered take-away pizzas and tucked in to those. *(Sod the cooking too.)*

Neither of us washed up *(sod that)* and, Henny Penny, the sky did not fall down.

Saturday 25th May
I did just four loads of washing comprising my clothes, bedding and towels. I refused to remark on the fact that no one else – yet – has done a thing. If they imagine they can wear me down by doing nothing, they've got another think coming.

*

I asked if anyone would like to come with me to Iggie's end of exhibition party this Friday. Tillie jumped at the opportunity. Now that she knows just how cool he is, she wouldn't miss it for the world. Lucas said there was no way he was ever going to any gallery again in his whole life, with art being a complete waste of time and only for plonkers. George looked like a rabbit caught in the headlights.

'Perhaps you should stay at home with Lucas,' I suggested gently.

'I'll be out at youth club,' said Lucas, undiplomatically.

'Yes, but Dad should be around in case you need him,' I said, hoping he'd take the bait.

'Nah. I don't need Dad!'

And then he realised what he'd said.

'I mean, I do need you Dad. Just not on a Friday night.'

Nevertheless, George will stay at home.

Sunday 26th May
As I'd not heard from Great Aunt Vi for some time, I called her.

'How's the house clear-out going?'

'I'm almost there – the point where I've kept everything I love and hold dear.'

'That's good,' I offered. *(Asinine comment of the day, Jill. Congratulations.)*

'It has been a redemptive experience,' she went on. 'Well worth it, not least of all because there's far less to dust. It's a huge benefit on the cleaning front.'

(Perhaps I should clear out our house.)

I asked if she had any other news. She considered the question for a second or two and then announced, 'I've become a trustee of a local charity.'

'Oh, that's interesting.'

(Three llamas ran, unbidden, across my internal video screen.)

'Yes. A rather unusual charity.'

(Four more wandered on and stayed there. Insolently.)

'It's called Leicester Loves Llamas in Lebanon. Otherwise known locally as The Five Ls. They count the two l's in the word "llamas".'

She mustn't discover that I knew of this charity. Or that I knew of it via Sue. If she did, she'd know that Sue had stalked her donations. Or perhaps she already knew: the charity may have told her.

'I didn't know there were llamas in Lebanon. I thought they were native to Peru,' I said, playing for time.

'Ditto. It's a long story.'

She embarked on a shorter explanation than Sue's original one, ending with, 'And now the charity's asked me to help them.'

'Why?' I asked with mock innocence.

'Why not?' she retorted.

'Well, lots of "whys". First, you don't like animals. Second, you're not keen on charities. And third, you've been clearing out your house because you're planning to ...'

(My sentence hung in the air. I was going to say 'die' but it seemed harsh, even if it was what Great Aunt Vi had said herself.)

She paused. I felt an icy wind blow south, rush under the gap below my front door and curl its chilly way round me.

'To answer your various points,' she said frostily, 'you're quite right. I don't like animals. Particularly those of the *human* variety.'

(Oh, oh.)

'I can't say that I have a soft spot for llamas either, but these ones are a long way away and I do recognise they require care. Second, I have never said a word against charities to you or anyone else.'

'Hang on, Great Aunt Vi. You're always disparaging about so-called "do-gooders" and those who knock on your front door asking for donations to this, that and the other.'

'My criticism has been aimed at individuals, not the organisations behind them.'

(This was rich but, in the narrowest sense, it was also true. I let it go.)

'Third. I have been clearing out my house to make my executor's task easier when I die – a word that I see you can't bring yourself to enunciate. Of course, that could be at any time within the next decade.'

(The next decade!?! That would take her to 104, and me to ... some other big number. The thought of being nice to her for another ten years was throat-cuttingly depressing.)

'Fourth – and I do realise that you didn't raise this but it was implicit in your previous points – I may be old, but I am mentally intact. In addition, I have years of experience, knowledge and wisdom from which others can benefit. In short, The Five Ls asked me because they saw what I have to offer.'

(No, Great Aunt Vi. They asked you because you inadvertently gave them a Tiffany vase and now they feel they should thank you by letting you be part of their organisation.)

'They'll be after your money,' I said, playing with fire.

'My dear. When you reach my age, everyone sees the coffin that shadows your every step and, thus, is after your money. What the fools don't see is that it takes a lot of funds to sustain a person to this ripe age and that what is left is next to nothing. It is my intention to die a pauper.'

'That won't be easy now that the workhouses have gone,' I retorted.

'Don't be silly. You know exactly what I mean.'

I gave up.

'Now, since I have some papers to read in preparation for The Five Ls annual general meeting, I shall have to go.'

*

I got straight on to Sue.

'Great Aunt Vi's become a trustee of The Five Ls. You're a hair's breadth away from being found out.'

'Jesus Christ and Holy Mother of God.'

She considered for a moment.

'I did ask them not to tell her that I was asking about a particular donation. Christ, I hope they're discreet.'

'Me too.'

'It's that bloody Tiffany vase being worth a small fortune,' said Sue. 'I expect they want to thank her or encourage her to give more.'

'My thoughts exactly.'

'Oh well, there's nothing I can do other than say my prayers. You could send a few up for me too.'

'I'll add you to the list.'

(As I put the phone down, a herd of llamas frolicked on to my internal video screen, halted and looked at me. They were smiling. Definitely. Bastards.)

*

Made love, followed by the don't-disturb-the-children post-coital nip to the bathroom. I have an anxious, guilty, unsettling and recurring thought that at this point in the proceedings, Tillie and Lucas will be texting one another from their respective bedrooms: *Over for another week.*

Common sense tells me they're more likely to turn a blind eye, parents making love being a thought too far.

Bank Holiday Monday 27th May
Although I keep George up to date on the Great Aunt Vi saga, I'm wasting my time. He's not interested. Nor are the children. They don't like the Aged Aunt and steer clear of her. They're not even interested in amazing events like the discovery of the Tiffany vase. Perhaps it's amazing only to Sue and me.

*

Another four-day working week. George and the children are in their element: more holidays. But for me, a bank holiday has lost its carefree gloss. Now that I'm a full-time housekeeper *(I refuse to write 'housewife' as women marry husbands, not houses)* a bank holiday is just like a Saturday or Sunday. All the jobs are still to be done. In fact, there are more jobs because the rest of the family is at home making a mess.

It *is* possible to be a great housekeeper. However, it is *not* possible to be a great housekeeper *and* a great something else: surgeon, politician, banker, writer, gardener, artist or designer.

Would Winston Churchill have been great if he had had to make three meals a day? Would he have risen to be a great leader if he'd had to do the washing up, put everything away, sort out shopping lists, do the clothes washing and the ironing, *and* bring up the children? Would he have ever found the time to build a wall or plant a rose garden, never mind write the odd book and become a great politician? Would anyone have even *heard* of him? Would it have been Clemmie who became famous? *(Not that her time was consumed by housekeeping either.)* Housekeeping: the bruised heart of gender politics.

Tuesday 28th May

Not a good day for the V&A's plumbers. Something like fifty toilets were out of order. It's half term and the museum had ten times the usual number of people passing through its doors. The place was teetering on the edge of lavatorial chaos.

Just before lunch, we were told that everything was now working. There was a stampede for the door.

*

Lucas is supposed to be revising for the school's annual exams which start next week. He's yet to start. And I'm determined not to nag. *(Exceptionally difficult.)*

Wednesday 29th May

Our twenty-seventh wedding anniversary. George was out to work before I woke, but I'd bought him a beautiful card at the V&A and left that in the bedroom for his return.

When he got home, he thanked me for it.

And that was it. No card in return. No small token of affection. Not even a kiss. Nothing.

Tomorrow I shall start divorce proceedings.

Thursday 30th May
Before George went to work, I told him I was hurt and cross that he'd paid no heed to me and our anniversary.

'I got that wrong, didn't I?' he said.

(I just looked at him. Tight-lipped.)

'I don't feel good about it, if that's any compensation,' he added.

(Sometimes I could clatter the man.)

'I'll try to do better next year,' he said.

(Next year? Next year! Does he think I'm going to be hanging around waiting? The man's not only forgetful and insensitive, he's an idiot too.)

'Sorry.'

*

He came home tonight clutching two bunches of carnations from Morrisons. He'd forgotten to take the 'two for the price of one' labels off the wrappers.

I decided to cut my losses and act with as much grace as I could muster. *(Not much.)*

As I write, they're glowing in the soft, pastel light cast by my bedside lamp.

Friday 31st May
Iggie's party at the Saatchi Gallery was the best fun Tillie and I have had in a very long time. The man's a dream. He has the gift of making everyone feel special, important and needed. He talked to me and then he moved on to Tillie, asking her about her plans for the summer and then university. It was all done with genuine interest. Also, as he was deft at introducing people to one another, everyone circulated, felt relaxed and confident.

Iggie looks quite different to how he did on those Tube journeys. He's put on weight and appears healthier. He's kept his head shaved and while his scars are visible, they're no longer livid. In fact, they're an artwork in themselves: neat lines and tiny, regularly spaced dimples where the stitches were.

I also met Arnold, the man who'd been with him on the Tube. Arnold is Iggie's studio manager and has worked with him for five years. He's lovely too. He said the pair of them realised that, unlike everyone else on the Tube journeys, I kept turning up on a regular basis. They were worried in case I knew who they were and was stalking them. I told him I was disconcerted by their regular appearance too and had even taken to moving down the Tube platform to sit in a different carriage to my usual one. Yet still there they were!

Not surprisingly, there weren't many people present who were on the Tube film. I'm guessing that most had been foreign visitors. But there were a good number of people who Iggie had photographed in and around London.

Tillie and I met everyone from dustbin men to City traders. No two people were alike, and the differences seemed to make the party work. Waiters came round with wonderful canapés, there was a great selection of drinks and, finally, a small band played cover versions of current hits to which we all danced. And I mean everyone: Iggie, Arnold, me, Tillie, the binman, the trader, the people from the gallery, the waiters and the drinks staff.

Tillie and I were on a high and so happy that, walking back to the Tube, we held hands all the way. That happiness prompted me to suggest, once again, that we go away together for a short break in the summer. And she was so happy, she said: yes.

My cup runneth over.

June

Saturday 1st June

Two weeks in with the new washing regime and George has used the machine for the first time. Tillie and Lucas have yet to touch it. It'll be interesting to see what Lucas does on Monday when he goes back to school. He has five plain white school shirts and all of those are in the washing basket. So, what will he wear?

*

Late afternoon, I searched Bonhams' website for the Tiffany vase. It's in a Ceramics and Glass sale on the 12th June at London's New Bond Street. I could go!

The e-catalogue showed it as the last lot before lunch. And it's a major item. Bonhams has given it a double-page spread with information about The Five Ls – how it's their most significant donation ever and will raise much needed funds for the charity. There's even a photograph of Great Aunt Vi smiling, sweet as pie – not giving one tiny hint of the venomous person she can be. And, last of all, information about how she'd bought the vase in a 1950s bring-and-buy sale and paid the princely sum of thruppence. Three pre-decimalisation pennies. The equivalent of one and a half pence today. Can you believe it?!

Bonhams had photographed the vase beautifully. It was lit to bring out the subtlety of all the colours – the greys, greens and black – and the way they flowed against and around one another. It was stunning. And there was the valuation: £30,000 to £40,000. I shook my head, still shocked by the sum.

I called Sue.

'The Tiffany vase is selling at Bonhams in New Bond Street.'

'That bloody woman and that bloodier vase.'

'Actually, I'm excited. I'm going to the sale.'

'What if Great Aunt Vi's there?'

'I don't think she will be. She hates London.'

'Yes, but what if she is? You've got to consider the possibility.'

'Look, I don't care,' I told her emphatically. 'I'm going. Can you come too? It's on Wednesday the 12th, the lot before lunch.'

'Can't. It's school. But look, if you go and Great Aunt Vi turns up, for goodness' sake have a rock-solid alibi for why you're at the same sale as she is. And whatever you do, *don't* let on that I know anything about The Five Ls.'

'Good thinking, Carruthers. I'm working on it already. I'll give you the low-down when I get back.'

'To be honest, Jill, I'm not sure I want to know anything more about that vase.'

I was surprised. 'Why?'

'Well, it's completely out of our hands. It's not really got anything to do with us anymore. All we can do is gawp like two children looking through a sweet shop window.'

'Speak for yourself. I don't feel like a child though, granted, I may be gawping.'

So I'm on my own. I've taken over Sue's earlier sleuthing and I'm thrilled.

Sunday 2nd June

Tillie and I decided that September is the best time to go away together. With a sense of great anticipation, we considered various destinations. Basel came out as the favourite, it being a less obvious but still interesting location compared to the usual high-profile cities.

While she revised, I trawled the Internet and eventually found an excellent low-cost flight and apartment deal. I showed Tillie, who responded with the same sense of inebriated near hysteria as me. And then I did the nerve-wracking, no-going-back bit of making the booking. We whooped and danced round the office, happy beyond description.

Monday 3rd June
Bliss! George was back at work and Lucas back at school. Lucas's white shirt looked suspiciously clean. How did he manage that? Anyway, despite this week being full of exams, he was blasé.

'Oh, who cares? They don't count, unlike the real GCSEs.'

'Actually, they show how well you're doing towards them,' I pointed out.

'Yeah. But so what? There's a year between now and then.'

'I care, and you should care too.'

'Well, I don't.'

Tillie, at this point in time, is the polar opposite of her brother: ambitious, driven and a hard worker, revising to a rigorous timetable. Sometimes I think they define themselves by not being like the other.

Tuesday 4th June
Half term is over for everyone, including the V&A. A few classes of schoolchildren, under the firm tutelage of teachers, were walking in neat crocodiles round the museum – as opposed to last week's rampant hordes racing round, beyond the management of anyone.

As we whipped through the lecturer's slides, learning far too much and too quickly, I decided that when I visit a museum it should be to see just one thing. And even that might be overdoing it. Perhaps just one aspect of one thing would suffice. We need to develop mindful looking. Slow and careful.

Since it was a sunny day, Annabel, Mabel, Lillian, Audrey, Rachel and I sat in the courtyard to eat our lunch. Toddlers, in their bathing costumes, were paddling in the pond. A light wind stroked the water's surface, sending a silver sheen of ripples racing from edge to edge.

Wednesday 5th June

Incognito is the look I shall aim for at the Bonhams auction this time next week, so if Great Aunt Vi is there, she won't recognise me.

But who shall I go as? It's not as if I can rifle through the kids' dressing-up box. *(Not that they have it any more, but a pink fairy isn't quite the thing.)* Think, Jill, think.

Thursday 6th June

Lucas ordered himself a RipStik online. It's like a skateboard but with a narrow, wasp-like waist and two wheels, each of which rotates 360 degrees. The website's reviews were mostly positive: 'My son loves his RipStik and even I've had a go on it.'

However, one person wrote: 'Within five minutes of playing with his RipStik, my son fell and was taken by ambulance to A&E, sirens blaring. He's had four operations for two fractured arms, two fractured legs and damage to his skull. Currently, he's learning how to talk and is having intensive physiotherapy to teach him how to walk. Don't, whatever you do, ever let your child use one of these dangerous, so-called toys.'

I told Lucas, 'If you're going to break anything, wait until your exams are over. And preferably do it after tea on Monday to Thursday when A&E is reasonably quiet.'

Friday 7th June

Dora arrived for lunch – a ham salad – which the three of us ate outside. I try to invite her when at least one of the children is home. Her eyes light up when she sees them and they're always pleased to see her too, though they're no longer spontaneous in their affections.

As a five-year-old, Tillie would throw her arms around Dora's ample waist, cushioning her head against her stomach and say, 'I love you.'

'I love you too, Tillie.'

Dora's life revolves round her extensive, close-knit family. Some years ago, when Tillie and Lucas were very young, one of Dora's many nieces became pregnant. I told the children that Dora was going to become a great aunt. Lucas burst into tears.

'What on earth's the matter?' I asked, surprised.

'Dora's going to become a great ant,' he sobbed. The fingers of his right hand raced across the table as he indicated one of his least favourite insects.

Today Dora was happy and, for the first time since she retired, I didn't feel overwhelmed by emotions.

*

Lucas's exams are over. He was singing round the house.

Saturday 8th June

Fergus came over for the day. He and Lucas played on the PlayStation, the trampoline and then had a mega-match of table tennis.

Although Fergus's parents complain about him being monosyllabic, he's chatty with us. At dinner he recounted stories of the ten times he's been stung by wasps. This included action replays, and his responses to them. It was all done deadpan and we were helpless with laughter.

*

Three weeks on and Tillie and Lucas still haven't washed anything. What are they up to? Their clothes look clean and neither of them smell. How are they doing that?

Sunday 9th June

George and the children were watching yet another David Attenborough programme, so I snuck upstairs. I've been thinking about my incognito look for the Bonhams auction. Inspired by a fashion shoot in this month's *Vogue*, I decided on the bohemian, gypsy style.

Rifling in the darkest recesses of my wardrobe, I unearthed an old Indian print dress from the 1980s – a little the worse for wear but it would do. I put it over some black leggings. Next I draped several fringed scarves artistically over my shoulders.

Checking *Vogue*, I saw the model was wearing plimsolls. Excellent: I have an old pair. Next, I raided my junk jewellery and pushed a ridiculous number of bangles on both wrists. Then I tried on the over-sized sunglasses I'd bought in New York three years ago. They hid a substantial part of my face and added a hint of glamour. Consulting *Vogue* a final time, I found a baseball cap – the very model that Lucas had bought on the same US trip.

I had to take the glasses off to see myself in the mirror. Wow! A bit weird, but wow! I definitely didn't look like me. Great Aunt Vi wouldn't stand a chance.

Pleased with myself, I went downstairs, opened the sitting room door and stood there, hand trendily on hip.

'Ta-dah,' I sang. 'What do you think?'

Their three faces turned to me and, simultaneously, the muscles on each of them went slack.

Eventually Tillie asked, 'What are you doing?'

'I'm trying out a disguise so Great Aunt Vi won't recognise me if she happens to be at Bonhams on Wednesday. Great, isn't it?'

'Mum, you cannot go out of the house looking like that,' said Tillie slowly and quietly. 'If you do, and any of my friends see you, I'll be a laughing stock.'

'But they won't recognise me! I'm incognito.'

'You're not,' chipped in Lucas. 'You just look like a worse version of yourself. You haven't fooled any of us. And the baseball hat looks stupid. Also, you haven't asked me if you can borrow it and no, you can't.'

I was stung.

'I don't look anything at all like this, normally,' I replied, indignantly. 'I wear jeans and tee-shirts like the rest of the world.'

'You look like a slob a lot of the time,' said Lucas, turning back to the TV. 'Ever since you've stopped work, you've stopped caring about your appearance.'

'No I haven't!' I was outraged.

'It's because you wear your old clothes most of the time,' said George diplomatically.

'That's because I'm doing the housework. You don't wear your best clothes for that!'

'Dora always looked smart,' Tillie pointed out. 'She'd wear a fresh outfit every day. And she was spotless, even when she'd finished cleaning.'

It's true. She always looked immaculate no matter what task she'd just completed.

'You're even wearing jeans with tears in the knees,' added Tillie.

'That's fashionable!'

'Not when they're old jeans, they're falling apart and they're not a designer brand. You used to care how you looked.'

'I did. I still do. Why didn't you tell me all this before?'

'We're telling you now,' said Lucas. 'It would just be nice if you looked good.'

I turned to George for support. He gave me a strained smile. A sort of, 'They're right, even if it's painful', kind of look.

'Well, thank you very much for your considered opinions,' I said angrily. 'I feel much better now.'

I slammed the door behind me. So this is it. Not only do I feel like a drudge most of the time, I look like one too.

I ripped off all the clothes and stuffed them in the wardrobe, fury battling with hurt, tears smarting my eyes. I picked out my very best dress and matching jacket, my sheerest tights, my smartest high-heeled shoes – all of which I'm waiting to wear for some extra-special occasion. *(What?!?)* I put my hair in a chignon, selected two discreet pieces of jewellery – a necklace and bracelet – made up my face, and rested the New York sunglasses on the top of my head.

I threw open the sitting room door.

'OK. How does *this* look?'

'Better,' said George, nodding his head in approval. 'Much better.'

'You scrub up well, Mum,' added Lucas. 'I'll give you that. Yeah, you can go out in that gear. You'll pass.'

Tillie didn't look convinced.

'You're definitely smarter, but the outfit's a bit passé.'

'This dress and jacket are only five years old,' I replied defensively.

'My point exactly. You could do with something new. But you're alright. We'll let you go to the ball, Cinderella.'

I laughed.

'But I'm not incognito like this.'

'You don't have to apologise for being yourself or being at Bonhams,' said George, firmly. 'Hold your head up high and if that wretched woman turns up, get in first and ask her why the heck she's at the same auction as you.'

Back upstairs, I took a long look at myself in the mirror. They were right. I looked smart, but the clothes were dated. And the rest of what I wore every other day? Old. Worn out. Worse, as I'd not had my hair coloured, the grey roots were shining through and the cut had grown out. I really had let things slide.

Monday 10th June

Tillie started her A-level exams in earnest. She has five – which doesn't sound much but the effort going into them is enormous. She came home saying the history paper hadn't gone too badly. Then she went upstairs to start revising for tomorrow's exam.

*

Lucas's RipStik arrived. He had the box open in no-seconds flat and left it by the front door, completely oblivious to the fact that George would fall over it the moment he walked in. Then he and the RipStik disappeared outside. In the interests of health and safety, I moved the packaging, but refused to put it in the bin as I'm attempting to house-train Lucas. *(Fifteen years on and progress is poor.)*

By dinner time, he could step on the RipStik, traverse the garage floor, nip through the doorway and continue down the garden path. He enquired if I'd like a go but I have a very well-developed sense of self-preservation. I asked Tillie not to try her luck either but wait until her exams are over.

Tuesday 11th June
The Tube to South Ken was full of the chattering classes: schoolchildren, their teachers and minders heading to the various museums. Children are always so brimful of excitement it's infectious and heart-warming.

Our lectures covered the role of the city in Renaissance Italy. I wrote so many notes that a muscle in my right hand flicked like an elastic band: in place, out of place, in place, out of place.

*

Tillie sat her second maths exam – weeks after the disastrous first – and said this one went well. Two down, three to go. We'll all be glad when they're over. Then we can have a brief rest before worrying about the results.

*

Lucas headed for the garage after school. Ninety minutes later, he came in hobbling. He'd fallen off the RipStik and hurt his knee. Fortunately, he hadn't damaged the most important thing: his *school* trousers.

'Why are you wearing your school trousers?' I yelled.

'You didn't tell me not to,' he replied indignantly.

And then we had one of those 'How old are you?' type conversations, straight out of The Frustrated Parents' Handbook or, as Lucas would see it, The Long-Suffering Son's Guide to Survival.

Wednesday 12th June
The big day at Bonhams! And I don't know why, but I had a stubbornly rebellious moment. Rather than dressing in version two of Sunday night's clothes, I opted for my first choice. If I want to be incognito – or my version of incognito – and look weird, so be it. Anyway, if the bohemian gypsy look is good enough for *Vogue*, it's good enough for me. *(Though I didn't have the baseball cap. Lucas had reclaimed it.)* Dressed and with sunglasses perched on my head, I checked in the mirror and felt my spirits rise.

By the time I arrived, it was late morning. I waited at the auction room door, looking for Great Aunt Vi. I'd concocted a credible cover story in case she was there: I was interested in a late Renaissance lot related to my V&A course.

As I couldn't see her, I slipped in and chose a seat near the door and two in from the aisle. If necessary, I could make a quick and easy exit.

I was just embarking on a swift fantasy about being the rich person I'd imagined I'd be as a child, buying great art at great auction houses *(a fantasy wrapped in a fantasy)*, when an image of the next lot came up on a large screen. It was a something-and-nothing glass decanter. Bidding started at a whopping £5,000 and then raced off. Literally. The prices leapt by £500 with each bid and the bidding was fast. I looked around in amazement. All fantasies had fled. Who were these people? Not any one I knew, for sure. The hammer came down at a walloping £10,000. For a grotty decanter which I wouldn't give house-room, never mind pay even 50p for in Oxfam!

I was breathless with shock, but already the next lot was up. A wine glass. Yes: one lonely wine glass. Pretty, I grant you, with double-twisted lines within the stem. Bang. Gone for

£18,500. I mean, you could trip and drop it on the way home. Leave it by mistake on the Tube. Knock it off a shelf while dusting. Is this what the rich did? Buy ridiculous things for silly sums? Shocking. Truly shocking.

The room started to fill as The Five Ls lot drew closer. A man, about my age, sat next to me. 'Right posh' as they'd say in Yorkshire. His suit was immaculately cut and tailored. A light scent of cologne *(or was it money?)* drifted from him to me. He nodded politely as he settled down and considered the catalogue resting on his knees.

And, at last, it was the Tiffany vase's turn. There was some shuffling in seats and then quiet, as if everyone was as nervous and excited as me.

The auctioneer explained that this was a special lot: a rare vase selling to raise money for a unique charity. And then, horror of horrors, he announced that the donor would be saying a few words. Great Aunt Vi's head appeared in massive form on the screen.

Appalled, I turned to the man next to me.

'Is that a two-way link? Can she see us?'

He looked at the screen as if contemplating it for the first time.

'Possibly. Though I don't know. Perhaps one should err on the side of caution and presume it does.'

He had one of those plum-in-the-mouth, rich English accents.

I gave my head a short, sharp shake. The sunglasses fell instantly to my nose. My heart beat faster and I broke out in a sweat. Great Aunt Vi was telling the story of how she'd bought the vase. I expected her to stop at any moment, lean forward to peer at us more closely and then, pointing a finger at me, demand, 'Jill! What on earth are you doing there?'

'I think my shoelaces have come undone,' I said to the man. I crossed my wrists, grabbed the bangles so they wouldn't clatter and draw attention, leaned over my lap, and pushed my head between our row of seats and those in front. If I hid down there, she'd never spot me.

'Can you see anything with those glasses on?'

My neighbour had joined me.

'Enough,' I whispered tersely. 'Thank you.'

He raised his eyebrows and sat back up.

Great Aunt Vi kept going for what seemed like an interminable length of time, ending by encouraging everyone to be generous in their bidding in aid of a particularly good cause.

She was gone. I sat up and pushed the glasses back onto my forehead.

She'd been replaced on the screen by the vase. Bidding started at £10,000 and was lacklustre, rising slowly to £25,000. My companion leaned towards me, smiling.

'Shall I buy it for you?'

I looked at him aghast.

And then he started bidding. Before you could say 'Bob's your uncle' the price started racing up. £28,000. £30,000. £32,000. The incremental leaps altered. £35,000. £38,000. £41,000. It was immensely confusing between bids coming from those in the room, those on the telephone and absentee bids placed earlier with the auctioneer. But the nutter next to me was definitely in the game.

Perspiration was leaking out of my armpits. My heart was fighting its way up to my mouth.

(How on earth was I ever going to explain this to George? Or Sue?

'Yes, I know it's sounds crazy and yes, on reflection it is. But the man sitting next to me bought it for me as a gift.')

'Please stop it,' I hissed furiously. 'You'll get me into terrible trouble.'

Leaning towards me again he murmured, 'Just having a little fun. It's for charity and the price needed a nudge north.'

I turned away, shaking my head. Who has the money – or confidence, or idiocy – to fool with nigh on £20,000?

The price was now at £50,000 and still rising, though the nutter had withdrawn from the field. The incremental leaps had altered again and each new bid raised the price by £5,000. At £65,000, the bidding slowed. By now it was clear that two people were in competition: one in the room, one on the phone. The audience was silent, alert, tense.

'£70,000,' said the auctioneer.

Was anyone breathing? I wasn't.

'£75,000,' he noted, accepting the bid from the room. Slowly he raised his hammer. The telephone bidder took a moment to re-consider and gave their assent.

'£80,000.'

The man in the room gave a slight shake of his head. The hammer came down. I was so nervous I nearly jumped out of my skin. The room erupted in cheering and clapping.

'£80,000,' said my neighbour, raising his voice above the noise. 'Double the top estimate and £50,000 above the low. That should help the alpacas.'

'Llamas,' I corrected, feeling suddenly and utterly deflated. 'Llamas. In Lebanon.'

People were starting to gather their bags and make their way to the door. All the excitement had drained out of me. Unbidden, tears had filled my eyes. I put my fingers to my face, surreptitiously wiping them away, hoping the man wouldn't see.

'Would you care to join me for lunch?' he asked, gently and kindly. 'It'll just be a modest, light bite.'

His sweetness upset me further.

'No,' I said, sniffing. 'I have to get back to clean the kitchen. Wednesday is kitchen cleaning day.'

(It isn't. Friday is. But I had to say something.)

'Can't you leave it?'

'No. Anyway, I could do with bashing something and

hitting the floor with a mop will be a good start.'

I stood up to make my way past him. Just as I was about to leave, I turned back.

'In March, I was offered that vase for £3.99.'

His eyes widened.

'Plus post and packaging.'

His mouth became 'O' shaped. Not a sound came out.

'And I turned it down.'

A tear slipped out of my right eye. I brushed it away angrily.

The man pushed his hand in his jacket pocket and pulled out a business card.

'If you ever fancy a coffee, call in.'

I took the card, not looking at it, shoved it in my bag and walked away.

'What's your name?' he called.

I turned round.

'Ethel.'

(Ethel? Where did that come from? Incognito was one thing, Ethel was quite another.)

I pushed my way into the hubbub of people and was gone.

Thursday 13th June

God knows how I got from Bonhams to Waterloo. I was blind with misery and fury. I cursed myself for not buying the damn vase when it was £3.99 plus the sodding post and packaging. I cursed George's strong personality and views that have the effect of inhibiting my own. I cursed myself for not standing up to the George who, when he's not in front of me, lives in my head and asks about any prospective purchase, 'Yes, but do you really *need* it?' I cursed the honest me who replies, 'No.' I cursed my lack of determination. I cursed my lack of greed. I cursed my ignorance for not spotting a gem when I saw one. I cursed the fact that no one, ever, has handed me £80,000 and never will.

As the train drew into my station, I pulled out the man's

card. Jeremy Osbert. He'd have to be called Jeremy, looking and sounding that swanky. Managing Director of Osbert & Small, purveyors of fine antiques with a gallery on Pall Mall. I tore it up and put it in the bin by the train door.

Walking home, I texted Sue.

- Tiffany vase sold for £80,000. Buyer's premium and VAT on top.

She replied almost straight away.

- LOL. Pull the other one.

- Have given up joking. Check Bonhams' website tonight for sale price.

I added a link.

Just before home, I bumped into some girls from Tillie's school. A crowd of year 10 GCSE art girls, I discovered by the ecstatic way they greeted me. They were so bubbly and happy that I was able to switch moods and respond in kind.

Once we'd parted, I switched back and continued down the street under my black cloud. I had the house to myself: Tillie was out and Lucas at school. I stuffed the boho clothes in the wardrobe and changed into my usual uniform of tattered jeans and manky tee-shirt.

*

For once, George and the children were interested in a Great Aunt Vi related tale. I gave them a blow-by-blow account, including the lunatic man bidding next to me.

They were all impressed with the price. Lucas said if he'd been given £80,000 he'd spend it on a flashy car even though he's too young to drive. Tillie said she'd travel the world and then pay for her university education. I opted for a hideously expensive handbag, a new kitchen and a luxurious bathroom. George said he'd save it as there wasn't anything he wanted.

'I wonder what your dear aunt is thinking?' pondered George.

'Presumably she's chuffed for The Five Ls,' I replied. 'She did, in the end, give the vase to them knowing what it was and what it could be worth. Even if it turns out to have raised an awful lot more money than expected.'

'Mmmmm,' said George. And wouldn't be drawn further.

*

After dinner, Lucas went back on the RipStik. He rode round the garage in tight figures of eight. Quite impressive.

He's not letting on about his school exam results. According to him, the teachers haven't marked the papers yet.

*

Just before I headed for bed, a text arrived from Sue.

- *Bloody fuck shit and hell. Have just looked at Bonhams' site. Will always believe you from now on. But don't tell me anything more about that vase. My heart can't take it.*

Friday 14th June
It was the first of the two English literature papers for Tillie. This is the subject she wants to study at uni. She came home in one piece but, rather than telling me how the exam went, she started berating me.

'I hear the so-called "performance artist" has been at it again.'

She held up her phone. It showed a photograph of me on Wednesday, walking home from the station.

'Where did you get that?' I asked warily.

'Instagram. WhatsApp. Facebook. Twitter. Snapchat. You name the social media and you're on it. Alice Donaldson, Charlotte Weitz, Lucy Koboyashi and Addie Nchebe were among just a few of the year 10 GCSE art class who showed me images of you or information about you. By now you're probably known by the whole school.'

'Blimey.'

'It would be my worst nightmare, were it not for the fact they think you're a media star.'

When I'd told the family about Wednesday's events, I'd missed out the minor detail of what happened on the way home from the station, hoping I'd get away with it.

'We told you not to wear those clothes,' she continued, 'and what do you do? You turn yourself out like some boho tramp.'

I looked at her sheepishly.

'But what do I know?' she asked rhetorically. 'The year 10s assumed you'd dressed like that because you're a "performance artist" working with Iggie Aitchison. "Performance artist" my foot. Pillock, more like.'

'That's a bit strong,' I said defensively.

'God! Mother!' She raised her eyes heavenward. 'And then you played along with their fantasy. Look!'

She thrust her phone at me, the forefinger of her right hand flicking through a series of photographs showing me posing and pulling my 'gypsy' skirt wide to give them the full effect of the Indian print.

'And what do the year 10s think?' she prompted.

'That I'm amazing?' I asked hopefully.

'Yes! They do! And how unlikely is that?!'

(Pretty unlikely, but what the heck.)

'Mum, you're incorrigible,' Tillie said, shaking her head. 'I'm hanging on by my fingernails at that school, hoping I'll finish before the year 10s discover you're not the person they think you are.'

And with that she went upstairs to revise for her final two exams.

*

Lucas has now admitted to receiving four results from *his* exams. They're graded at GCSE level, though he's only half-way through the course. He was crestfallen about some of them – notably French in which he got a 6. Overall though, he's done very well. Just not as well as he'd like. *(So that blasé attitude hid the fact that he did care after all.)*

Saturday 15th June
Hacked off about the Tiffany vase and being done out of a small fortune, I decided to sell Great Aunt Vi's unwanted Wedgwood gift and try to make some money from that instead.

The morning was spent photographing the service in various arrangements: afternoon tea set for four, dinner service for four, two tureens, a gravy boat and sauce boat and so on, until I'd accounted for the whole damn lot. It took hours, but I enjoyed the creative process of making the items look attractive.

I put just one of each of my various, multiple sets up on Gumtree, stating that the buyer had to collect. Now I have to wait.

Sunday 16th June
George and I walked to Frankie's for her fiftieth birthday party. Sam was opening bottles of champagne, filling glasses, answering the front door and generally ensuring everything ran smoothly while Frankie – fabulously slim, nowhere near a diabetic waistline and looking far younger than half a century – mingled among her guests.

Archie and Seb had set up a camp in the garden to entertain all the children. They'd accumulated a number of different sized boxes which some children were drawing on while others were playing in them.

Two little girls – perhaps four and six – in matching pink summer dresses, had found a tall box in which they both fitted and disappeared when the flaps were pulled down. They ran up to their father in the kitchen.

The elder one said, as she led him out of the door, 'You pretend that you've planted us in the box. Then you forget about us and we'll suddenly jump up and you'll be surprised.'

He dutifully 'planted' them, carefully folding down the flaps and wandered once round Sam's vegetable patch. As he passed the box, the two girls burst through the top. He leapt back in amazement.

'Good Lord! I forgot about planting Rose and Iris. What an extraordinary surprise!'

They jumped up and down with delight, beaming from ear to ear. Then asked him to do it all over again. Which he did.

*

No takers on Gumtree. Yet.

Monday 17th June
Once a mother, always a mother. One of the children went to the loo in the small hours of the morning. As they never do this, and I didn't hear the person go back to bed, I got up to check on them. I couldn't find anyone and, when I peeped in each bedroom, both were in their respective beds. I went back to mine wondering if I'd dreamt it all.

Will I still be doing this when they're forty-two and are staying with me because their husband or wife has told them I'm due a visit? Will we bump into one another on the landing in the middle of the night, me wondering if they're well, them wondering if I'm senile?

Tuesday 18th June
'Where have all my plain white work shirts gone?' George asked this morning. He was dressed in boxer shorts, peering into his wardrobe and riffling through the empty hangers. 'All I've got are patterned ones.'

'Are they in the wash?' I suggested.

We looked at one another and, simultaneously, knew what had happened.

'Lucas?' we shouted in unison.

He drifted up the stairs from the kitchen, in no race to start his school day.

'What, bunnikins?' he asked, airily.

'Where are my white shirts?' roared George.

'Keep yer shirt on mate,' he replied carelessly.

'Lucas, this is serious and don't be rude! I had at least ten white shirts in my wardrobe. Unworn. And now they've gone. Where are they?'

'How should I know?'

'Because you're the only other wearer of plain white shirts in this family.'

Tillie had joined us from the bathroom, scrubbing her teeth and foaming at the mouth.

'Well,' said Lucas slowly. 'It's like this. Mum's got her new regime of doing your own washing. And Tillie and I thought there's no point doing any washing until the clothes have run out.'

'Your *own* clothes,' George reminded him.

'She never said that.'

'It was implied.'

'So, I've used up all my white school shirts, I've been through the shirts that fit me from the school's Lost Property and I've just about used all of yours. There's one left for today. I was planning on doing some washing tonight.'

Tillie, on hearing her name, had nipped back to the bathroom and locked the door.

'Tillie, come out here now,' George called.

The toilet was flushed and she reappeared.

'So whose clothes have you been borrowing?'

'No one's!' she told him, indignantly.

'Have you done any washing yet?' I asked.

'Bras by hand and overnight.'

I nodded, impressed.

'And pants?'

'I just buy a new pack when I run out.'

I raised my eyebrows.

'And how many pairs do you now own?'

'Mum! This is a very personal subject but seeing it's you – probably about forty.'

'And how about you?' I asked Lucas.

'I'm still turning mine.'

I frowned. 'What do you mean?'

'I wear them one way out one day and then turn them the other way out the next day. That way they last longer.'

'I've got the picture,' I said. 'It doesn't sound very nice.'

'Well, you've not noticed me smelling or anything, have you?'

I hadn't. Actually, I was impressed at their resourcefulness. I'd never think of doing anything other than wash my clothes, it being the simplest option.

'Right. This stops now,' said George. He pointed at Lucas. 'Tonight, *you* do your washing and tomorrow,' pointing at Tillie, 'You do yours.'

'But I don't need to, Dad,' replied Tillie. 'I've got loads more clothes to wear yet before I run out.'

'I don't care,' he said, calming down now that he'd given them an ultimatum.

'OK,' she said breezily. 'But I'll do what I like when I've left home.'

*

Ironically, given this morning's domestic run-in, we had a lecture at the V&A on the most expensive material in Renaissance Italy – cloth of gold. *(Magnificent but probably unwashable.)*

I came home to find Lucas on his third lot of washing and what he'd already done was hung on the line down the garden.

'You're a good lad,' I said to him, putting my arm round his shoulder and kissing his cheek.

'You're not that bad yourself, Mum.'

He kissed my cheek.

'By the way,' I asked, 'what happened to the shirts you took from Lost Property?'

'I returned them afterwards. I'm not washing other people's crap!'

(Ah, if only I'd had the same attitude years ago.)

Wednesday 19th June
George has pasted a rota above the washing machine. Under the new, stricter rules, each of us has to use the washing machine on specified days and fill it with not just our own clothes but the clothes of others too. That'll thrill Lucas.

*

Still nothing from Gumtree.

Thursday 20th June
Tillie had her final A-level exams today: history followed by English literature. When I asked how they went, she grimaced and then broke into a big, beaming smile.

'They're over! I'm free! No more revision! My time is my own!'

And then, just as quickly, she burst into tears, exhausted from revising forty hours every week for the past twelve weeks. I put my arms round her and held her tight. She's worked hard because she wants to go to Durham University, for which she needs one A star and two As.

And even if she doesn't get those results, she'll go somewhere else. The point is, she'll be gone. So I cried too.

*

Fifteen plain white shirts to iron. Fun. *(Not.)*

Friday 21st June
Lucas came home armed with the rest of his school exam results. He's done really well: mostly 8s and 6s with one or two 9s. However, he was disgruntled with the overall grades.

Tillie – aka Miss Sensible – said it would be pointless getting 9s now across the board, as it would leave you wondering why you weren't sitting all your GCSEs this year rather than next. And that cheered Lucas up.

Saturday 22nd June

Still nothing from Gumtree. I thought thousands of people were supposed to see these ads? What if the Wedgwood is so old-fashioned no one wants it? What do I do then? Send it to Oxfam? *(Or The Five Ls?)*

*

Lucas was wearing swimming goggles, a pair of Marigold gloves and using the wooden toaster tongs to put clothes in the washing machine.

'What are you doing with my tongs?' I asked appalled. They're my most useful kitchen gadget, preventing us daily from electrocuting ourselves every time we extract a piece of bread that's wedged itself in the toaster.

'There's no way I'm touching other people's pants,' he said, waving the tongs at me.

'But we'll never be able to use them with food ever again!'

'You could wash them. The dishwasher would sterilise them.'

'Lucas. You don't need tongs or Marigold gloves or swimming goggles to protect yourself from other people's underwear. You can just wash your hands after handling them.'

'What? And catch Ebola? Or E.coli? Or some other dreaded disease? No thanks.'

There's only so many fights worth fighting. I left him to it.

Sunday 23rd June

Out of the blue, an email arrived from Iggie. He'd like to make a photographic portrait of me as part of his next body of work and could I come to his studio in Brixton on the 3rd July? He'll send a taxi to pick me up, along with any props I'd like to bring.

Wow! How amazing! What a request! I've never had a portrait made of me. And what an opportunity! Perhaps the year 10 girls are right. Perhaps I am a performance artist. *(Well, in my dreams. But it could be fun. And it's certainly a break from the usual, tedious routine.)*

'Yes!' I replied. 'Will be there.'

But what does he mean by 'props I'd like to bring'?

Monday 24th June

Tillie and I went to Selfridges on Oxford Street where she chose a pair of vertiginous heels to go with her ball dress. The Leavers' Ball is on Friday.

In Marks & Spencer, I bought an expensive Spanx-like, super-reinforced slip to hold my body in shape. Despite Total Workout, my stomach still rolls over the tops of my jeans in an unappealing way. The only thing that I look half-decent in is my swimming costume, which holds me so tightly I'm flattened to a better shape. So this seemed worth trying.

I looked, briefly, at other clothes but as I haven't decided what to do about my full but dated wardrobe, I didn't buy anything else.

Tuesday 25th June

We had a 'handling' session of majolica in the V&A's pottery department. Except it wasn't, as we weren't allowed to handle anything, it all being far too precious. That was left to the curator wearing purple protective gloves.

*

Finally, a response from Gumtree. Some woman in Berlin *(Berlin, for God's sake!)* who'll be back in the UK in early July wants to know if she can come and see the Wedgwood then? Of course she can. No one else wants to.

Wednesday 26th June

A well-needed, catch-up day. I made breakfast, put the washing on, put the dishwasher on, took Lucas to school, went to Morrisons for the main shopping, put it all away, hung out the washing while Tillie unloaded the dishwasher, went to the opticians for an eye test, called in at the bank and post office, came home, made coffee, caught up with emails, made lunch and sat outside with Tillie, watched a daddy blackbird feed a baby blackbird a snack between flying lessons, sorted out the family finances, brought in the washing, did the ironing, made the evening meal, washed up, laid the table for breakfast, had a bath and tumbled into bed. A relatively peaceful fifteen hours.

*

I keep thinking about what to wear to Iggie's studio. Should I go in the five-year-old outdated but smart outfit I didn't wear to Bonhams? And what about my props? A handbag? An umbrella? My specs? Is this how I want to appear in a portrait?

Thursday 27th June
As Tillie, Lucas and George were glued to the television, I had a private moment to try on the new Spanx-like slip. It's the width of a ten centimetre tube and clung to my head as I pulled it on. I thought I'd die of suffocation. After a lot of tugging and wriggling, I finally managed to roll the thing down. It attached itself with such force to my hips and thighs that I could barely move and had to waddle, penguin-like, to the landing mirror to see how I looked.

Was I transformed into the lovely young thing I'd been at eighteen with the waist size of a *Vogue* model? Did it flatter my contours, miraculously turning fat into beguiling curves? Did it, at the very least, flatten the stomach and minimise my bum?

No, it did not. It might have glued itself to my hips and legs, but my stomach was sticking out as much as it normally does. More so than in my swimming costume. Why???

It took twenty-five minutes to wriggle my way out of the damn thing. After fifteen minutes, with my arms pinned above my head, I had a panic attack and lay down on the bed to recover. Trapped in a tight-fitting tube, it wasn't easy to either lie down or get back up. I sweated so profusely trying to extricate myself out of the thing, that I must have lost at least half a kilo.

I don't think I've ever hated an item of clothing so much. What I need is a Victorian corset, reinforced with whale bones.

Friday 28th June
To ring the changes *and* feel better about the sight of my stomach squashed flat in my super-slimming swimsuit, I opted for the pool rather than Total Workout. First, though, I nipped to the loo, then stood on the scales. 'Struth! I've put on two kilos – the very same two kilos that took five months to come off. I'm back to where I started in January! How can that be?!

Swimming up and down the pool, I devised a new strategy. No chocolate, biscuits, cake, butter, cream, cheese or crisps. For one month. Then I'll get back on the scales. I have a will of iron and I can do it. Back at home, I settled down to a mid-morning sugarless coffee accompanied by no biscuits.

*

Tillie went to the Leavers' Ball dressed in her beautiful 1950s gown. She'd put up her hair, made up her face and wore one of my necklaces. She looked lovely. She sauntered out of the house to meet her friends. My gorgeous girl whom I love with all my breaking heart.

Saturday 29th June
The Ball went well, and Tillie thoroughly enjoyed herself. The best thing, for me, was that George picked her up at midnight.

*

God tested my iron will for one full, cruel, sugar-scented and fat-filled hour. I was cast as the person manning *(womaning?)* the cake stall at Lucas's sports day. I sold zillions of cakes and ate not one. Not even a smear of chocolate topping. Not even a crumb.

Lucas came eighth out of the ten boys running in the 400 metres race. It's not his thing. The school focuses on outdoor sports: rugby, hockey, cricket and athletics. They do offer table tennis and badminton for those – like Lucas – who prefer their exercise indoors. But in the big scheme of things – in the director of sports' view – they don't count. Those are games for wimps, the namby-pambies, the happy-clappers. Losers all.

Sunday 30th June
If too much time passes without a call to Great Aunt Vi, I feel guilty. She's not my responsibility, but I act as if she is. Don't ask me why.

'Harmondsworth,' she barked, after the sixth ring. It made her sound like a place in west London.

'Hello, Great Aunt Vi, it's me. Jill.'

'Yes, I can tell that.'

Silence.

'I'm just calling to find out how you are?'

'I'm fine.'

(Nothing else. She uses silence as a weapon to make the other person feel uncomfortable and inadequate.)

'It's been a while since we spoke,' I said with false gaiety, searching for an opening.

'It certainly has. I thought perhaps you'd left the country.'

I laughed. 'No such luck. Anyway, *you* could always call *me*.'

'True. Although I feel it is incumbent upon the young to take care of their elders.'

'Great Aunt Vi, you've never let *anyone* take care of you. Not even for a millisecond.'

'Possibly not. But it would be nice to see someone trying. Now, what do you want?'

And just at that moment, my mouth declared independence from my brain. I heard myself say, 'I'm coming to see you.'

(WHAT? What are you doing? This is your Great Aunt Vi, the

gorgon, who you are talking to. Why would you want to visit her? Isn't it enough to talk to her over the phone?)

'WHAT?' she yelled.

I wasn't sure if she was shouting because she too was outraged at the idea or because she hadn't heard. Despite protestations from my brain, my mouth motored on.

'I'M COMING TO VISIT YOU,' I yelled back.

'There's no need to shout,' she replied tartly. 'I'm not deaf. So when are you arriving?'

(Zip it, I told my mouth. Back out now before it's too late. But my mouth was enjoying its autonomy.)

'I could do a week on Thursday.'

'Thursday the 11th is perfect,' she said.

(Stop it! There's no need for this.)

'I'll aim to be there for midday. I'll take a taxi from the station.'

(Oh, for God's sake.)

'Perfect. I'll make a meal. You've not turned vegetarian or lost your marbles and gone vegan, have you?'

'No,' I replied smartly.

'I'll look forward to seeing you then.'

The phone went down crisply at her end.

I sat there, stunned. What's happening to me? Why are parts of me striking out? Why aren't I in control? Why am I a mess? And, worst of all, what will happen next?

July

Monday 1st July
Oh God, why have I chosen to visit Great Aunt Vi? I asked Tillie if she'd come too, but she pulled a face and walked away. There's not a single hope in hell that Lucas will join me. And there's no way that George will take a day off work to hold my hand. I logged on to cheaptraintravelfornervouswrecks.com and bought my ticket. The deed is done.

*

I'd vacuumed the stairs and was making my way into the bedrooms when an idea popped into my head about what to wear and what to take to Iggie's studio. Got it!

Tuesday 2nd July
Well, I finally hit a topic that I couldn't give a tuppenny-toss about on the V&A course: Italian small-scale bronze sculptures. I mean, really?

*

It was a quick meal of sandwiches for Lucas and me at tea time before we raced off to prize-giving evening. It's a three-line-whip for at least one parent to attend. Fail to turn up and your son is slung out of the school.

They're generous with prizes, but it's dismal to sit through two hours of clapping the feats and successes of other people's children while your son sits on the sidelines. Though in fairness, most of the boys sit on the sidelines.

Wednesday 3rd July
I had everything ready when the taxi arrived at ten. An hour

later, I was at Iggie's studio and relieved to see he wasn't surrounded by assistants. It was just him, me and Arnold. We sat down and, over a cup of coffee, talked about the portrait. Or rather, I talked.

I want it to be true to who I am. And what I feel is that, although I have various roles, currently the dominant one is that of cleaner. Hence I'd brought my cleaning clothes: jeans with tears in them, an old tee-shirt, apron, my ancient falling apart ballet slip-ons which I use as indoor shoes, and a grip to hold my hair so it doesn't get in the way. I'd also brought the vacuum cleaner and, for added authenticity *(albeit contrived)*, a used duster.

Iggie listened intently. I could tell his mind was racing with possibilities. He and Arnold kept shooting looks at one another and they were all positive.

We considered whether the backdrop should be plain white or the rough and tumble bricks and mortar of the studio wall. After positioning me against each, Iggie decided on the white background with the paper curving invisibly at the base to become the floor too. He didn't want anything detracting from me and what I was doing. Also, a white backdrop is timeless and placeless.

And what I was doing in the portrait was vacuuming, my eyes set on the floor just beyond where I was cleaning. I wasn't smiling but concentrating on the task in hand.

Over a couple of hours in which I tried various poses, Iggie took literally hundreds of images. The three of us looked at a select few on his computer.

He's very clever. I don't know how he did this, but he's captured me ostensibly looking at the floor but actually appearing to reflect on some inner thought. Or rather, some inner turmoil because I'm not remotely happy. *(Is that how I look when I'm cleaning?)*

The pristine white backdrop worked incredibly well.

There's no dust or dirt in sight anywhere. What you have is me vacuuming an apparently infinite area of perfectly clean floor space. All to no purpose.

'It's brilliant,' I told him, impressed by his compositional and photographic skills.

'*You* were brilliant,' he replied, generously. 'It was your idea.'

'*Our* idea. We all worked on it.'

For a brief moment, he put his arm around me. And I didn't mind that arm. With some men it could have been predatory, but with Iggie it was brotherly.

How do I describe how very much I enjoyed today? How exhilarating it was to express my ideas and find they sparked more ideas in Iggie and Arnold too? How fundamentally thrilling it was to work with people open to unexpected possibilities? How amazing when everything came together and what emerged was an arresting image? How extraordinary to be liked, appreciated and wanted? I came home on a high.

My only reservation was lunch. Iggie quizzed me about my life and because I rarely have the chance to tell anyone anything I yacked on. Probably far too much.

Well, what's done is done. Working with him is over too, but boy was it fun!

(Oh, and his scars are much better. Soon they'll just be pale lines on his scalp.)

Thursday 4th July

Despite just starting the new diet, I stepped on the scales. Oh, the slings and arrows of outrageous fortune! I weigh more than last week!

How can that be? I've not touched a slice of cake, not eaten any chocolate, had no ice-cream and only put a smear of butter on my bread. *And* I've taken as much exercise as previously. So how can I be heavier? It defies logic.

*

The German woman – Johanna – who replied to my ad on Gumtree emailed to ask if she could see the Wedgwood tomorrow. As she's the only person who's shown any interest, I hope she wants it.

Friday 5th July
Johanna arrived just after I'd laid some of the Wedgwood out on the kitchen table, as if for a meal. It looked attractive and I was tempted – momentarily – to keep it for myself.

Johanna was taken with it too. She was also bright, knowledgeable, witty and fun. The pair of us hit it off straight away.

It turns out she runs a stall every Saturday in Greenwich Market selling vintage house-wares from the 1930s to the 1980s. Twice a year she goes to Berlin – where she's from – and sells at a vintage market there.

'Well, I've got a lot more than this set, if you're interested,' I told her.

'Really?' *(A guttural roll of r's. I do like accents.)* 'Can I see?' *(Ken I see?)*

I showed her the two crates in the garage.

'Gott im Himmel,' she remarked, shocked, as she unwrapped tureen after sauce jug after sugar bowl. 'I've never seen so many pieces or in such pristine condition. Are you selling it all?' *(I'fe nefer seen zo meny...)*

The long and the short of it is that she's bought the lot. We loaded the crates into her van.

'Let's stay in touch,' she said, as she counted out a bundle of used £20 notes into my ready-and-waiting palms. It wasn't within a gnat's whisker of what the Tiffany vase had sold for, but it was a long way better than nothing.

'Come and see me in Greenwich!' *(Green Witch. Oh, stop it Jill.)*

I will, definitely.

*

It was the final day of year 10 for Lucas. He rang the doorbell, staggered in red-faced, sweating profusely and carrying three bags of books, which he dumped at my feet. Then he fell to the floor.

'Oh God. Last assembly and it went on all afternoon. The temperature in the chapel was incredible and the windows wouldn't open. Then I had to empty my locker and carry all these books, the bus was too hot and I thought I was going to die. I need something to drink.'

He crawled to the kitchen and was soon revived by a glass of water and a Magnum White. He announced, with great pride, that he'd gained full colours in music *and* been handed a special tie by the headmaster to commemorate the occasion. I asked what full colours meant. He hadn't a clue, but the fact that he'd been awarded something was what mattered.

Then he switched into holiday mode and raced down the garden to play on the trampoline.

Saturday 6th July
Lucas's report arrived in the post. The school stopped sending them via the boys long ago. Too many were lost in transit. *(Reports, not boys.)*

Despite it being addressed to George and me, Lucas ripped the envelope open milliseconds after it hit the doormat. 'Six 9s!' he yelled. 'Cool! It's more than I've ever had before. You've got to see this, Mum.'

The six 9s were excellent news. George and I focused on them and praised him to the high heavens. We didn't say anything about the rest of the report.

French: 'I was alarmed to see that Lucas arrived for his speaking assessment with supporting notes that contained just one word.' *(Did it say, 'Help?')* 'Lo and behold, he immediately had stage fright. It took three attempts until he was able to deliver the excellent speech of which I knew he was capable.'

English: 'Lucas's exam results were not a good reflection of his class work. He needs to add more detail to answers and extend his vocabulary.'

Chemistry: 'Lucas has had a relatively successful year, though it could have been better.'

Lucas's written assessment of his year: 'I have learned many things in year 10 including how much I hate chemistry.'

*

This evening, Lucas and I packed his case in readiness for tomorrow's school trip to Iceland, where the boys are adding to their GCSE geography studies on the topic of 'the restless earth'.

Sunday 7th July
We were at Heathrow by sunrise. Lucas spotted his school group in the far distance.

'Well, thanks Mum for bringing me. See ya.'

And off he ran.

I had a revelatory moment where I understood my value in his life: useful on occasions, but otherwise an embarrassment to be dumped instantly.

It was impossible not to be hurt.

*

Iggie phoned. He started by explaining that he had planned to do a series of portraits of various people from *Now You See it, Now You Don't*, starting with the me-as-a-cleaner portrait. But he'd had a re-think.

For a heart-sinking moment, I thought: he's going to tell me he's sorry but he isn't going to use the portrait after all and then apologise for wasting my time *(and raising my hopes that I was part of an amazing creative project)*.

But he didn't. Instead, he said he'd like to do the whole darn body of work based on portraits of *me* in my various roles as I'd explained to him over lunch: housekeeper, wife, mother, graphic designer, gym bunny and student. He'll photograph me dressed for each part and with just a few props – as in the first image. *(So all that talking paid off!)*

'Would you like to work on that with me and Arnold?' he asked quietly and politely, adding, 'It would be a collaborative process.'

Would I? Would I??!!! I was jumping up and down on the basement floor, wondering how to contain my excitement.

'I'd love to!' I replied. 'I'd absolutely love to work on this with the two of you! I can't think of anything better. When shall we start?'

We begin on Tuesday 16th. I'm going dressed for the V&A. My academic-student look.

George is pleased for me in his understated kind of way *(that is, you can't tell but I think he's happy)*. Tillie was half-pleased, half-jealous. Lucas doesn't know because he's away and probably wouldn't care anyway. And I am UTTERLY THRILLED.

Monday 8th July
Tillie is bored. Actually, she's been bored for days. It only took her a week to recover from A-level exams. She's cleared out all her notes, returned her books to school, erased unnecessary files from the laptop, tidied her desk, tidied her wardrobe, tidied her room and is now twiddling her thumbs. She's so bored that she's even resorted to helping me around the house – wonderful for me, but dreary for her.

As an antidote, we packed a picnic and headed to Green Park where we spread our blanket under a tree and settled in for a delicious lunch. The sun was shining, the sky was blue and the temperature perfect for lounging around. For the rest of the afternoon we ate, drank, chatted and watched everyone. Nosey-parker heaven.

Tuesday 9th July
The final day at the V&A and I've signed up for the next course – Late Renaissance to Baroque – starting in September. I do realise that at least half the enjoyment I gain from these V&A days has nothing to do with the course and everything to do with what's around it: the people I see on the train and Tube, the sights I see while walking, the lecturers, what they wear, how they speak and the other people on the course. And being away from home. But isn't that the point of the day? That it brings much more than just one thing?

Most of my new friends are signing up too. I'll have the joy of seeing them in the next academic year. It was truly exciting to have that end-of-term, yippee-it's-the-holidays feeling after many years' absence.

Wednesday 10th July
Tillie's school's end-of-year concert: the last for upper sixth formers. The evening began with solo recitals from three exceptional students: a soprano, a pianist and a harpist. They were followed by a performance of Karl Jenkins's *Songs of Sanctuary* sung by students from the massed choirs of the junior and senior schools, with Tillie among the latter. I adore children's voices. There's a heart-touching quality to them: pure and true.

That leaves two more points of contact with the school: A-level results and, in December, prize-giving.

*

All day, on and off, I've been thinking about tomorrow. Nervously. Can't wait. *(Can't wait until it's over.)*

Thursday 11th July Part I
Well, I might have known that a day involving Great Aunt Vi was not going to be ordinary.

Dressed in my best clothes *(and yes, they really are tired and need replacing)*, I arrived at Leicester station late morning where I bought a large bouquet of flowers, then took a taxi to Great Aunt Vi's.

When I told the driver the address he said, 'Oh, that's Miss Harmondsworth's house. I know my way there like the back of my hand.'

That was the first surprise. I asked him how.

'Everyone knows Miss Harmondsworth. She's famous round here.'

Second surprise. She's famous in our family, but I thought *we* were the limit. And he'd said it with proprietorial pride as if I was the outsider, not him.

'How do *you* know her?' he asked. His voice held a hint of suspicion.

'She's my great aunt.'

'A great woman too,' he added, switching his tone to one of approval. 'You're lucky to be related to *her*.'

Clearly, he'd only witnessed the best of Great Aunt Vi. Perhaps she saved the worst for the family.

'I am lucky,' I replied, trying to sound loyal and not sarcastic. 'But why is she famous in Leicester?'

'Her philanthropy,' he said with great pride. 'She's made a big donation. I expect you know that.'

I knew far more than I was supposed to know and, as I didn't want to start compromising that knowledge, I tried a tactical approach.

'She's very modest and doesn't say an awful lot,' I commented.

'It's that Tiffany vase that did it. Did you know about that?'

He turned round to look at me. I gave the kind of vague nod which I hoped could mean anything.

'She gave it to The Five Ls. That's a charity, local to round here. Of course, she didn't know it was Tiffany and when they found out and offered to give it back to her she said, "Keep it. I've given it to you. It's yours." They put it up for auction in some fancy place in London and it went for a huge sum. I shan't say what in case you don't know the details and Miss Harmondsworth wants to tell you the good news herself. Well, then the charity wanted to let everyone know about her generosity. Next thing she's in the papers and on the local radio and even the telly. She's quite some woman!'

(Not 'arf.)

'And of course, our cab firm's been busy for weeks on end while she's been clearing out her house, taking everything she doesn't want to The Five Ls.'

Third surprise. Alarm bells rang. Surely her spring-clean couldn't keep a taxi firm busy for *weeks*?

'Mind you,' he carried on, 'once it got out about the Tiffany vase every crook within fifty miles wanted to burgle her house, thinking there was more where that came from.'

'Good God.'

'But we sorted it. Put the word out that the Tiffany vase was the only thing of value in the whole house. I can tell you that, nice as Miss Harmondsworth is, she's got a lot of rubbish. No offence,' he added.

'None taken,' I said, thinking of her war-time Utility furniture, functional but ugly.

He pulled up outside her semi-detached Edwardian house and gave a cheery wave to Great Aunt Vi, who was waiting at the front gate, wearing her usual uniform of tweed skirt topped with a short-sleeved jumper from a twin-set. Familiar, brown, lace-up brogues graced her feet. I thought of the shoe box containing my letters and which once had held an elegant pair of stilettos: impossible to believe they'd ever been hers. Her hair was tied up in a French twist, the same style she's had since the first time I clapped eyes on her.

'My darling Jill,' she said, her arms open, her mood hail-fellow-well-met.

I presented her with the flowers, then followed her into the hall. But I stopped almost immediately and listened. Something was wrong. Great Aunt Vi turned round to watch me and as she did so, I noticed this wasn't a casual gaze but a sharp, assessing one. She was looking to see what I'd noticed. But what *had* I noticed?

'Don't stand there gawping,' she said, interrupting my thoughts. 'Come in the sitting room and tell me your news.'

I walked into that familiar room. Except that it wasn't. Familiar, that is. It was a room stripped bare of everything but the essentials: a carpet, two casual chairs and a television. No cabinets full of trinkets, no shelves full of books, no pictures on the walls, no occasional tables overloaded with knick-knacks, no settee, no cushions, no antimacassars. Nothing.

And then I realised what had been wrong in the hall. The sounds had echoed off the walls, ceilings, floors and windows, dancing up the staircase and rattling round the bedroom floor corridor. I was in an almost empty house. My blood ran cold.

She ushered me to one of the two chairs, as if everything was the same as before.

'Coffee, darling?'

A tray with a jug of coffee, two mugs, some milk and sugar was lodged on the floor by the side of her chair.

'What on earth's happened?' I asked, shocked.

She smiled at me innocently. 'What do you mean?'

'The room, the house – it's almost empty. What have you done?'

'I told you I was having a spring-clean,' she said reasonably, as if mollifying a child.

'You didn't say you were applying a scorched earth policy.'

She sat back and pondered this.

'True,' she said, more soberly.

For a moment I saw her thoughts turn inwards. And then they came back.

'But I did tell you that, having started, I was finding it hard to know quite where to stop.'

'Do you think you might have gone too far?' I asked quietly.

Her eyes narrowed and she looked at me, hawk-like.

'Definitely not,' she said in a cold tone that warned me *I'd* gone quite far enough and that the subject was closed.

Instead, we chatted of this and that. She'd made a pleasant lunch of Coronation chicken followed by strawberries and cream. We ate in the dining room, also stripped of its usual furnishings, and sat either side of an old, baize-topped card table, our knees almost touching. The crockery was a hotch-potch selection from various ancient sets, which was curious given that she'd kept four place settings from the Wedgwood she'd sent me.

Afterwards, I excused myself to go to the bathroom upstairs. On my way, I passed two bedrooms. Their doors were open and both rooms were completely empty, save for threadbare carpets. The bathroom was similarly denuded with just the essentials of toothbrush, toothpaste, soap, flannel and denture accoutrements lining a single shelf.

The house that I had known was gone. Of course, I knew about the piano and wardrobe being sent to Sue and Robert. There must have been additional items which reached other relatives. But the disappearance of so much that was familiar was heart breaking. It didn't matter that Great Aunt Vi's furniture and possessions were old, plain and tatty. Or that there was far too much of everything. They were hers. Belatedly, I realised that they were mine too: landmarks stretching back to my childhood. My parents' home was gone, and now Great Aunt Vi's was all but gone too.

I came downstairs, my heart in my boots. Great Aunt Vi saw my misery and, before I could say anything, opted for a distraction tactic.

'Let's go for a stroll round the garden,' she said cheerily.

Great Aunt Vi is a fine plantswoman and her garden, at

least, was unchanged. Her roses were out in abundance, the foxgloves were monumental, the irises and lilies elegant in stature and rich with colour. We strolled to the end where she had a simple raised bed full of fruits and vegetables. As she talked, my focus wandered to the compost heap and the discreet rubbish dump which lay by the boundary hedge.

Something white, lying on the ground, caught my eye. Great Aunt Vi was chatting about her pak choi and fingering the fat leaves of a particularly fine specimen. I turned to look at the white thing. It was a painted board attached to a post. I could just make out the words "For Sale". It was an estate agent's sign. Except that it was hand-painted in Great Aunt Vi's script.

'Great Aunt Vi,' I interrupted. 'Have you sold your house?'

Thursday 11th July Part II written on Friday 12th July (all I did was write)

It was phenomenally upsetting. For me, that is.

'Ah,' she said, as she realised I'd discovered something she hadn't intended me to. She pulled herself up to her full height, gazed back to the house, then turned and looked me in the eye. 'Yes. Or to be more exact, I'm in the process.'

I held on to a wooden plant support, stared at my feet and blinked hard against my tears. Of course, I should have realised as soon as I walked in the house: she had cleared it with the intention of leaving.

'Where are you moving to?'

'That's none of your business,' she snapped angrily, and turned to walk away.

My own mood switched just as quickly. I wasn't taking that tone from anyone.

'Stop right there,' I said forcefully. 'If nothing else, I need to know where to send your Christmas card.'

To my amazement she did stop and turned round.

'I haven't finalised either the sale or where I'm moving to.

When I have, I shall let you know.' She was trying to moderate her tone.

'But you *love* this house,' I said, returning to my normal voice. 'It's been your life. Look at the garden. You have created a thing of beauty. You're as physically and mentally able as me. You could stay here forever. Why move?'

She sighed and, for a second, her shoulders drooped.

'Let's go in and chat.'

What transpired was that she'd started the year intending to clear out all the extraneous detritus around the house so that on her death there would be less for her executor *(whoever that was)* to do. But the more she sent to the charity shop, the less she wanted in her home. And the less there was in her home the more she didn't want to be in it any longer. Then she had the idea of leaving the house completely.

She'd contacted five estate agents, received estimates for the house's value, was shocked at the fees for selling, and decided to do the job herself. Hence the hand-made "For Sale" sign.

Within three days of it being up, a young couple had expressed interest – Pippa and Matt, who live in a smaller house at the other end of the street. With their two daughters, four-year-old Grace and two-year-old Lily, they needed more space.

They loved what they saw: the extra rooms and the large garden. A price was agreed and now they're in the middle of exchanging contracts. At completion, the furniture that remains in the house will be sent to The Five Ls and Great Aunt Vi will move on with a handful of boxes.

I had to face the inevitable: my ancient, irascible, mercurial, idiosyncratic aunt was moving to the one place left for an elderly person.

'What's the address of the old people's home?' I asked miserably.

She looked stunned.

'Good God, Jill! I may be old, but I'm not gaga. I am not,

definitely *not*, moving into an old people's home. Or a care home.' She tapped the forefinger of her right hand on the card table, emphasizing her point.

'You don't have to be gaga to go into either, and it's got to be sheltered accommodation of some kind if you're taking so little.'

She waited a moment, watching me closely, her eyes narrowing.

'You're fishing. You're hoping I'll tell you. But I won't.'

I said nothing but I could feel my lips pursing with irritation and frustration.

'Look, the reason why I'm being cagey is that I don't want to jinx myself by saying something and then it all falling through. It's not personal to you. It's personal to me. When all the contracts are done and dusted, then I will tell you what I'm doing.'

I sighed, wondering what else there was to say.

'Well, if you need help moving, George and I will do everything we can.'

I thought we'd probably both gone as far as we could with that particular conversation. I changed tack.

'The taxi driver told me you're famous round here.'

'Oh that,' she said, dismissing it with a flick of one of her long, bony hands.

'But you're a media star. I was told you've been in the newspapers, as well as on the telly and radio.'

'All true,' she conceded. 'It was over that vase in the back bedroom. The one you wanted. At first I thought I'd keep it, but then I decided it was just more junk and I sent it to The Five Ls. They discovered it was made by Tiffany, of all people, and offered it back. But having given it to them, I felt they should keep it. They, in turn, sent it to auction and it raised a tidy sum.'

There wasn't a single apology for not giving it to me when she changed her mind. The temptation to thump her was almost overwhelming. But I'm a fully signed up, non-violent, card-carrying pacifist. She didn't even bother to mention how much the vase sold for. I took my meagre, pathetic revenge by not giving her the satisfaction of me oohing and aaahing over the vase being Tiffany or enquiring about its sale price.

'But I'm back to being a nobody now,' she said, smiling and folding one hand over the other in her lap.

'I had my fifteen minutes of fame too, recently,' I said brightly, thinking I'd tell her about Iggie's Saatchi Gallery exhibition.

'Jolly good,' she replied and stood up, brushing one hand against the other as if ridding herself of some dirt.

A flame of fury rose in my chest. She was not interested in me. Not one iota. Not one miniscule molecule. After a lifetime living on her own, there was only one person who mattered: herself. It was time for me to go.

But, as I did so, I was assailed by another emotion: sadness. For this was likely to be the last time I would see her dear old home. The loss made my chest ache.

'Well, Great Aunt Vi, it was interesting to see you,' I said opting for a higher truth that over-rode both bitterness and sorrow.

She held me at arm's length.

'Thank you for coming.'

And then she did what she never does. She kissed me on the cheek.

(What am I to make of those mixed messages?)

Saturday 13th July

Lucas arrived back from Iceland.

'How was it?' I asked.

'Alright.'

'Was your hotel OK?'

'Yeah, 'cept I had to share with that tosser Tomma who can't sleep without snoring.'

'What were the geysers like?'

'Yeah. Good.'
'Did the restless earth move?'
'Sort of.'
'And the food?'
'Crap. No pizzas.'

I was presented with a suitcase of dirty washing as if it was a gift.

'Nice try,' I said, and reminded him about the washing regime.

No presents. Not even a bar of soap from the hotel bathroom.

Sunday 14th July

A quick turnaround: Lucas washed his clothes, they dried in the sun, I ironed them and then the majority were repacked. Tomorrow he's off – with Max – for a four-day criminology taster course at the University of Birmingham.

Monday 15th July

Lucas and Max took the train together. It's the first time Lucas has travelled any distance without us. Last night we gave him step-by-step instructions on how to get from here to the university. He was nervous, but not as nervous as us. Still, at least he's got Max. It's not as if someone's going to abduct *two* teenage boys, is it?

Tuesday 16th July

Exciting – another day with Iggie and Arnold. They're such special men: intelligent, fun to be with, not egotistical, their energies focused on making the best creative work they can.

I changed into my V&A clothes at the studio after we'd worked out how best to position the props. We took Iggie's desk and, from another studio, borrowed a moulded plastic chair – the kind you find in every institution up and down the country – and placed them against the same plain white backdrop as in the previous photograph.

I sat at the desk, my open notebook in front of me, my favourite fountain pen in my right hand and a ruler clutched in my left fist. I looked up as if watching a screen of slides at the V&A: alert and ready for the off. I was focusing on a poster of *The Adoration of the Mystic Lamb* from Jan van Eyck's The Ghent Altarpiece – which Arnold had pinned behind Iggie and his camera.

It's an extraordinary work, the colour palette so brilliant that it almost looks as if it's come straight from *The Wizard of Oz*.

It shows the sacrifice of the lamb – the symbol of Christ's slaughter for our salvation. It's a well-built, robust animal standing four-square and completely oblivious to the strong, steady fountain of blood spurting from its chest into a goblet. The lamb is surrounded by angels and, at a slight distance, four distinct groups: churchmen, saints, martyrs and lay people.

Very cleverly, and after the photograph was taken, Iggie inserted the painting behind my image so the audience can see what it is that I'm looking at.

And what did he capture of me this time? Curiosity, eagerness, awe and a sense of wonder – the latter so open and radiant that it verged on the spiritual. It was as if I was one of the acolytes in the painting.

Iggie has this uncanny ability to capture far more than I think is expressed on my face when I'm sitting in front of the camera. It's a revelation to me that he sees my internal life, then somehow draws it out and transports it into an image.

We're going to fit in one more session before the end of the month, when we're all heading off on our different holidays. And we've agreed what we're doing next.

Wednesday 17th July
Back to reality: washing, ironing, shopping, cooking and catching up with emails. I don't mind the housework when the previous day has been stimulating. In fact, it's a calming contrast. And it's an opportunity to do some thinking.

Thursday 18th July
Tillie spent the day upstairs packing, unpacking, repacking, un-repacking and re-repacking for her and Kaya's trip to the Gentlemen of the Road festival in Lewes.

Lucas returned home from his criminology course – wildly enthusiastic. The course had been brilliant. He'd stayed in a four-star hotel with a room and ensuite bathroom all to himself, the food had been delicious – a pizza option every evening – and the last night had included a gala dinner with celebrity guests who he recognised from the telly.

I thought he was winding me up, but he assured me it was all true. He rated the whole experience as ten out of ten and thanked me for sending him. I'll just repeat that because it's amazingly nice to write: HE THANKED ME FOR SENDING HIM.

Friday 19th July
I phoned Sue this evening to spread the word, albeit belatedly, about Great Aunt Vi's imminent move to God-knows-where. She already knew!

'How?' I asked indignantly.

'She told me,' replied Sue affably.

'But when?'

'About two weeks ago.'

'And you didn't think to tell me?'

'I presumed you knew.'

'But how could you know for sure unless you discussed it with me?'

There was a pause at the other end of the phone. 'I hadn't thought of that.'

I was shocked to discover she wasn't applying the same open policy as me. If I find something out, I share it. It suggested that she wasn't as interested in the news as me, or worse, that she wasn't interested in me.

'Well, in future, please tell me anything you find out,' I said, incensed.

'Aye-aye, Captain,' she responded flippantly.

'So, I suppose you also know where she's going.'

'An old people's home.'

'*What?* She told *me* she definitely wasn't going to one of those.'

'Oh, well, maybe she's not.'

'For goodness sake. Did she actually say, "I'm moving to an old people's home"?'

'Am I being interrogated?'

'Yes. And I haven't got out the thumbscrews yet. Now answer the question.'

'No, she didn't. I just presumed she was.'

'Well, she told me she wasn't. But she has got rid of almost all the contents of her house.'

'Or given it to poor unsuspecting relatives like us,' said Sue. 'Which reminds me. You know she gave me that wretched piano and we had a communal sing-song with all the residents?'

'Yes.'

'You'll never guess, but it's turned into a regular occurrence. We so enjoyed the get-together round Great Aunt Vi's piano that once a month we meet in someone's flat and have a party. A sedate party, but a party nonetheless.'

'What do you do? Smoke pot while sitting round a coffee table?'

She ignored my jibe.

'Thus far, we've had an evening of canasta, another playing

bridge, and a tasting night when Harry made canapés and cocktails. I'm introducing the first Monopoly night this weekend.'

'Good grief, you know how to live.'

(But I did note that while no one else was named, Harry got a mention. Could romance be in the air? Could the virgin Sue be about to tumble in love?)

'What's Harry like?' I ventured.

'Middle-aged, fat and going bald,' she said flatly.

(Or perhaps not.)

'The point I'm making,' Sue continued, 'is that Great Aunt Vi's generous-stroke-malicious-stroke-mischievous act of sending that ancient piano has led to this wonderful community development. We're thinking of venturing further and having a night out at the theatre.'

'It sounds ...'

I searched for an appropriate word. I was thinking it sounded rather like the social calendar of an old people's home.

'Fantastic.' *(That covered it.)* 'Anyway, to get back to the original subject: have you any idea which geographical location Great Aunt Vi is moving to?'

'None at all, and I couldn't care less.'

'God, you can be heartless.'

'I don't know why *you're* interested,' she replied tartly. 'What good has she ever done you?'

'Actually, I'm fond of her.' *(Though perhaps not as fond as I was before I discovered how fond she is of herself.)* 'I had some interesting holidays with her as a child, she always turned up trumps on birthdays and Christmas, and she's the only elderly relative I've got left.'

'You want your head seeing to. She's a waspish, malevolent, nasty old woman who's nearly always up to no good.'

'Well, there is that,' I conceded.

And I still didn't know where the old bat was going.

*

Tillie's taken herself off to the festival. I gave her strict instructions to text me once a day so I know she's OK. Today's text: *Arrived.* Why do I receive monosyllabic messages when she sends friends whole essays?

Saturday 20th July
This morning's text: *Fun!* Tomorrow, my loquacious daughter will be home.

Sunday 21st July
Tillie arrived at lunchtime looking spectacularly tanned and radiantly happy for just forty-eight hours near the sea and despite little sleep. Perhaps I should try it.

Monday 22nd July
I made it to Total Workout, my regular attendance not totally working out this month because of all my other commitments. But the good thing is I don't huff and puff as much, or ache as badly as I used to. I'm definitely fitter, even if the body still isn't that beautiful.

Tuesday 23rd July
Mindfulness, which I'm reading slowly, suggests a ten-finger gratitude exercise. Each day you count ten things for which you've been grateful in the last twenty-four hours. The aim is to appreciate the small things in life, as well as the large.

I do this some nights when I can't sleep. Either I struggle – wondering what came after the third good thing – or I haven't got enough fingers. The difference is not always in what happened in the day, but my attitude to it. Some days my cup is half-empty. Others it's half-full.

Today:
1. I watched George concentrate on his image in the mirror as he did up his tie, and thought how handsome he looked.

2. Tillie had a lovely day out in Battersea Park with friends.
3. Her happiness is infectious.
4. Lucas went to Max's house where they played on Max's PlayStation. He's easily pleased.
5. I am well.
6. It was a beautiful day, the sun shone and the temperature rose to the low 30s.
7. I can stand in any of the rooms at the back of this house and see the greenery of our garden and the neighbours' gardens. The view is as good as any in the countryside. *(Well, OK, not really like the countryside, but for London it's peerless.)*
8. Interflora sent an email ad for a bouquet of flowers. They looked so beautiful that I ordered a bunch for Edith. She adores flowers.
9. I read a short story from J. D. Salinger's *For Esmé with Love and Squalor*. This may be the best book of short stories I will ever read. Salinger is a genius. An unsettling genius at times, but a genius nonetheless.
10. I didn't once go near the chocolate cupboard.

If I had to write ten bad things about the day I'm not sure I could, because they've now been diminished by the good. There's a moral in there somewhere.

Wednesday 24th July
Another session at Iggie's – the last until September. He's closing the studio for August while he and Arnold take their separate holidays, and I have mine with the family in the mountains of Switzerland.

This image featured me as a sportswoman. *(Don't laugh.)* I'd dressed in my usual hotchpotch outfit for Total Workout – old sports bra, tired tee-shirt, ancient fleece with a hole at one elbow, vintage leggings and antique trainers. I had considered buying some new kit so everything matched but that's not the me who goes to the gym, and I want these photographs to be honest.

Arnold had sourced an extra-heavy netball – the kind we throw to one another as part of the Total Workout warm up. Using the white backdrop – which will nearly always appear throughout the series of photos to provide an important, neutral consistency – we decided that, out of shot, Arnold would throw the ball to me and I'd run into the shot, jumping to catch it.

Easier said than done. It took some time for Arnold and me to become proficient, and for me to appear in the right place. It was also a test of Iggie's skills to take a shot of someone moving fast and yet capture a perfect, still moment within that. What I thought was going to be simple was far from it. Exhausting, too.

I must have run and jumped hundreds of times and had to keep stopping for a rest. It was a warm day and the lights made the studio hotter still. *(I've definitely lost several tonnes in sweat.)*

By mid-afternoon, Iggie said he'd got what he needed.

And what had he got? My worst fear had not been realised. Iggie's photograph did not parody an older woman trying to stay fit. Quite the opposite. It showed me intent on catching the ball and doing it in as athletic a way as is possible at this stage in my life. In fact, even if I say so myself, I looked good. Better still, because I'm leaping and reaching up with outstretched arms, my portly stomach is pulled in. I look like the slim version of me I've always wanted to be. Utterly, brilliantly wonderful. I could be a life-affirming role model for the over-50 woman: strong, healthy, sporty, determined and happy. *(Actually, a life-affirming role model for myself.)*

We set a date for the next photograph and agreed on the subject and props. Now I just have to persuade the props to come too.

Thursday 25th July

Edith phoned: she loved the bouquet. It filled three vases, which she's distributed in her kitchen, sitting room and bedroom –

the three rooms she uses most.

Friday 26th July
I worked like stink all day: packed, made sandwiches for the journey, told the neighbours we'd be away, wrote a shopping list for our return and put it on Ocado, and closed down the house in readiness for our departure.

George took five minutes to select the clothes he'd take, then asked how it took me so long to do the rest. I have not one clue about money-laundering law but sometimes I'd like to swap jobs for a day. I could mess up his work, and he could be shocked at what he's required to do at home.

Finally, before heading to bed, I hopped on the scales. Then hopped off. The day before a family holiday is not the time to be worrying about weight. *(Wow! Common sense! How did that enter my life?!)*

Saturday 27th July
The temperature in Zurich was in the high 30s. It was only as our train hauled itself into the mountains that the heat dropped to an acceptable level and the sweet scents of grass, alpine meadow flowers and pine trees wafted through the open windows. My heart rose.

From Kandersteg station, we walked to our apartment. And what a place! It's on the first floor of an old converted farmhouse and is a perfect picture postcard of the original wooden Swiss chalet. A balcony stretches along the side of the building that faces the sun. All the windows have wooden shutters with small heart shapes cut out of their centres and window-boxes full of orange, red, purple and white geraniums in full bloom.

The interior, with its wood cladding, smells like a forest. Despite the season, the beds are made with the fattest duvets I've ever seen, each plump within a white cover. They look like small, snow-clad mountains. I expect miniature skiers to appear over their tops and race down their slopes.

Best of all, we have a spare bedroom with two single beds. When Heidi and Peter arrive we'll be able to put them up too. *(Not sure what we'll do with the goats though.)*

Sunday 28th July

Hi Frankie,

Am in my dream Swiss house – a farmhouse that dates back to the late eighteenth century, complete with original furniture.

Spent our first, very hot day walking up a smallish mountain and discovering how hard that is.

Hope your Corsican holiday goes well. Loved your birthday party! Jill xxx

Monday 29th July

Dear Edith,

If you were here, you'd be wondering why you'd bothered to leave home. The rain is torrential and unrelenting. Still, it was beautiful yesterday.

We walked round a lake where Tillie and Lucas discovered three salamanders on the footpath, picked them up and put them in the grass. The highlight of the day.

Love, George, Jill, Tillie and Lucas

Tuesday 30th July

George can't believe his luck. We've made love every night. Not sure what's got into me. It must be the Swiss mountain air. Plus happiness. And no housework.

Wednesday 31st July

Made love again and then – in what I thought was a post-coital moment of bliss – George asked, 'Are you having an affair with Iggie? Or Arnold? Or indeed anyone else?'
(??!!!???)

August

Thursday 1st August – Swiss National Day *(for what it's worth)*
Honesty being the best policy, I reached out a hand to George's under the duvet and said gently, 'Yes. I am.'

'I knew it,' he replied bitterly. He whipped his hand away.

'With you! I'm having an affair with you!' I replied half laughing, half outraged.

He looked at me disbelieving. 'You can't have an affair with your husband. The very term "affair" suggests an extra-marital relationship. It's implicit in the word.'

He was going all legal on me, his default mode in times of stress.

'OK. Then I'm not having an affair,' I replied lightly. 'Not with Iggie, who's young enough to be my son and who I don't fancy sexually, though I like him very much as a non-sexual friend. Nor am I attracted to Arnold. And for the record, neither Iggie nor Arnold have shown any sexual interest in me. Thank God. No one else is interested. Not now, not any time this century and probably not since I met you. And anyway, I'm a mono … '

I was trying to think of the word to describe someone who has one sexual relationship at a time.

'Monomaniac.'

He turned to me. 'I'm not sure you mean that.'

'Oh, George. I'm not having an affair. I've never wanted an affair. You're the one for me. I'm loyal, loving, boring. There is no one and nothing in my life but you.'

He gave a weak smile. 'It's just that you've been unusually interested in sex these last few days, it made me wonder.'

'It made me wonder, too. I think it's a combination of

happiness, not being exhausted by the housework or my London life, and not feeling time-pressured.'

I reached out for his hand again.

'Sorry,' he said sheepishly. Then added, 'I hope this won't interrupt our current record.'

And just to show it hadn't, we made love again.

Friday 2nd August
I've had two brilliant ideas. First: I could use the money from selling Great Aunt Vi's Wedgwood to buy myself some new clothes. Second: I could ask Tillie to help me. She has excellent taste, plus she's honest and will be a good fashion guide.

When I put this to her, she was interested but cautious.

'You mean, I help choose the clothes?' she asked.

'I'm relying on you.'

'And you're prepared to step outside your comfort zone of jeans and tee-shirts?'

'Yes. Though there's nothing wrong with jeans and tee-shirts.'

'If they're stylish.'

'Exactly. That's what I need.'

'OK.'

I was about to hug her but she put up a hand, blocking me.

'First, though, you have to clear out your wardrobe and chest of drawers because they're crammed full of crap.'

(See what I mean?)

'True. Though I do like some of that crap.'

She raised her eyebrows in a you-must-be-mad kind of way.

'Will you let me help clear out your clothes too, then?'

I didn't have much of a choice: something had to go because there wasn't room to add anything new.

'OK,' I replied decisively. 'Out with the old and in with the new!'

And then we hugged.

*

Made love yet again. George's doubts over my fidelity have evaporated.

Saturday 3rd August
Dear Great Aunt Vi,
We're staying in a beautiful old Swiss farmhouse – refreshingly different from home. Talking of which, I hope your house sale (and purchase?) is/are going well.
Remember, George and I are happy to help with the move. With fond wishes, Jill xxx

Dear Sue,
Text me the minute you hear any news on the Great Aunt Vi front. Am relying on you. God knows why.
Jill x

Sunday 4th August
There's a tube of Easy Glide in the chest of drawers by my side of the bed. I presumed it was to make the drawers slide more easily. Then I put my glasses on. It's the Swiss version of KY Jelly. It cost the equivalent of £21 – a sufficiently high enough price to put you off sex.

Monday 5th August
Dear Frankie,
Am becoming proficient at walking for hours up near-vertical mountains. Was thinking smugly of how fit I must be when I was overtaken by a woman about my age who was running! She had the body of a twenty-year-old Olympic athlete and was so not out of breath she even greeted me as she passed.
Comforted myself with the thought she'll need knee replacement operations before I do.
Jill xx

Tuesday 6th August
As we're all exhausted, we promised ourselves to take the gondola up to the highest mountain, gawp at the view and then take the gondola back down. We managed everything but the last bit, a challenge being irresistible.

But a thousand metres is a big drop, and it took several hours to walk back to the valley floor. Now we're even more tired. Hips hacked off. Knees knackered. Feet fucked.

Wednesday 7th August
In the apartment, there's a cupboard full of polishes, creams, detergents, pastes and unguents for removing every speck of dirt on every surface known to man. Or woman. There are even cleaning things for cleaning things. I've not tried one of them.

Thursday 8th August
I hardly dare write this given George's concern, but I spend a lot of time thinking about Iggie. Any moment for quiet reflection and there he is. I mull over the lunchtime conversations we had. He's a private person, but he has told me about the craniotomy: of the terrible headaches before it was diagnosed, the nausea, vomiting and drowsiness. And then, most frightening of all for a photographer, the deterioration in his vision.

He says he's the luckiest man on the planet because the doctors did find out what was wrong with him, that the tumour was benign, it was removed completely and now his vision is fine. He peered into the dark, silent, vertiginous abyss, and returned.

Of course, you can't go through something like that and be unaffected. In the short term, he can't drive, he's had to give up football – contact sports are to be avoided for obvious reasons – and he tires easily. So easily that after a day's shooting, he takes the next one off to rest. Which means that, at most, he manages two days of commercial commissions beyond the day with me.

'It's my second chance at life,' he told me quietly. 'I'm learning about myself and other people.' He turned to look at me fully. 'Now I'm learning about you.'

There was nothing sexual in the comment. He'd offered it in the tone of voice that a psychotherapist might use. But I had a sense that in some way I'm a cipher: what he's learning will lead to something else.

I'm learning about me as well. Paradoxically, I'm learning about myself through his eyes: he reveals a person I don't wholly recognise. It's not the me I see in a mirror but a heightened version: both more intense and more emotionally honest.

Is my year off a second chance at life for me? Is it a chance not simply to remove the stress of work, but to make major changes — albeit within the limited framework of family life? Am I being thrown a lifeline too?

Friday 9th August
The mountains are covered in miniature cowslips, purple gentians, fragile edelweiss, pools of tiny pinks along with white and yellow daisies whose heads wave in the breeze. The beauty of all this is breathtaking. I want to remember it always, knowing this is where I belong: among these dizzying wonders.

Saturday 10th August
A ten-hour journey. Stepping out of the train in London, we were hit by the smell and feel of pollution.

Sunday 11th August
The weather was sublime. By tea time all eight loads of washing *(shared equally between us all)* had dried on the line. We dusted and vacuumed the house from top to bottom. Tillie and Lucas complained, but it hadn't been done for weeks.

This evening, I stripped off and checked myself in the

mirror. Not bad. After two weeks of walking, my muscles have toned up. I resisted stepping on the scales. I'll leave the good news until the end of the month.

Monday 12th August
Spent all day working through the 600-odd emails which came in over the holiday. Several offered ways to increase the length of my penis. *(Does 'Jill' sound like a man's name in other languages?)*

Emailed Fay to meet her later this month.

Tuesday 13th August
Tillie and I cleared out my clothes.

'We need some rules,' said Tillie, opening the wardrobe.

'Do we?' I asked anxiously.

'If you've not worn something for two years, it's out.'

'That's a bit strict.'

'And if it's got a hole in it and you've not mended it, it's out. Or if it's just plain horrible, it's out.'

'You make my clothes sound hideous.'

She looked at me and said nothing.

'OK. I'll go along with it. You win.'

I will not give a blow-by-blow account of the day. Suffice to say we wrangled over many items, and I lost every time. My wardrobe is now full of a motley assortment of hangers and no clothes. The chest of drawers is equally empty, bar a lonely bra and a few pants to tide me over until we reach the shops. Almost every garment bought since 1990 is neatly folded in one of fifteen black bin bags at Oxfam *(including that wretched Spanx-like-doesn't-suck-your-stomach-in slip).*

Although it was hard to part with some items, I feel pleasantly liberated, cleansed, ready to be a new me. *(Slightly anxious, too.)*

The purging had a second benefit: it distracted Tillie from

worrying about her A-level results – due on Thursday.

Wednesday 14th August
Harvey, Riley and I *(all at art college together)* met in Soho for our annual get-together. We ordered chocolate-topped cappuccinos, then got down to catching up on our past year.

They're both working full-time and were shocked to hear that I'm not. I explained about the year off with the option to do work if I fancied it. They looked at me as if I'd just landed from Mars.

'You're either working or you're not,' said Harvey.

'Well, sometimes I work and sometimes not. Mostly not. The point of the year off is to find out what I want to do.'

'Doesn't make sense to me,' said Riley, shaking his head. 'I mean why would you *not* want to work?'

That told me everything. Riley loves his work. He loves his clients. He even loves the clients he says he hates. Harvey too. They're in the thick of it, and they're happy.

'The thing is,' I said, 'I'm sick of it.'

They looked at one another and I could see the silent message passing between them: she's lost it.

'Well, if you're sick of it – then stop,' advised Harvey.

'But I might be offered a really tantalising piece of work and then I'll want to do it.'

'And have you?' asked Riley.

'No.'

There was an uncomfortable silence while we all hugged our coffee cups and stared at the frothy dregs.

'I don't get it,' concluded Harvey, looking to Riley for help.

'Well, never mind. Just accept it,' I said as lightly as I could. But I was dejected. Damn it, I wanted their approval.

That's the problem with men. Everything's black and white. Open and shut. Love it or hate it. Take it or leave it. Do it or don't do it. But don't hover between the two.

I saw myself alone, perched on the periphery of the design world. The very far periphery.

*

Afterwards, I walked to John Lewis on Oxford Street where Tillie joined me for lunch. That perked me up.

'I've drawn up a list for a capsule wardrobe,' she said, pulling out a piece of paper from her handbag as we tucked into salads. 'Two pairs of jeans, two skirts, two smart dresses, a jacket that will go with all of those, four tops that will go with the skirts and jeans, two jumpers, a pair of knee high boots, a pair of ankle boots, one pair of shoes, a handbag and then new underwear. You'll be able to mix and match so that you have a style suitable for every occasion.'

It made sense. But it sounded like a lot to purchase, even if it was far less than we'd thrown out.

'We can make the most of the tail-end of the sales *and* buy from the new autumn season's clothes. You'll be bang on-trend,' she continued. 'The right colours, the right cut, the right style. Wow, Mum, you're going to be amazing!'

And I am. It took hours, and I've never undressed and dressed as many times in one day nor seen the changing rooms of so many shops. But between John Lewis, Jigsaw, Warehouse, Hobbs, H&M and Marks & Spencer we bought everything on her list. And it was fun! I tried on a g'zillion items *(to use Tillie's terminology)*, nearly all of them outside my comfort zone. I did not buy my habitual tight-fitting tee-shirts which highlight my rolls of fat, but instead chose loose-fitting – though definitely not baggy – blouses and tops that hide what's underneath while also making me appear slimmer. What I'm now sporting is a new outline: chic, elegant, up-to-date.

I spent every last penny from the Wedgwood sale. I am exhausted but elated. I couldn't have wished for a better, wiser, smarter shopping companion than Tillie.

And we didn't once talk about tomorrow.

Thursday 15th August

The big day. The day on which the next few years pivot for Tillie. For me. For us all.

I was wide awake by four a.m. worrying, but Tillie slept on unperturbed. She went to school at nine expecting to join her friends collecting their results, but they'd all arrived at the crack of dawn and departed long since. In fact, she was the second to last person to turn up.

The headmistress always talked about education being a marathon and that pupils must pace themselves for the fourteen-year long haul from reception to upper sixth. With that analogy in mind, I thought there'd be teachers waiting at the end of the educational process to cheer the girls in as they staggered past the finishing line of A-level results. I was wrong. There was just one teacher and she was obviously eager to go home. To say it was anti-climactic would be the understatement of the year.

But to the main event: three cheers for Tillie because that clever young woman got one A star and two As, which is exactly what she needs for Durham University.

I hugged her, chock-full of love, pride and joy. And then she burst into tears.

'I'm happy, really,' she said, gulping for air and then bawling some more. 'It's just I'm so relieved I got what I wanted. And I'm really glad I'm going to Durham. But I'm hugely sad about leaving home. And though I'm excited, I'm also frightened, Mum.'

That did it. I cried too. We were *both* looking at the end, and we were both scared. School is over, home is over. University and an independent life beckon. *(Well, for her.)*

She mopped herself up and phoned George and the rels to tell them the good news before hitting social media. Most of her friends had done fine, though one or two were going through Clearing.

It was time to celebrate. I dragged Lucas from the PlayStation and drove the three of us to Marks & Spencer, where we bought every delicious food we've ever fancied. Lucas grabbed pizzas and crisps. Tillie opted for hotdogs, hamburgers and salads, while I filled the trolley with various breads, fruit, a pile of profiteroles and a bottle of champagne.

We pigged out over lunch and groaned our way through the early afternoon during which Frankie phoned to say Archie had got three A stars *(brainy or what?)* and is going to King's College, London to read history. Excellent news. George came home early and we tucked into more pizzas, hotdogs and hamburgers, all washed down with champagne. This is the life!

*

I've just worked out it is six weeks and two days until Tillie leaves home on September 28th. That's forty-four days in total. Or one thousand and fifty-six hours, of which she'll be asleep for four hundred or thereabouts. That leaves six hundred and fifty-six hours awake and in which to enjoy her company. That doesn't sound too bad. *(Does it?)*

Friday 16th August
Great Aunt Vi had posted a congratulations card to Tillie and a £50 cheque. *(Sent from her usual address. No sign of a house move yet.)*

Tillie spent the morning reading about Durham University and the accommodation in her chosen hall – Trevelyan or 'Trevs' to give it its popular name. There's a myriad of online forms for her to fill in. By lunchtime, she felt sick with nervousness about her forthcoming departure.

One of her friends texted to say she'd been looking at her university's website and just seeing the title of her course had given her a panic attack. We laughed, each of us having been close to that state too – though for different reasons.

Saturday 17th August
More cards for Tillie. Everyone's making her feel special. She went to work at Morrisons and even the store manager said how proud he was of her. She's walking on sunshine.

Sunday 18th August
We put on our glad rags *(for me, my new dress, matching jacket, shoes and handbag)* and went for a late afternoon meal at the Wolseley on Piccadilly to celebrate Tillie's success.

It was grander than anywhere we'd ever eaten before. Lucas wanted to know which of the patrons was rich and famous. The elderly rich tend to wear their wealth, but everyone else dresses down to the point of scruffiness. Also, we're hopeless at identifying celebrities. I could fall over Justin Bieber and never know it was him. *(He'd never know it was me either.)*

Tillie and I had a croque monsieur each, while Lucas had a beef-burger, and George ordered chicken with mushrooms. For pud, Tillie chose vanilla cheesecake, George had treacle tart and Lucas opted for another beef-burger. *(I resisted every sugary option on the menu in my quest to shed weight.)* It was all scrumptiously delicious.

Piccadilly, which was heaving as we went into the Wolseley, was quiet when we came out. We sauntered to the station, enjoying the evening air as it cooled, the dark coming in too early – a sure sign that summer is on the wane.

A lovely day. My wonderful family. My beautiful children. Tillie, my shining star.

Monday 19th August
Clutching a wodge of my money, Tillie and Lucas went to Decathlon – Lucas to kit himself out with trainers, socks, badminton racket and shuttlecocks ready for school in September, and Tillie with trainers.

They know I expect a contribution for all clothes purchases

but, in a moment of generosity, I said I'd treat them. Tillie argued against this. I could see Lucas behind her with an anxious ticker tape crossing his forehead: 'Shut up! If you pay, I'll have to pay too.'

When Tillie realised the decision wasn't up for negotiation, she said, 'You're such a kind person.'

And Lucas added, quite sincerely, 'Mum *is* kind.'

I nearly fainted with shock.

Tuesday 20th August

I'm putting aside as much of my time as possible to be with Tillie. Today involved us in a university-related expedition to Covent Garden. She signed up for an inexpensive mobile phone contract, bought an academic year diary and called in at the Apple store to find out about the cost of new laptops. *(Breathtakingly expensive and, she decided, not for her.)*

We bought salads and picnicked in the garden behind St Paul's – the actors' church. A young man strode up the church steps wearing knee-length shorts, an open-neck shirt and the highest pair of platform stiletto shoes I've ever seen. Tillie's bet was that he was the vicar.

Wednesday 21st August

Tillie spent the day with her friends. Lucas played on different screens all day, avoiding eye contact with me, and neither of us mentioned tomorrow.

Thursday 22nd August

Lucas drifted from his bed to the loo and back again all night. I spent it listening to him and worrying about his GCSE results.

It was pandemonium in the school hall. The year 11 boys were waiting for the results of the ten subjects they'd sat in the summer. The year 10 boys, with their one full maths GCSE and half RE, were gathered at the side of the hall. On the dot of ten o'clock, the head of exams called for quiet in the kind of commanding voice that made me feel like I was a sixteen-year-old who needed controlling.

He explained how the results would be handed out, how the school didn't encourage re-marking and concluded portentously, 'I hope you've all got what you wanted. You have certainly got what you deserved.' I almost laughed because by this stage I was teetering on the edge of extreme nervousness/hysteria and would have found anything funny.

Lucas went off to his classroom and didn't reappear. Other boys were emerging with their pieces of paper. Finally, Lucas came out, beaming.

'I got two 9s,' he said, waving his paper in the air.

I was genuinely gob-smacked *and* utterly thrilled.

'Lucas, that's fantastic!'

I could hardly believe it. Two 9s! Of course, it's what I wanted him to get, I just didn't think he'd do it.

I hugged him, rubbed his back, stroked his arm and kissed his cheek, all the time telling him how brilliant he was.

'I must be clever,' he concluded, amazed.

'Of course you're clever!'

Back at the car, he phoned Tillie, George, Edith and Great Aunt Vi to tell them the good news, then spent the whole day being pleased with himself.

This evening we went to Pizza Express, where he managed to eat three courses including a 'to die for' chocolate bombe.

I hope he remembers just how good it feels to be successful, and that this will motivate him to try hard with his full set of GCSEs next summer.

Oh, but I am totally elated that he pulled it off. I couldn't be more pleased for him. George too.

And Seb, Frankie's youngest son, achieved straight 9s in his GCSEs. Joy in their household, too.

Friday 23rd August
Several cards arrived for Lucas, including ones from Edith and Great Aunt Vi, both of whom had sent money. *(Still no mention of a house move from Great Aunt Vi.)*

Tillie spent the day agonising over which clothes she should pack for her week's holiday in Derbyshire with Amy and family. She must have tried on every possible combination before deciding, six hours later, which seven outfits to take. *(Perhaps I could have selected a capsule wardrobe for her.)*

As they're setting off at the crack of dawn, Tillie spent the night at Amy's house. I drove her there and hugged her goodbye before we rang the doorbell and the leaving became public. Amy's dad answered, his whippet Saxon standing by his side.

This makes him sound like the head of a working class family from the kind of Yorkshire town I grew up in. Actually, the family's posh. They live in a detached Georgian house, own a painting by Lucian Freud and a small sculpture by Elisabeth Frink. You can't get much better than that round here.

Saturday 24th August
I trotted off to Fringe Matters on the high street. There's something about hairdressers' mirrors that's particularly cruel. I looked like an old hag: roots showing, hair long grown out of its original style to the point of raggedness, split ends waving free. The mirrors at home never show me like this. They know if they did, I'd throw them out.

The hairdresser followed the usual highlighting routine: put in dozens of foils, left me to roast under a heater, took them out, washed my hair and directed me back to the chair for the cut and blow-dry.

Under the hum of other dryers, I heard myself say, 'I'm going for a change.' *(It's that woman back again – the one who decided I should see Great Aunt Vi. She's developing a life of her own.)*

'Really?' asked the hairdresser, shocked.

I've been coming to this salon since the dinosaurs died, and always have the same style: straight, long hair reaching to mid-way down my back, trimmed by a couple of inches.

'Yes. A bob. Cut just below my jaw-line and with a few subtle layers, to soften the look.'

She considered my instructions, running her fingers through my hair.

'Yes. I think that'll suit you.'

The results are fabulous. I feel fantastic. Younger. Stylish. Good looking. And, most important of all, NOT the drab woman who walked into the salon two hours earlier.

When I arrived home, Lucas asked where I'd been.

'The hairdressers. What do you think?'

I pirouetted so that he could appreciate the full effect.

He looked, chewed the inside of his cheek and shrugged his shoulders. 'Can't tell the difference.'

'Oh, Lucas!' I said, exasperated and irritated. 'It's completely different. And even if you can't see it, just pander to me for once.'

A few minutes later, George came in from the garage where he'd been tinkering with the lawn-mower in lieu of actually cutting the grass. He remarked straight away on how good I looked. *(Lucas had definitely nipped out to warn him.)*

*

Text from Tillie: *Wet. Holiday house dry. Happy.*

Is this what the rest of my life with Tillie is going to be like? Terse messages sent from afar?

Sunday 25th August

Perhaps as a way of saying sorry for yesterday's remark, Lucas brought me a tray of tea in bed. Or rather, a tea pot and a mug. When I asked about the milk, he pointed out that it was in the tea pot with the tea. It tasted fine and I didn't say anything because he meant well. But I was astonished that, even though we drink tea at every meal, he's never noticed that the tea and milk are served separately. *(Or perhaps he has and thinks it's arcane.)*

*

Tillie's text: *Amy's mum is dream cook. Had crab followed by grouse for supper.*

Well, thank you very much, Tillie. For years I've slaved over a hot stove with hardly ever a 'that was delicious' remark. And then she finds a mum who's better. *(Not that I'd ever cook crab. Not never, ever in a million years. And probably not grouse either.)*

Bank Holiday Monday 26th August
The sun shone! A bank holiday and the sun shone. How rare is that?!

*

Text: *Rain stopped. Hill appeared. Walked. Love Saxon. Please, please, please can we have a dog?*

*

Our sex life has gone to pot. Made love for the first time since Switzerland. If we keep up this rate, we only need to do it four more times and it'll be Christmas.

Tuesday 27th August
A brilliant day! Lucas went to Fergus's house. He and his three sisters had each invited a friend while their parents were at work.

Late afternoon, I drove over to pick Lucas up. Belle, Fergus's twin sister, opened the front door, grabbed me by the arm and propelled me at speed through the house.

Belle is fifteen, frighteningly well organised and has the kind of leadership skills which, one day, will result in her running the country.

'Excellent timing on your part,' she remarked as she ushered me into the sitting room. The furniture and carpets had been pushed away from the windows. 'You can take over my position. There's a full bucket of water by the patio door. Try not to let too much into the room, but in case of any accidents I've put towels on the floor. You've got to defend the house against the boys outside as well as the little ones: Harriet and her friend Cam have jumped ship. I'll be in the kitchen guarding the back door with Lucy. Eve is upstairs with Danshu firing from the bedrooms.'

She thrust a huge plastic gun in my hand – eighteen inches long and six inches wide.

'This is the barrel. When it's empty, you unscrew it and refill it from the bucket. It's currently full and you're ready to go.' She moved to leave the room. 'Just remember: don't let the boys or the little ones in the house. We're depending on you.'

With that she slammed the door behind her. I heard her run down the corridor to the kitchen, where mayhem was breaking out with screams and shouts.

As I couldn't think what else to do other than what I'd been told, I positioned myself to one side of the patio door, searching the long grass of the overgrown garden for any sight of the enemy. A yell came down from upstairs as thirteen-year-old Eve spotted one from her vantage point.

'Downstairs gunner, boy at nine o'clock. Give him what you've got.'

I couldn't see anyone and it took a second or two to work out where nine o'clock was in relation to me and the garden. I fired the gun in that direction and heard a satisfying gasp as Fergus was hit. He retreated, but not before firing a blast of water at me which caught my legs. I nipped back behind the patio door in case he fired again.

It was quiet for a few moments, and then six-year-old Harriet sidled up to the house with her sweet-faced friend beside her.

'Who are *you*?' she asked, looking up at me and smiling, one arm behind her back.

'I'm Jill, Lucas's mum.'

And with that she swung her gun forward and blasted me full in the face. Her friend followed suit.

As fast as I could, I raised my gun and fired at their backs as they raced into the long grass.

Belle and Lucy were doing a great job of keeping the boys from the back door. In the lull, I reloaded my gun. As I did so, I noticed the grass starting to move. A fresh shot of water caught me in the back as Lucas lifted his head. Then he realised it was me.

'What the fuck are *you* doing here?'

'Language,' I said. 'Is that how you talk when you think I'm not around?'

'Jesus wept.'

'I came to pick you up, but Belle hauled me in to defend the house. So here I am.'

I smiled, took aim and caught him full in the chest. He grinned and let rip with his super-gun. He caught my left hip. Water ran down my trousers and into my shoes.

'Serves you right, Mum!'

He blasted more water my way, then ran off.

The fight continued for some time as the boys and little ones regrouped, tried various tactics with varying degrees of success, and we kept the house from being invaded.

All our buckets of water ran out at about the same time, which was probably just as well as we were all soaked. Belle called a truce and told everyone to meet in the kitchen.

We sat round the table and I'm glad to say that no one batted an eyelid at me being there. I was accepted as a fellow wet combatant.

Belle gave Harriet and Cam fresh towels to wrap around themselves. Then she produced drinks and biscuits before racing round the house, gathering all the soaked towels from the doors and windows. She put them through the washing machine's spin cycle and ordered Lucas and Fergus to hang them on the line. Meanwhile, Eve and Danshu were despatched to return all the rooms to their original order.

After a warming cup of tea, I poked my head round the sitting room door. You could not tell what had been going on just fifteen minutes earlier. The parents will live in blissful ignorance.

Lucas and I chattered all the way back home about who did what, which were the best sight lines and who got the wettest. We were high as kites.

*

Tillie: *Knew you'd say no. You're a hard, cruel woman. What's wrong with dogs?*

Wednesday 28th August
Dora came for lunch and was astonished by how much Lucas has grown – very satisfying for Lucas, who is quietly proud of his height.

He went off to play on the PlayStation while Dora and I launched into a catch-up conversation covering family news, health, the state of the Tory and Labour parties, the size of handbags, the multiple uses of bicarbonate of soda and local road works.

I gave her a birthday present and card, which she protested over.

'Dora, you mean the world to me.'

This was the first time I'd been able to say anything about my feelings for her, and I had to stop at that because I was welling up. *(And I'd thought I was beyond tears.)*

*

Tillie: *Dog walking morning and evening. Langoostines (?) for supper. Cool.*

Thursday 29th August
Clad in my other smart dress and the match-with-everything jacket, I met Fay for lunch at the Royal Academy. It's outside our usual stomping ground, but she was seeing a client nearby and it suited her to meet there.

We kissed cheeks and then she held me at arm's length.

'Wow! You look amazing. New hairstyle, new clothes and, I think, a new woman!'

That's Fay to a T: generous in all her comments.

As work is picking up at Ellis Hatcher, she asked if I was interested in taking on any jobs. I thanked her, but said no.

It was such a beautiful day that afterwards, I decided to walk back to Waterloo, cutting through St James's. On Pall Mall I noticed the fascia for Osbert & Small, purveyors of fine antiques. The name rang a bell. Now how would I know an antiques shop on Pall Mall? I slowed down to peer in the window.

Then I remembered Bonhams and the man who'd sat beside me. The one who had ostensibly been bidding in my interest and had driven up the price of Great Aunt Vi's Tiffany vase. The one who had looked kindly at me and who had, very sweetly, offered lunch while I fought back tears. The one who had handed me his business card and said: call in if you're ever passing. Jeremy Osbert. That was him.

I walked on, recalling that day. At the National Gallery, I stopped and leant my back against the sun-warmed wall of the Sainsbury Wing, taking in Trafalgar Square and the tourists. I had a free afternoon. I didn't have to go home straight away. I could take up the offer. Plus, it was a lovely August day in London, and I was happy, buoyed from seeing Fay.

I walked back down Pall Mall and stopped at Osbert & Small's window. Beyond the displays in the far left corner, Jeremy Osbert was sitting at a fine antique desk. His head was bowed as he concentrated on the papers before him, a fat-barrelled fountain pen held in his right hand. I paused for a moment, quashing a last-minute doubt, then pushed the plate glass door open. Jeremy lifted his head and put down the pen.

'Good afternoon,' he said, friendly but formal with his impeccable, plum-in-the-mouth-public-school accent.

'Good afternoon, Jeremy.'

His focus sharpened. For a brief moment I saw him struggle with his memory. Then his face lit up.

'Ah! It's Ethel the bohemian kitchen cleaner. Welcome.'

He walked round the desk and came towards me with open arms and genuine warmth. The subtle scent of his after-shave drifted towards me. This time I recognised it. Chanel. Bleu de Chanel. The one thing that George wore but only rarely. We shook hands and he, like Fay, stepped back and took a good, hard look.

'Very smart. Very chic. A fresh identity. And definitely *not* a kitchen cleaning day. So what's it to be? Coffee, as I promised you? Or tea because it's the afternoon? Or would you prefer corporation pop?'

I laughed.

'I've not heard that expression in years,' I told him. 'And you're neither a northern man nor related to one.'

He raised an eyebrow. 'Don't assume too much. But what's it to be?'

'Decaffeinated coffee, if that's possible, please.'

'It's possible. Two ticks. Look round the gallery while I dish up the drinks.'

It was an elegant and sophisticated place selling a mixture of oil paintings – both figurative and pastoral – large items of furniture including a gilt-edged chest of drawers, and a variety of period accessories: wine glasses, decanters, trays and ancient mirrors. Not a single item was priced.

'What do you think?' Jeremy emerged from the dark recesses at the rear of the gallery carrying a fine silver salver on which were crowded two coffee cups, matching sugar bowl and milk jug. He put the salver on his desk and drew up a chair for me.

'You have fine taste. I could live happily with almost everything you're selling.'

'Thank you,' he replied smiling.

He was in his early forties and slim with an attractive squeaky-clean look, as if he'd just emerged from shaving. He was also dressed immaculately in a suit that had to be hand-made. Elegant yet informal. His eyes were a cerulean blue, the irises etched with a fine black line that made his gaze compelling. There were tiny crease lines either side of his eyes, a sure sign of someone who smiled and laughed a lot. I liked him instantly.

He handed me my coffee.

'So, Ethel, what brings you my way?'

I took my business card from my handbag and passed it to him across the desk.

'Jill. Jill Baxter. I was travelling incognito that day at Bonhams.'

He raised his eyebrows as if asking a question, but I wasn't going to say. Not now.

'I'm a freelance graphic designer,' I continued. 'Mostly working on websites. I met a fellow designer for lunch at the RA. Someone I used to work with. To be accurate, I *was* a freelance graphic designer, but I'm trying to give it up.'

'Now, why would that be?' He leant back in his chair, smiling encouragingly and watching me carefully.

'The short version? I was fed up, tired, lonely, unstimulated and wanted a change. I've taken a year off – to find out what it's like not working while also leaving the option open to take on jobs I can't resist.'

He nodded slowly, listening to what I was saying.

'And travel? People who take a year off usually go and see the world. How about you?'

I laughed.

'I'm a full-time mum of two teenagers, and wife to a workaholic husband. I run the house and our lives. We take a family holiday in the summer when revision and exams are complete.'

He crossed his legs and looked at his right foot as he rotated it slowly.

'So,' he said, switching his attention back to me and saying light-heartedly, 'in summary, your year off means you've not got a job, you've not got an income, you're not travelling with friends to Cambodia, Laos or Vietnam, and you're still a slave to the family.'

I took a sip of coffee and, momentarily, plunged into misery. Maybe that's all it was. Maybe I was kidding myself. Maybe it was just a fantasy. Was I peering at what might be possible, and not actually having it?

But then I rallied, for the sun was high in the sky and I was equal to the day. 'It's the best I'm going to get at this stage of my life. The highlight is that I'm now doing a course in art history at the V&A. Which I could never have done when I was earning an income.'

'I know the V&A's courses. Which one are you studying?'

He'd taken my business card, seen my web address and was keying it into his laptop.

'Well, last academic year it was Late Medieval to Early Renaissance. And this September, I'll be starting on Late Renaissance to Baroque.'

'The Baroque through to the Rococo is the main period for this gallery, though I sometimes catch the tail-end of the Renaissance.' He leaned towards me, smiling. 'We'll be able to have learned conversations, if you come back for another coffee.'

'I'd like that, though you'll be learned and I'll be learning.'

'One can always learn from another. Sometimes it's the innocent eye that sees the most.'

He turned to the laptop and looked through my website.

'It's impressive,' he commented. 'Some big company names: BP, Unilever, GlaxoSmithKline. And nice work too. You've got a sharp eye and a good hand.'

He turned back to me.

'I'm wondering if you could do something for me?' he asked casually.

'What?'

'Would you cast your designer's eye over *my* website and let me know what you think?'

My heart started to sink. As soon as I say I've worked on web designs, people ask me to comment on their site. I should say I'm a mortician's assistant. That would shut them up.

'I'll pay, of course. Let's say £250. For half a day's work. I'm sure you're worth that.'

I nearly bit his hand off. In the heady days before the recession, I charged £500 for a full day. Now I can't get even half of that. The vertiginous fall in fees was another reason why I'd become fed up with my profession. Call me fickle, especially given I'd just turned Fay down *(though her fees wouldn't have been as high)*, but my heart started to rise.

'Alright. I'll do it.'

'I want everything: the good, the bad and the ugly. And don't just write a report. Come and tell me what you think. Over coffee. And bring your invoice.'

So that was it. We resorted to small talk, finished our coffees, shook hands and I came home. Flushed with success.

I've taken a brief look at Osbert & Small's website. They definitely need help.

*

Tillie: *Don't like potted shrimps. Amy & me walking hours with Saxon.*

Friday 30th August
Went to Total Workout. As I've hardly been this month, I thought it would be excruciatingly difficult. It wasn't. In fact, I seemed to be more supple despite doing less exercise. How does that work? Is everything in my life counter-intuitive?

I nipped down to the changing rooms, went to the loo, stripped off and weighed myself. So, here it is. After two months of self-monitoring and abstinence, I have lost....

HESTER THOMAS

half a kilo.

Does five hundred grams sound more impressive?

No! It's UTTERLY PATHETIC. It's beyond pathetic. It's ABYSMAL. It's HIDEOUS. Weight loss is a completely misery-inducing experience. I mean: what is the point? What *is* the point?

*

Tillie: *Sick of dog poo. Picking it up or watching Amy pick it up. Gone off dogs. Can't wait to see you! xxx*

Saturday 31st August
I was ridiculously excited to see Tillie this evening. She was, briefly, taken aback by my new hairstyle but then was enthusiastic and declared I looked, 'Cool.' *(Well, what more could I want?)*

Oh, it's good to have her home. She was full of all the things they'd done and seen and eaten and how amazing Amy's mum is at cooking everything and anything at the drop of a hat. Still, when I asked her what she'd like for supper, she opted for baked beans on toast.

September

Sunday 1st September
How does September *know* it's September? The early morning was crisply cold and there was a new scent in the air. Not autumn, but a forerunner: a gentle warning that soon the leaves will turn as the trees ready themselves for the long chill of winter.

George spread the substantial contents of the compost heap across the flower beds, then set a bonfire within its brick surround. Tillie invited a few friends for the evening and together they barbequed sausages over the embers, eating them wedged between bread rolls. This was followed by roasted, squidgy marshmallows. Lucas, who'd been given a surprising dispensation to join them (though for the food only) said they were scrummy.

*

I've been calling Sue, without success, for several days. Perhaps she's on holiday.

Monday 2nd September
Tillie was thrilled to come along to Iggies's studio, but I had to bribe Lucas with a promise of lunchtime pizza. Before the words 'cantankerous teenager' could escape my mouth, Arnold had roped him in to help with the lighting. Lucas's mood shifted. He revealed himself to be bright, happy, amenable and fun to be with. *(Arnold's single, no partner, no children and fancy-free. But perfect dad material.)*

Today's portrait was about my role as a mother. I know it's cheesy, obvious, boring and hackneyed but I just couldn't think how to present myself in this role without the children. It's a triple portrait and they're my props. *(Truly. As well as the loves of my life.)*

We'd all dressed in whatever we fancied. Tillie decided on a smart look: wide-legged, pale blue linen trousers topped with a tight-fitting, sleeveless shirt, her face made up beautifully and her hair brushed to a long gloss. Lucas chose jeans and tee-shirt – fifteen-year-old casual, though with the added detail of new Nike trainers.

And me? Well, I'd gone for an unfussy look: mum at home in comfortable jeans and a loose-fitting blouse that managed to hit that perfect note of untailored yet smart.

We stood on the white background paper which ran in a gentle curve to become the wall behind us, disconcerted and self-conscious in an unfamiliar setting. Iggie was taking images in rapid succession even though we weren't posing. *(He wouldn't want the pose.)* I inserted myself between Tillie and Lucas, putting my arms around their waists, anchoring us all. Lucas giggled as if I was tickling him, pulling his upper body away from me. Tillie did what she tends to do in moments of quiet: she put her head on my shoulder. I leaned mine towards her while turning slightly to watch Lucas and his giggling, squirming antics. And though we moved around into different positions and stopped being quite as silly and embarrassed, that shot was the best.

Taking the photograph at this point in time is especially poignant: knowing that Tillie will leave soon and that it's not just me but Lucas too who will be left behind. I was moved to tears by the images. For they capture love. Mine for Tillie and Lucas, Tillie for me and Lucas's for life.

*

Tonight I read the remaining chapters of *Mindfulness*. And then I put it on a high shelf because there's no point kidding myself – I'm never going to do the associated meditations. It's a book for people who are stressed – mostly because they're frantic in a frantic world. Just as I used to be. I'm not saying life is perfect but between this year off and the long and relaxing summer, I'm probably the most OK I've been in a long time.

*

I still haven't got hold of Sue. There's been no answer to calls or emails. Surely she'll be back at school any day now?

Tuesday 3rd September
A half-day of paid work reviewing Osbert & Small's website. It's pretty dire: functional rather than professional. For a start, the corporate identity differs from that on the gallery's fascia. There's nothing about who Osbert or Small are in terms of the people behind the names. *(Is there a Small person?)* And while there are a few items of furniture featured, there's very little information about each and no mention of prices.

What's there are the essentials. But there could be much more. Products, informative descriptions, a news page, a blog, and links to social media. The photography could be better, a different typeface would look more attractive and page layouts could be improved.

I made copious notes, then rewrote them in a logical order. When I talk to Jeremy everything I say will be coherent and provide a framework for what could be a really compelling site.

Next, I called Fay with a proposition. Then I phoned Jeremy. I'm seeing him next Friday – the earliest date we could both manage. Finally, I typed my invoice.

Wednesday 4th September
The start of Lucas's autumn term, year 11 and GCSEs to work for. Not just one and a half, but nine of them.

*

After the midweek shop, I called Sue. Lo and behold, she answered.
'Hello stranger! Where've you been?' I greeted her.
'Oh, hi, Jill.'

She sounded sleepy, though it was after ten o'clock.

'Have I woken you?' I asked, surprised.

'Mmmm. Not really. I've been awake for a while but haven't got up yet. It's the last day before school starts and I'm making the most of it.'

There was a strange rustling sound in the background, as if the duvet had taken on a life of its own and was shuffling round her mattress.

'I've been calling you for days and was starting to wonder if you'd gone on holiday. Or moved.'

'Neither actually, though I did go to Rhodes for a week in July. Didn't I send you a postcard?'

'No. Did you get mine?'

'I think so.'

She sounded incredibly vague for someone who is normally on the button.

'It was from Switzerland. I asked you to let me know of any developments on the Great Aunt Vi house-moving front.'

'Oh, that. Yes, I do remember.'

'You don't sound interested.'

'I'm not.'

There was a sound, like a cough, in the background. Sue lives on her own and has always done so.

'Have you got someone staying with you?' I asked. 'I can call back if now is not convenient.'

'Err, no. And no.'

I was trying to work that one out when a deep male voice whispered, 'Coffee or tea?'

(Bloody hell fire! Sue has a lover!)

'Look, I'll call you back another time,' she said, suddenly focused and alert. 'Now don't go worrying about Great Aunt Vi. She knows how to look after herself. And you're not her mother. Bye!'

(Not her mother? I know I'm not her mother! And besides

which, who was the man? Was he the cause of the rustling duvet? The virgin Sue with a man in her bed? A considerate man at that. And she was still in bed after all those hours. All those hours of what? Making love? Sue? Good grief!)

Thursday 5th September

Last night, as we were eating our evening meal, I told George about Sue and her lover.

'You don't know they're lovers,' he said, putting a slice of bacon topped with baked beans in his mouth.

'But I heard the duvet rustling and moving. It had to be him.'

'It could have been her. I do like a fry-up. There's something deeply comforting about baked beans with egg and bacon.'

Tillie and Lucas were eating their food with great care and in silence, not making any distracting noises that might interrupt our flow.

'What do *you* think?' I asked them.

Startled, they looked at one another and then at me.

'About what?'

'Oh for goodness sake! About what you've been listening to. Sue and her lover. Or Sue, her noisy duvet and the nice man offering her an option on tea or coffee.'

'Sounds cool,' said Lucas.

'I've no idea,' replied Tillie. 'All adults seem weird to me. Even though I am one, I still see them as an alien species.'

*

I spent much of today mulling over Sue and The Man. When I wasn't pondering on them, I was busy packing and chivvying Tillie to do the same. She and I are off to Basel tomorrow for our long weekend – the final holiday of this lovely summer.

George and Lucas are having a boys' weekend and are hatching plans around films and food.

*

The next photograph at Iggie's studio is me as a wife. I'm racking my brains to come up with an idea for it. I mean how do you portray a wife? Or rather, me as a wife? I can't take George as he's unwilling to be part of the shoot. *(I don't want him there, either. I'm territorial: this is my project with Iggie and Arnold. Though, oddly, I didn't mind Tillie and Lucas being involved.)*

I have had various thoughts but either they're clichéd *(photograph of my worn-out ageing hands, with engagement and wedding rings)* or liable to lead to divorce *(me lying in bed watching the ceiling while a George look-alike lies on his side facing away from me, fast asleep).*

I've sent emails to Iggie and Arnold for help. Arnold replied, 'Ask Iggie'. And Iggie wrote, 'You're the wife. You come up with the idea!!!'

Great.

Friday 6th September
Up with the lark for a flight to Basel. We have a tiny but well-designed apartment, complete with small but perfectly formed kitchen, bathroom and sitting-cum-bedroom.

As it was a glorious day, we walked to the old part of Basel, bought ourselves a picnic lunch and ate it within the cool shadows of the old town hall. And then we explored.

I hadn't realised central Basel had such a rich history. Many houses date back to medieval times and are stunningly preserved.

Tillie was spooked by the lack of people. She's used to the hustle and bustle of London. Basel has a population of around 200,000 – about 20 per cent less than that of our borough but spread over about four times the area.

This evening, when I called home, Lucas was just back from the local takeaway with a pizza for his tea. It hadn't crossed his mind to buy one for George, who was still at work.

When I pointed this out he said cheerfully, 'He can eat toast.'

There was the whiff of Marie Antoinette in his solution.

Saturday 7th September

Tillie suggested we take the train to the old university town of Freiburg in Germany. We travelled through very beautiful countryside: vineyards to the east with the mountains of the Black Forest rising behind them in serried ranks. To the west was the plain through which the Rhine flows and, far beyond that, the Vosges mountains of Alsace-Lorraine.

A vast market dominated Freiburg's cathedral square. Stalls were piled high with summer produce: tomatoes, lettuces, beans, potatoes, radishes, kohlrabi, strawberries, raspberries, apples and plums. There was bread, cheese, salami, bottles of kir, honey and baskets of beautiful flowers. We bought a selection of inexpensive bread, cheese, fruit and vegetables to eat over the next couple of days in hideously expensive Switzerland, then strolled through the streets window-shopping and people-watching before heading back to Basel.

We called home after our delicious evening meal of German market foods. George and Lucas had been to see a film, eaten lunch at Nando's, then walked home. I haven't heard the pair of them sounding as happy in a long time.

Sunday 8th September

We spent all day in the Kunstmuseum, starting with the kind of medieval paintings seen on the V&A course. They were interesting, but the focus on religion was overwhelming.

Fortunately, in the adjacent room, there was an extensive collection of nineteenth and twentieth-century works by Swiss artists, including a particularly lovely painting of a young country boy lying flat out across some hay, deeply asleep and oblivious to the world.

Over the course of the day, with numerous breaks for food and drink, we managed to see almost every painting. Tillie is an excellent companion. She has a keen eye, is interested in the different methods of painting and articulate in her observations.

I called home only to find I was interrupting film night. George had made a chicken curry, which he and Lucas were eating while watching *Django* on TV.

Inspired by some of today's paintings, I emailed Iggie with an idea for how to portray me as a wife. I think it will work. Anyway, they've got a few days to source the props.

Monday 9th September
Drawn like a magnet to all things connected with design and safe in the knowledge that Tillie likes the subject too, I suggested we visit the Vitra Design Museum, just over the border in Germany.

Our first impression was disappointing, for the bus delivered us at Vitra's factory campus – where they make furniture and accessories for home, office and retail environments. Our hearts sank.

We were told, by a very nice receptionist, that a tour for English-speaking people left in an hour's time at midday. Our hearts sank further. We loathe tours. But, as there wasn't anything else to do, we agreed – reluctantly and miserably – to go on it. The receptionist directed us to the design centre to while away the time.

And then our hearts started racing. For the design centre, otherwise known as the VitraHaus, was breathtaking. Created by architects Herzog & de Meuron, it consists of twelve long gabled houses stacked at intersecting angles to form a five-storey structure. Completely inventive and totally whacky.

Inside, it's a showcase for Vitra's products. We were free to try out every piece of furniture placed within room-sets – from funky design office to quietly tasteful contemporary home. We spent sixty blissful and exhilarating minutes testing every chair, table and sofa, and imagining ourselves living the kind of life which went with each room. The accessories – lights, shelves, tableware, trays, pens, computers – were all in keeping with their particular set and everything, absolutely everything, was inspiring, beautiful and covetable.

We had to tear ourselves away to go on the two-hour factory campus tour. I thought this was going to be a case of gawping at assembly lines of workers and breathing in dusty wood shavings in dirty environments. How wrong could I be?

The campus was full of extraordinary buildings, each created by an architectural icon. Zaha Hadid designed the fire station. Frank Gehry constructed his first European buildings here in 1989 with the Vitra Design Museum, the Museum Gate and one of the factories. Tadao Ando built the conference pavilion. Other buildings were created by Nicholas Grimshaw, Álvaro Siza and SANAA. There was even a geodesic dome paying homage to Richard Buckminster Fuller. So much outstanding architecture to see in such a short time!

We ran to catch the bus back to Basel, picked up our suitcases, headed to the airport and were home by seven thirty.

*

Lucas was eating his dinner: two pieces of toast. George was still at work, pursuing yet another crisis in dirty money. The kitchen sink was full and the floor was covered in crumbs. The whole house had the faint air of neglect.

Tuesday 10th September
Exhausted! Unpacked, washed *(my)* clothes, dealt with the backlog of emails and post, tidied up – I could have spent all day doing that alone – and, finally, made an evening meal.

Wednesday 11th September
It's curious what being away reveals. George realised, within hours of me leaving for Basel, that while he can just about manage to keep up with the demands of a job in a London legal firm, he cannot manage to do anything extra in the

house. Hence Lucas was eating a takeaway on Friday night and George's evening meal consisted of Lucas's suggestion – toast. They did have a good weekend together, but everything else fell by the wayside.

Well, it's good to know that I'm needed and to know that George knows I'm needed.

Thursday 12th September
The Wife Photograph. I do hope George isn't offended by it. It won't lead to divorce, but he may not be pleased. On the other hand, it is accurate.

I sat at a dinner table laid with the cutlery and dinner service we use every night at home. There were two place settings: one for me facing the camera and, opposite, the other for George. I had a plate full of food: roast chicken, roast potatoes, carrots, broad beans, bread sauce and gravy. There was nothing for George. Just his place setting and his empty chair. Behind me, there's a vacuum cleaner, a duster, a variety of cleaning materials – Domestos, Cif, Pledge, and an ironing board with a neat pile of ironed clothes on top of it. I'm not eating yet. I've just taken a discreet look at my watch. And that's it.

Because that's my life: the woman who keeps the house clean and tidy, does the ironing and the shopping, prepares the evening meal and then hasn't the husband to eat it with because he's still at the office working. Of course, the children are usually there to share the meal. But for this image we left the children out as it's focusing on my role as a *wife*.

I've gone past anger and frustration on the subject of George's absences, as has George. *(It's no fun for him either.)* I look weary and resigned in the photograph, but there's stoicism and dignity too.

What I particularly like about this image is that it's witty. The viewer, positioned beyond George's chair, stands in for him. Each time someone looks at this image they'll be a shoo-in for George – regardless of their gender and whether they know it or not.

*

I had a brief phone conversation with Frankie. She's busy getting Archie ready for university. He starts next Monday and, even though he'll be living at home, he's anxious and worried.

Friday 13th September

Wearing a new skirt and top, my matches-everything jacket along with my tan knee-high boots, I headed off to Osbert & Small to report back to Jeremy on the website.

A young woman, dressed simply but elegantly, was managing the gallery. She greeted me like an old friend. Jeremy emerged from a room at the back and *he* greeted me like a member of his family: a hug then a kiss planted on each cheek. I've not felt as welcome anywhere in a long time.

'Come into the back office, where we can talk without interruption,' he said, leading the way.

A man of about the same age as me was sitting at a round table. He pushed back his chair and stepped forward. He was tall, his grey hair well-cut and brushed back from his forehead. His clothes were carefully chosen for dress-down Friday: loafers, blue chinos, a purple gingham shirt open at the neck and a herringbone tweed jacket. A blue handkerchief with green polka dots poked nattily out of the breast pocket. As he stretched a hand towards me, his shirt-cuff shot out from the jacket revealing silver cufflinks in the shape of World War II spitfires complete with distinctive yellow, blue, white and red enamel circles on their wings. His hands were manicured, the skin brown and soft, his fingers long, the nails trimmed.

'Hugo,' he announced, in a broad Yorkshire accent. 'Hugo Small. Jeremy's partner.'

'And husband,' added Jeremy.

It wasn't what I was expecting: neither the accent nor the

relationship.

'Lovely to meet you,' I said, hoping my good manners covered my surprise. I moved to sit in the chair he was holding for me.

'I detect a fellow Yorkshire patriot,' said Hugo. 'Though there's not much left of your accent. Not compared to mine. But there's summat there.'

'Ay,' I said, giving him the full works. 'Tek us t'Ilkley and as'll talk like t'best of 'em.'

He laughed, enjoying the joke. Now I knew where Jeremy had picked up the reference to 'corporation pop'.

'We thought we should both hear what you have to say about the website, given its importance to the business,' Jeremy said, sitting next to me.

'Just t'explain. I'm more of a sleeping partner, if you'll forgiven the pun,' said Hugo, sitting on my other side. 'My main job is running an 'edge fund in Mayfair. Funny that, in't it? An auld Bradford boy running an 'edge fund.'

'Not quite so unusual if you're an old Bradford *Grammar School* boy,' I replied, sensing there was far more to him. He'd never have survived in 1980s Bradford with a name like Hugo unless he had a less than usual background.

Jeremy bit his lips, crushing a smile. But he couldn't stop the corners of his eyes from wrinkling.

'Ay. Mebbe,' said Hugo, refusing to give up his past for free. 'Anyway, there it is. This place is me second business and it's important. I don't want to see 'owt neglected.'

I wasn't fooled. I grew up with men and women like him. People who thought they could disarm anyone by using the local brogue as cover for their intelligence. People who were as sharp as knives and who watched you like a hawk. Apart from which you didn't get to be as apparently wealthy as Jeremy or Hugo by being an idiot. Hedge fund managers *(and when did you hear of an unsuccessful one?)* were astute, intelligent, quick-witted. I was being tested.

I pulled out my laptop and took control of the meeting. I brought up their website and talked through all the positive things about it. And then I paused and asked what they thought it should do to further Osbert & Small's business?

That got them thinking, and we had a good discussion, ferreting out ways in which it could enhance their trade – the very ways in which it was currently failing them. Having got them to set the scene, it was easy for me to describe the site's weaknesses. And, after that, I talked through everything that could be done to make the website work far better for the business – encouraging buyers to the site, to the gallery, to the products and to Jeremy.

'What d'you think, Jeremy?' asked Hugo.

'I think we need a new website.'

Hugo turned to me. 'Ay, lass. You've 'it nail on t'head.'

'Thank you.'

I was pleased with myself. It was some time since I'd run a client meeting and my sparkle was still there. But I had to be careful that self-satisfaction didn't make me overstep the mark.

'Do you think you could sort it out for us?' Jeremy asked. 'Could you manage the redesign?'

'No,' I replied. This was what I'd rehearsed at home. I'd considered the possibility of Jeremy asking me to create a new site and my heart had sunk. I'd be back doing the kind of work I no longer wanted. 'It's too big a job for me. You need a team of people with different skills – structural IT *and* design – to work on this.'

It was an honest answer, and it left me independent. Penniless, but independent.

'Oh dear.'

Jeremy was downcast. As if he thought he'd solved a problem only to find it was still in his hands.

'But I know a design consultancy that can manage it for you.'

I keyed in Ellis Hatcher's website.

'They're very good, have lots of experience and charge sensible fees. I've worked with them for many years and can honestly say that their creative work is outstanding.'

I slid Fay's business card between the two of them. Hugo picked it up.

'I've asked if they'd be interested in working with you, though, for reasons of privacy, I avoided your company name. They'll be happy to hear from you. Just mention me and they'll understand the connection.'

'Well, that sounds like a grand move,' Hugo said, pushing back his chair. 'We'll think it over.'

I put the laptop in my bag and drew out the envelope with my invoice, passing it to Jeremy.

Hugo had already picked up his leather portfolio and was making his way out of the door to his hedge fund. Jeremy turned to me.

'Well, that was marvellous. Disappointing, though.'

His juxtaposition of responses threw me.

'I thought you'd work with us. Solve our problems. Wave your design wand and put everything right. Just like that.'

I smiled.

'Ellis Hatcher will do all that. You'll be in safe hands.'

Still, he didn't look happy.

'Look, call in some other time, won't you?'

So, there we are. Job done.

To tell the truth, I was both pleased and dissatisfied. Pleased because the meeting had gone to plan. Dissatisfied because well, I like Jeremy. And I've managed to write him out of my life.

Saturday 14th September

An invitation, printed in gold italics on luxuriously thick white card, arrived in the post. George and I are invited to Great Aunt Vi's house-warming party on October 12th.

There's no indication of where the party is being held, other than Leicester.

'I take it we're not free,' said George, displaying his usual party spirit.

Yes, we are! I don't care what George does or doesn't want to do, wild horses wouldn't keep me away from this particular event. Apart from which Tillie leaves a couple of weeks earlier. We'll be in need of some distraction. Or rather, I will.

(Only two more weeks and my lovely Tillie will be gone. My heart is breaking.)

*

This afternoon, mainly in an attempt to distract myself from sad thoughts of Tillie's departure, I went to Greenwich Market to see Johanna and her vintage-ware stall – Everything but the Kitchen Sink. She recognised me straight away, came round and embraced me.

'Sehr schön,' she said of my new look. 'Very sophisticated and considered.'

Very was pronounced *fery*. I smiled.

'Not like me!' She pointed to her apron, protecting her clothes.

'You look lovely,' I said, for below the apron she was wearing a bright red, three-quarter sleeve tee-shirt, a denim skirt, bright red tights and blue court shoes to match the skirt. She'd tied her hair up in a loose bun. Escaping wisps hung attractively. 'But where's the Wedgwood?'

'It's in storage for Berlin.'

Bearlin.

'I'll take it next spring to a special market near my old home. It will be loved.'

Shoppers were gathering round the stall.

'Come round the back and help. When we're not selling, we can talk.'

Vee. Ken. I'm a sucker for accents.

I stayed for an hour and a half and I don't know where the time went. We both sold a variety of items. Mine included a Minton cup and saucer, a Worcester fruit bowl and three T.G. Green Cornishware blue and white striped storage jars which I'd dearly have liked for myself. *(Not that I need anything.)*

And when we weren't selling, we talked about what was on her stall, what we liked and disliked, and the roles certain brands or items had played in our lives.

As I was about to leave, Johanna wrapped a Spode Italian design mug in pale pink tissue paper.

'It's for you,' she said, putting it in my hands. 'For helping. And for fun. Come back.'

Kom beck.

Oh, Johanna, I will.

Sunday 15th September

I phoned Great Aunt Vi.

'Hello! It's Jill. How are you?'

'Oh, hello, dear. I'm very well, thank you.'

She sounded relaxed and happy.

'We received the invitation to your party and yes, George and I would love to come.'

'Excellent. I shall add you to the list. Sue's coming and she's bringing her young man.'

(Young man??!)

'Oh, who's that?' I asked, mock-innocently.

'Let me see. I'm just looking down my list. Ah, yes. This is him. Harry.'

(Harry! The same name and, no doubt, the same person who lives in her apartment block. The one she dismissively described as 'middle-aged, fat and going bald.' Ah ha!)

'He sounds very nice,' she continued.

'You've talked to him?'

'Briefly. He answered her phone once. I thought I might

have the wrong number, but he very nicely explained that it was Sue's flat and he was answering while she made a meal.'

(Got his feet under the table, then.)

'I'm pleased you can come,' she continued. 'The arrangements are this: first, absolutely no presents. Second, arrive after midday. Third, leave by midnight. Fourth, when you arrive in Leicester, call me on this number and I'll give you the address.'

'You could give it now.'

'No. I shall give it on the day. I'm making no exceptions. If I tell one of you, you'll tell the others. This is my life and my new home. I shall share it with you on the 12th of October and not a moment before.'

'Fair enough.'

I hadn't got the energy to argue. Apart from which, I was dying to tell George the news about Sue and Harry. Nevertheless, I wasn't going to leave without a little digging.

'When are you moving?'

'I've moved. I'm talking to you from my new residence. I took my old telephone number with me.'

'Good grief! That was fast. And I did say we'd help you.'

'I know, but I'm quite capable of managing on my own.'

'What can you see from your front window?'

'Jill, I'm too long in the tooth for you to catch me out with your silly trick questions. The view, as you will discover, is delightful.'

'And what are the other residents like?'

She paused and I felt the atmosphere change from sunny to wintry. I wondered whether the phone would be slammed down or, alternatively, if her hand would corkscrew its way along the line and out through the phone to grip me by the throat.

'They too are delightful,' she replied. 'Truly delightful.'

I was shocked.

'You *have* moved to a home!'

'Of course I have. It's *my* home.'

'I meant a *care* home.'

'I know exactly what you meant. You will find out in due course. Until then you will just have to wait. Goodbye.'

I sat for a moment, considering. Had I heard sounds of other people in the background? Any residents muttering? Any staff ushering an elderly person and their zimmer frame along? Was there the irritating squeak of a wheelchair as it made its way over a cushioned vinyl floor?

There was nothing. Not another voice sotto voce, not a creak, a grind, the sound of a plate being put on a table or cutlery being picked up. Not even an external sound of a car passing or a motorbike racing along. Nothing. Nil. Zip. Only Great Aunt Vi.

Where the hell *is* she?

Monday 16th September
George is complaining about our sex life again. He even complained after we made love. Not about the quality but the quantity.

I should add "Make love" to my list of things to do each day. *(Well, not every day.)* But even then it would end up at the bottom, not be done and have to be added to the following day's list. My morning intentions are good but by the evening they've evaporated, sleep being far more attractive. And important. I do my best, but it's just not good enough.

Tuesday 17th September
Tillie was excited about the two of us going to Morrisons to buy the household items she'll need at university and considering how everything will look in her new room.

Suddenly, I recalled how George and I went shopping for her baby clothes when I was eight months pregnant. My idea was that we'd spend a happy half-day strolling round our local shopping centre, make careful decisions about types of clothing including sizes and colours, discuss the pros and cons of flannelette crib sheets versus polyester, and ponder the environmental impact of different types of nappies before concluding which was best for our baby.

George's idea was to nip into Boots and purchase everything in as short a time as possible, then head straight to work.

We did just that. It took twenty-seven minutes. He then caught the train into central London while I staggered home with several bulging bags. I could have cried.

Now, here I was, almost nineteen years later, with that beloved baby having grown up, buying the essentials for her new life, independent of us. The thought almost bolted me to the ground. I wanted not to walk into the shop, or buy the goods or, ultimately, say goodbye.

But I did as I always do. I swallowed hard, pretended everything was fine and tried to match Tillie's excitement.

And it was exciting. Unlike George, she wanted to think carefully about every purchase. We took our time, considered options, looked at prices, weights and volumes, smelled shampoos and bath gels, wrinkled our noses at some, agreed on others. It was much more like what I'd hoped for when she was yet to enter the world.

But then, half way round, in the biscuit aisle, she stopped abruptly and said, 'I don't want to leave you.'

It undid me. I burst into tears.

'You don't need to cry,' she said, laughing. 'You've still got me for just over another week yet!'

(As if that was anywhere near enough!)

This process of leaving is the start of an enormously important part of both our lives. I know it will, mostly, be lovely for her. I'm just not sure about what it will be like for me. I keep seeing a chasm and me on the edge of it.

Wednesday 18th September
A new academic year at the V&A studying the Late Renaissance to the Baroque: 1500 to 1720. There were plenty of familiar, welcoming faces – among them, Annabel's. We made our way through the excited students and hugged.

After lunch, a gallery tour included the study of a beautiful, painted terracotta bust of Henry VII. His head was slightly turned to the right as if someone has just said something very quietly and he was trying not to miss anything. His wasn't a face from the past, but a person you might pass in the street now – neither handsome nor ugly, but keenly astute.

Thursday 19th September
My birthday! Fifty-five years young.

Tillie made a beautiful chocolate cake. *(The first year I've not had to make my cake and eat it.)* We had the traditional birthday tea of sandwiches, crisps, Cadbury's fingers, party rings and pineapple pieces on cocktail sticks. *(A 1960s tea. The only thing missing was jelly in pretty paper cups.)* And then I opened my presents.

Tillie and Lucas gave me a cookery book and a lovely bunch of sunflowers, which are extravagantly large and such a bright yellow that I find myself smiling every time I look at them. George presented me with a cheque to buy myself a present as I couldn't think what I wanted. Friends and relations had sent slippers, a necklace, chocolates and a bar of Chanel No. 5 soap.

Oh, what joy to be cherished, loved and spoiled!

Friday 20th September
I keep pondering the curious issue of my visual identity: that I appear familiar to myself in mirrors and family photographs but look completely different in Iggie's images. After some considerable thought, I've realised that when I look in mirrors I always have the same expression, and I think that's

something to do with ensuring I recognise myself. That's one aspect of my identity.

But it doesn't explain the other Jill – the woman who Iggie sees and reveals. Perhaps that's why he's a great photographer. He's finding the fleeting moment, what lies behind or lies in front and is unfamiliar. *(Unfamiliar to me, at least.)* The man's clever.

Saturday 21st September
An amazing call from Iggie. He showed his gallerist, Ann-Marie Larnier (who owns Seed Gallery) the series of photographs he's been taking of me. Apparently, she was deeply impressed and wants to show them, as opposed to the work that featured at the Saatchi Gallery exhibition, at Frieze London early next month. *The* major annual commercial art show! Where the world's leading galleries show the work of their most important artists! Wow!

As Iggie needs to work with his print-maker to produce the portraits to the size and quality he requires, we won't be making any new images for some time.

He was insistent that I come to the launch. And even better, he said he'll pay me, retrospectively and going forward, for my work as a model! *(As a model!!!)* Actually, he was apologetic about this. He'd started out thinking it was a one-off shoot, but now that it's become a series he wants to put it on a formal basis.

I hadn't minded not being paid. In fact, I hadn't even thought about it. It was fun and totally different to anything I've ever done before while calling on my creative skills too. But it's a professional arrangement now. Excellent. I love professional arrangements, especially when they're fee-paying. And it's good money too – on a par with Jeremy's website consultancy fee.

I shared the news with Tillie and Lucas about Iggie's photographs, including the image of the three of us, featuring at Frieze London.

Tillie looked pleased and then despondent because she won't be able to attend the launch. And then she looked pleased again.

'You can't have everything,' she said, cheerfully. 'Apart from which I'll be having the time of my life in Durham. But take loads of photos. I'll put them on social media and the GCSE art class can eat their hearts out!'

Lucas was unimpressed.

'You'll come to the launch, won't you?' I asked.

'Will Arnold be there?'

'Definitely.'

'Then probably.'

I'll take that as a yes.

Sunday 22nd September
Just under a week to go, then life as I have known it with a daughter I love beyond passion will be gone. How am I going to bear this? I thought grief was for the dead. Now I realise it covers other partings too.

I'm on an emotional rollercoaster: one day happy, next day agonisingly sad.

Monday 23rd September
Tillie and I went to a country park run by the neighbouring local authority. It's beautifully maintained and includes a recently opened café where we ate lunch outside. *(If I eat any more salads I'm going to turn into a cow and start producing pats.)*

We walked through the grounds, admiring the topiary work, the deep English borders still full of flowering plants, and a sunken garden.

'None of my friends would be seen dead in a place like this,' said Tillie cheerfully. 'I don't mind because I can see how beautiful it is. And I'm loving having this time with you.'

'Oh, thank you so much, Tillie,' I responded, gratified and, simultaneously, shocked to realise how out of touch I am with what a young person would like to do. *(Though as soon as she said it, I realised it was blindingly obvious that 99.9 per cent of 18-year-olds would not want to go for a walk round a park with their mother.)*

We linked arms. 'This time is extraordinarily important for me too,' I told her.

And, like an old couple, we leant into one another, touching foreheads, and sauntered back to the car.

Tuesday 24th September

Fay phoned. Jeremy has asked for her consultancy's help with Osbert & Small's website. She's going to meet him tomorrow. I know they'll get along well, and Ellis Hatcher will create just the site that Jeremy and Hugo need. Job done. *(Perhaps I could take up commercial match-making as a new career? Or maybe not.)*

Wednesday 25th September

I'm exhausted by the stress and distress of Tillie going. Only two more days. I trudged up the street to the station on my way to the V&A and my whole body ached. If there had been a bed at the side of the road, I would have tumbled into it.

Tillie was bored to tears, having failed to find any friends to spend at least part of the day with. Nearly all have started university already.

This evening she said, 'I just need to go to Durham to get the going over with. Then I'll be OK.'

(Part of me thought: no, no, no! And another part thought: yes! I wish we could get it over with too, because the waiting is unbearable.)

At bedtime, I went to kiss her goodnight – something I did throughout her and Lucas's childhoods, but which I rarely do now as they're usually in bed after me. Sitting by her side, I said lightly, 'I have to kiss you twice because soon you won't be here for me to kiss at all.'

I snuggled my head into the space between her neck and the pillow. I drew in the scent of her and thought: I must remember this.

'Oh, don't be soft, Mum.'

She laughed and wriggled so much that I almost fell off her bed.

'You can kiss me,' yelled Lucas from his room. 'I don't mind.'

That boy has ears out on stalks. But I did go and kiss him, all the same.

Thursday 26th September
Misery and most of it my own fault.

Tillie came in for dinner after her final shift at Morrisons. Lucas had already left the table and there were just the three of us. She was tucking into her food when I decided to tell her about my plan to visit her, mid-term.

She set down her knife and fork.

'Mum, I can't possibly see you. I have lectures Monday to Friday and all the study work plus essays to do. I'll be far too busy.' And then she added with finality, 'I'll see you when I get home at Christmas.'

I was stung.

'Surely you can see me for a few hours.'

'I thought you were talking about a weekend.'

(Well, in my dreams maybe.)

'If I came for the day, we could have lunch together. You do have to eat between all your hard work.'

'But it's such a long way to travel for a meal. I thought you'd want to stay.'

'I've never talked about anything other than seeing you for a meal. Ever. Even when we were looking round universities a year ago.'

(I was just hoping she'd change her mind in the interim and be longing to see me. A case of projection if ever there was one.)

'That's true,' she conceded begrudgingly.

'Look, I don't have to come at all. I can leave it until Christmas. It's not a big deal.'

(Racing in at number one among The Biggest Lies I Have Ever Told.)

Nothing more was said, in either compromise or apology by either of us. I went to do the washing up in order to bring things to a close and to stop myself from crying in front of the two of them.

Tillie finished her meal and went upstairs.

'*I* love you,' said George, coming up behind me at the kitchen sink and putting his arms round me. 'I suppose she feels it's her adventure and we're not part of it. Even if we're the people who helped make it happen and are bank-rolling it.'

I'm hurt and sad and miserable. And about two millimetres away from crying most of the time.

Friday 27th September

Final day. Partly to ensure that life goes on after Tillie and Archie go to university – even if Archie's still living at home – Frankie and I have organised to meet up next Thursday.

In the middle of packing, Tillie decided we needed to make a last-minute trip to the local shopping centre in order to buy a cheap and cheerful dress in which to go clubbing.

'This is exactly why I love London,' she said excitedly as we walked round the nearby market. 'You've got Afro-Caribbean people playing music. There's fruit and veg stalls selling ethnic foods that we haven't a clue how to cook. There's a fish stall with the fish baking in the sunshine and giving off a stomach-churning stench. There's a guy over there lying on the pavement wrapped in pristine blankets and you can't tell if he's homeless or an art installation. I mean, it's just bonkers. I love it! I love London!'

(I wanted to say: well then, stay. Go to university in London. Live with us. You don't have to go to Durham. But, of course, she does.)

*

This evening, we went to the local Indian restaurant to mark Tillie's imminent departure. On the way back, she took my hand in hers.

'I'm sorry about yesterday. I didn't mean to hurt you.'

'I didn't explain very well what I was proposing,' I said, building my side of the bridge.

'That's why I thought you meant you were staying for days.'

'No. Just for a few hours.'

It sounded so pathetically short that I had to fight back the tears. I had wanted much, much more.

It was, ostensibly, a lovely evening if you ignored the fact that my heart was tearing in two. In bed I started to cry about her going, about the fact that this intense period of mothering and nurturing her over eighteen years is coming to an end and with it, my role. Once I started, I couldn't stop. George cuddled me but the tears kept running down my face, long after he'd turned away and gone to sleep.

Saturday 28th September

We were up at five o'clock to eat a hasty breakfast. George packed the car, then the four of us stood outside the front door – Lucas bleary-eyed and keen to get back to bed – as we took a series of group 'selfies' and photographs of Tillie on her own, radiant and animated.

All the way up the A1 there were cars just like ours, laden with boxes and bags, topped by a tell-tale duvet. Gradually, the majority peeled off for Nottingham, Sheffield, Leeds and York, until there were just a few of us left for Durham and universities even further north.

Outside Trevs hall of residence a tall young woman, gripping two table tennis rackets, guided our car into a parking place outside the college. A line of five other women in cheerleader outfits with extra-short skirts and shaking extra-large pom-poms, screamed whoops of greetings as Tillie stepped out of the car. Such energy and enthusiasm was infectious: it was impossible not to feel thrillingly excited for her.

A posse of eight students descended on the car, emptied the boot and interior in no-seconds flat and took both Tillie and belongings up to her room.

Cara, a second-year student, led us at a more sedate pace. Trevs is a rabbit warren. Were it not for Cara *(and I have mixed feelings about this)* we'd still be wandering round the college wondering where Tillie was and how we'd find her.

Her room was small, bare and imperfectly formed: six walls and each of a different length. But by the time we'd unpacked – with Tillie's personal items, familiar ornaments and photos adorning the shelves – it looked homely.

Cara returned to take Tillie for the registration process. As George and I needed to start on the long journey home, we shared a few last hugs. Tillie looked enormously happy and waved briefly, before walking away.

As we left, I noticed a large, multicoloured, hand-painted sign outside the college: 'Don't worry, parents! We'll look after them!' Even I smiled.

The dreaded day was over. Tillie was fine. Also, the weather was wonderful and, as we raced south, the distant Yorkshire hills looked sublime.

*

And that's it. You have your baby, you raise her for what, at times, seems like forever. Then when she leaves, you think: only eighteen years and they just flew by. Your arms are empty. What happens next?

Thank God Lucas is still at home.

Sunday 29th September
I woke up with a frightened start in the middle of the night. Tillie isn't here. Is she safe?

I gave myself a firm talking to. She's most likely tucked up in bed, just like me. And, anyway, what can I do? We've taught her what we can and added our soprano line to the chorus of safety advice she's had from school and university.

*

Mid-morning, a text arrived saying she could Skype at midday, the only time she had free.

She looked perky despite being at a Freshers' party until the early hours of this morning. *(So, perhaps, not tucked up when I woke up!)* I'm not sure when we'll talk next. Possibly Christmas. She has a lot of administrative tasks to sort out immediately, and then there's all the Freshers' activities before the lectures start at the beginning of next week.

I stripped her bed and put everything in the wash. Later, remaking it, I gathered her teddies in my arms before settling them on her pillow.

'Don't worry. She's coming back,' I whispered to them. 'Not for a while, but she'll be home some time. You'll see.'

Monday 30th September
I'm trying to look at Tillie's leaving from George's, Lucas's and Tillie's points of view. George says he's sad, but that it's a natural step and one which we've encouraged her to take all her life. He thinks, too, that things might be better for Lucas, who will receive more of our attention.

Lucas says he's thrilled she's gone. But I know he'll miss her. For one thing, he won't have anyone to help him with his maths homework. *(He's at a level way beyond George and light-years ahead of me.)*

And Tillie? Well, she's ridiculously excited about being at Durham and all that's happening in Freshers' Week. Which is good. It would be very difficult if she was deeply reticent and we were having to persuade her to stay there. *(There will be students who are struggling, even at this early stage. I saw their ilk when I was at college.)* There are a lot of positive things.

But none of this stopped the tears from rolling down my cheeks all the way through Total Workout.

October

Tuesday 1st October
It's hard to stop crying. Any thought of Tillie is setting me off. By mid-morning, I'd turned into two people: the crying person and a detached onlooker telling me I was heading in a direction which, the further I went, the more difficult it was going to be to get back.

I went for a swim because it's hard to swim and cry without gulping in so much water you're likely to drown.

A text arrived mid-afternoon:
2 busy 2 talk. Having gr8 time xxx

*

I keep thinking of Jeremy and wishing I hadn't closed the door on that potential friendship. Ah well, at least there's Frieze London to look forward to tomorrow.

Wednesday 2nd October
I chose my clothes carefully for this evening's opening of Frieze London. My aim was to wear something different from any of the combinations in Iggie's photographs. I wanted to make a statement: creative, casual and smart. I think I pulled it off: black knee-length pencil skirt, eye-catching long-sleeved fuchsia jersey blouse, smart jacket and high-heeled shoes.

Lucas and George came too, as did Fay, who's an admirer of Iggie's work. The place was heaving with gallerists, artists and their studio associates, relatives, buyers, friends, friends of friends and a few down-and-outs. *(Probably famous artists.)*

We made our way through the crowds to Seed Gallery where Iggie, Arnold, the gallery owner Ann-Marie Larnier and her staff were mingling among clients.

Iggie had had the photographs printed slightly larger than life-size. They made a terrific impact, the colours dramatic and mesmerising.

It was odd to see people scrutinising and talking about them. From what I ear-wigged, the comments were complimentary. Then someone turned round and recognised me. The next thing I knew I was being treated like a film star, made to stand in front of Iggie's work so everyone could take photographs. It did wonders for my ego. I haven't felt as self-confident, self-assured and happy in a long time.

When they'd all finished, I sidled up to George. He was examining *The Wife* portrait, ironically standing in place of himself – the person who hadn't been at the meal.

He sighed deeply. 'I've never really thought what it's like for you when you've made a meal and then I don't turn up. Now I know. Sorry.'

I squeezed his hand and kissed his cheek.

Iggie came over and asked George if he could photograph him in front of *The Wife*, both facing the image and then with his back to it. Amazingly, George agreed. *(He's normally averse to photographers unless they're taking an image for his firm's website.)*

Arnold pushed his way through the crowd and congratulated me.

'You do know, don't you,' he said, leaning in and speaking close to my ear so I could hear over the noise of the crowd, 'that you're Iggie's muse?'

'What?' I asked incredulously, pulling a face in disbelief. 'A past-middle-aged-woman becoming the muse of a young man. Pull the other one, it's got bells on it.'

He drew himself up to his full height and regarded me, then leaned in again.

'It's a great compliment. He's never focused on one person before. There's definitely some magical chemistry going on between the two of you. Just look at the photographs.'

I did. And deep down I know he's right, but I'm not going to think about what he said. Whatever 'it' is, those photographs have worked thus far. I don't want to jeopardise anything by analysing what's going on and possibly destroying it. Creativity can be fragile and elusive, and some things are best left alone.

Lucas pushed his way through to talk to Arnold and I took photos of Iggie's work, the party, the people, their clothes, the canapés, the champagne, George, Lucas, Fay, Arnold, Iggie, and then a selfie in which I look totally joyful and slightly barmy. I pinged them off to Tillie to do as she wants on social media. Thirty seconds later, she replied.

Cool! Looks amazing – party & Iggie's pics. Love the 1 of us. Love u. xxx

I talked briefly to Ann-Marie, who is not only beautiful but shrewd, too. She explained that the end of last year and the start of this had been terrible for Iggie: his declining health, the discovery of the tumour, albeit benign, the craniotomy to remove it and the long road to recovery which he is still on.

Taking my hands in hers she said, 'You brought him back to life. He was trying hard to stay positive, but it was almost too much. On the Tube, to and from the hospital when he was making the film – and that was to keep himself sane by focusing on an artwork – he realised that no one noticed or cared. Then you sat opposite him and saw him. Really saw him. And you kept turning up even though each journey he took, he chose a different carriage. He felt you were sent. And now he's much better physically and emotionally. Creatively, he's moving in a new direction and the clients love it. It's like a dream. I do hope you keep working together.'

I was tremendously moved and grateful for her insight and generous comments. But it made me realise that I'm the one who should be doing the thanking. Because in a funny kind of way, Iggie's been *my* saviour. I was at a low ebb when I saw his exhibition at the Saatchi Gallery, and now I'm not. *(Well, with the exception of how I feel about Tillie, which is bloody awful.)*

*

We came home at midnight, but I was buzzing with excitement and couldn't sleep. I've never been anyone special – not publicly special – but tonight I was. And it was amazing!

Thursday 3rd October
Frankie and I met for coffee which I really needed because my eyes were drooping with fatigue. I told her all about last night. She was pleased for me and said that if it ever happens again to take her along as she could do with some glamour in her life too.

Moving on to home territory, she reported that, after a nervous start, Archie had settled into student life, commuting to King's College from home.

I saw a gulf open between us. Her life continues unchanged. Mine is altered, irrevocably, and she has no idea.

*

Fay emailed a thank you for last night and asked if I'd join her later in the month running a workshop for students. Said yes. *(Grateful for any distraction.)*

I sent an email to a select number of friends and acquaintances about my appearance in Iggie's photographs at Frieze. Some of them might get there in the next couple of days. Oh, and I received the biggest bouquet of flowers I've ever seen from Ann-Marie. She wrote, 'Thank you for helping Iggie in every way.'

Friday 4th October
Text from Tillie:
 Absolutely love it here!
 Followed by a string of emoticons.

Saturday 5th October
A milk float – a sight never seen for decades in this area – drove past carrying half a dozen bottles of milk and hundreds of bottles of Evian water. Wondered if I was hallucinating.

Sunday 6th October
Mid-afternoon, George and I Skyped Tillie. She's had a wild week of planned parties, followed by unplanned parties, ending with last night's bash marking the conclusion of Freshers' Week and the start of studying. Despite the expenditure of vast amounts of energy combined with almost no sleep, she looked surprisingly well.

Monday 7th October
I've received a good assortment of emails and texts from friends and acquaintances who went to Frieze, and all with sweet comments. Another bouquet arrived too, this time from Iggie and Arnold. *(Should I send them one? What's the etiquette of mutual congratulations?)* Frieze closed last night. Oh, but it was lovely while it lasted!

*

I keep lurching from being OK about Tillie – not necessarily happy but alright – to feeling sick. Between the high of Frieze and the low of Tillie's absence, I'm an emotional yo-yo. The good thing is, I've almost stopped crying.

Tuesday 8th October
I'm wasting hours running from my mobile phone to the computer to the landline answering machine to check for messages from Tillie. None.

With a bit of luck, by this time next week I'll have stopped acting like a lovelorn teenager.

*

An email arrived from Catherine Cohen, head of art at Tillie's old school. She's seen Iggie's photographs of me at Frieze. Apparently, this work complements the Contemporary British Photography module on the GCSE art course. She wants me to ask if the year 11 art students can visit him at his studio, and whether I'll talk to them about my role as his model. These are the same girls who saw me in the film at the Saatchi Gallery, and who are now in their final year of GCSEs.

Even though Iggie now refers to me as his model, it's still odd to hear that word in the mouths of others. I'm not exactly your average model: fifteen-years-old, no breasts, no hips, anorexic thin, long legs and pretty face. In fact, I'm an anti-model model.

Anyway, I forwarded the email to Iggie.

Wednesday 9th October
Just before I left for the V&A, Jeremy called. The clouds parted, the sun shone.

'You have to come and see me,' he said, in his beautiful plum-filled voice.

'Why?' I asked, laughing with happiness because he'd phoned.

'I have a delightful diptych which even the V&A would love to get its hands on. It's a marvel.'

'Well, Jeremy, that beats "come up and see my etchings" any day. If I didn't know you were a happily married man, I'd think you were after me.'

'I am after you, but not in *that* way.'

I could hear the mischievousness in his voice, the same mischievousness which had prompted him to bid on the Tiffany vase.

'How about next Tuesday?' he asked.

I checked my diary.

'That's fine. And how's the website redesign going?'

'Excellent. But don't worry about that. Let's concentrate on the diptych.'

I detected a slight edge to his voice on the subject of the website: I'd washed my hands of it and he didn't want me near its redevelopment. Good.

That's it! He opened the door and I'm walking towards it. Joy of joys!

*

At break-time, three people came up and remarked on my appearance at Frieze. They quizzed me about my ongoing relationship with Iggie and asked how many other artists I'd modelled for in the past. *(LOLs, as Tillie would say.)*

Thursday 10th October
Iggie's happy to host the year 11 art students. He and Arnold will talk about the studio and his work, I'll talk about my role in this current project, and then we can answer any questions. I've arranged with Catherine Cohen for them to visit in November, after half term. We're aiming to restart work on the project that month.

*

Yippee! A text:
Loving lectures! Skype at w/e xxx

Friday 11th October
Swam, emptied bladder *(not in the pool)*, stood on scales. Oh God. Drank a skinny latte. If only it was me, not the latte, that was skinny.

Saturday 12th October
Not your average Saturday. In fact, not like any Saturday ever before. It was Great Aunt Vi's house-warming party.

While George worked, I spent the entire train journey to Leicester staring out of the window and wondering what kind of home she'd be in. Sheltered accommodation? A horrible but easy-to-navigate bungalow on an ill-kempt estate? Or, my worst fear, an old people's home with the stomach-churning scent of stale urine competing with Dettol?

We phoned for her address while queuing for a taxi and, a few minutes later, pulled up outside a mint-new apartment block featuring glass floor-to-ceiling curtain walls. Inside, gawping in wonder and lost for words, I pressed the button for her floor. 'Penthouse apartment' was incised in a shiny brass plate next to it.

'The *penthouse apartment?*' I asked incredulously when the lift doors closed behind us. 'Do you suppose she's borrowed someone else's place to hold the party?'

George shrugged his shoulders, as bemused as I was.

The lift stopped, the doors opened and there, waiting for us, was the Aged Aunt.

Except this was Great Aunt Vi, Mark II. This woman was clothed in a smart, black, tailored dress that hugged her slim figure, opaque black tights and elegant low-heeled black pumps. A pearl necklace complemented the dress. A single pearl studded each ear. Her hair had been cut into a short pixie style that fringed her face and ears. Her face was simply made up with foundation, rouge and a deep red lipstick.

'Great Aunt Vi, you look beautiful,' I said, gasping. 'Breathtakingly beautiful.'

'Darlings! How wonderful to see you both. And you, Jill, look particularly attractive. I see we've both had something of a make-over. Welcome to my new home. You're the first to arrive. Do come in.'

We stepped into my ideal ultra-modern habitat. It featured a large, light-filled living space encompassing kitchen, dining and sitting rooms. Sunshine poured in through the window-walls and glass doors, the latter opening on to a wrap-around balcony from which there were spectacular views over the city.

'Fifi will take your coats and I'll give you a quick tour before any more guests arrive.'

A young woman welcomed us, then disappeared with our coats. Great Aunt Vi stood between us as we admired the main room. As well as having a chic built-in kitchen, the well-chosen and complementary furnishings were by designers whose work I drool over: a famous Barcelona chair by Mies van der Rohe, leather sofas by Jasper Morrison, dining chairs and table by Charles and Ray Eames, lamps by Isamu Noguchi and a wall clock by George Nelson. Most magnificent of all was a black Steinway grand piano, its lid open and flanked by a fat leather stool wide enough for two people to play a duet.

She steered us through three sublimely elegant bedrooms, one with an ensuite bathroom, the other two sharing a bathroom tiled in coloured glass and with a huge shower capable of firing water at The Body Beautiful from every angle.

'Great Aunt Vi, it's truly the loveliest place I've ever seen. But how on earth could you ...'

I faltered.

'Afford it?' She cut in quickly and sharply. 'Yes, I thought it wouldn't take you and your money-laundering husband long to cut to the quick.'

George raised his eyes heavenward. A long breath whistled quietly through his pursed lips.

'Well, it's easy,' she said tartly. 'I sold my house, which turned out to be in a highly desirable location due to the outstanding local state schools. And I sold a rather valuable Tiffany vase.'

I looked at her, stumped.

'I thought the money from the Tiffany vase went to The Five Ls.'

I'd been at the auction. I'd seen it sell.

'It did.'

I thought some more, wondering what it was I didn't understand.

'I don't understand,' I said.

She took a deep breath.

'There were two vases.'

'What?'

I looked at George, but he was busy gazing at the ceiling.

'There were *two* vases,' she repeated. 'A pair. One on the right-hand side of the mantelpiece in the back bedroom, and the other on the left. But whenever you children came to stay, I always put the one on the left away. I liked those vases and I didn't mind the idea of one of them being broken by an over-zealous child, but I didn't want to lose both of them.'

'But when I came to your house as an adult, there was only ever one vase.'

'I always put the other away. Old habits die hard.'

'So, when The Five Ls discovered your vase was Tiffany and it sold for a nice sum, you still had hold of the other one?'

'Yes. And I sold it. Privately. Through the auctioneers, to the person who bought the first vase. It's highly unusual to have a pair of vases and, as a result, the second one fetched an even greater sum.'

I was lost for words. She'd had two vases and neither of them had come my way. Not that she was obliged to give me either of them, but she had asked what I would like from her house all those months ago. And she'd deliberately withheld both vases. Conflicting emotions were fighting in my chest: fury at her treatment of me and admiration at her canniness. Having seen what the first vase was worth, she'd realised the sale of the second could bring enough money to change her life.

'As a result, I could buy whatever I wanted. I saw this place advertised in the local newspaper – radically different to anywhere I'd lived before. This was the show flat, complete with everything you see here. I told the agent, "I'm a cash buyer. Knock £20,000 off the price and I'll take the lot: the flat, the furnishings, everything. No chain, no hassle. Right now." Of course, he thought I was demented. It's the problem with old age. No one ever believes you're of sound mind. But he checked my credit rating and within the hour accepted my proposition.'

I decided grace and good humour were called for. 'I'm very pleased for you and I can't describe how much I like the apartment. The only issue is – how quickly can I move in?'

George shot me a warning look.

'You can't. I've already got two lodgers. You've met Fifi. Then there's Trillion, her friend.'

'Trillion's a good name for someone living in the lap of luxury. Rhymes with millions!'

I laughed at my joke, giddiness overtaking me. George poked me in the side with his elbow. His lips had become a thin line.

'She's a second-year student studying history of art at the university and Fifi's in the same year doing medicine. Now I have an income as well as two wonderful companions.'

With each new revelation, Great Aunt Vi rose higher and higher in my estimation. She was proof-positive that anything was possible, regardless of age.

The doorbell rang.

'I must go and see to my other guests.'

Within an hour, the apartment and balcony were heaving. The guests included a handful of Great Aunt Vi's contemporaries, a greater number of younger though still elderly ladies from her civil service days, and neighbours from her old street.

They included Pippa, Matt and their children – the family who'd moved into her house. I knew who they were the moment they arrived. The little girls, Grace and Lily, raced towards Great Aunt Vi, who knelt on the floor. Grace threw herself in Great Aunt Vi's arms while Lily plonked herself on her lap. They were completely relaxed. You'd have thought they'd known one another for years.

But the greatest surprise was this: Great Aunt Vi's face

was transformed. She was smiling – a soft, sweet, pure and unrestrained smile – quite unlike anything I had ever seen before. Those two little girls had done what no one else had ever achieved: they had captured her heart.

George, standing beside me, remarked, 'Well, I'll be damned. The old codger's in love.'

It was a profoundly tender sight, so touching that it seemed voyeuristic to stare. We turned away and, as we did, the chatter and laughter in the room diminished to a sibilant hush. All eyes turned to the apartment entrance where the world's most handsome man had entered.

There was a sharp, collective intake of breath and not just by the women in the room. Tall, elegant and broad shouldered, his face featured high cheek bones, a long slim nose, closely shaven square jaw and green eyes that took in the whole room as he smiled. We all smiled back. It was that simple.

And who had her arm entwined with that of the world's most handsome man? Sue. Virgin Sue. Looking radiant with happiness. *(It looked like middle-aged, fat and balding Harry had been well and truly dumped.)*

Conversation resumed but the tone had edged up a notch as if everyone was expressing the same thought albeit in different ways: wow!

I pulled George over to greet them. Sue and I hugged and her chap held out his hand.

'Harry,' he said.

(Harry?!? How many Harrys did she know?)

'Pleased to meet you,' I replied, then as George engaged him in conversation I hissed in Sue's ear, 'You said Harry was middle-aged, fat and bald. Who's *this*?'

'The same person,' she hissed back.

'What happened? Did he have a body swap? For God's sakes, he could be the next James Bond.'

She laughed. 'As I didn't want you being too interested in

my new relationship, I was putting you off the scent.'

She made me sound like an overly keen bloodhound. I could have clocked her.

'Well, all I can say is bloody hell and what an amazing catch, you lucky woman.'

'Thanks!' She grinned.

Not only was Harry ridiculously handsome but he was also a lovely, amiable, chatty person who was, of all things, a librarian. I mean, why would he be a librarian when clearly he's some kind of classical god deigning to set foot on earth? And what do people do in his library? Come in and pull out a book as an excuse to stand and stare at him? I might have to move to west London. Possibly this month.

When Harry and Sue moved on to circulate, I went in search of Trillion and Fifi. Apparently, they've been best friends since starting university. And they were completely taken with Great Aunt Vi.

'She's such a sweetie,' said Fifi. 'If we're in late, she gets out of bed to check we're OK.'

'That's a turn up for the books,' I said. 'Whenever I stayed with her as a child she was an absolute stickler for having me in bed by some hideously early hour and making sure I stayed there until the next morning.'

'But we're not children.'

'True. But don't you find her a tad mercurial at times?'

'You mean bad-tempered?' asked Trillion, laughing.

'The words never passed my lips.'

'Oh, she has her moments. But mostly, she's very kind.'

I raised my eyebrows in disbelief.

'She thinks *you're* cool,' said Fifi. 'She's always talking about you. You're the only relative who offered to help her move, the only one who thanked her for the gift she sent earlier in the year and the only one who calls regularly.'

I was completely floored. Great Aunt Vi has never provided

such feedback. *(And anyway, if I'm that great and she's that appreciative why didn't she offer me one of those two Tiffany vases?)*

'Don't worry, we *will* look after her,' Trillion remarked.

I was reminded of the sign outside Trevs College, and I nearly said, churlishly: good luck because no one else has ever managed – but thanked them instead.

Time passed in a haze of introductions to new people, lots of drinks and delicious designer food. George and I were circulating again when Sue reappeared. Now she was accompanied by a tall and elegant woman with blonde shoulder-length hair. A tight-fitting evening dress clung below her broad shoulders to a slightly nipped in stomach and slimmer hips, emphasising an almost androgynous figure. Her green eyes were heavy with mascara, the lids coloured with shades of mauve to accentuate the sockets. Her lips, pulled in a tight moue, were pillar box red. She glided towards us and as she did, I tried, desperately, to think who she reminded me of.

'How lovely to see you again! I'm Debbie,' she said. She'd tempered the original voice with a slight coquettish femininity.

She gave George the back of her hand to kiss. After the faintest of pauses, he lifted it to his lips.

'Pleased to meet you too,' he replied looking her in the eyes, adding flirtatiously, '*Darling* Debbie.'

My mouth dropped open. This was a side to George I'd never seen before. How come everyone I know is suddenly turning into someone I don't know? What's going on? And, after all these years, do I need to keep an eye on George?

'What do you think?' asked Sue, a smile stretching from ear to ear. 'Isn't she wonderful?'

'I thought you were called Harry,' I said flatly.

'Only when I'm a man.' She smiled, the lips full and attractive. 'When I'm a woman, I'm Debbie.'

She paused for effect.

'Get it? As in Debbie Harry? The singer?'
(Of course! Blondie!)
'When the occasion arises, I take her role. Well, on the piano, that is.'

With that she walked to the piano, carefully settled herself on the stool and played the complete works of Debbie Harry. *One Way or Another, Hangin' on the Telephone, Sunday Girl, The Tide is High, Denis, Dreaming, Heart of Glass* – they all had an airing. And every time she raised her eyes from the keyboard, she looked at Sue. Sue looked back and the only word to describe the two of them is *smitten*.

As for Debbie's performance, it was faultless. But, more to the point, she'd adapted every song to suit the event, jazzing up or softening down most of the melodies so that they embraced a softer musical line beyond which guests could still talk to one another.

'Congratulations, Sue,' I said. 'You've clearly bagged yourself a remarkable man. Or do I mean woman?'

'Thanks. It's what Harry does to earn a little extra income beyond the regular day job. Though he's not charging Great Aunt Vi,' she added hastily. 'It's his present to her. Amazing, isn't it?'

'I'd go for amazing,' I said, nodding.

'Amazing, too, how my life's turned out and all because of Great Aunt Vi's unwanted gift of that old piano.'

George was looking at his watch. He had legal papers to read on the train home, and I was flagging. Surprises are exhausting and we'd had the average decade's worth within one afternoon. We found the Aged Aunt and said our goodbyes.

'I can't express sufficiently just how beautiful you look,' I told her, 'how wonderful your apartment is, or how fortunate you are to have found such intelligent and kind flatmates. I wish you every happiness in this new stage of your life.'

'Thank you, Jill,' she said courteously.

I kissed her soft, warm, papery cheeks which were still lightly scented with the Coty L'Aimant she always favoured.

And then we left.

Sunday 13th October
I lay all day in a dark room reeling from the shocks of yesterday. *(OK. That was my fantasy.)*

Pinged off a text to Sue: *Congratulations, you dark horse. Looks like you found the man who ticks all the boxes. Hope he realises what an amazing woman you are too.*

Think I might be jealous.

*

Tillie texted to say she can't Skype until tomorrow. To be honest, I'm glad. I need a break from the emotional rollercoaster.

Monday 14th October
Tillie's exuberance took me aback. Happiness and energy, life and loveliness poured out of her. Was she always this happy when she lived with us? Had I forgotten already?

As she leaned her head forward, I wanted to kiss it. I knew exactly how silky her hair would feel and how her skin would smell. My chest ached. It was all I could do not to weep – not for Tillie, but for me.

We told her all about Saturday: the surprise of Great Aunt Vi's new home, her being in love with Grace and Lily, and then the bolt from the blue of Sue, Harry and Debbie.

'We felt like two old farts,' said George.

'You're nice old farts,' said Tillie. 'You're *my* farty parents, and I love you just as you are.'

Tuesday 15th October
I put together another smart outfit from my capsule wardrobe and went to Osbert & Small. The same young woman as last time greeted me with just as much warmth as before, this time

introducing herself as Sukie. She, like Jeremy, was super-nice and made me feel special.

Jeremy was talking to a customer who was admiring a hideous chest of drawers complete with scary, gold, winged caryatids at each corner. He gave a discreet wave.

While Sukie went to make coffee, I looked round the opposite side of the gallery to Jeremy and the customer. I recognised about half of the pieces. Clearly, there was a healthy turnover rate. High prices were not an issue.

The customer left, and Jeremy came over.

'That was Mr No-Name. He comes in once every few weeks to admire the commode mazarine.' *(Commode??!! I thought commodes were portable loos for poorly people. They are in Yorkshire.)* 'It doesn't matter what I do to encourage him to tell me his name, he won't. He loves that piece. And, then he goes away to think about it. Again. Perhaps, one day, he'll buy it.'

We kissed cheeks.

'But to business. This is what I wanted to show you. Sukie's familiar with it, but I'm sure she'll enjoy seeing it again. It's a little beyond the boundaries of my period but when I saw it I thought of you. And then I had to have it.'

I couldn't suppress a smile. His flattery was ridiculous but it appealed to my sense of humour.

The three of us sat at the gallery desk: Jeremy in the centre, Sukie and I at either end. He opened a central drawer, handed me a pair of white, lint-free gloves, put a pair on himself and then drew out a small object wrapped in tissue paper. Carefully, he peeled back the layers. Inside lay a closed diptych, its old, stained oak panels hinged on one of the two long sides. He opened it and laid it in the palms of my hands.

'Tell me what you see.'

And then I had a curious, out-of-body experience. Part of me detached herself and sat on the empty, fourth side of the table, opposite Jeremy but turned towards me, a look of mild amusement on her face as I described the diptych.

'The left panel shows the Virgin Mary holding the infant Jesus. Mary looks at him while he looks at the viewer, baby and viewer establishing a spiritual relationship. The gold background marks Mary and Jesus as different from ordinary mortals. The link with Byzantine icons is clear, though here the figures are not stylised. They're human.'

I paused for a moment, swapping a quick glance at the other me. She was smiling encouragingly.

And then I described the other panel. 'The male figure – probably the donor who might be a merchant or diplomat – faces and prays to Mary and Jesus. His fur-lined cloak, pearl rosary and gold cross mark him out as wealthy. Behind him is a house interior with a family crest painted on a window. If I knew whose crest it was, I'd probably know the name of the donor.'

I was running out of things to say. The other me across the table raised her eyebrows and gave a slight nod as if to say, 'Go on. There's more.'

I recalled, from the V&A course, how diptychs were used.

'This would be a portable item for the donor to take on his travels. Where possible, he'd hang it from a nail on the wall, quite high up, and pray to it.'

The other me beamed, pleased.

'Not bad. Not bad,' Jeremy remarked. 'Do you have any idea about the artist's identity?'

I didn't, and there was no obvious mark. But I added a thought.

'It looks northern European with its dark and sombre colours. There's no hint of the lovely light captured in the background of Italian diptychs. It's not as meticulous as Dürer. Perhaps the school of Dürer?'

I came to a halt. I looked up at the other me. She winked and was gone.

'It's the right era,' Jeremy confirmed. 'What if I said

"Rogier"?'

My jaw dropped and my heart started racing. I breathed in deeply trying to stop myself hyperventilating, fainting and dropping the wretched diptych.

'You surely don't mean Rogier van der Weyden? As in arguably *the* most famous and sought-after early Netherlandish painter?'

'That's the one!'

My hands fell in slow motion towards the desk. Jeremy quickly and deftly removed the diptych from them.

'I've never held anything as precious and valuable in all my life,' I told him, shocked that he'd casually entrusted me with it. 'How much is it worth?'

'Ah. Now then. Discretion is everything. Let's say between eight and ten.'

My mind had gone to mush.

'Hundred thousand pounds?' I asked, incredulity making my voice rise in horror.

He looked at me, amused, a smile catching the edges of his lips and playing in his eyes.

'Million.'

I gasped. 'Oh my God! Jeremy! And you really bought it because of me?' I recalled his apparently rash bidding at the Bonhams auction when he offered to buy me the Tiffany vase.

He nodded and smiled with such a look of openness and pleasure that I knew it was true.

'Of course, I'll sell it,' he added, rapidly bringing the subject back to earth. 'Now look, the donor is Philip de Croÿ. That's his family crest. The diptych was made in around 1460. It's a bit of a find on my part. But, given its size, I haven't a clue how I'll display it.'

Out of the dark recesses of my memory, I recalled a travel agency on the high street which always filled its window with A4 sheets of paper, each featuring a different holiday offer.

One day the window was empty except for a single, tiny piece of paper, slap-bang in the middle. Every passer-by stopped, compelled to read what it said.

'This is what you do: you clear out the gallery window entirely. Then, in the centre, you place a metre-wide, floor-to-ceiling cream coloured 'wall'.' *(Just like the one we use at Iggie's.)* 'On that, at a height usual for devotional paintings in medieval times, you hang the diptych. And put a spotlight on it. It'll be dazzlingly eye-catching.'

I smiled, pleased with the simplicity of my idea.

He turned to Sukie.

'I think she's got it!'

'I think so too!' she said.

I looked at the pair of them. The penny dropped. It had been another test, with Sukie rather than Hugo as Jeremy's fellow judge. But what was I being tested for?

He passed the diptych for her to wrap and signalled for me to follow him to the back room.

'I've put your cheque in an envelope.'

He rummaged among a few papers on the circular table and, as he handed me the envelope said, 'Look. I think you should come and work for me. One day a week. Learn the trade. You'll love it. And you'll be a great asset. What do you say?'

I just stood there and stared at him. Silent. Struck dumb. I'd never ever even in my wildest dreams considered such an idea. Not even the teensiest, weensiest flicker of a thought. I was stumped.

'But you've got Sukie,' I said lamely.

'She wants to work four days a week and spend Fridays with her young daughter. She and I could show you the ropes, and then you can take her place. How does that sound?'

(Bloody fucking brilliant.)

'But what will Hugo say?'

'Oh, he already thinks you're the bee's knees.'

(Really? He's clearly a man of great discernment and taste. But where's the rest of my fan club?)

'Well, I'll have to think it over,' I replied, trying to stay calm.

I paused, wondering what this alternative life would be like. I'd be completely out of my comfort zone. Completely out of the house. In a completely different world.

'I've thought it over,' I said. 'And I accept.'

He smiled, winningly.

'Excellent. Let's shake on it.'

*

George took the news in his stride – including the information that Jeremy is happily married to Hugo and therefore neither of them is sexually interested in me or me in them. Lucas wanted to know how it would affect him and, when I said it would mean he'd have to open the front door himself on a Friday after school, he couldn't have cared less. Tillie replied to my text:

My clever Mum! Love you lots xxxx

Wednesday 16th October
Jeremy sent a contract for me to sign. I start work after the half term holiday on the second Friday in November.

*

I longed to tell all my friends at the V&A, 'Oh, I've got a job with an antique dealer on Pall Mall. Yesterday, I held a diptych by Rogier van der Weyden.' But I couldn't think how to say it without it coming out in a lofty, bragging kind of way. I kept my mouth shut.

*

I didn't expect today's lectures to be interesting, even if, potentially, they are now critical to my new job. They were: The Printed Book in Venice, Print Techniques, and German Prints. Despite having spent a lifetime working in design – and much of it in print design – I knew nothing about the birth of metal type printing.

But I have pushed back the boundaries of ignorance. Indeed, the subjects were fascinating. Yesterday, I was blind to the history of type design. And now I see.

Thursday 17th October
The V&A's history lessons came in the nick of time, because today Fay and I ran a workshop on typographic design with second-year graphic design students at Central St Martin's school of art and design.

I was able to tell them about the history of printing in the fifteenth and sixteenth centuries and how the invention of moveable type was revolutionary – arguably on a par with the invention of the Internet. I explained how the first printed books were pale imitations of previously hand-written, illuminated manuscripts, but that they changed as designers put their minds to the look of a printed rather than a hand-written page. And then I moved on to the roles of designers and printers being interchangeable until type designers started to emerge – which brought us to today. The students were keen to learn and Fay was impressed.

At lunchtime, I told her about the job offer from Osbert & Small. Curiously, she was less surprised than me.

'He's a dream client for us on the website, and I can see that you and Jeremy would hit it off.'

'Really? How?'

'Oh, Jill!'

She said it as if it was self-evident. I must have looked as vacant as I felt for she added, 'Think about your sense of humour. And you're a fresh pair of eyes for him. I'm immensely pleased for you. It's the change you needed.'

She's right. It is.

Friday 18th October
After Total Workout *(getting better, growing stronger)* I spent the day packing for our holiday. Arak, who is joining us, came home with Lucas on the school bus. George was home by six, ready for a two-week holiday: one in Suffolk and one at home.

We're staying in Kersey, a tiny village in Suffolk. It took some time to find the cottage in the profound dark of the countryside, but what a gem! It's a sixteenth-century thatched half-timbered house with low ceilings, a massive fireplace with attached bread oven and enough beds and bedrooms to sleep a small class of children. *(Or even a class of small children.)*

We ooohed and aaaahed, had a cup of tea and then fell into our respective beds.

Saturday 19th October
Kersey is breath-taking. It's full of ancient houses, most of them chocolate box-top pretty. The hill on which our house sits leads down to a ford. From there, the road runs up steeply to an Elizabethan pub and various higgledy-piggledy old houses. Jars of home-made jam, bags of apples and great fat orange pumpkins are for sale outside some of them. This is fantasy England. And the amazing thing is, the only tourists it's crawling with are us.

We went for a walk round Kersey's perimeter where there were pheasants in abundance. Arak had never seen one before. Every time he spotted *any* animal he shouted, 'Kill it, kill it!' in a manic, excited manner.

On our way back, I heard him whisper to Lucas, 'People hate snails and kill them, but I love them. Don't tell anyone.'

Sunday 20th October
We drove to the National Trust's Melford Hall. The boys explored the house in about ten minutes and concluded it was a shame the Trust didn't let people play hide and seek as this

was the ace place for it.

George and I took our time. I felt obliged to study every piece of furniture, painting or object that looked like it had been made between the late Renaissance, Baroque and Rococo periods in order to improve my knowledge for when I start at Osbert & Small. But I'm giddy with happiness about the job and it was difficult to take anything in.

I really need this holiday. What with Tillie leaving, the success of Iggie's show at Frieze, the offer of the job at Osbert & Small – it's all been such an up and down time *(or rather a down and up time)* that I need a break. I need time to step back and draw breath, to reflect and rest.

Monday 21st October
Today it was Ickworth – National Trust again. I enjoyed the servants' quarters most of all. Apparently, the boot boy – perhaps the lowest of the low – was recruited at the age of fourteen and worked from seven in the morning to ten at night. *(Sounds like my working day. Though, fortunately, I don't sleep in a narrow bed with inadequate blankets, located in a cold, damp, subterranean corridor.)*

*

Kersey has no street lights. At night, looking out from our bedroom window, I can see a few distant rooms, their open-curtained, bright interiors floating untethered in a field of blackness. Not a sign of a flickering television or computer screen. Just warm fires burning and a few discreet lamps. It's as if I am looking through a telescope of time at England as it once was.

Tuesday 22nd October
We mooched round Clare's antique shops and art galleries. The boys found a couple of old cap guns for sale, but the shopkeeper refused to sell them unless they had an adult with them.

'What will your parents say if you go home with a cap gun?' I asked Arak.

'Oh, they won't mind,' he said cheerfully. 'My brother has one already.'

They made their purchases. Fortunately, since the guns didn't come with caps we were spared the sound of firing. Nevertheless, on the drive back, the pair of them 'shot' at everything they could see. Lucas insisted that he enter the house first in order to kill the drug dealers who would be inside. Arak said he'd cover Lucas's back. And in they went. George and I stood on the front doorstep looking at one another: me in amusement, him in despair.

*

A text arrived from Iggie. Seed Gallery has sold two photographs – *The Cleaner* and *The Wife* – to private collectors! He's thrilled, Ann-Marie's thrilled and I am too. But it's a bit weird as well: two people are going to have me hooked on their walls. Where will I be? The sitting room? The dining room? A bedroom? *(Creepy.)* Or a lavish loo?

Wednesday 23rd October
Another walk. Lucas and Arak took their guns and 'shot' every pheasant, pigeon, sheep and horse they could see. Arak stopped at one point to carefully remove the tiniest snail from the footpath and put it under a hedge before he continued on his shooting spree.

George is suffering from suppressed stress, finding the raised noise levels and surreal behaviour of Lucas and Arak almost intolerable. I don't mind them. It's interesting to see how Lucas is when he's with another boy. It's a revelation to discover that what I'd always taken as his normal behaviour with us is in fact a formal version of the far more relaxed, imaginative and free person that he is with Arak. *(Foolishly, I always thought it was the other way round.)*

Thursday 24th October
After lunch, following a trip to Gainsborough's House, we played a new variant of whist that Arak taught us. George, who has stopped being on his best behaviour because that's another thing that was causing him to be stressed, angrily took Arak to task for some of his moves. Rather than being offended or even alarmed, Arak looked at George and burst out laughing. Instinctively, he knew this was the real George and was triumphant that he'd finally unearthed him.

Friday 25th October
We were in London by midday, dropping Arak off at his house. As Arak's mum hugged him, he closed his eyes and on his face was a look that combined relief with near ecstasy. The boys are such contradictions: aggressive and combative at one moment, loving and tender at another.

Saturday 26th October
Mid-morning, I walked into our bedroom to find Lucas sitting in my corner chair, half naked and with wet hair, running the hairdryer at full blast close to his bare stomach.

'What are you doing?'

He jumped with surprise.

'Bloody hell, Mum. You should stop creeping up on people.'

He turned the hairdryer up higher and pointed it at me. My hair and clothes started billowing.

'I wasn't creeping,' I yelled over the blast. 'I was walking into my bedroom. To repeat myself: what are you doing?'

He reduced the blast and turned it back on himself.

'I'm trying to see how close I can get the hairdryer to my skin before I have to stop because it hurts too much.'

'That's bizarre.'

'It's fun. It really hurts even this close.'

Just then, the phone rang. As I went to pick it up, he turned the dryer off so I could hear the caller.

It was Edith. She started to chat and as she did so, I watched Lucas become instantly bored and then, in his boredom, raise the hairdryer nozzle to his open mouth. I waved madly with my free hand while mouthing, 'Don't do that!'

I caught his eye and he stopped, just before his lips wrapped round the nozzle. He suddenly realised what he was doing, took the hairdryer away from his mouth and burst out laughing. I hit my forehead with my hand and looked aghast in exactly the same manner that he does with me when he thinks I've done something stupid.

Afterwards, I wondered why I hadn't simply shouted at him. He could have died because I was being polite to Edith.

Sunday 27th October
Housework. Hoovering. Cleaning the bathroom. Dusting. Dreary. It makes a huge difference not having Tillie doing her fair share. It also makes a huge difference to the amount of dust: there's far less. Who'd have thought that one person's absence could have such an impact?

Monday 28th October
George and I are unhinged at the moment. I blame it on Tillie. Her departure has shifted the usual equilibrium.

George, who was appalled at the waste of windfall apples in Suffolk, is picking up every apple in our garden. He has filled all the shelves in the garden shed: cookers on one side, eaters on the other. Today he moved on to the kitchen. By lunchtime, every surface was covered.

I asked him what he plans to do with them. He says he'll cook an apple crumble. I pointed out that he needs just eight large apples for that, while we must have about four hundred in the kitchen alone. He hasn't started cooking yet because he's too busy picking the produce.

And me? I'm spending hours wandering up and down the high street in search of clothes I don't need. My capsule wardrobe is perfect. But I'm sad about Tillie, and this is what I do when I need comforting. I've bought one jumper, two long-sleeved tops, a dress and four thermal vests. I know these are all surplus. I'm just trying to plug the gaping hole left by her not being here. I know it won't work, but I'm doing it anyway.

Tuesday 29th October
George has been miserable for almost ten days with headaches, stomach pains and – oddly – sore feet.

But tonight he was better. He smiled continuously for an hour. He laughed and the light came back into his eyes. Why? Because we had a Skype call with Tillie.

She was full of her usual bounce and energy, bursting with things to tell us – lectures she'd been to, tutorials she hadn't understood, parties that lasted from sunset to sunrise, and meals at mad hours.

It feels as if she's been away for years. *(Thirty-two days, actually. Not that I'm counting.)* At the close, George looked like a new man. The lines of pain and fatigue had disappeared from his face. He smiled and was happy.

*

Following the example of Kersey's citizens, I put two boxes of apples – cookers and eaters – at the end of the drive with a 'Help Yourself' sign. By lunchtime they'd all gone. A couple of people had written thank you messages on the boxes. I refilled both boxes with more apples and they all went, too.

Wednesday 30th October
George has gone to Edith's for three days in order to tackle all the household and gardening jobs she can no longer manage.

*

I put out two more lots of apples before I left for the V&A, and asked Lucas to replenish the boxes if they emptied. He did, and then saw two men get out of a car and put all the apples and the boxes in the boot! He reckons they'll sell them. Well, that's the end of that venture. Still, at least I've got rid of all the apples in the kitchen.

Thursday 31st October
By dusk, children dressed in Halloween costumes were out trick or treating. I put a few bars of chocolate by the front door in case anyone called. They rarely do.

Ironically, would-be witches and ghouls are unnerved by the darkness of our drive, the pitch black of the bushes and the ponderous branches of the trees creaking above them. It's an empty set waiting for a Hammer horror movie.

No one called.

November

Friday 1st November

Belatedly, I phoned Great Aunt Vi to thank her for inviting George and me to her party.

'You took your time,' she retorted irritably.

I ignored the barb and focused on flattery, saying how much I liked her house-mates.

'I was always a good judge of character,' she said with smug self-assurance. 'Years of working in the civil service and meeting all branches of the public from the wise to the wily soon teaches you how to spot the good 'uns.'

Moving on to what seemed a non-contentious subject I asked, 'What have you got planned for this week?'

'That's none of your business,' she snapped with vicious anger. 'I don't know why you always think you have to pry into my life.'

The sudden switch in mood took me aback. Why does she have to be unsettlingly mercurial?

'Actually, I was showing interest in your life,' I explained reasonably. 'That's all. But if you find it insulting, I can be uninterested. Like this. Oh crikey, is that the time? I must go. Bye.'

I put the phone down and felt extremely pleased with myself. Thirty seconds later it rang. I held it to my ear, not saying a word.

'That was extremely rude of you,' said a very angry person, before she slammed her phone down.

I put mine back on its cradle. And laughed.

*

Lucas and I were glad to see George back from Edith's. We may not see much of him when he is here, but when he's not we definitely miss him.

*

Just think, this time next week I'll be starting my first day at Osbert & Small. Truly exciting! *(A bit frightening too.)*

Saturday 2nd November
Tillie's sent daily emails this week, which has been lovely. In my blind-as-a-bat way, I missed the point of this until the phone rang mid-morning.

'Mum, it's me. I'm not missing you, but I've had the strangest week waking up every morning and thinking that when I open my eyes I'll be back in my own bedroom. Then this morning I heard you shout "Breakfast" and that woke me up. But you couldn't have and I thought, "That's weird, what's going on?" As I've just realised I have no work to do this weekend, can I come home?'

'Of course you can.' *(Yes! Yes! My girl's coming home!)*

'I have to go back tomorrow, but if I leave now I could be with you by late afternoon.'

'And you could come with us to see the fireworks on the common.'

'Cool! And can we have an evening meal together and then play cards like we always do on a Saturday?'

'We were planning to do that anyway.'

'Oh, and Mum, can we go to a National Trust place tomorrow? Like we used to when Lucas and I were little?'

'Definitely.'

'I'm on my way. I'll text you when I get to London.'

I ran up the stairs shouting, 'Tillie's coming home! George! Lucas! She's coming back for the night.'

'Well, that's nice,' said George, emerging from the bathroom. He gave me a hug.

I was phenomenally excited and set about the Saturday jobs

with energy and zeal, finishing them in half the usual time. It's extraordinary what happiness can do.

At five o'clock, Tillie texted to say her train was arriving at our local station. I grabbed my coat and boots, and speed-walked up the street to meet her. And there she was, coming down it. We were like a scene from a 1940s movie. We both started running and fell into one another's outstretched arms, laughing and hugging.

Tillie was brimful of excitement and, over the evening meal, answered our myriad questions about what it's like living in Durham. She loves the city, not least of all because it's like a village: stand in the middle of it and you can see the countryside. She's established a routine of lectures, work and leisure. The work is hard, but manageable.

After dinner, we walked to the common to watch the firework display and then came home to play the new kind of whist that Arak taught us on holiday. Lucas won. It's the one card game he likes because, thus far, he's always beaten the rest of us.

Lucas, George and I were much happier this evening. Tillie's such a bright light and a joy that her good mood is infectious. Without her we are wounded and not our better selves.

Sunday 3rd November

Tillie slept in until ten – as did Lucas. After a leisurely breakfast, we drove to the National Trust's Emmetts Garden in Kent.

We have many happy memories of this place, especially when the children were much younger and we played hide and seek among the azaleas, rhododendron bushes and maple trees. But I don't think we've ever visited the garden in autumn, and the season's colours were spectacular. Tillie and I held hands or linked arms for most of the woodland walk, and when we didn't she picked sweet chestnuts with Lucas for George to cook later.

We ate lunch in the café, walked through the final part of

the garden, then headed back to London. Tillie packed her bag while I made her a picnic for the journey. The three of us walked her up to the local station – she didn't want us to take her to King's Cross.

We'd managed to fit such a lot into less than twenty-four hours and all of it without trying hard or stressing over the time. It had worked perfectly.

Sometimes life hands you an enormous gift and that was this weekend.

Monday 4th November
Tim, the elderly piano tuner, arrived for his annual appointment. As I removed the music and clutter from the top of the piano, he explained how he used to visit this house when he was a teenager.

'And just there,' he said, pointing at the alcove, 'was a pinball machine. Oh, we loved playing on that. There was a juke box *and* a pool table in this room, too.'

We worked out that this must have been in the first half of the 1960s and was three house-owners ago. Tim was initially attracted by the owners' two daughters, who were of a similar age to him. However, once he discovered the pinball machine, that became the main focus. And not just for him but quite a few of the local boys.

*

Johanna texted to ask if I could help her at Greenwich Market this weekend. Christmas shopping starts earlier each year and she needs an extra pair of hands. Replied: yes.

Tuesday 5th November
I dressed in casual clothes for the year 11 GCSE art class visit to Iggie's studio. I did wonder if the girls would think it odd that I wasn't in a more outlandish costume such as the Bonhams bohemian outfit they'd seen me in during the summer. But that

went out with the general wardrobe clear-out. And if I turned up in something similarly whacky, Iggie and Arnold would first have a good laugh and second ask what was going on. I opted for normal.

Anyway, the girls weren't interested in me. It was Iggie they'd come to see and they were ridiculously excited. They did – eventually – sit quietly and listen to what he had to say about his background, various working methods depending on who he's taking photographs of, the process of staging a shoot, selecting a final image, manipulating it if necessary and then printing it.

I talked about what it's like working with Iggie and Arnold, how we consider what image to shoot next, what props we need, how we set them up and then the hours it takes to get the photograph that Iggie's satisfied with.

At question time, a girl in the front row asked, 'Why did you choose Mrs Baxter as your model?'

Iggie looked at his feet for a moment, then switched his gaze to something outside the window before returning to the student.

'Because she came into my life by chance and she looked interesting. You can see that in the images we're making. She's fully present and, at the same time, she's completely different in each. Beyond that there's something ineffable and that intrigues me.'

It's curious, because I see it too. As do Arnold and Ann-Marie, and presumably the buyers. Yet none of us has a clue what it is.

*

George came home from work just before the Baxter household's lights-out time. It was way past the hour to celebrate Bonfire Night. In fact, Lucas and I were in our PJs. We didn't manage to celebrate last year either. The fireworks and sparklers are still under the stairs waiting to be used. God knows when.

Wednesday 6th November
Lunch with Dora. She gave a debrief of who has what ailments in her family, what their treatments are, how it's affecting them and what their chances are of a full recovery. Her diagnoses are consistently dire. And then we discussed maple syrup, Marks & Spencer, moths, longitude and latitude, and South Africa – a country that neither of us has ever visited yet which, it turns out, we have strong opinions on, including its politics, people, flora and fauna.

I gave her two bags of cooking and eating apples and, because they were far too heavy to carry, drove her home.

For the first time since she retired, I felt fine about her arriving and leaving. Perhaps, at last, I'm recovering.

Thursday 7th November
Went to Total Workout. It's almost easy-peasy these days. I can throw that lead ball around like a pro. Got on the scales afterwards.

There is no rhyme or reason as to why I gain or lose weight. The numbers rise or fall regardless of the exercise I take or the food I eat *(or don't eat)*. I'm plagued by the bad weight fairy. Why is she picking on me?

*

Tomorrow's the big day. I'm nervous. Excited too. I've laid out my clothes in readiness. Another mix-and-match job from my capsule wardrobe – smart and professional. I've tried everything on *(it fits)* and I look fine. Tillie would be proud of me.

Friday 8th November
Osbert & Small opens at ten and I was there on the dot for Sukie to let me in. She's working throughout November to show me the ropes. In December, it will be just Jeremy and me in the run-up to Christmas. Scary.

Sukie was her usual lovely self. I instantly felt like one of her oldest, most cherished friends. Jeremy greeted me with open arms, then made a small welcoming speech.

My first day was completely overwhelming. There's vast quantities of everything to learn. Sukie started with the basics: how to operate the landline and mobile phones, how to work the coffee machine *(I need a barista degree to master that alone)* and how to manage all the different types of client payments.

She went on to explain the gallery's security systems. As I've signed a secrecy agreement on that, I can't even discuss it with myself here in these private pages. Suffice to say they're discreet, sophisticated and strong. If a tank drove in the front window, it would be the one to suffer.

The three of us keep the furniture, paintings and works of art free from dust. The cleaning cupboard includes different types of dusters, brushes of every shape and size, and even a specialist hand-held vacuum cleaner which you strap round your waist and hold in two hands. Apparently it's used for tapestries and other materials. I can see I'll need another degree to manage the cleaning.

Jeremy showed me the computer and physical files he keeps for every item in the gallery. Some are small, others encyclopaedic. They provide the complete history of each art work: its provenance, whether it was commissioned and if so by whom, where it was made, when, who made it, with what materials and where they were sourced, the techniques of manufacture and finishing, what it originally sold for and through whose hands, countries and sales houses it has passed before landing in Osbert & Small. And of course, there's all the supporting paperwork to validate each piece's authenticity.

Jeremy said I should read each file and memorise as much of the contents as possible. That way I would, eventually, be able to talk knowledgeably to customers. He must have seen the horror on my face. It's not that I'm not interested. But I felt crushed just looking at the size and quantity of files. The words 'bitten off more than I can chew' danced before my eyes.

He put a calming hand on my shoulder.

'You don't have to learn everything today. It takes everyone years to master.'

He went on to explain how each file includes the item's sale price and what this can be negotiated to before referring to him.

I was comforted by a familiar face. Mr No-Name came in again to view the commode mazarine. Sukie went to talk to him this time. There's something very special about her personality. She's neither too familiar nor too formal but knows how to make each person relaxed. It's a real gift to be as lovely as she is. Anyway, despite her charms, she didn't manage to discover his name. And he still hasn't made up his mind about the piece.

By the end of the day I was exhausted, suffering from acute information overload. But I've promised myself I'll start reading the commode mazarine file next week. And maybe ask about the diptych too. There was no sign of it today.

Saturday 9th November
I wrapped up extra warm for my day at Greenwich Market. Fortunately, we were very busy selling and I didn't have time to feel the cold.

Unlike Jeremy's august emporium, there's little to learn about Johanna's vintage kitchenware, most of which I'm familiar with anyway, being of a similar vintage myself. We supplemented what we sold with more goods that Johanna had stored in boxes under the stall. In the few quiet lulls we chatted away like old friends.

She has led a completely different life from me: single, itinerant, carefree, switching careers from nurse to travel guide to book-keeper and now a seller of vintage crockery. I suppose when she's had enough of this, she'll reinvent herself again. I really admire her for that.

She's also straight as a die and paid me for my work. I tucked the money in my purse and quietly smiled to myself at my bipolar life working at opposite ends of the second-hand market. Ironically, they both pay similar rates.

Sunday 10th November
Lucas is schizophrenic about schoolwork. Most of the time he's laid-back to the point of being comatose. He's given George and me strict instructions not to hassle him about what he's doing, how he's doing it, why he's not doing more of it or any of those irritating things that parents do with their offspring. We're not to worry because, it's *all under control.*

Then an exam looms. His self-confidence and bluster drain out down his long legs. Fear sets in, followed by panic. Why? Because he hasn't done sufficient work all along. I know that. George knows that. In his heart of hearts, Lucas knows it too. But he is never ever, in one billion years, going to admit it.

Suffice to say, his GCSE French oral exam is on Tuesday and he's nowhere near ready for it. He wrote out what he's going to say and sent it to Tillie for a second opinion. She told him that it requires more work. That's the polite version. She even made some suggestions about how he can improve it. Now he's panicking. If he could ingest the French dictionary, he would.

He is, at this very moment, sitting on the loo trying to memorise what may be the French equivalent of utter dross. He doesn't have any supporting notes either. Not yet and maybe never.

Monday 11th November
Amid the worry of the French oral exam, Lucas forgot to mention that he has a GCSE history controlled assessment essay to write today. He slipped that into the conversation on the way to school. Fearing the worst and trying hard not to show my frustration with him, I asked him – calmly – if he had prepared for it over the weekend.

'Of course! What do you think I am? A numpty?'
(???!!!)
'What did you do?'
'I wrote up all the notes I could take in with me and learned the quotes.'
'And how are you feeling about it?'
'Nervous.'

I watched him slouch his way into school, weighed down by worries.

This evening, though, he burst through the front door, fired his imaginary machine gun at me, then announced that the exam had been 'ace'.

The most ace aspect of it had been several boys turning up with more than the two allotted pages of notes and, as a result, not being allowed to sit the exam.

'Never mind them. How did it go for you?'
'Just brilliant, Mum. I wrote seven pages of superb historical detail peppered with a piquancy of perfectly inserted quotations from famous figures.'
'I hope the person who marks your essay is able to recognise your genius.'
'Bound to. Now, in celebration, I'm off to make myself a hot chocolate. See yah, bladderins.'

Next: French.

*

With perfect timing, George has gone to work in the USA for a week. Transatlantic money-laundering. Just before he left, he managed to sit on his one and only pair of glasses. The lenses were intact but the metal frames were bent beyond wearing. He's bought himself an emergency pair of ready readers at Heathrow and left muggins here to take the glasses to the optician's.

Tuesday 12th November
As I was going to bed last night, Lucas announced he'd got the

squits. He's still got them now, going to the loo three times before we were due to leave for school.

At breakfast, he slipped it into the conversation that he has a GCSE chemistry practical THIS MORNING as well as his GCSE French oral this afternoon.

I phoned the school to explain he wasn't well, and that I'd bring him in for each exam and then take him home again.

Currently, it's four in the afternoon and I have been to and from Lucas's school three times. First, to take him to his chemistry exam; second, to bring him home; and third to take him for the French oral. I have to drive there once more tonight as it's parents' evening.

The chemistry practical went well, but he was just about in meltdown by the time we arrived at school this afternoon.

Ten minutes later, he came out cock-a-hoop. He'd remembered everything but one word and the French teacher – not his usual one – had remarked on his fine language skills. Let's hope it wasn't sarcasm.

*

In between trips to and from school, I took George's glasses to the optician's to see if he could mend them. The optician looked up George's record and announced, in a loud voice which combined horror with smug satisfaction, that George last had his eyes tested six years ago. I sensed all the customers behind me, who'd been browsing the racks of frames, stop and switch their attention. There was no doubt, he continued, that George's eyes would have deteriorated in the intervening years and that the lenses were completely inappropriate. Everyone gasped – apart from me. It's a shame that George is never present to witness these occasions.

The optician did manage to resurrect the glasses, and I made an appointment for George to have an eye test.

*

An email arrived from said husband who is in Connecticut. Or rather, an email popped up with a subject-line but no content:
Snow here.
George has never believed in wasting words. *(The sentence: I love you, is three words too long.)*

Lucas is mightily pissed off. He'd give his eye teeth to be there where there's snow, rather than here legging it between exams and toilets.

He's not the only one who'd like to be somewhere else.

Wednesday 13th November
Parents' evening wasn't exactly a thrill a minute. Some teachers were positive about Lucas's progress, but the majority were non-committal. The main criticism was that he doesn't give sufficiently detailed written answers to questions and frequently fails to use the particular vocabulary or phraseology expected at GCSE level.

I'm at my wits' end. Sometimes I think I should emigrate – alone – to Australia and come back when all the exams, worry and stress are over.

Thursday 14th November
Went to the gym, ordered a coffee and almond croissant, read *The Times* and cracked the fiendish-rated sudoku. Very satisfying. *(Though it won't have contributed much to The Body Beautiful Project.)*

*

A second subject-line only email arrived from George:
Still snowing.
Can't he think of anything else to say? Like: missing you. Wish you were here. Can't wait to be home. *(That last one's really stretching it.)*

Friday 15th November
Day two at Osbert & Small. I'm getting the hang of the coffee machine. I can create lattes, cappuccinos, Americanos, filtered, frothy, caffeinated or not. Well, the machine does it really. I just press the buttons. But at this rate, I'll soon be creating swirly hearts in the centre of the froth.

It's surprising how many customers would like a drink and even how many customers there are. Not that anything's selling like hotcakes. But there is a discreet turnover.

The customers are fascinating. I thought they'd all reek of money. Some do: they're well dressed, have impeccable manners and speak with plummy southern England accents. But the rest of them are, well, what can I say? Ordinary. They could be me or Sue or Dora. There's just no way of knowing who's got the cash.

When Sukie and I nipped out for a quick lunch, I quizzed her about her background. She studied history of art at Edinburgh University and then went to Christie's Education to do a postgraduate degree in art world practice. Since then she's worked for Jeremy and Hugo. She has a two-year-old daughter, Belle, and is a single mum. Belle goes to nursery while Sukie works.

Back at the gallery, I looked up the file on the commode mazarine. I can't stand the thing, but that's irrelevant. It doesn't stop me appreciating the craftsmanship and skill that has gone into its making, or the history that lies behind it. I found myself engrossed, as if reading a thriller. It suddenly struck me that memorising most of this information is not going to be a huge problem because it's gob-smackingly extraordinary. I feel like a medieval peasant peering in at a king's palace, my eyes stretched wide in awe, taking in every detail in order to be able to recount it all later to my poverty-stricken friends back home.

Anyway, I now know all there is to know about the commode mazarine and can talk about trailing lion paw sabots, foliate scrolls and flower-head ornaments with the best of them. *(As long as I can remember all this by next week and it hasn't been erased by more pressing household matters such as the contents of the shopping list.)*

In all the excitement of the commode mazarine, I quite forgot about the Rogier van der Weyden diptych. Rats. Must remember to ask next week.

Saturday 16th November
Another enjoyable morning with Johanna at Greenwich Market – selling and yacking. I was home in time to greet George back from his USA trip. Mercenary beasts that we are, Lucas and I were both hopeful of a present.

George explained that yesterday afternoon he had gone with good intentions to the local shopping mall. *(My heart leapt: George in a shopping mall! Hooray for the USA!)* But then he'd been overcome by disgust at all things materialistic and turned tail. *(My heart sank back to its usual place. Possibly lower.)*

Our 'presents' consisted of the freebies he'd picked up through the week: two packets of crisps, two bars of chocolate and two in-flight wash bags. Lucas is always thrilled by these things. He only turned his nose up at the ear defenders, pulling a face when he discovered they'd been used.

In fairness, I did receive a bunch of red carnations which George bought at the exit of our local train station. Their red hearts beat angrily against the sterile white of my kitchen. *(Just having a Sylvia Plath moment.)*

Sunday 17th November
Tillie Skyped. She was radiantly happy and that made both George and me happy too. Lucas popped his head into the camera's frame for a quick hello, then ran downstairs to the PlayStation on which he knows he can mess around uninterrupted while we chatter.

I asked her if – potentially – she'd like to work for Johanna in the Christmas holidays. As I can't manage both a Greenwich Market job and prepare for Christmas, this could be a good solution for everyone. She nearly bit my hand off.

Monday 18th November
George went for an early morning eye test and yes, he does need new lenses. He chose a frame with the optician's help. *(I'm putting my money on the optician: he may be smug but he has good taste in glasses.)*

Tuesday 19th November
Lucas's sweet sixteenth birthday. Although excited about its arrival, he wasn't prepared to wake up earlier than normal in order to open his presents and still get to school on time.

Instead, he opened them when George came home this evening. Such restraint in one so young.

Tillie sent him a frisbee, George and I gave him jeans, a tee-shirt, a book and lots of chocolates, while the rels sent him money.

I made a chocolate cake, decorated with Smarties and candles. We ate that after we'd been to Pizza Express on the high street. Since the staff know him well, they sang happy birthday before presenting him with a complementary knickerbocker glory. He was mightily embarrassed but very pleased.

The phone rang all evening with people wishing him happy birthday – including Tillie. By the end of the day, he was glowing with happiness. My beautiful boy.

Wednesday 20th November
Am worried about George. Actually, I've been worrying for some time. It's a sign of how much I'm worrying that I've committed these worries to paper.

He's home so late and so often that I'm worried he's having an affair. Could all his worries earlier in the year about me having an affair with Iggie really have been him projecting his guilt on to me? Is George capable of such tortuous thoughts or behaviour?

And what of his reaction to Harry? Or rather Debbie? Is he interested in her? Has he been hot-footing it over to west London? Is he bisexual? Or gay? Or the plus sign that appears at the end of LGBTQIA? *(And what does it stand for anyway?!)*

Also, he's been less interested in sex recently. He's never been not interested in sex. *What's* going on?

I'm thinking of hiring a detective to stalk him when he comes out of work. Alternatively, I could stalk him. *(But then his tea wouldn't be on the table when he got home, he'd wonder where I was and perhaps think I'm having an affair.)*

*

Iggie texted. Seed Gallery has sold two more photographs: *The Academic* and *The Mother* – my favourite. One has gone to a private collector overseas and the other to a collector in the UK. Wow! To think I'm collectors' material! *(A bit bizarre too.)*

Thursday 21st November
Sue phoned. She won't join us for Christmas as she always has done, since she and Harry are off to Mauritius for alternative festivities.

'Does "alternative" mean Debbie's coming along too?' I asked mock-innocently.

'Actually no,' she replied. 'It means we'll be taking yoga classes in the morning and having therapies in the afternoon.'

'And what will you be doing on an evening?'

'Mind your own business, you nosey old prude!'

There was an edge to her tone.

'Blimey! I was only trying to be funny!'

'Well, you're not, so stop it,' she continued crossly. 'Being a transvestite does not affect Harry's sexuality one iota. Let me tell you, he's all man.'

(Whoa! TMI! I hadn't asked for all this. Really, I had only been teasing. But perhaps I shouldn't have.)

'Sue, I honestly didn't mean to imply anything. I apologise. I think Harry's terrific. If anything, I'm a tad jealous of what you both have. Of course, I love George but when you've been together for two centuries, most of the gloss has gone. And for you two it's shiny new.'

My apology seemed to mollify her.

I wouldn't mind Christmas in Mauritius. Or afternoon therapies. Or even sex in a hot climate. *(Though I doubt George would believe that. And I'm still worrying about what's going on with him.)*

Friday 22nd November

A steady number of people stop to look in Osbert & Small's window. One or two at any given time. But today, as I approached, there was a small crowd of seven or eight, peering at something just beyond their usual line of vision. I sidled up and joined them, curious to see what had caught their attention.

It was the diptych! And it was displayed exactly as I'd suggested to Jeremy. A metre-wide, floor-to-ceiling, cream coloured 'wall' had been placed in the centre of the window and on it he'd hung the diptych just above the normal sight-line – at a height usual for private devotional paintings in medieval times. He'd put a single spotlight on it, and it shone.

My idea had worked. I felt both proud and pleased.

'What do you think?' asked Jeremy as I stepped through the doorway.

'Casting aside all modesty for just two ticks, I think it looks brilliant,' I replied, smiling.

'Hugo and I put it up on Sunday. Since then, we've never had as many people attracted to our gallery window. Nor had as many come in.'

'Crikey.'

'And our sales are up too. It's worked an absolute treat. And all thanks to you.'

'Crikey. Again.'

I didn't know what to say. I'm not used to compliments coming thick and fast. The usual rate is about one every six months.

'And it's great timing being near Christmas. Commercially, it ticks all the boxes.'

'I'm really pleased for you, Jeremy. It's lovely when things go well.'

'Which makes it all the more important to get the new website up. It's going live in December. We'll launch it along with our Christmas party. I told all our customers about the party in the autumn newsletter, but we'll send out the invites today. First, though, you need to nip along to Ellis Hatcher's photographer to have your image taken for the website.' He handed me an address in Soho. 'Then when you get back here, write a description about your background and send it to the designers.'

The visit to the photographer's was quick and easy: I felt like an old hand after all the work with Iggie and Arnold.

Back at Osbert & Small, and to give me an idea what to write, I asked Sukie what she'd composed. She found the file and turned the computer screen in order for me to read it. It was the usual stuff: education, specialist professional interests and career experience. But what caught my attention was her name. Sukie Rothschild. *Rothschild?!*

'So,' I questioned, choosing my words carefully, 'are you part of the famous, centuries-old, international, hugely rich Rothschild family?'

She smiled that lovely disarming smile. 'Yes. But I'm an outlier on the very far reaches. I'm not weighed down with money.'

I considered this for a moment or two. There's a very simple way of working out someone's worth in London.

'Where do you live?'

'Chelsea.'

'In a hovel?'

She laughed.

'No. I have a nice home.'

'But not that poor either.'

She smiled again, and I smiled back because even if I was bitter and twisted and jealous of rich people *(which I'm not, though I am amazed at how much money some of them have)* I could never think ill of Sukie. *(But am I the only person round here who is ordinary?)*

I wrote my blurb for the website:

Jill Baxter studied graphic design and spent many years working with international consultancies creating magazine and web designs. She is studying art history – Late Renaissance to Baroque – at London's V&A museum. Her interests provide a complementary overlap with those of Osbert & Small's, where she is the new member of the team, available every Friday.

It makes me sound half-decent. Jeremy read it and turned to me.

'You left out your work with Iggie Aitchison.'

'How do you know about that?' I asked, surprised. I'd never mentioned it to him as it seemed irrelevant.

'Because,' he said smiling, 'Hugo and I went to Frieze and saw those extraordinary portraits he's made of you.'

A thought flashed through my mind that they'd been the buyers of one of the portraits. *(I wasn't sure how I felt about that.)* The same idea must have raced through Jeremy's mind.

'We haven't bought one,' he said. And then, grinning mischievously from ear to ear, added, 'Yet.'

I included a new sentence:

Currently she is working with Iggie Aitchison, the well-known contemporary photographer, on a series of portraits. In addition, she is studying art history etc etc

Jeremy gave his approval and now the file is with Ellis Hatcher.

I printed out all the Christmas address labels, stuffed the invitations in the envelopes, posted them and that was that. Another day in the world of antiques.

*

Googled 'Private Detectives' to find out how much it will cost to have George followed. S'truth! What a lot of money! And what a waste if it turns out he's not having an affair!

Saturday 23rd November
Despite being extremely tired *(Fridays are amazing but draining days – how can learning be completely exhausting?)* I hauled myself out of bed and made it over to Johanna's stall.

I tackled the issue of December. Johanna needs help but, as I'll need whatever spare time I have to prepare for our family's celebrations, I can't give it. I suggested Tillie would be happy to work for her and explained that she's had sales experience in Morrisons *(if that's what you can call stacking shelves).*

'She will be perfect,' Johanna replied with confidence, as if she'd known Tillie all her life when in fact she'd never met her. 'But I want you to promise me one thing.'

'What?' I asked, surprised.

'That you return in the new year after she's gone back to university.'

'Oh, I'd love that!' I told her, pleased that she thinks there's more we can do beyond the festive season.

And then I tackled the next subject. She listened carefully, we discussed the date, logistics and timing, and then she agreed. Perfect.

*

Tried following different people to and from Greenwich,

testing the detective skills needed to do the same with George. It turns out I have the attention span of a gnat. I'm too easily distracted by shop windows, other people and traffic lights.

Decided I couldn't take the strain any more.

'George,' I said, after we'd finished the evening meal and Lucas had gone upstairs. 'Are you having an affair?'

He looked me in the eyes.

'No.'

I paused.

'Sure?'

'Sure.'

The kitchen clock ticked. Five long seconds elapsed.

'Why are you asking?' he enquired.

'Because frequently you're home late. Because you're not interested in sex. Because you acted strangely with Harry and I thought you might have swapped sexual sides. Because you're not the same.'

He raised his eyebrows and sighed.

'There's a lot on at work. All legal, not sexual.'

'But what about Harry? I mean, Debbie. You kissed her hand. I saw the look in your eyes. You called her "darling".'

'And you think it's significant?'

'It could be. You don't kiss my hand and call me "darling".'

'You're jealous of a transvestite?'

'Stop it! You know that's not what I mean. It's just not the kind of thing I'd expect you to do. Also, your eyes changed. They became soft. They became ...' I was searching for the right word. 'Loving.' And then I felt really upset because if they ever did that with me, I missed it.

He waited, his fingers resting on the side of the table, the forefingers lifting and falling with a gentle motion.

'I was playing along. Nothing more, nothing less. Harry was having fun as Debbie, I was having a moment's fun with her.'

'But what about your eyes?'

'I don't know what happened with my eyes. They felt the same.'

'Well, they weren't.'

He shrugged his shoulders, defeated, as if everything was beyond him. As it was beyond me too.

'Don't forget,' I said quietly but firmly, 'that I am your wife.'

'As if I could forget.'

Then he smiled and reached out his hand across the table to mine.

'And as for not being interested in sex, I'm just too tired from the demands of my job.'

'Truly?'

'Truly.'

'Does that mean I don't need to pay a private detective to follow you? Or do it myself?'

'Definitely not.'

*

Washed up, went to bed and made mad passionate love. *(Will that solve anything?)*

Sunday 24th November

If it's not one thing, it's another. Crisis talks over breakfast: we're all depressed about how long it takes to clean the house without Tillie. We took an executive decision: we'll clean half the house one week and the other half the next, reverting back to the original schedule once she's home and contributing to the dirt. We put the new plan into effect this afternoon and it was better. *(It was even better when Dora did it.)*

*

Am worrying whether – or not – George is lying.

Monday 25th November
As I had an early dental appointment and needed to leave home before the school run, Lucas caught the bus. He left ten minutes after me, locked the front door, then noticed three police cars parked at the bottom of the drive. He sauntered past, hoping he'd find out what was going on. Two policemen, wearing blue gloves, were searching the public bin that sits outside next door's house, while several others looked on.

'Got it!' said one, and he pulled out a brick-sized package wrapped in brown paper and cellophane.

'And here's another,' remarked the second policeman, holding an identical package.

'Drugs,' announced Lucas this evening when he told me. 'Presumably the bin's a drop-off point. We've been living in the centre of an illegal drugs empire and not known it! How cool is that!'

He texted Tillie, who was suitably impressed.

*

No dental work needed. Phew.

*

Can't stand worrying over George and his possible mendacity. Have decided to opt for a simple *(possibly blind-eyed)* life and believe him.

Tuesday 26th November
Back to Iggie's studio to continue the series of images. He's aiming for a set of eight. Five down, three to go. Today's image is me as a great niece.

Johanna arrived promptly in her van and, between the four of us, we unloaded all the Wedgwood. We stacked the pieces on the floor around the space where I would pose, sitting cross-legged the crockery towering either side of me. After that, Johanna left to scout round the local charity shops.

I'd brought the box of cards and letters which Great Aunt Vi had sent earlier in the year. These we mounted on the photographic 'wall' behind me, alternating the picture side of one card with the written side of another.

Surrounded by symbols of my relationship with Great Aunt Vi, I sat trying to capture a look of love and frustration – which is how I feel about the Aged A. It was impossible. We looked at the stills and for once I just looked silly: gormless and confused.

For the next attempt, I closed my eyes and thought about her, seeking a mindful meditative state. And I stayed like that, semi-comatose until Iggie said he'd finished.

Afterwards it's a little like sweetie time. The three of us gather round his computer to see what treats he's captured.

Oh, but sometimes I don't like what he does. I don't like what he sees. Great Aunt Vi provokes many things in me: love, sympathy, anger, frustration, irritation, hurt and occasionally bitterness. But not bliss. Not ever, never bliss. And yet there it was on my face.

All I can put it down to is the meditation. Not Great Aunt Vi. *(And I wasn't even meditating on her being dead! And how cruel a comment is that?)*

Johanna returned, just as we were dismantling everything. As we carefully put the final box of Wedgwood in her van, I asked, 'When are you going to sell it?'

'Next spring, at Bazaar Berlin.'

She saw my nonplussed expression and explained, 'It's an annual fair for arts and crafts including vintage-ware. The Wedgwood is going to be the centrepiece for my stall. I hope you'll come and help!'

It took me a couple of seconds to realise what she'd said.

'Go to Berlin with you to sell Great Aunt Vi's Wedgwood? Really?'

'Of course!'

'Oh, Johanna, I'd love to! Thank you. I've never been to Berlin.'

'We can stay in my apartment and, on an evening, I can show you the city.'

Cool! *(As the kids would say.)*

I couldn't wait to tell George and texted him on the way home.

He replied with his usual subject-line only message: *Portfolio*.

He's described it exactly! I'm building a portfolio of jobs. It's the new way of working and I'm right there on the cusp of the curve!

*

The elation didn't last long. Tillie Skyped and for once she wasn't on form. She was overwhelmed at the weekend, when a combination of fatigue and problems with an essay on Beowulf had left her weepy and low. She claimed to be back to normal, but I spotted the odd moment of watery eyes. I'll be very glad when the term is over and she's back home where she can rest and I can look after her. Seventeen more days.

Oh, I do miss her. It's all very well telling everyone that I'm fine and that everything goes on as usual. It doesn't and it's complete bollocks. A major part of me is limping through life pretending all is well, but desperately waiting to see my golden girl.

Wednesday 27th November

By chance, at the V&A, I saw the lecture list for the twentieth century course. I was horrified to see that branding, the subject on which I've spent thirty-three years of my life, is discussed in just one hour. This slight approach to a substantial topic made me realise just how superficial all our lectures must be. Of course, if you have one hour then you can only say the most basic things. But it was a revelation to realise that what we're probably getting in every lecture is the idiot's guide.

Thursday 28th November

Another epiphany. I watched Lucas walk on stage at the school concert to play in the percussion group and saw myself. Never before have I seen myself in him. His face and physique have always been variants of George. But his diffidence, the physical way in which he carries that uncertainty combined with his determination to do his best – it's all me. I smiled from the pure joy of realising we are mother and son, son and mother.

This coincides with the two of us enjoying one another's company as we forge a fresh relationship in Tillie's absence. We have a gun fight most afternoons when he arrives home from school. A text book, jammed into his shoulder, becomes his automatic weapon. I whip the shapers out of my boots, firing my two machine guns at him from my hiding place at the turn of the basement stairs. We carry on like this until one of us runs out of ammunition or dies, the body jerking in the last throes of a dramatic death.

After a suitable pause, we get up and go to the kitchen. I make a cup of tea, and he makes a mug of hot chocolate topped with a spectacular whirl of cream.

Friday 29th November

My last day with Sukie. It's nerve-wracking to think that next week, it'll be just me and Jeremy. I know I can ask him anything, but somehow it's easier to ask Sukie. She keeps telling me I'll be fine, and I keep trying to believe her.

Today, she showed me how to dust and clean the works of art, whether paintings or ceramics. The paintings are mostly large and sturdy so, as long as you hold one corner steady, there's not a lot that can go wrong. But the ceramics are another matter.

We emptied a display cabinet, dusting each item and then putting it back. There were two matching platters which featured overlapping large leaves from different plants, some of which extended beyond the natural edge of the plate. They were painted in vibrant, bright colours – greens and yellows – so modern in their design that they could have been made in the 1950s, though they were actually from the eighteenth century. George would love them and, in a moment of happiness and generosity, I thought perhaps I could push the boat out this year and buy them for his Christmas present.

Jeremy was hovering nearby.

'I love these,' I told him as I held one at arms' length. 'They're incredibly contemporary.'

He came over.

'Beautiful aren't they.'

Nothing has a price on it. You have to look in the file for that, but I was thinking perhaps a couple of thousand pounds for the pair. I've never, ever spent that much on George. For the last decade my budget has hovered around £40. But I could lash out.

'How much are they?' I asked.

Jeremy took the platter and admired it. Then turning to me he said, '£22,000.'

(What????)

'Each.'

(Well, that puts paid to my idea of generosity.)

Reading my mind, he went on, 'It's because they're extremely rare and in mint condition.' He turned the platter over. 'In addition, there's this.'

The base included the symbol of a red anchor.

'It's one of the marks of the Chelsea porcelain factory, founded in 1745 and the first important porcelain manufacturer in England. The red anchor means it was made some time between 1752 and 1756. It's one of the most forged marks because it's easy to copy. One must always be sure to have a rock-solid provenance for each piece.'

The moment he showed the red anchor, my heart sank.

'Do you know what, Jeremy? If I'd been better informed earlier this year and while it was for sale with The Five Ls charity shop, I'd have got hold of that wretched glass vase that you and I saw in Bonhams, and I'd have looked for a maker's mark. Then I'd have known it was Tiffany – and bought it. And instead of Great Aunt Vi selling it for a ridiculous sum in aid of some misplaced llamas, it would be sitting on the chest of drawers in my bedroom. Or I'd have sold it and be wallowing in money.' *(Enough to pay for those two Chelsea porcelain platters. Oh, insult piled on injury.)*

Jeremy looked at me, appraising what I'd said. Sukie stood quietly at his side.

'Ah. I'm guessing that Miss Violet Harmondsworth, generous donor to The Five Ls, is your venerable great aunt?'

I nodded. The happiness I'd felt just a few minutes earlier, anticipating a generous purchase for George's Christmas, had leaked out. I was as flat as a pancake.

'And the reason why you were fiddling with your shoes in the auction room and actually hiding from what might have been a two-way screen, was because she wasn't supposed to know that you knew about the vase?'

I stretched my lips in a defeated grin.

'How *did* you know?' he asked.

I sighed and explained about the whole sorry saga: Great Aunt Vi's Machiavellian character, her clear-out, her offering me the chance to choose a memento followed by her prompt denial of it, Sue's detective work, her contact with The Five Ls, the local antique dealer, Bonhams' identification that Great Aunt Vi's vase was Tiffany, and then its sale.

I'd run out of things to say. Jeremy let the silence hang, carefully replacing the two platters in the cabinet. Sukie was looking at the floor, her face a portrait of sorrow.

'Well!' Jeremy remarked turning back to me and in the jolliest voice imaginable given the circumstances said, 'You have nothing to berate yourself about. Tiffany glassware is about the most difficult to identify in the whole of the antiques world.'

I was taken aback.

'Really?'

'There's no single, simple way of identifying it. Yes, some of his pieces were signed, but signatures are easy to reproduce and they don't signify authenticity. You can find Tiffany pieces marked L.C.T or L.C. Tiffany Favrile., Inc or Louis C. Tiffany Favrile Inc, or with numbers, or numbers and a letter prefix, or numbers and a letter suffix. And any of those could be fake, too. You have to be an expert and know what you're looking for: the product, the shape, the colour, the finish, the lustre, the provenance. Your Great Aunt Vi hadn't a clue, had she?'

I shook my head. 'No. But the local antique dealer looked at the vase's base and made an offer on it.'

'How much?' Jeremy asked.

'A tenner.'

'He was making a mean punt. If he'd thought it was the real thing, he'd have offered more. It was pure luck that what was a beautiful piece of glassware was identified as a beautiful piece of Tiffany glassware.'

'Two pieces, actually. She'd always kept another matching vase hidden. Her logic was that if, as children, one of us broke one vase she'd still have the other. She's since sold the second vase and used the proceeds to buy herself a mouth-wateringly wonderful contemporary apartment full of famous designers' furniture and accessories.'

Jeremy's jaw actually dropped. But not for long.

'Antique story of the year!' he yelled, recovering himself. And then roared with laughter.

Sukie looked up at me and started smiling. It was a kind smile. A consolatory smile. A smile that acknowledged I'd been stuffed and there was nothing I could ever have done about it. And then she started laughing too because Jeremy's laugh was outrageous and infectious. Before I knew it, I'd joined in: Jeremy looked funny, and I suddenly saw that the story was both ridiculous and comic too.

As we calmed down, something changed in me. I felt lighter, happier. I was free. Of anger, sorrow, guilt and acrimony. It wasn't my fault. I hadn't made a mistake. It was just life.

Jeremy pulled a beautiful, deep blue silk handkerchief from his top pocket, wiped his eyes and blew his nose.

'Of course, Sukie and I will never tell a soul,' he said soberly. 'Discretion is all.'

'Oh, it's all out in the open,' I said breezily. 'Great Aunt Vi has told me about both vases.'

'No, it's not,' he said. 'It *demands* discretion. She does not want the world's media landing on her doorstep. And the buyer requires privacy too. It will go no further than these four walls.'

I was surprised. Did it really require that much prudence? I thought of the taxi driver putting the word out to all the local thieves that she had nothing else worth stealing. The local and not-so-local burglars would never believe that story if they heard about the second Tiffany vase. Jeremy was right.

'Thank you,' I said. 'Thank you for enlightening me on all these matters. I feel much better now.'

'My pleasure!' he replied. Then he turned to the display cabinet and locked it.

*

It's not the end of Sukie and me. We're friends now. We'll see one another at the Christmas party and we've agreed to meet socially next year. A Baxter and a Rothschild. Now there's a combination.

Saturday 30th November
George and I went to collect his new glasses. They suit him. He moved his head around to take in both the interior of the

optician's and the shops beyond. A smile spread across his face.

'I can see everything clearly. It's amazing. I feel like a bionic man.'

He insisted we walk up and down the high street, where he described all the notices and adverts that we passed with the awe of a blind man whose vision has been restored.

December

Sunday 1st December
My Christmas season starts today with all the extra jobs that, somehow, must be crammed in between all my other commitments. *(How?)* What with Iggie, Jeremy and the V&A combined with the boring, regular household jobs, there's not a moment to spare. Tasks include:

1. Write Christmas cards and send the overseas ones before final posting date
2. Wrap presents, post and distribute as necessary
3. Plan what to cook pre-Christmas, write shopping list, buy and cook
4. Plan what to cook for Christmas Day and beyond, write shopping list etc etc
5. Put decorations up.

Oh, to be a carefree child again and have an adult manage everything.

Edith is coming for Christmas, even if Sue isn't. I wondered, for a millisecond, if I should invite Great Aunt Vi. In mitigation, I did tell her several years ago that she has an open invitation. *(Please God, don't let her take it up this year.)*

First, though, I gave Lucas his Advent calendar. Tillie texted to say she was thrilled I'd sent one to her.

Monday 2nd December
Cyber Monday and I'm totally smug. My self-satisfied smile stretches from one ear to the other. I bought nearly all the presents throughout the year *(mostly in the sales)* and put them

in the present box with yellow Post-It notes attached saying who they're for. There's not much more I need to purchase.

I told George he can buy Edith's presents. *(God help her.)* The last time I did this, he spent ten minutes on the phone to The White Company and then collapsed in a chair, exhausted by his contribution to the festive season.

Tuesday 3rd December
Lucas's drum exam. I never mention he plays the drums, because he doesn't. That is, he goes to the lessons but never practises in between. Despite this – and amazingly – he has progressed to Grade 5.

Late morning, I picked him up from school and drove to the exam centre. He was so excessively nervous, I thought he would faint from hyperventilation.

'Look, I can't cope with driving and you passing out at the same time,' I said with the kind of sympathy only a parent can show. 'Breathe slowly and deeply and calm down.'

He was shaking by the time we arrived. I couldn't imagine how he'd hold the drumsticks.

His teacher took him to a practice room while I sat alone in the waiting area opposite a vending machine. I stared at it for a few minutes, then gave up and inserted every coin I could find in my handbag. A Twix, a Mars bar and a Milky Way dropped out. I checked no one was looking, then gave the machine a whacking good kick simply for being there. A moment's silence and a Cadbury's chocolate bar dropped down. I stuffed it in my handbag. Emergency rations. I ate the rest, all sickeningly sweet. *(Sod The Body Beautiful Project.)*

Lucas said the exam went OK apart from the play-along where he gave a drum accompaniment to an unknown piano piece performed by the examiner. He and the examiner started and ended together but went their separate ways in between. *(A metaphor for so much of life.)*

*

Weighed myself at bedtime. Fat loves my body: it sticks around. Slumped into a deep depression.

Wednesday 4th December
Osbert & Small's Christmas party. I was there for six o'clock, ready to provide whatever help was needed. Except it wasn't.

Jeremy and Hugo had hired caterers. Pretty young things – female and male – wafted their ways round the room carrying silver salvers on which were placed various drinks, or mouth-watering and theatrically styled canapés. But best of all was the gallery. Jeremy and Hugo had decorated it, and all I can say is they have breathtakingly good taste based on the concept of less is more.

The Christmas tree was amazing. Not just because it was the real thing *(unlike at chez nous, not that it's up yet)* but because of the 'baubles'. Each was a miniature replica of an item in the gallery. They included a petite silver and gold standing cup and cover; an exquisite emerald and diamond snuffbox; a portrait of Hortense Mancine, Duchesse de Mazarin which would fit in the palm of a hand; a small alabaster portrait of Louis XIV of France looking suitably imperious; a bronze statue of Henry IV on horseback; a pixie-sized pair of gauntlets complete with articulated joints; a mini-armchair with gilded frame and scarlet silk damask upholstery; and a diddly copy of the Rogier van der Weyden diptych with the world's tiniest hinges.

I presume everything's a cheap and cheerful copy, though the light did bounce off the 'diamonds' on the snuffbox in a disconcerting way.

The rest of the room had been carefully styled. Bowls of oranges pierced with cloves sent out a delicious mixture of scents. Over-sized snowflakes covered the tops of antique furniture. Lamps had been lit and carefully placed with the result that the room looked inviting and cosy.

In the centre of the gallery was an Apple laptop, showing Osbert & Small's new website, the pages gently sliding from one to another. And what a difference! The identity has been resolved, the pages are uncluttered, the content flows, the products look tantalising and the information level is just right. Best of all, there is a photograph and information about the oldest junior in the universe: *moi*.

Sukie, Jeremy, Hugo and I had a quick meeting. Sukie and I were required to talk to as many clients as possible; Jeremy and Hugo would introduce us.

Don't ask me for names. I met an inordinate number of people and was reeling. By the end of the evening, several were far jollier than when they'd arrived. In fact, we had to move some of the more easily breakable ceramics for fear they might be knocked over.

I did recognise one person: Melanie Adams, my course director at the V&A.

'This is the best party of the Christmas season,' she said, kissing my cheek. 'It's an outstanding gallery. Have you seen the Rogier van der Weyden in the window?'

'Not just seen it but held it.'

She looked surprised. Then she leaned closer and asked conspiratorially, 'Are you going to buy it?'

I managed to keep a poker face.

'Not this week.'

'Can I take it you're a client?'

She was angling for an answer.

'I work here.'

'No! For how long?'

'A month.'

'You dark horse. And you never told us!'

Actually, I've hardly told anyone. Just Fay, Johanna, Iggie and Arnold – beyond George and the children. For the moment I'm hugging the news to myself, savouring the joy.

But, I suppose, in some minor way I was launched tonight – along with the website and the Rogier van der Weyden diptych which shone, thanks to the spotlight, like a beacon in the dark, winter street.

All evening Hugo and Jeremy introduced me to clients as 'one of us.' I walked home on air.

Thursday 5th December
As Fat Face is Tillie's kind of shop, I went there to buy her birthday presents. I wrapped the skirt and top, added a card and some money, then posted the lot. With a bit of luck, they'll be there for Monday.

I had hoped to share the day with her, but she didn't invite me. Still, it's the end of term next Friday. Can't wait.

Friday 6th December
No Sukie as my side-kick and prop. Just Jeremy and me. Luckily, the day went well. Jeremy, whose temperament is never less than sunny, was positively glowing when I arrived.

'I've done it,' he announced, beaming.

'Done what?' I asked, taking off my coat and hanging it in the back room.

'I've sold the diptych.'

I came out and glanced at the window to make sure I hadn't missed something. It was still there.

'That didn't take long.'

'I had three potential buyers.'

'How did you resolve that?'

'As in an auction. They kept outbidding each other until only one was left. And he, she, or it, is now the happy owner.'

'You don't know who bought it?'

'Of course I do, it's just that I can't say,' he said, adding darkly, 'I can tell you it's an individual and not an institution.'

'How come it's still in the window?' I asked.

'We agreed it would stay here until the close of Christmas Eve. It's part and parcel of our Christmas decorations and a great draw for customers.'

I thought about the significance of its departure date.

'You're telling me that someone has spent £10 million on someone else's Christmas present?'

He raised his eyebrows and smiled, drawing an imaginary zip across his lips.

'Well, I'm only saying this because there's just you and me in the gallery right now but, bloody hell! Who gives a multi-million pound Christmas gift? I mean, what kind of cracker's going to look like it's worth pulling with the Christmas dinner after that?'

He pursed his lips and tilted his head from side to side, considering.

'Probably one with a hefty diamond as the novelty.'

I shook my head. He knew people *(and possibly I knew them too from the Christmas party but didn't know that I knew them)* who were wealthy beyond my wildest imaginings.

'Fun, isn't it?' he remarked, smiling.

*

We were kept busy almost all day. Clients *('Not customers, Jill')* were Christmas shopping. Most bought relatively modest gifts *(relative in relation to the price of the Rogier van der Weyden diptych)* in the thousands and tens of thousands of pounds. *(It's shocking how quickly I've come to think of thousands of pounds as not being a huge sum when I'm here.)*

In a post-prandial lull, I asked about the look-alike 'antique' ornaments on the Christmas tree.

'Exquisite, aren't they?' Jeremy remarked, walking over to the tree and admiring them. 'They're all perfect, authentic and unique copies created, wherever possible, in the same materials as the originals.'

'You mean the diamonds are real diamonds?'

I had to check because it was hard to believe.

'Oh, yes. Hugo and I have everything copied the moment it arrives. We're creating a collection of a collection. We source eminent craftspeople from around the globe. Each Christmas, we show the best of this year's miniatures on the tree. And then they go into a bank vault.'

I looked at him, then I looked round the gallery with its handsome and valuable works, absorbing all he'd said.

'Jeremy, that's the smartest, cleverest thing I've ever heard of.'

He smiled.

'Just think: every client who's ever bought from you will want the miniature. Everyone who's seen a sale fall through their hands will want the miniature. Every collector of each artist or maker will want the miniature. Collectors of miniatures will want a miniature. You're creating the equivalent of the V&A's Baroque to Rococo gallery in miniature. It's utterly brilliant.'

'Of course, it's expensive,' he added soberly. 'It makes a huge hole in our profits, but you could say it's a sort of pension.'

My mind was racing.

'You must have hundreds of them. How many years have you been trading? They'll be worth a fortune.'

'We're hoping so.'

'Jeremy, you're a genius.'

'Hugo too,' he added modestly. 'I couldn't do anything without Hugo.'

Saturday 7th December
Spent the morning with Johanna at Greenwich. Then raced home to start the epic task of writing Christmas cards, tackled the pile of ironing and made the evening meal. Half a day in paradise, the other at the coal face.

Sunday 8th December
Lucas, George and I are getting along much better than we have in a very long time. Probably since Tillie left home. *(Sad,*

but true.) It's not that we didn't get on well before, but we're definitely getting on better now. Having lived under Tillie's shadow all his life, Lucas can now be his own person. His own peculiar, eccentric, madcap and happy person.

It's ironic that, just as we work out how to live together, Tillie's about to burst back upon the scene.

Monday 9th December
Tillie's nineteenth birthday. We sang 'Happy Birthday' down the phone, ending in a drum-roll from Lucas. She's going out this evening with a group of friends for a celebratory meal.

The oddest thing was not making a birthday cake, preparing a birthday tea or celebrating with her. It felt completely wrong.

Tuesday 10th December
As per usual, I was on my own at Lucas's school's Christmas concert. George was still at work. Fortunately, I'm good friends with another of the solo parents – Adam's dad, Neil. He and his wife have divorced, spectacularly acrimoniously. They both arrive separately at school events and never speak. I do talk to her as well, though obviously not when he's near. *(Motto: never take sides.)*

Shockingly, and because I'm not used to sustaining such long breaths, I felt faint after a few verses of 'The First Noel'. Fortunately for Neil, I didn't faint. He's a small slight man and I might have done him in.

Wednesday 11th December
End of term at the V&A. Melanie Adams arrived to introduce the day.

'Before our final day of lectures, I have some very special news. One of your fellow students has accepted a job with Osbert & Small on Pall Mall. I'm sure many of you know this antiques gallery, not least of all because it specialises in art works from part of our period. The owners, Jeremy Osbert and Hugo Small, are shrewd buyers, always managing to purchase the very finest example of a particular piece of furniture, painting or art work. But, most important of all, let me tell you who our talented student is.'

She paused for effect. People were turning to their neighbours or looking around to see who it could be. I'd gone brick red and was sitting stock still.

'It's Jill Baxter who's at the back of the room. Stand up, Jill, in order for us all to see you.'

Everyone started applauding. Instantly, a vision of Jeremy and Hugo appeared in my mind. They were both smiling at me in an encouraging way, though there was a hint of steeliness in Hugo's eyes.

'Thank you,' I said, switching to professional mode. 'Of course, I'd never have got the job without the knowledge I've gained from this and the previous course I studied here at the V&A. I owe a debt of gratitude to Melanie and her colleagues. Melanie's description of Osbert & Small is correct. It houses an extraordinary collection of art works, breathtaking in their quality, rarity and provenance. I work there on a Friday. If you'd like to visit, do call in. If you want a more informed conversation, talk to Jeremy Osbert who is there Monday to Saturday.'

As I sat down, Annabel leaned over and took my left hand in hers. 'Why didn't you tell *me*?' she asked.

'Because I've only just started working there and I didn't want to say anything here because it might seem like showing off. Melanie only found out by chance.'

At lunch, I was surrounded by people congratulating me and wanting to know more. My popularity, which has been limited, reached an all-time high.

Thursday 12th December
I'd just fed the shop-bought Christmas cake eight tablespoons

of brandy in an effort to make it taste home-made and was feeding myself the ninth when the phone rang.

'I thought you should know about Christmas,' said a sprightly voice from Leicester.

(Oh, please God, I know this is a mean thought in a generous season, but don't let her come here.)

'I'm spending Christmas with Pippa, Matt and the girls.'

(Thank you, thank you.)

'I can't imagine a nicer family or better children,' she continued.

(I don't care how rude you are, Great Aunt Vi because God has answered my prayers. You're not staying with us and that's all that matters.)

'Well, that's lovely,' I replied.

(Dear God, just one more request. Please let Pippa and her family only see the good side of Great Aunt Vi, and may we be protected from her forevermore. Thank you. Amen.)

'I've posted the Christmas presents to you,' she went on. 'It's the usual things – cards and money for the children.'

She hung up.

And that's how, this year, I got off scot-free.

Friday 13th December

Tillie's final day of term. I sang all the way through making the breakfast, getting dressed, walking to the station and even at work. Jeremy raised a questioning eyebrow.

'I've got Tillie-itis. She's coming home.'

He smiled and nodded understandingly.

Today's lesson at Osbert & Small was on how to find antique 'gems'. Long story short: it's like looking for a needle in a haystack. And Jeremy turns out to be rather good at it: a combination of skill and instinct.

*

By early evening, I was stood at the end of platform four at

King's Cross, hopping from one foot to the other and grinning madly with wild excitement, waiting for Tillie's train. It pulled in and vast numbers of people poured out. Eventually, I spotted her, pushed my way through the crowd and threw my arms around her at the same moment she threw hers around me.

'Oh, Mum, I've really missed not being hugged by you,' she said, holding me tight. 'I never realised how much we cuddled one another.'

'I missed you too, Tillie,' I said, forcing back the tears. 'I missed you more than I thought possible.'

We struggled through the Underground with her various large and heavy bags which, it turns out, are stuffed full of dirty clothes.

I was about to put the first load on when Lucas burst into the kitchen.

'That's not fair – you're breaking the rules,' he declared. 'It's every man, woman and teenager for themselves in this house when it comes to washing. Tillie should do her own.'

'Oh, Lucas,' I replied. 'It's my small way of welcoming her home and treating her.'

'Well, you shouldn't. Dad and me never get treated.'

I sighed. Tillie had hardly been back five minutes and an argument had already broken out.

'It's OK, Mum,' said Tillie in a conciliatory tone. 'Lucas is right. I'll do my own.'

I stepped back and let her while Lucas looked pleased with himself. Well, he's got a point.

*

Tillie has spread her belongings across the hall, kitchen, sitting room, bedroom and bathroom. *(Was she always this messy?)* But the very good news is that she's here for an amazing thirty-one days. Thirty-one whole days. Heaven!

Saturday 14th December
Over an early breakfast, Tillie waxed lyrical about the comfort of being in her own bed, in her own bedroom, in her own home and how there's nothing quite like it. And then she headed off to Greenwich Market to work with Johanna.

The day went well for them. They sold almost everything, including all the extra items stored under the stall. Even better, Johanna has booked a stall for tomorrow and Tillie's going back to earn more money.

*

This evening, we put up the Christmas tree and decorations. Tillie and Lucas focused on the tree, hanging all the decorations we've collected over the years. George and I wound the fairy lights in and out of the stair balusters from the top to the bottom of the house, and framed paintings and photographs in every tinsel colour we could find. It looks wonderfully festive. The fairy lights twinkling in the dark are magical.

Sunday 15th December
Tillie went to Greenwich and I headed off to meet Iggie and Arnold at the studio. We aim to finish the final two photographs before Christmas by working this and next Sunday, these being the only days we can all manage.

Today's image was me as a graphic designer. I've thought about this image for weeks and, mostly, been stumped about how to portray the role. Anyone watching me work in recent years would have seen a woman sitting at a computer – looking no different from a secretary, a call handler or myriads of other administrators staring at their screens.

A graphic designer's role is that of a visual communicator. *(Ironically, the same as Iggie's.)*

Well, who knows if what the three of us created today will work but it was my best *(and only)* idea. During last week, I created a new font and made the word *Believe* out of it. With more than a fair share of jiggery-pokery – otherwise known as computer manipulation at which Arnold is particularly good – we came up with the image. I'm standing against the usual backdrop, with *Believe* printed in black on it. I'm holding open my laptop, staring at the screen from out of which hundreds of pieces of paper with the same printed word – *Believe* – are tumbling. The floor around my feet is covered in them.

As a graphic designer I always worked on projects I believed in. I put my heart and soul into the work. I believed. Yet, in the overall scheme of things, much of it was ephemeral and, in recent times, I wondered about the value of what I believed in. It was the fact that I couldn't sustain my belief that contributed to me taking this year off.

Iggie understands. He's going through a transition too – switching from commercial to artistic work. We're each trying to be true to ourselves. *(It's fortuitous that we're doing it together.)*

For years, I loved being a graphic designer. You can see that passion in the photograph and you can see too, the disbelief and dismay as I watch the words fall from the laptop. It's a photograph of not just any graphic designer but me, at the very end.

Monday 16th December

Tillie and I spent most of the day in the office, working. I kept stopping to watch her as she wrote an essay, her whole being focused on the task. In the end I gave in, walked over and put my arms around her, kissing her face. She leaned in.

'I love you, Tillie,' I said.

'I love you, too,' she answered and kissed me on the tip of my nose.

*

I'd finished ordering a few last-minute stocking-filler presents on Amazon, when the doorbell rang. It was Lucas who'd forgotten to take his key to school.

'I passed,' he said waving a piece of paper victoriously.

'Passed what?'

'The drum exam!'

'That's amazing! How do you do it when you never practise?'

'I'm just brilliant,' he replied, letting his school bag fall from his shoulder to the floor. 'You've never appreciated how smart I am. Why practise when you can pass without any effort?'

I decided now wasn't the time to remind him about his nervousness before the exam. Instead, I read the examiner's notes. Lucas had done very well on each of his three pieces. He had, however, failed the play-along. The examiner had written: 'A cacophony in which each of us played different rhythms in contrasting styles, though we did meet at the start and finish. Listening skills could be much improved. Lucas's, not mine.'

I laughed.

'Well, you did fantastically well,' I said. 'It deserves a celebration at Pizza Express. Phone your dad and tell him to meet us there after work.'

Tuesday 17th December

I'm beginning to flag and mentioned this to George.

'What's made you tired?' he asked, as if I had no excuse.

I paused in shock: why is what's glaringly obvious to me not glaringly obvious to him?

'Because I get up at quarter to seven every day and work through until ten every night. Plus, because of my day at Osbert & Small, I have to cram in four days' household management into three. Or, if I'm at Iggie's, into two. Plus, Christmas adds even more work. Plus, I'm fifty-five years old.'

He considered what I'd said and then replied grudgingly, 'Well, if you put it like that.'

We both fell silent. I simmered, feeling distinctly unappreciated, thinking about how hard I work on our home life. Meals are planned, the shopping's done and there's always food on the table or keeping warm in the oven for George when he comes home from work. The beds are changed, the bed linen washed, everyone's clothes ironed, aired and put away in cupboards or drawers. I do much of the cleaning, organise household and car repairs, find and book every holiday, and sort out all the bills. I help the children in every way I can and always go to see them in school plays and concerts. George rarely has to do anything other than work for his law firm. But that didn't quite touch it.

I sat smouldering, wondering what it was that was *really* bugging me. And then I worked it out. Yet again, George has failed to book a single day off over Christmas. He's got the statutory bank holidays but nothing else. Are we the only family in Britain who spends most of the Christmas break with one of its key members absent?

The children and I tackled him about this last Christmas and he *promised* that this year it would be different. It isn't.

I went ballistic. At the end of my tirade, George sighed and looked crestfallen. He didn't need to say anything. I know the patter and it's all true. He is one of life's workaholics. He's employed in a sector which hires workaholics. He lives in an era when, if you're lucky enough to be employed, then the contract between employer and employee takes precedence over all others. We just have to lump it.

Wednesday 18th December
Tillie went out with her friends and I started wrapping presents while listening to the Christmas CD that Lucas's school produced last year. I sang along lustily with the senior choir and wept at the beautiful soprano voices of the junior boys.

It's wonderful to have Tillie home. Life feels just right, as if everything has slotted back into place. I know it's exceptional to have her home now, but the fact is it feels normal. The exceptional part is when she's not here.

Thursday 19th December
It was Lucas's last day of term and, this evening, prize-giving at Tillie's school.

It's hard to believe she left school *this* year. It seems such a long time ago already. Still, it was lovely to see her friends back from university, each of them radiantly happy.

Tillie, like all the ex-year 13 pupils, was awarded a certificate and book token for her A-level results.

And that really is the end. Fourteen years and, finally, finished.

Friday 20th December
Two scary things and one miraculous thing happened today at Osbert & Small. The first scary thing was that in the early afternoon lull, Jeremy went to Christie's in King Street to view a forthcoming sale AND LEFT ME ON MY OWN.

I had just positioned myself at the desk trying to look composed and authoritative when in walked Mr No-Name. He headed straight for the commode mazarine. I gave him a couple of minutes then went over, introduced myself and shook his hand.

'I'm not going to tell you anything about this wonderful piece,' I said, 'because I know you know far more than I'll ever know.'

He looked at me, nodded, then turned back to the commode. We stood looking at it in silence.

Eventually he announced, still watching it as if it was an old friend, 'I've come to say goodbye.'

For a horrible moment I thought he must be dying. But he looked healthy enough.

'Are you leaving the country?' I asked tentatively.

'No. It's just that I've decided not to buy it. This is my swansong visit.'

I relaxed.

'Well, that's just as well,' I said cheerfully.
'What's just as well?'
'That you're not buying it.'
'Why?'
'Because it's sold.'
He turned to me, his eyes wide, aghast.
'Is it?'

I gave what I hoped was an enigmatic, inscrutable look: something that neither confirmed nor denied what I'd just said.

And then the second scary thing happened. Mr No-Name's face crumpled and he burst into tears. They coursed down his cheeks and his shoulders shook. I snuck a nervous look at the door, fearful that Jeremy would return to find me with a crying client.

I rushed to the desk, grabbed a box of tissues and handed them to him.

'Would you like to sit down?' I asked. I pulled out the eighteenth-century armchair with its gilded frame and scarlet silk damask upholstery *(that features in miniature form on the Christmas tree)* and placed it in front of the commode *(also on the tree)* so he could cry and see it at the same time.

'It's because I love that commode,' he explained through gut-wrenching sobs.

I've never seen anyone as passionate about an inanimate object. I love lipsticks and handbags, but I've never cried over either. Still, each to his or her own.

'In that case,' I told him decisively, 'you should buy it.'

He looked up at me.

'But you said it was sold.'

'I was trying to make you feel better about not having bought it.' I pulled an apologetic face. 'Sorry. It's still for sale. And really, if you feel this strongly, you *should* buy it. When you feel passionately about something – when it calls to your heart – it means it's incredibly important.'

He tapped the handkerchief to his cheeks. The sobbing had stopped.

'You're right. If I walk away, I'll regret it for the rest of my life. I've been in and out of this place more times than you've had hot dinners, wondering what to do. I thought I'd finally made up mind. But I was wrong. I'll buy it.'

'You will?' I asked surprised.

It was such a swift turnaround. I didn't know whether I was coming or going.

'I know how much it costs,' he said. The tears had stopped and he'd become business-like. 'Reduce it by ten per cent and I'll pay the deposit now and sort out the rest of the funds today.'

Fortunately, having read the commode's file, I knew what Jeremy was prepared to let me or Sukie negotiate down to. At ten per cent, I was within my limit.

'I accept,' I said, smiling. I put out my hand and he shook it.

And that was the miraculous thing: I'd sold the commode mazarine. All done and dusted in thirty minutes and Mr No-Name already gone to his next appointment.

When Jeremy walked back in the gallery, I was over-excited and almost pounced on him as he wiped his feet.

'You'll never guess what I've done!' I didn't wait for an answer. 'I've sold the commode mazarine!'

He studied my face to see whether I was being serious.

'Really! I've sold it! To Mr No-Name. Except I know his name now. And you'll never guess what it is?'

'Go on.'

'John Smith.'

'You're joking.'

I shook my head. 'No. Not about any of it. Do you think he changed his name by deed poll to make himself anonymous? Mind you, there was a John Smith who was a Labour politician and there's a John Smith's Brewery, so there's a few well-known versions of them about.'

I was gabbling with exhilaration.

'Congratulations! Now sit down and tell me all about it.'

I did, including the good price that I achieved for it *(not that I was really responsible for that, but still)*, the substantial deposit Mr No-Name/John Smith paid on his debit card *(imagine having that much in your current account)* and then the conversation he had with his bank to transfer the balance to Osbert & Small's account today.

'But how did you persuade him to buy it?' asked Jeremy, incredulous.

'Oh well, you know, diplomacy, a well-honed patter, years of sales experience,' I blustered. Then I told him the truth.

He shook his head in amazement.

'It's the strangest sales technique I've ever come across and I hope you'll tailor your approach to each client, but it worked and you're an absolute marvel. Well done!'

It was my last day before the Christmas break. We locked the doors at six and as we parted I said, 'I love working here, Jeremy. I love applying my little bit of knowledge from the V&A course. I love learning about the business. I love the clients. I love Sukie. And you and Hugo are just the best. Thank you for offering me the job.'

We set off on our separate ways, me whispering a quiet goodbye to the Rogier van der Weyden diptych which will be gone by the time I return and which I'll probably never see again.

It was raining. The pavements were wet and black. The street was busy with commuters heading home. I put my umbrella up and, as I did so, a posh voice bellowed down Pall Mall.

'See you in the New Year, Ethel!'

I put on my best Yorkshire accent and yelled back, 'Ay! See yer son.'

I turned away, laughing, knowing he was laughing too.

Saturday 21st December

Tillie's working in Greenwich all weekend putting in as many hours as Johanna wants: money is everything.

I made a venison casserole, an Irish lamb stew and a vegetarian roasted tomato and goat's cheese tart with thyme – all to go in the freezer and be eaten over Christmas. Then I decorated the Christmas cake. George made lunch – a cold collation of ham, cheese and salad. He volunteered to make supper too until he decided it was too much like hard work and that fish and chips from the local chippy would be far better.

Sunday 22nd December

It was an emotional day for Iggie, Arnold and me: excitement at creating this last image, fatigue from the hard work we've put into the project, and giddiness because there's an end-of-term feeling. At the close of today, we've finished!

The final photograph in this body of work was me as myself. Which is where this whole project started in July. Back then I'd presented myself as a cleaner – because that's what I was.

And now? No, definitely not a cleaner. A worker, yes. But now I'm back in the world of professionals: Jeremy, Hugo, Johanna, Iggie and Arnold. I feel much better about myself and the turns my life has taken. I'm far more confident and happier, too. I've become someone with a purpose. Several purposes, actually. It turns out I have a lot to offer *(as well as a lot to learn)* and people want me. People I've come to really like.

What did I wear? What props did I use? What pose did I choose? What look was there on my face? Well, I'm not saying anything because all will be revealed at Seed Gallery next year. For Ann-Marie Larnier arrived unexpectedly at lunchtime to catch the last shots and, out of the blue, announced she'll feature this series of photographs in a solo show dedicated to Iggie in the spring. We were all taken aback and hugely pleased.

As it turns out, today is not the end. We'll all be involved in the press launch at least. As to what happens beyond that, who knows? Will I continue to be Iggie's muse? Maybe. Maybe not.

I'm immensely fond of him. We've provided one another with an outlet for our respective creativity at a crucial time in both our lives. Of course, I'd love that to develop further. But we'll see.

Monday 23rd December
On the morning news the weather forecasters promised a terrific storm. Beyond the kitchen window, a crow slid sideways across the sky, opening and closing its wings in slow motion to control its turbulent flight.

Tillie and I met Edith at Euston. By the time we'd reached the local station, the wind was stronger and the rain was not so much pouring down as hurling itself horizontally. We arrived home battered and drenched.

The gale has become even stronger. I'm writing this in the semi-dark, having turned off the lights and opened the curtains to watch the trees in the back gardens as the wind races through them. Next door's conifers are taking the worst of it. I can't recall having heard such a wind before. It's like a Tube train rushing down a tunnel towards us, the sound increasing until, just as you're thinking it can't grow any louder, it's swept past and gone.

Christmas Eve Tuesday 24th December
The storm has blown itself away. All is calm, though the garden is strewn with fallen branches.

In the kitchen, Edith was tackling the pile of clothes that need mending. To keep her company, I made brandy butter and then pastry in readiness for the mince pies.

Just before lunch, Lucas and I walked to the high street to collect the turkey. As we came back, all my energy leaked out and, by the time we opened the front door, I was ready to collapse with fatigue. Simultaneously, I was fighting evil thoughts about George and why he wasn't here to help.

Mid-afternoon, Tillie asked me to drive her to the nearest Tube station – which is not-so-near – where she was meeting a friend. I didn't know the route, but she said she did.

She didn't. We ended up on the A3 racing along with thousands of other motorists towards deepest, darkest Surrey. I panicked and Tillie simultaneously cried while texting her friend to say she'd be late.

Somehow I got us off that hideous road, found the Tube station, deposited her and drove home even more tired and stressed. And then I shut the car door on my left hand. Fortunately, my right hand *(which seemed to be acting independently of my brain)* caught the door at the last millisecond, diminishing some of its force.

Though my fingers were crushed rather than broken, the pain was excruciating. I headed to the bathroom, weeping, applied masses of arnica cream and sat nursing my hand, unable to make the mince pies or the evening meal.

When George arrived home at four, I was suffering from a venomous mix of self-pity, anger and frustration.

'I'm giving you a year's notice,' I told him. 'If you don't take time off work next year to help me manage Christmas, I promise you I will not be here on Christmas Day.'

I explained what needed cooking, where the recipes and ingredients were and left him to it. He exited the room grumbling, 'I'm tired too.'

I don't know why I said anything about the recipes. George is congenitally unable to follow any instructions. He and Edith made the mince pies in muffin tins. Edith insisted the pastry lids didn't need sticking to the pastry bases. As a result, they all lifted in the oven and the mincemeat went everywhere.

'Look on the bright side,' said George when I arrived in the kitchen. 'Because the lids aren't stuck down we can scoop up the contents and put them back in the individual pies.'

'The *burned* contents,' I said.

'No one will notice when they're covered in brandy butter.'

Still, the slow-cooked belly of pork smelled delicious and tasted good despite him not following that recipe either.

After the kids headed for bed, George and I put all the presents under the Christmas tree. When we finished, it looked like the perfect image for a Christmas card.

I turned to him.

'It's wonderful. And it's sad.'

'What's sad?'

'That you don't know what's under any of those wrappings. That I've done everything for the children this Christmas, as I have for the last nineteen years and you have done nothing. You have missed out on far too much.'

I said it not in an accusatory tone, just factual.

He put his hands in his trouser pockets. His shoulders slumped and he looked at his feet. For a moment I thought he was going to cry. And, for a moment, I was tempted to console him. But instead, I went to bed.

Christmas Day Wednesday 25th December

There is a perfect moment on Christmas Day, when the turkey is in the oven, warmth and mouth-watering scents are drifting from the kitchen and circulating round the house, we're in the sitting room opening our presents and everyone is, quite simply, completely happy.

At that point, everything that has gone before makes this particular moment worth it. There is nothing quite like being surrounded by yet-to-be opened presents with all their exciting secrets, as well as freshly opened presents with all their surprises sprung, plus mounds of wrapping paper strewn around the room. It is the essence of loveliness.

I received a beautiful Middle Eastern cook book, a casserole in which to create some of the recipes, scented soaps, perfume, a lipstick and various books. Iggie had sent an A2 size, framed photograph of me, Tillie and Lucas which I shall treasure forever. And Johanna, bless her, had sent a Spode Italian design jug to go with the mug she gave me earlier.

More importantly, what did I give? Well, everything that everyone else wanted and probably too much more. The main thing was that they were all pleased.

Just before lunch, Sue called on an exceptionally clear line from Mauritius.

'Happy Christmas, darling,' she chirped. 'I'm lying by the pool, clutching a tall, cold drink, having the best-ever Christmas in my life with my favourite friend and wonderful lover, Harry. Say hello, Harry.'

'Hello sweet, scrumptious cousin-y kind of person,' cooed Harry. He passed the phone back to Sue.

'Blimey, how much have the pair of you had to drink?' I asked.

'Not a drop. Other than iced tea. We're the prime examples of what happiness can do for you.'

(Perhaps I should go to Mauritius next Christmas. And remember to take George too.)

*

I called the gorgon.

'You're lucky to catch me,' she said breathlessly. 'I'm just on my way to Pippa and Matt's.'

We swapped quick Christmas messages and I was about to put the phone down when she added, 'And don't try calling me until January. I'm going away tomorrow.'

'Where?'

'Klosters.'

'Klosters, as in Switzerland?' I asked, surprised.

'The exact same. Fifi's parents are renting a chalet and they've asked me to join them.'

I saw disaster. Icy pavements. An easy slip followed by a broken wrist, leg or far worse, a hip. The irreparable hip that leads to hospitalisation, pneumonia and death.

'Great Aunt Vi, is that a good idea?' I asked soberly.

'An excellent one. I'll be in the best hands. They're both doctors. I've bought all the right winter clothes and I'll rent the skis locally.'

'You're going *skiing*?' I was horrified.

'It's what you do in Klosters in the winter. Not downhill for me, but cross country. Can't wait. Now I really must go. Happy Christmas!'

And she'd gone. Hopefully, not for good. *(Though that mightn't be too bad either.)*

*

We spent a very long time eating lunch, then staggered to the sitting room to watch the first of the multiple Die Hard films that Lucas received. Afterwards, we considered eating another meal but instead opted for plates of toast – or in Edith's case a bowl of Shreddies – watched another Die Hard movie, and then went to bed. A perfect day.

Boxing Day Thursday 26th December

A completely indulgent day in which we snacked on mince pies with brandy butter – George was right: the latter makes the former edible – ate more turkey and drank more wine. We voted against starting the Christmas cake as we were just too full and watched two more Die Hard films.

Friday 27th December

George went to work and the rest of us slobbed round the house, snacking on leftovers from Christmas Day or whatever else we fancied. Dinner consisted of smoked salmon and a loaf of home-made soda bread. *(I did do one productive thing today.)* Pudding was Christmas cake, followed by too many chocolates during an extended game of whist.

Saturday 28th December
While George took Edith to Euston station on her homeward journey, Tillie and I went to the Paperchase sale in Tottenham Court Road for our annual purchase of notebooks and birthday cards.

Afterwards, feeling chipper and in need of exercise, we walked west on Oxford Street, south down Regent Street, across Piccadilly, along Lower Regent Street, east along the Strand, over Waterloo Bridge and to the station. Then home. And we chatted all the way.

It is impossible to describe how happy I am with Tillie home. We are restored as a family. I am restored and reinvigorated as a mum of two young people. My heart is overflowing with love for both of them. But particularly for Tillie, for whom I have few chances now to show how much I care.

Sunday 29th December
Aliens have taken Lucas in the night and left me with a looks-the-same-but acts-differently version.

He was in the office revising. Voluntarily. I expressed surprise.

'It's mock GCSEs after the holidays, you know,' he said irritably, as if I wasn't taking his studying seriously enough.

Actually, I didn't know. He hadn't told me previously.

'You're working,' I stated, wondering what was going on. 'Without being asked.'

'These are important exams, Mum. I need to do well in them. Now if you don't mind, I'd like to get on.'

It's definitely not Lucas.

Monday 30th December
A motorbike despatch rider arrived on the doorstep.

'Parcel for Mrs Jill Baxter,' he said, handing me a small package wrapped in brown paper. 'Needs signing for.'

I wasn't expecting anything and hadn't a clue what it could be. In the kitchen, I tore off the brown paper and then smiled. I'd revealed another layer of paper but this time expensive wrapping paper with several strands of multicoloured raffia holding it together. A note, written in Jeremy's dramatic hand fell on to the table: *To be opened just before midnight on New Year's Eve.*

I've put the gift on the chest of drawers in our bedroom where I can savour its promise. I love surprises. *(But what can it be?)*

New Year's Eve Tuesday 31st December
This is it. The end of my year off. Time to assess how I fared with my January New Year resolutions.

1. I will end a lifetime's habit of agreeing to every piece of freelance graphic design work I'm offered.
   - ✓ Yup, I managed that. I only took on the charity work and the review of Jeremy's website. Paradoxically, my refusal to design his new site prompted him to think of another way in which he could employ me. And that has worked out superbly. Never *(before this year off)* would I have thought that turning down work would lead to something better. *(A lesson to be learned there, methinks.)*
2. Instead of working, I will do something nice.
   - ✓ I signed up for the V&A courses. It's partly due to them that Jeremy thought about employing me.
   - ✓ And it was the journeys to the V&A that led me to Iggie and Arnold, the inclusion in the Saatchi Gallery show and, from that, a professional relationship and warm friendship. Of course, I'd never have managed the creative aspects of that connection without my background in

design. But more than that, Iggie discovered something in me that I never knew and still don't understand. Only the gods know what went on there.

3. Embark on The Body Beautiful Project and lose some weight.
- ✓ Mmmmm. Not sure if I deserve this tick because the least said the better. Let's face it, this is an ongoing project. Probably over a lifetime. I stepped on the scales this morning and – ta-dah – I weigh exactly the same as I did this time last year. Nowhere near the five kilo target that, for two milliseconds in January, I thought was possible. On the other hand, I haven't put on weight. Oh, what the hell, I'll be generous and count it as a success.

4. Take more exercise.
- ✓ I'm definitely fitter. Between Total Workout and the housework, I've toned up my body. It's not perfect but it's definitely better.

5. Write this diary.
- ✓ I did it! I charted the whole rollercoaster year: the downs *(and boy, there were a lot of those but worst by far was my heart breaking over Tillie leaving home)* and the ups *(where I am currently: Tillie's home and I love the way my life is panning out in various directions).*

What this assessment ignores are the malevolent machinations of Great Aunt Vi and their effect on my year. She deliberately refused to give me either of the Tiffany vases and, instead, sent exactly what I didn't want – the Wedgwood service. And yet – ironically – good came from that. For in refusing one and giving the other, her actions led me to meet Jeremy and Johanna. The work that I do with each of them and the richness of these relationships is far greater than anything I'd ever have realised from a vase which, let's face it, I'd never have known was Tiffany anyway.

What can I conclude? That by stopping work I found the time to let new things come into my life. To be brutally honest, I can't claim responsibility for all of them. I never set out to work in a Pall Mall antiques business, nor to become a photographer's muse, or work on a market stall. But I did have the wit to grasp opportunities as they arose.

Now I have a future – a new future – completely beyond my vision at the start of this year. It's wildly different, it's hugely exciting and life is never going to be the same again.

*

I was giving myself a proverbial pat on the back when the phone rang.

'Great Aunt Vi here.'

The tone was stern-don't-mess-with-me-I-mean-business.

'I thought you were in Klosters.'

'I am.'

'Are you alright?' I asked solicitously, fearing the worst. 'No falls or broken bones?'

'Don't be ridiculous,' she snapped. 'Now look, I can't spend all day speaking to you on an expensive call from Switzerland. I'll cut to the chase. As you know, my circumstances have changed dramatically this year. For the better, I might add. However, they do mean that I have had to revise my will.'

I was having a sense of déjà vu. And I wasn't bothered. I was a successful, smart, articulate, professional woman who could stand her ground.

'I've decided to appoint *you* as executor,' she continued. 'The sole executor.'

'I think I've been here before,' I told her, pretending to recall the facts. 'About a year ago when you announced I was your sole executor. As I remember, you snatched the task away from me and gave it to Sue. And just as she was recovering from the shock, you decided she wasn't good enough and you told Robert that it was his job. For all I know, you went round the rest of the cousins delegating it to each of them.'

'What I did – or didn't do – is none of your business.'

'But it is,' I cut in. 'If you appoint someone to be your executor you are asking them to take responsibility, to ensure your wishes are carried out after your death. It's not a frivolous assignment to be touted willy-nilly round your family.'

'You're being impertinent,' she hissed.

'I'm being honest.' I paused for effect and then continued. 'I will be your executor on the basis of two provisos. First, that you don't ask anyone else.'

I stopped for a moment to let that sink in. I knew full well I couldn't stop her doing whatever she wanted, but I did want her to know I wasn't a pushover.

'And second,' I said, equally seriously but knowing this would never happen, 'you leave that wonderful apartment and all its furnishings to me.'

There was a long silence in which the air became as thin and cold as it must be on the mountains above Klosters. And then the sound of a low, avalanche-like rumble increased in volume as it raced towards me.

'You've got a NERVE.'

The phone clicked off. I laughed. I haven't a clue who will end up being her executor, but I do know who will inherit her estate. And I'm very happy for those two little girls.

*

George came home early. We ate dinner, watched a film and were just about to go to bed when I remembered the fireworks I'd bought for Bonfire Night the previous year.

'We could set them off!' I suggested.

George and Lucas went to find them.

'What about your present from Osbert & Small?' asked Tillie.

I'd forgotten about it. The pair of us went upstairs. While Tillie plonked herself on the bed, I sat in my armchair, the beautifully wrapped gift in my lap looking almost too good to open. But I pulled the raffia loose and the paper fell away revealing a midnight blue box. Inside, tucked in folds of gold silk, was the miniature copy of the commode mazarine that had hung on the Christmas tree.

It was perfect in every detail: a thin, delicate sliver of onyx covered the top surface. Below were two fitted drawers set within a carcass supported on cabriole legs each headed by gilded and winged caryatids, the bodies of which trailed to lion paw sabots. It was decorated with panels of foliate scroll and flower-head ornaments. The detail was breath-taking: the maker had captured every element and replicated it exactly.

'What is it?' Tillie asked, coming over to see.

'It's a copy of the piece of furniture I sold just before Christmas.'

She looked at it in my hand.

'It's a bit weird.'

I nodded. One of the drawers had the tiniest key imaginable in its lock. I turned it carefully and the drawer opened. Inside was a piece of folded paper.

In miniscule script, Jeremy had written: *Commemorating your first sale and looking forward to a new year in antiques. With love, Jeremy & Hugo.*

'That's extraordinarily kind and unbelievably generous of them,' I said, touched to the core. I knew what these pieces meant to them.

I tucked the commode back into its box.

'Do you like it?' asked Tillie.

'I do,' I said. 'What I like most of all is why they've given it to me.'

I could see her taking that in, wondering whether or not to give me her opinion and then deciding against it.

I broke the silence. 'Come on! The fireworks must be just about ready by now.'

George and Lucas were waiting for us with the lighter. The fireworks went off with satisfying whizzes, pops, hisses and flares, while the rockets shot up into the night sky with blood-curdling screams. Last came the sparklers. We raced across the lawn drawing silver circles against the dark sky.

There was still an hour before midnight but, true to form, George and I headed for bed. Tillie and Lucas settled into the settees in the sitting room 'talking' to friends on social media.

*

And that was my year off. My rollercoaster year off. The year in which I became a new, better person. I'm never going back to the old freelance graphic design life. Ever. My sights are set – resolutely and happily – elsewhere.

(I'll tell George tomorrow.)

Acknowledgements

Enormous gratitude goes to Robert Nelson in Melbourne for understanding everything instantly and for being so enthusiastic. When I started this project, Chris Russell knew far more than I did about how to write a novel and was generous in sharing her knowledge and providing oodles of positive criticism. Paul Crane of Brian Haughton Gallery in St James's kindly explained how an antiques business in that area of London might run. He also offered a detailed description of the two eighteenth century matching platters that I spotted in his gallery and which now feature in the novel. Michelle Finlay helped hugely with the blurb and offered wisdom gained from her many years in the publishing industry.

Allison Parkinson and Teresa Forrest never gave up nudging. Teresa led the way to the printers, KMS Litho Ltd in Hook Norton, where Chris and Ali were always helpful. Robert Barkshire provided the great cover design. Veronica Davis was chief cheerleader. (If you ever need bolstering, she's your woman.) For years Joan Abel listened to the developing plot lines and recognised the greater reasons behind the writing of the novel. Thank you also to Betzy Dinesen, Maggie Lawrence, Frances Leong, Ana Prada, Nick de Ville, Daphne Tomkins and Jane Vearncombe.

Finally, thank you to Bill. I'd be lost without you.